Dear Michelle

From the desk of
Author
Cherisse M Havlicek

The Love and
Family is Every
thing!

Cherisse
Nov 2019

Love Consumes The Chill

A Present / Past Saga

By

Cherisse M Havlicek

The Lewis Family Tree

Elizabeth (Beth) Palmer and William Lewis

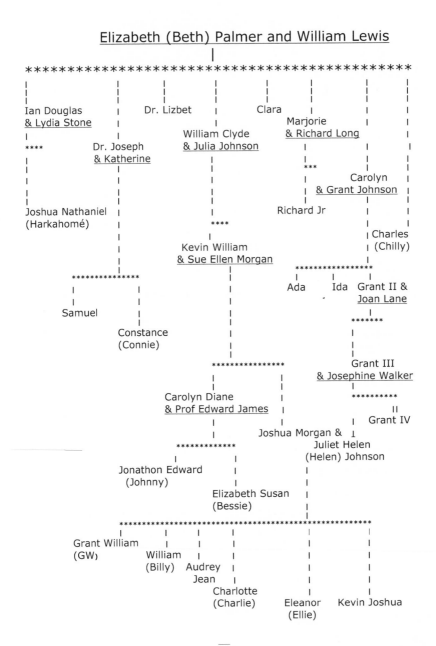

```
Ian Douglas          Dr. Lizbet          Clara
& Lydia Stone                            Marjorie
                  William Clyde          & Richard Long
****      Dr. Joseph    & Julia Johnson
          & Katherine
                                         ***
                                              Carolyn
                                              & Grant Johnson

Joshua Nathaniel                 Richard Jr
(Harkahomé)
                    ****                            Charles
                Kevin William                      (Chilly)
                & Sue Ellen Morgan

         ***************                 *****************
                                         Ada    Ida  Grant II &
                                                      Joan Lane
     Samuel
                                                     *******
         Constance
         (Connie)
                                                     Grant III
                     ****************                & Josephine Walker
                                                     **********
                     Carolyn Diane                        II
                     & Prof Edward James                    Grant IV

                                   Joshua Morgan &
                *************          Juliet Helen
                                       (Helen) Johnson
           Jonathon Edward
           (Johnny)
                          Elizabeth Susan
                          (Bessie)
       *****************************************************
   Grant William
   (GW)              William
            (Billy) Audrey
                    Jean
                       Charlotte
                       (Charlie)      Eleanor    Kevin Joshua
                                      (Ellie)
```

The Masters
Family Tree

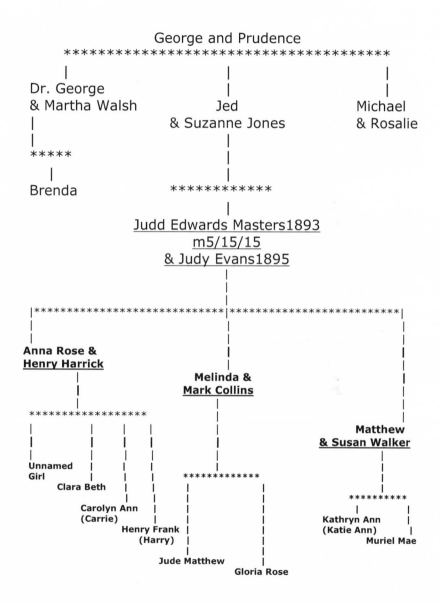

George and Prudence
****

Dr. George
& Martha Walsh

Jed
& Suzanne Jones

Michael
& Rosalie

*****

Brenda

****

Judd Edwards Masters1893
m5/15/15
& Judy Evans1895

|***************************|*************************|

Anna Rose &
Henry Harrick

Melinda &
Mark Collins

Matthew
& Susan Walker

****

Unnamed
Girl

Clara Beth

Carolyn Ann
(Carrie)

Henry Frank
(Harry)

Jude Matthew

****

Gloria Rose

****

Kathryn Ann
(Katie Ann)

Muriel Mae

DEDICATION

This novel is dedicated to those who have loved me and taught me that caring for others is the greatest gift we can give.

My mother was a no-nonsense woman who fought every fight for those she loved. In the end, we fought alongside her as she fought to hang on, while battling cancer.

My husband, a retired police officer, was a no-nonsense man on the job. At home, he took care of his aunts, disabled cousin, and his mother. Now that he is sick, it is his turn to be the person who needs care.

They both showed me that dedication to the ones that you love, is a blessing that you give and get.

****

ACKNOWLDGEMENTS

I need to thank all my prepublication readers. I couldn't have written a single word without the caregivers for both my husband and my mother. Thank You – Penny, Tammy, and Sheryl. I need to thank my editing friend, Marnie and my sister-in-law, Judy, who unselfishly came to Michigan to assist me with my mother's last few weeks and edit this novel in her spare time. I love and thank you, Judy, and her husband, my brother Sam. As usual, I need to thank the loves of my life who have taught me everything and have believed in me, so that I can do what I thought impossible. Thank you, Doris, my beautiful mother. Thank you, Allan, my loving husband. Thank you, Arthur & Alisse, my children who are behind me, yet kid me every step of the way.

****

This novel is a work of my imagination. The towns of EL Dorado and Lawrence in Kansas are real. The towns of Bartlesville and Nowata in Oklahoma are real. But Pennysville is made up as are all the events that happen to my characters in this novel. All my characters are the work of my imagination. Any similarity to persons deceased or living is merely a coincidence and nothing more.

ONE
January 5th, 1896
A Sunday in a small town in Oklahoma

It has been ten long years since he last saw the Indian. A warrior stands before him where a young brave once stood. But Sheriff Charles Palmer Lewis recognizes him immediately. He shouts across the barroom, "Harkahomé! Stop right there! Put your hands up in the air."

The six-foot-three adopted member of the Cheyenne tribe who lived with the Lakota's, smiles but follows the Sheriff's orders. "And what if I don't? Are you going to shoot me?"

The saloon gets quiet and the drinkers at the bar all take a step away from the Indian. With his hands, still up, Harkahomé takes a giant step toward the six-foot-eight redhead and repeats. "Are you going to shoot me?" A gasp escapes from the lips of the saloon girls.

"Now, why would I do that?" The sheriff has his hands in position to draw. He squints in total concentration. His hands slowly relax as he takes a giant step toward the Indian. "What brings you to Oklahoma?" he says in a measured tone, and he takes another step forward.

"I thought I would visit my old uncle. I heard a rumor that he lives here in Pennysville. I heard other rumors, as well." He also takes another step forward.

"What exactly did you hear?" The sheriff asks.

"I have heard that a redheaded 'Navoualevé' was sheriff. Is it you?" Harkahomé smiles.

"So I share the honored Cheyenne title of 'Too tall'?" The sheriff points to his chest. "The townspeople gave me a star and everything."

"What were they thinking?" Harkahomé asks.

"I think, they thought no one else would be crazy

enough to apply for the job. The last two sheriffs were killed in their first month of office."

"Oh so, they were desperate then? How long have you been in office?" The Indian takes another step forward.

"Two years, now." The sheriff responds.

"You must be good." Harkahomé shakes his head in disbelief, as he says this.

The sheriff says, "I must be."

"And modest?" Harkahomé adds.

"It runs in my family," the sheriff chuckles.

"So, have you seen my old uncle? We used to call him Chilly."

"Only when I look in the mirror. And that isn't too often." The two men have taken enough steps to be face to face. Sheriff Lewis continues, "Nephew, it is so good to see you. Can I call you Joshua or do you prefer Harkahomé?" They wrap their outstretched arms around each other and heartily slap each other's back.

"Whichever you like Uncle. I wish I could say that it was good to see you. When was the last time you took a razor to your face? Do people take you seriously with that ridiculous red fuzz on your chin?"

"They better, if they know what's good for them! Everyone calls me Sheriff or Sheriff Lewis, now. I haven't been called Chilly, since I left the Cavalry. What are you doing this far from the tribe?"

His nephew, Joshua Nathaniel Lewis, only six months younger than himself, has been living with the Cheyenne since 1878. He and his mother were rescued by a young Cheyenne brave from the carnage, that was taking place in the little town of Oberlin, Kansas. "You look more like Will every day! If he was clean shaven like yourself, you could be his double. Of course, being a Cavalry man, he would never grow his curly hair into braids like you have." The sheriff's older brother, Colonel William Clyde Lewis, took the then 14-year-old Chilly on the search for

Joshua, soon after his disappearance.

"How is Uncle Will? Is Gram Beth and Grandfather still alive? I think about them often and thought that I would venture to Kansas and visit them."

The saloon has gone back to its usual loud atmosphere. The sheriff leads his nephew, to a table, but before he sits, he calls out to the bartender for two beers. "My father passed away back in '91. My mother is still going strong. Will and Julia are great and they have a son Kevin. I am his Godfather. How is your mother? I bet your half-brother Avonaco is all grown up. Surely, you have a wife by now?"

"Why, do you?" Harkahomé fires back.

"I haven't felt the need." The Sheriff shrugs.

"I thought I wanted to marry one woman," the Indian continued. "I loved her but she was the missionary's daughter. He would not allow it, because of how I was raised. He came to preach about Jesus' love for all people but as a human, he couldn't live by his God's teachings. Even though I was born a white man, I still wasn't good enough for her and she refused to disobey him." He takes a long drink of his cold beer. "Mother passed away two years ago. She and her husband Kanuna died within days of each other, from a sickness that went through the tribe. My blood-brother, Degotoga, is married to three squaws and has many, many little ones already. Avonaco has four sons, too."

"That cannot be, he is only about 18-years-old now."

"Yes, that is how it is done, with our people."

"Were you serious about going to Kansas? January isn't the time for traveling, if it can be helped. Late Spring would be much easier. That is something we could do together. I haven't been home since Father's funeral."

"That is why I have come to find you. I hoped you would take me to Lawrence. I have been away too long and do not know if I would be able to fit in, if traveling by myself."

"You might want to cut your hair and grow some man-whiskers and buy some real clothes. Wait, then you would look just like Will! Mother will be so tickled. She has been praying to see you again. Do you realize, it has been almost twenty years since your Mom and Dad left Lawrence with the cattle drive to Oberlin? Who knew that they would never get back home." The sheriff pauses a moment and looks at his drink before him. "Strike that, my mother knew. She grieved for you all from the moment that you left. When word of the massacre reached her, she was devastated. She didn't smile for at least a year. She was in a very bad way until Will found out from your step-sister, Ayita that you were still alive."

"I still cannot believe that Ayita saw the resemblance between he and I. She was only seven or eight-years-old. I was only eleven but she saw that I looked like my grown uncle Will? I wonder what became of her and her mother?"

"Will got them all settled in Montana. After that, I don't know. Have you eaten, Joshua? I could go for a huge steak, right about now."

"I could eat my horse, right now."

"Is it a good horse?"

"No, he is old and half-starved."

"He would be too tough to chew, let's get the steak, instead."

***

After the two get seated at Big Momma's Diner and have ordered their steaks, they start to reminisce about being raised as brothers more than uncle and nephew. Joshua's father was co-owner of the farm with Chilly's father. Even though they had their own little house on the farm, they were inseparable.

"Do you remember when we snuck into Carolyn's

room and cut her hair?" Chilly starts. "She earned the name 'firecracker' that day! She was so mad!!"

"You got your nickname that day too!" Joshua adds.

"Yes, but that was later. Father asked me why we cut her hair and before I could answer, Carolyn said that I was jealous of her and copied her red hair. That is when father said we were as different as fire and ice. She teased me and called me Chilly Charlie and it stuck. How about the time you caught those bullfrogs and put them in both Marjorie's and Carolyn's beds?"

"I couldn't sit down for a week after that escapade." Joshua is quiet for a moment. "All in all, it was a wonderful way to grow up."

"Both Marjorie and Carolyn are mothers themselves now. If you can picture that. Carolyn has three children but Marjorie only has one little boy, poor guy is very sickly. Oh, here comes our steaks." Chilly waits for the waitress to put his plate down, so he can look at her as she bends over.

"This looks delicious." Joshua comments as he picks up his knife and fork.

"It sure does." Chilly's eyes do not leave the waitress. "Josie, sweetheart; meet my long-lost nephew, Harkahomé. Isn't he a handsome fellow with his clean chin and his long braids?" He leans in to whisper something in her ear. She turns bright red and with a smile, slaps the sheriff across his face.

"Josie, I can arrest you for assaulting an officer."

"I'd like to see you try! It would mean you wouldn't be invited up to the house, anymore."

"Oh, but I would have you in my cell, to do with as I please."

"Sheriff Lewis, how improper!" She goes to leave pretending to be mad, but stops and turns back to him. "I get off at ten, tonight, Sheriff. You and your nephew can buy me a drink."

Chilly smiles at his nephew. "We might just take

you up on that, Josie. What do you think Harkahomé?"

"I don't have any other plans. Got a friend? Or two?"

"He's a chip off the old uncle's block, wouldn't you say, Josie?"

"I don't know if the town can handle two like you, Sheriff."

TWO

January 5th, 1959

A Monday in Chicago, Illinois

Carrie Ann is unpacking her third box. "Clara, so far, I do not love Chicago. The snow has been falling nonstop for 48 hours. The roads are impassable. The University is having snow days, and here I am in unpacking hell. Why did I bring so much stuff?" She says as she sits cross-legged in her pedal pusher pants and her men's style shirt that she has buttoned down only half way and has tied the remainder around her waist.

"I have no idea. All you needed was a wardrobe and books. Sissy, you have more than our parents had when we moved to EL Dorado in 1946!" Her older sister Clara Beth is dressed in a wide skirt and a smock top that she wears when doing housework.

"I was just thinking about that. I feel overwhelmed with starting college a semester late, in a new city. Mother moved with three little ones to start her second restaurant. I am just beginning to appreciate the inner strength Mother had."

"Of course, Father was always at her side," Clara reminds her.

"We should be so lucky as our parents and grandparents were, to find our soulmates! True love, it is out there for the both of us. I know it."

"Spoken like our mother's daughter!"

"It was very hard to leave Mother. I cannot imagine *not* talking to her every day. That is why I took you up on your offer to room with you. You look just like our mother." Carrie confesses.

"And you don't? Same heart-shaped face, same brown eyes, same widow's peak, same small button of a mouth. Father had nothing to do with either of our making, apparently. Harry, though, is Dad's double. Gray

15

eyes, Roman nose. His voice is starting to change from a boy's squeak to father's low timber."

"It was squeaking more than timbering over the Holiday."

Clara Beth is opening a box marked 'TOPS'. After rummaging through it for a moment, she looks up. "Carrie, this is all bras! There are no blouses in here."

"I know but I did not want the movers to look in a box that said 'Bras', now, did I? Besides, under every top is a different bra."

"That is the difference between us. You are blessed with Aunt Melinda's ample bosom. I got mother's 'secret' weapon, as she calls them. Secret because they never showed, no matter what sort of top or bra she wore." She looks down at her own figure. "Flat as a pancake! It is just not fair, at all."

"Oh, but you have the brains in the family, Clara. All the teachers expected so much from me because you did so well. It was very hard to follow the famous brilliant mind of Clara Beth Harrick."

"You never had any trouble with grades."

"I had to work hard for them. You never studied, but aced every test. It was always easy for you."

"Well, you received Mama's cooking and sewing skills. I can barely boil water. After living my whole life in restaurants, I still can only make coffee."

The phone rings in the living room of the tiny two bedroom flat on South Paulina Street. Clara gets up off the floor and goes to it. "Harrick Girls residence, Clara Beth speaking." This makes Carrie giggle.

"Oh, how are you doing, cousin? Happy New Year." Clara is silent for a bit. "I enjoyed the Holidays at the Plantation house, very much. So, did Carrie. She is settling in very well. You want to talk with her? Hang on." Clara puts her hand over the mouthpiece. "Cousin GW wants to talk to you. Are you in?"

Carrie is up in an instant. "Of course I am in!

Don't be silly. Give me that phone." She crosses the two rooms in a swift second. "GW, how good of you to call. Happy New Year." She listens for a moment. "The Annual Valentine Ball in EL Dorado? It is on Saturday the 14th? I don't think I can come in, because of classes. You want me to fly in to Wichita Airport? Are you crazy? Anna Harrick's daughters do not fly!" She looks at her sister and rolls her eyes. "GW, that is too extravagant of an expense for a simple dance." She listens quietly for a while. "I understand that your Great-Great Grandfather was the founding organizer for it, and that it funds the hospital each year, but . . ." She is quiet again. "Does your mother know that you want to pay for me to fly out and fly back for one weekend? She does? If you are lying, GW . . . I will be very upset with you." She laughs. "I'll think about it. Call me on the weekend and I'll give you my answer. I haven't even started college and you are trying to whisk me back to the country." She listens, again. "You know I enjoyed seeing you over the holidays. Okay. Please, call me Sunday evening. I will give you my answer then. Have a great evening, GW." Carrie hangs up the phone and with her head down, she walks back the boxes.

"Did I hear you right? He wants you to FLY in for a dance? Money means nothing to that side of the family. Why doesn't he fly me in, also?" Clara Beth shrugs and goes back to getting rid of the chaos in her apartment. "He always had a thing for you, Carrie. As far back as I remember."

"I did not know that until the day after Christmas. He asked me to go on a sleigh ride. He held my hand and admitted to his lifelong crush that he has had for me. I must admit, I have always thought he was so nice and handsome."

"Doesn't it feel a little weird? We were all raised together. I know that he is not related by blood, but I think of him as a little brother. Don't you?"

"Not at all! I have always thought him dreamy, but

beyond my reach. The Lewis family is so rich, and though Mama thinks of his parents as her adopted brother and sister, I always felt they were so removed from us, especially after we moved from Lawrence. They were raised in two mansions, one in EL Dorado and the one in Lawrence. Mama and Father worked seven days a week for them."

"Mama and Daddy worked seven days a week for us, Baby Girl. They wanted to give us a college education and every other thing that was denied them during the Depression. The Lewis family bankrolled both restaurants. Or didn't you know that?"

"I did, and I know that you are named for Clara & Beth Lewis. And I was named for Carolyn Diane Lewis. We are connected in every way but blood, which makes it okay to date Grant. If he can afford to fly me in for a dance, I think I will just let him. Mama will be happy to see me, too. I know she will make me call before and after the plane takes off and she might hold her breath while it is in the air, but she'd be happy for me. I think I will go." She nods *yes* to herself and then is silent.

Clara Beth gives her a minute to think about it. "Are you all right?"

"Why wouldn't I be?"

"You just beat yourself up so, during that decision-making process. I thought you might have pulled something." Carrie Ann grabs a big pillow from the couch and throws it at her big sister. "If you are going to treat me like that, I may just move out of this frozen city. How did I let you talk me into this?"

"You wanted to learn fashion design and Chicago has the best schools for it. Me living here was just a bonus. That and Chicago-style pizza pie! Let's call out for delivery! I am famished from all this work."

"Let's get our facts straight first, Big Sister. Pizza pie was the reason for the move, fashion design and you were the bonus! I want sausage, and peppers and black olives on it, please."

***

An hour and a half later, the sisters are down to their last pair of boxes. The pizza pie still has not been delivered. Clara Beth says. "I think I should call the pizza parlor and see if they forgot us." Suddenly someone starts pounding on their outside door. "Well, it's about time." Carrie goes to her purse for the money while Clara answers the door.

Thoroughly covered in snow, the pizza pie delivery guy says weakly, "Delivery for Harrick?" Then he pushes the snow off the top of the box so that the name Como's Spicy Meatball & Pizza Pie shows.

"Oh, you poor man, please come in and warm up. Did you walk the five blocks?" He nods as Clara grabs his arm and leads him in. "I didn't realize that the storm had gotten so bad."

The man trembles as he says, "You need to put that in a warm oven to heat it up. So, sorry!"

"We'll do that. Can I heat you a cup of coffee or make some tea? I feel so bad that you had to walk the whole way." She takes the pizza pie to their kitchen which is too small to eat in. She turns on the oven.

"The streets are filled with snow. No one is getting anywhere by automobile. The streetcars are having trouble because of snow on the electric lines. The routes that still have the trolley buses can't maneuver around all the stuck cars. It is awful out there. This is the worst storm in years, they say."

Clara Beth takes their glass coffee pot, with this morning's coffee in it, from the back burner and removes the stem and the grounds basket from it. She turns a burner to 'light' and strikes a match to ignite the burner. "Coffee is but a few hours old and will take just a minute to heat you a cup. We can put a fresh pot on for you, it would be no trouble."

Carrie walks up to him. "Here is your money. I've included a tip for your trouble." She blushes, as she says. "Please stay a moment and un-freeze yourself. We insist."

The young man blushes, also. "Please do not trouble yourselves over me. I must get back to the parlor. This is one of our busiest days ever. My father is up to his ears in dough and my sister Sophia is taking orders. I am the only one on delivery. My good-for-nothing cousins Luigi and Antonio still have not made it in. We live above the restaurant so . . ."

Clara Beth turns off the stove and puts the pizza pie into the warm oven. "We know everyone's name but yours?"

"I am Gianni."

"I am Clara Beth and this is my sister Carolyn Ann." She shakes his still gloved hand.

"I go by Carrie Ann, if you please. My older sister is so formal about everything." She now shakes his hand.

"Pleased to make your acquaintance. Just moving in?" He says as he points to all the empty boxes piled up.

"My little sister is. I have been here for three years. I am a senior at the University of Chicago. Carrie is a late start freshman. She did one semester back home at the Community College."

"That's nice for you, both. I have gone to the School of Hard Knocks, as they say. We've had the pizza pie parlor my whole life and while I'd like to go to Art school, I am the one who will take over the family business. Why am I telling you two beautiful sisters this? I must get back. As my father says, 'We Gotta Maka de Pizza Pie! Mama Mia!'" He says with a thick Italian accent.

"Our mother and father own two diners in Kansas. I don't think they expect either of us to take over. Maybe our little brother Harry but not us. I burn toast and Carrie wants to go into fashion design."

"You don't own an electric toaster?"

"I do, but I still manage to burn it. Carrie will do all the cooking for us. That is my reason for letting her live with me. I am tired of eating out."

"I came here for the Pizza Pie!" Carrie exclaims.

"It should be warm enough to eat and I am unfrozen so I will let you enjoy it. Any time you want a personal delivery, just call the parlor and ask for Gianni."

Clara Beth laughs, "I bet you say that to all the girls."

"My hand to God, I have never said anything like it."

"Thank you, Gianni. We appreciate the service and you." Carrie Ann bats her eyes.

"Miss Carrie, I think you are flirting with me."

"My hand to God, I have never done that in my life!" She says with mock innocence. "Whatever do you mean?" She says with a fake southern accent.

"Oh, I better get back, I feel I would be in big trouble hanging out here any longer. Ladies, it has been a pleasure. Come into the Parlor sometime. We have excellent service. Well, when my good-for-nothing cousins show up, that is."

After Gianni leaves, the girls eat the pizza pie like they haven't had food in days. When full, Clara Beth looks at her little sister. "So, you like Gianni?"

"Not really, I just like to flirt. How about you? Could you go for an Italian?" Carrie tilts her head and winks at her.

"Tall, dark and handsome can be my type. He was awfully cute. If you go for that sort of thing. I like tall crew-cut-blonde god-like men"

"Like Oliver?"

"Yes. I guess he would fill that bill, wouldn't he? How about you?"

"I don't know what my type is. I am not about to limit my options, this early in my life. That is why I am not sure if going back to EL Dorado to dance with GW is such a good idea. I want to see how things go, here."

Clara Beth is now looking out the window at the snow scene from hell. "Things are not 'going' at all in this storm. Why did it wait until you get here to be so bad? I wanted to take you to the Museum of Science and Industry, the Art Institute, The Shedd Aquarium and a few jazz clubs to give you a well-rounded view of the Chicago life. We will be stuck in this apartment for a week, by the look of things out there." Clara Beth says with her head on her hand, staring blankly.

"It's a good thing that there are three convenience stores and five restaurants within five blocks of us. The benefits of city life. Gianni's place most likely would have great spaghetti and meatballs. We can have that tomorrow. Italian restaurants are Mama's favorite. That and Chinese. Remember when the Chinese place moved to Lawrence? Mama had us eat there three times in the first month they were open."

"Oliver took me to 22nd and Wentworth to the area called Chinatown. It was like being in China itself. The street signs are even in Chinese. None of the shop windows have ads in English. Everything is so exotic! If Mama comes for a visit, we should take her there. We should go this weekend. Oliver can take us." Clara decides.

"So I will be a third wheel?"

"If you haven't met anyone by the weekend, I will have Oliver bring a friend. Or you can call Gianni." She gives her a wink.

"Clara Beth, you are a bad influence, I think."

THREE
January 6th, 1896
A Monday in Pennysville, Oklahoma

"Sheriff? Sheriff? Are you back there? Just thought you might want to know. The morning stagecoach is an hour late. There might be something wrong. SHERIFF, DO YOU HEAR ME?"

The sheriff wakes up in the small back room of the town's Sheriff's Office, where Chilly has been living since becoming sheriff. "Give me a minute, Elliot. I will be right out." Chilly calls back out to the man in the office.

He looks to his nephew. They are both still dressed. He vaguely remembers coming back to the office at about four in the morning. He rubs his eyes and looks at his pocket watch. *How is it noon already?* "Elliot, if you are still out there, make yourself useful and put on a pot of coffee."

"Already on it, Sheriff."

Joshua is holding his head as Chilly shouted for coffee. "Who hit me? And why are you yelling so loud?"

"I think he was Jose Cuervo. You had a lot of tequila, my nephew. The girls thought you were quite entertaining, though. I purposely don't usually drink that much. It always invites trouble the next morning. And his name is usually Elliot!"

"Yes, Sheriff?"

The sheriff ignores Elliot. "Joshua, you go back to sleep, while I attend to this matter." Chilly walks to the pitcher at the basin and pours water to splash on his face. He looks in his four-inch square mirror. "Maybe you are right, this red fuzz needs a trim. Or a lion tamer!"

"Took the words right out of my mouth."

"Sheriff!" Elliot is calling again.

"I am coming, Elliot!" he shouts out. Then turns to Joshua who is sitting up. "I'd call him Elliot, the Idiot, but

---

23

he is our Post Master, and one of the ones who hired me. And those are just the first two reasons why the name fits."

Without another word, Chilly grabs his gun belt, straps it on, and leaves the backroom. He passes through the long hall that has two empty jail cells on either side before he opens the door to the Sheriff's office.

Elliot is pouring the sheriff's coffee. "I started this before I called out to you, Sheriff. I know how you are before your coffee."

"Thanks, Elliot. Now what is this business with the stagecoach?" He sits down at his desk and Elliot brings him the cup.

"The eleven o'clock coach is over an hour late. Jerry has the Sunday night run and Jerry is always early. Never late."

"Where is this stage coming in from?" Chilly says as he sips his coffee, loudly.

"Bartlesville, on its way south to Tulsa. Jerry's girl is in Tulsa and he is always in a hurry to get back to her after his weekend runs."

"Let's give it another hour or so before we get all worked up. Jerry might have taken the weekend off and the new driver might not know the road as well as Jerry or has Jerry's incentive to get to Tulsa. Run down to the diner for some ham, three eggs and toast, please, for two."

"Two? You have a guest, Sheriff?" he says with a smirk.

"Get your mind out of the gutter, Elliot. My nephew, Joshua is visiting." Just then Joshua comes into the office.

"Did you call me?" He is scratching his stomach. "Did I hear breakfast is coming? I am starved."

The five-foot, forty-year old bald Elliot is just staring up at the exceptionally tall Indian in front of him. "This is your nephew?" he asks timidly.

"I am Harkahomé of the Cheyenne." He holds out his hand to Elliot. "I was born Joshua Nathaniel Lewis."

Chilly interrupts by saying, "You can call him whatever you want, just don't call him . . ."

"Late for a meal!" Joshua finishes the sentence. "Chilly and I always ate every morsel of food in the house, growing up."

Elliot asks, "Chilly?" He looks from the sheriff to the Indian.

"I'm sorry, that was our nickname for my Uncle. Is there any place to take a bath in this town?"

Chilly answers. "The Barber has a tub and will even pull a tooth, if you have a need for it. Joshua, you've inspired me. I am going to the barber shop, too, for a bath and a shave, right after we break our fast. If the stagecoach is still missing, afterward, would you like to help me track it down?"

"Don't you have a Deputy for that?"

"I will if you say yes." There is a gasp from Elliot and Chilly turns to him. "Are you still here? My eggs are not getting cooked with you standing there, gawking." Elliot grabs his hat and runs out the door.

"That's your Post Master? Are you sure he can read?"

"I haven't seen much proof so far. So, since we have a few months to kill before Spring arrives, want to be my Deputy?"

"I don't see why not. I am not doing anything else."

"Is that your answer for everything?"

"Pretty much, lately."

"I feel there is more to that story. On our way to the barber, I need to send a few telegrams. One to Mother and a couple about the stagecoach."

***

After their baths, Chilly gets his hair cut above his ears. Joshua has his middle-of-the-back braids cut, but leaves his hair long enough to pull into a knot at the back

25

of his neck. Joshua gets a full smooth shave and Chilly has his beard trimmed down to a short, neat goatee. They go back to the telegraph office to see if there has been any word from the Bartlesville or Tulsa stagecoach offices, but nothing has arrived so far. And neither has the stagecoach, itself.

"If you are going to look for the coach with me, you will need a badge. Do you have a gun belt?" the Sheriff asks as they walk back to the office.

"No Uncle, just a rifle."

"Are you a good shot?"

"I was the best in the tribe. The Colonel & Pa taught all of us well, if you recall. I can still see your sisters, trying to hold guns bigger than they were while aiming. They were all good shots, also."

As they walk into the Sheriff's office, Elliot greets them. "Sheriff, what are you going to do? It is after three, and the stage is now four hours late." Elliot is wringing his hands.

"Were you expecting something on that stage, Elliot?"

"My Aunt Martha and little cousin Brenda were coming out from the Bartlesville Depot. I am fearful that they were on that stage but I have no way to know. They may have stayed another night in Bartlesville and waited for the afternoon stage. The stage is only late when there is a bad reason."

"Sorry, Elliot. I sent a telegram to the Bartlesville depot to find out what time they departed, the employees' names and the passengers' names, and what was on its manifest. I haven't heard back from them yet. I do not want to start out without that information."

Chilly goes to his desk and takes something out of the top drawer. "Here, Joshua. Pin this badge on your chest. Boy, I cannot get over how much you look like my brother, the Colonel, especially with your braids cut off. Did you want to borrow a shirt and pants and complete the conversion back to a white man?"

"Not yet, Uncle. I am very comfortable in the buck skins sewn by my mother. If we are going on a hard ride, I do not need to feel uneasy."

"Would you be uncomfortable with a gun belt with a Colt .44 in it? Can you shoot with a pistol accurately?"

"I will be fine with both, Uncle."

"Joshua, you never called me Uncle while growing up. Why are you doing so now?"

"My people taught me to respect my elders and people in authority. You are both, though you are only six months older than myself. I'd hate to hang . . ."

"For six months!" Chilly finishes his sentence. "You are taking all my best lines, Harkahomé." He turns to Elliot. "Give me a description of your aunt and cousin."

"I have never met them. They lived back east my whole life."

"Do you know their ages at least?"

"I know Aunt Martha is my mother's youngest sister and she is older than me. But nothing else."

"So you are of no use to me here. Start rounding up a few men for a posse. Get Tom Baker, George the Blacksmith, then go to the Kirby Ranch and the Endeavor Ranch. See if they will spare me some ranch hands for a few days. Volunteers only."

The door to the Sheriff's office suddenly opens and a young man runs in. "Sheriff, you have three telegrams." He hands him the envelopes. "I will wait outside in case you have a reply." He walks out the door as fast as he entered.

Chilly is already reading the first telegram. "This one is from Mother. She says her prayers have been answered, and she awaits your return in the Spring. Then she adds, she is praying for our safe journey to Lawrence." He looks up at his nephew. "I can see the tears of happiness in her eyes, now." He hands the telegram to Joshua.

He rips open the next one. "This is from Bartlesville. The stage left on time with two employees, Jeff Williams the driver, and Pete Scroggins riding as the shotgun. They had five passengers." He looks up at Elliot. "Sorry, Elliot, your aunt and cousin are listed, along with a Scott Jones, a Sadie Miller and a Rusty Banner. That sounds like an alias if ever I've heard one." He chuckles to himself. "Their load includes the payroll for the Dawn of the West Mining Outfit in Tulsa. Six hundred dollars would be in that strong box."

He rips open the last envelope. "The Mining outfit is getting their own posse together, and are headed this way from Tulsa. The regular driver Jerry is home. Seems he got married on Saturday." He looks up at Elliot. "Go get that posse ready. Send in the telegram man. I need to send one more message. When I have enough men here, we head out!"

***

It is less than an hour later, that ten men crowd into the Sheriff's small office. "I want you all to meet my nephew, Harkahomé, formally of the Cheyenne tribe in Wyoming. He has agreed to be my permanent Deputy. Tom Baker, since you worked for the stage line some years ago, I want you in the lead to find the coach. Can you do that?"

"Yes, sir. Sheriff."

Harkahomé is next to his uncle and asks, "How far is Bartlesville?"

"It is twenty miles which is a twelve-hour ride, on a good day. That is why I telegrammed the Sheriff of Bartlesville to form a posse and meet me on the trail. Depending on where the trouble lies, he might beat us to the stagecoach."

"That was a good idea, Uncle."

"I am not as dumb as you look, Nephew."

28

"I think we look alike except for our coloring." Everyone nods in agreement.

"Okay, men. Keep your guns holstered until you see my gun out, not before. Do you understand?" He looks at each man. "Can you obey that order?" A few mumbles and grunts are heard. "We will find the coach, some of you will escort the coach back here. Then we will search for the person or persons responsible for its delay. Agreed?" More grunts. "Good. Let's mount up." They exit the office.

Elliot does not leave. "I feel I will be of more use to you here, Sheriff. I am not good at confrontations. As you recall, you saved my life the morning you became Sheriff. I am just not good in a fight."

"Do not worry about it Elliot. Not everyone is." The six-foot-eight sheriff pats the man, nearly two feet shorter, on the shoulder. He puts his hat on and walks out. He says as he is mounting his Morgan horse. "Everyone ready? Then Tom – head north!" Tom kicks his horse into gear and takes off as the rest of the posse follows close behind.

***

The Sheriff and his posse have ridden hard with little luck. Tom says that they are past the halfway point to Bartlesville. They are camped early for the evening, as it is a moonless night, and the temperature has dropped to just above freezing. They have two fires lit and all the men are huddled around them, shivering. Elliot packed a mess kit for the group with cans of bean, salt pork, beef jerky, coffee and hard tack. One of the men shot two rabbits. The rabbits are roasting on makeshift spits. The men are complaining about the temperature."

Chilly says, "You don't know cold. When my brother the Colonel and I were looking for Harkahomé back in 1880, we were in snow up to our knees and the cold

29

wind froze the snot to your mustache."

Harkahomé interrupts, "You were only 14, Uncle, and you did not have a moustache to freeze."

"True, but I had to watch Will's snot cake up on his mustache! I do not know how your tribe survived those harsh winters in teepees."

"The summer after you found us, a missionary came to us and taught us to build long houses. They kept out the cold better and we slept in them during the worst nights. The braves did not like it because it was hard to share a blanket with your woman with so many snoring sleepers."

"Still better than freezing to death, wasn't it?"

"I do not know. I had not shared a blanket with a woman to compare the two."

"And have you shared a blanket with a woman, yet?"

"No, Uncle. I have not married, or shared a blanket."

"Oh, Joshua, when we get back, I will take you out and fix that."

"I do not want to wed, Uncle. I want to go to Lawrence."

Chilly starts to laugh. "I was talking about the blanket activities, not marriage. God forbid, we get all mushy like the Colonel or Carolyn's husband Grant. Marriage changes a guy. I am not interested. I like to come and go as I please."

"That is what Josie said about you."

"What did she say?"

"Charming Charlie comes and goes as he pleases. She did not seem too happy about it. So, you have shared her blanket, Uncle?"

"A gentleman does not kiss and tell."

"But you are no gentleman, Uncle."

Chilly laughs so hard that he spits out his coffee. "Joshua, you wound me with those words. I was raised a gentleman, when the need calls for it. And I am a 'take charge with no apologies' kind of a guy all the rest of the time."

"And you say you are not like your brother Will?"

"I did not say I was not like him. I said that I did not want to end up like him. A glorified farmer, hosting grand balls just so that he can dance with his wife."

"It does not sound like a bad life, Uncle. You just have not found the right woman, yet. Neither have I. We have not been lucky like the Colonel."

"Right now, I will be lucky to find the stagecoach, just broken down and no foul play, involved. If it was held up, usually the passengers are permitted to continue their journey. If both employees were killed, they would be stranded, unable to find their way. Or it might just be a broken wheel, and everyone is fine, just inconvenienced. We should run into them or the other posse, early tomorrow, either way. I am going to turn in."

He calls out. "George the Blacksmith and Harkahomé will take the first four-hour watch. Dillon Hurly and Dustin Crowder, take the second watch. Henry and John Worthington get the last watch before sun-up. If we are out another night, I will pick on six other men. Agreed?"

Everyone settles in for a long cold sleep in their bedrolls. Harkahomé and George take turns walking around the sleeping men, all of whom are snoring and checking the horses during their four-hour shift.

FOUR
January 6th, 1959
A Tuesday in Lawrence, Kansas

Helen walks out of the large eat-in kitchen and goes to the staircase. "GW, William, Audrey, Charlotte, Eleanor, and Kevin! It is time for breakfast! Chop, chop kids."

"We are coming, Mommy." The youngest girl, Eleanor, shouts down. "But, Audrey won't leave the bathroom."

"Come, use one of the other ones. We have five, for goodness sake." Their demure thirty-six-year-old mother has her arms crossed over her chest. "Seriously, children, we have enough bedrooms and bathrooms that there should be no fighting at all! Now come down for breakfast." She shakes her head as she walks back into the kitchen. Her husband of nineteen years, Joshua, is drinking his coffee. "I swear, I feel more of a circus wrangler than a mother, most days."

The six-foot-tall, dark blonde grandson of the Colonel, puts his cup down and crosses over to his wife. "I think a circus would be easier, than getting six children to school on time. Just breathe, Helen. If Gram Beth can wrangle seven children . . . " He sees Helen roll her eyes. "I am sorry, I know you are tired of me comparing you to her but she is in our blood and so is her strength."

"I think we need to find another Anna. I feel that I have not been able to catch up since she moved out to EL Dorado in '46. Even while running the restaurant, she managed to keep everything running smoothly in our house and hers."

"I think they broke the mold when they made Anna. Carrie Ann seems to be the most like her. But outside of her, there is no one like her, anywhere."

"Listen to you, that is why I was so jealous of her when we were first wed. I didn't know how to compete with her. I knew that you idolized her."

"Yes, and now you agree with my assessment of her." He enfolds Helen into his arms. "It is you that still makes my heart beat faster, when you walk into the room. Sweetheart, I will go upstairs to get the children moving. You make yourself a cup of tea and relax."

"Thank you, Joshua, you always make me feel better."

"That is my life's mission." He bends to kiss her forehead. Then he turns around, goes out of the kitchen and up the stairs. "GW, William, Audrey, get your little siblings downstairs. Now!"

Helen turns to the stove and takes the kettle off to fill it with hot water. She lets the water run exceptionally long to drown out the children bickering amongst themselves. She gets the kettle back on the stove and goes to get herself a cup. When she turns to put it on the large diner style island, she is startled by her oldest standing there. "Oh, GW. Good, time to have breakfast, please. Are the others almost ready?"

"Yes, Mother. Father is bringing them down shortly. I need to talk with you and father, once the little ones head off to school." GW is as tall as his father and has light brown hair that always turns blonde every summer. He is a freshman at the University of Kansas and looks the most like his father than any of the others.

"That sounds serious. Are you all right?"

He crosses over to her and bends down and gives her a kiss on the forehead, just as his father had moments before. "Never better, mother, but I do need some advice regarding a personal matter."

Before she can say a word, the kitchen is suddenly packed with children, followed by their father. "Here they are, Helen. All clean, dressed and ready for breakfast."

"And just in time! Cereal is on the table and I have your lunches packed." The three oldest sit at the island but the three little ones sit at a children's table off to the side. They have three redheads in the family, Audrey, Charlotte and Kevin. William and Eleanor both have dark curly hair like their late great-grandfather.

"Hurry, children, the school busses will be here in fifteen minutes. Not much time to eat and go back upstairs to brush your teeth. So, hurry!" Their father says.

The next fifteen minutes, flies by and the children are off to their schools. William, 16, and Audrey, 14, go to the high school. Charlotte, 12, Eleanor, 10, and Kevin, 8, go to the elementary school.

The whole house seems suddenly dead quiet once the last bus leaves. Helen comes back into the kitchen where GW and Joshua are still sitting at the counter. "Let me go to the bathroom, GW, and we can have that talk. Okay?"

Joshua looks up from his second cup of coffee. "We wouldn't dream of stopping you!"

"Very funny!" Helen says as she rushes to the bathroom, right off the kitchen. "Gram Beth never mentioned in her journals that having six kids can affect your ability to hold a cup of tea in your bladder for more than fifteen minutes! That would have been useful information!"

"I don't think GW needs to hear it, though."

"Why not? Men should know what a woman goes through baring his children." Helen says from the bathroom. They can hear the water running then a flush. Helen always uses the sound of water to cover the sound of her going because what happens in this bathroom can be heard as if there was no door at all between them. After she washes her hands, she exits the room. "Wow, that feels better. Now what do you need to talk to us about?"

"Carrie Ann Harrick." He says simply.

"What about her?" His mother responds.

"I am nuts about her. We went for a sleigh ride before she moved to Chicago and I told her. She says she has feelings for me, also. I called her yesterday and invited her to the Annual Valentine Ball. I told her that she should fly to Wichita and we would pay for it." GW holds his breath, waiting for his mother or father to object to the notion.

"You feel that strongly for her?" Joshua asks.

"I have been in love with her since we were eight years old. Maybe even before that."

"It's about time that you finally admitted it, and did something about it." Joshua looks to his wife. "Our boy is growing up."

"So, you are not mad that I offered to pay for her to fly out?"

"I cannot say that I am exactly happy but you have made the first move." His father says.

"I think it is time he reads how the Colonel won his Julia during the Cheyenne-Kansas war. They wrote letters to each other until he convinced her to marry him just days after seeing each other for the first time in four years." Helen says with pride.

"Those must have been some letters!"

"They were, we have those also. It is the best way to win a long-distance gal to your side."

"You think I should write Carrie Ann letters?

"Not just letters but love letters." His mother corrects him. I will find the box of letters and Gram Beth's journal while you are at school. Aren't you going to be late? What time is your first class, today?"

"Not until 10:30, but I need to go to the library, so I will be off. Thank you for not getting mad at me. I was worried." He holds out his hand for his father to shake it and goes to his mother and gives her a hug. "You are the best parents, ever." He says as he races out the door.

"See, and you thought you weren't doing it well." Joshua says.

"One down and five to go! Then I will know if I have succeeded."

FIVE
January 7th, 1896
A Tuesday in Oklahoma

The last two watchmen got the fire roaring and the coffee on as the sun came up over the horizon. Harkahomé is the first to rise though he had four hours' less sleep than most of the men. He pours two cups of coffee, then walks over, and puts one down to shake Chilly. "Uncle, the sun is up and so must we be. I feel we will have a long day ahead of us."

"I am up. I swear, I am just twenty-nine but when I sleep outdoors like this, I feel ninety-two!"

"Is that how old we are? I have not thought of my age in years."

"You will not be twenty-nine until May, Joshua."

"Still, it is strange how different we have grown apart yet are still very similar. Do not you feel it so? Uncle?"

"I try not to have deep thoughts or feelings before my first cup of coffee, nephew. Pour me a cup, will you?"

"Sorry, Uncle. This is your cup." He hands the hot cup from the ground to Chilly.

After the sheriff takes four long loud gulps, he shouts to the men. "Let's get a move on. We need to find the coach. Anyone left alive, will not survive another cold night like the last." The men roll up their blankets, repack their horses and within fifteen minutes they are all back on the trail with Tom in the lead.

***

It is a few hours later that Tom slows down to point out to Chilly a dust cloud coming toward them. "Must be a large group on horseback. Since it is on the trail, I would assume it isn't Indians, but we can never be too sure. Do we want to ride or hide?"

"I think we will just wait for them. No need to hide." He turns to the men. "Everyone dismount. We will take a short break and wait for the Bartlesville sheriff to arrive."

It takes a quick half hour for the other posse to catch up to them. Chilly is standing in the front to greet them. Two men dismount and approach Chilly. "Are you Sheriff Charles Lewis?"

"Yes, sir. Are you Sheriff John Lucas?"

"I am."

Chilly squints to look at the Bartlesville Sheriff. "Damn man, what happened to you? You've gained thirty pounds since you left the Cavalry!" The two men hug and pat each other on the back.

"It's called the love of a good woman, who loves to cook." He looks to the tall man beside Chilly. "Is this your nephew, Harkahomé? He looks just like the Colonel!" John Lucas holds out his hand for Joshua to shake.

"You know my Uncles, Sir?"

"Served under the Colonel when he was a Major and Chilly served under me when I was a Major. I am the one who told him about this position being open."

"Did you know about the two dead sheriffs before he came here?"

"They were fools. Your uncle is no fool."

"That is your opinion?" Harkahomé asks.

"Excuse me, I am standing right here! John, have you seen anything of the stagecoach? We haven't."

"About two miles back, my scout thought that he saw fresh tracks go off the trail. I sent him ahead while I came for you. The rest of my posse is waiting for us, there."

"I thought that four men was a little light for the dust cloud we saw rising." Chilly turns to his men. "Breaks over. We have a coach to find." Everyone quickly mounts up and rides out following Sheriff Lucas.

A half an hour later they meet up with the other five

men in the Bartlesville posse and follow them in the direction that the scout went. The scout was careful to ride parallel to the tracks so as not to disturb them, Chilly is told. Chilly points out the stage tracks to Joshua. "It doesn't look as if they were in a hurry to take this detour. I wonder what made them take this turn. Elliot told me that the driver, Jeff Williams has made this run lots of times, so he did not just take a wrong turn."

The trail is downhill and leads to a wooded area. As soon as they get in the woods, they see a path where a stagecoach might fit. As they proceed two by two it takes another half an hour before they come across the stagecoach parked next to a small pond. There are no horses or men in sight but there is a fire lit. There are several ladies sitting around the fire. The posse of men dismount, and the ladies stand up and dust themselves off.

The matronly woman is the first to speak. "Thank God, you've come to help us. This has been just awful."

I am Sheriff Lewis out of Pennysville and this is Sheriff Lucas from Bartlesville. What's happened? Where are the men and horses?"

"Indians!" She exclaimed. "They forced us off the road. The driver thought he could hide here in the woods but they found us. They stole the team of horses and all the weapons. The man riding shotgun was shot and so was the driver. The Indians left us here to rot."

"Where is Jeff and Pete and the other men?" asks Chilly.

"They said that they were going to find help. Didn't any of them find you?" Says the dark haired young lady.

"No we haven't seen them. Are you Aunt Martha Masters?" Chilly asks the eldest lady.

"I know you can't be my nephew Elliot. From what his mother wrote, he never grew past five feet."

"Yes ma-am, I think that is true. Elliot is the town Postmaster and he sort of runs my Sheriff's office. He was very concerned about you and sounded the alarm that something was wrong. Are you and your daughter unharmed?"

Chilly looks at the two young ladies standing next to Martha. The dark haired one has on a very colorful dress and a large feathered hat. The other is wearing a smartly tailored traveling suit. It is identical to her mother's, except for the color. Martha's is black, while Brenda's is royal blue. She has a small blue bonnet covering her very blonde hair.

"We are not harmed." Brenda says in a small shy voice.

"Not harmed? I was supposed to start work last night at Penny's Parlor and Saloon. Do you know how much money I missed out on? I deal twenty-one and I am very good at what I do."

Harkahomé speaks. "Do you know which tribe it was?"

"No, if you've seen one Indian, you've seen them all." Says Martha with distaste.

Chilly says in a very loud authoritative voice. "Ladies, I'd like to introduce my deputy and nephew, Joshua. Also, known as Harkahomé of the Cheyenne."

Martha holds her head up higher and stands a bit taller and says, "Present company, excluded." But does not apologize.

The two sheriffs and their deputies leave their side and go to look at and around the stagecoach. "Something doesn't add up here." Chilly says to the others. "The tracks that turn off the trail had no hard-riding men on horseback with it, and the tracks weren't made by a fast-moving coach, being pursued."

"Why would Elliot's aunt lie and the other women agree to it?" Joshua asks.

"That is another mystery, isn't it? Is the strong box up there?"

Tom climbs on top to look. "Not here, sheriff."

"Any blood, bullet casings or bullet holes?"

"Just casings as far as I can see."

Chilly whispers something to his nephew then they go back to the women. "Miss Brenda, can I ask you a few questions?" He takes her by the elbow and leads her away from her mother. Joshua leads the other girl in the opposite direction. "Miss Brenda, when did the shooting start?

Brenda looks at her hands as she speaks. "We were still on the main trail, I think. Things happened so fast."

"I am sure they did. When were Pete and Jeff shot?"

"Who?"

"The driver and the shotgun man."

"I do not know. They were hurt when we came to a stop."

"Thank you, Miss Brenda. You live in Bartlesville or just passing through?"

"We were visiting relatives in Kansas, on my father's side. My father's baby brother Jed and his wife just had a baby boy. They named him Judd. And he has the Master's light blue eyes. They are living in Hope, Kansas. So, we have come from there. We just decided to visit Elliot, last minute."

"Thank you Miss Brenda. You can go back to your mother."

Chilly and Joshua go back to Sheriff Lucas on the other side of the stage. He says to them, "We have to locate the missing men. If it was Indians, the women and the horses would be gone but I doubt the strong box. What I see is that the men, horses and strong box are gone, and the women are lying about it. Tom, hook up horses to the stage and let's get everyone to town. Sheriff Lucas, we are closer to your jurisdiction; do you want to investigate this case, or shall I?"

"I think you have the larger number of jail cells. I think there are going to be many arrests made before this gets sorted out. I yield the jurisdiction to you. I will stay here and look for the men or any clues as to which tribe of Indians were involved. I will come to Pennysville with my findings, as soon as I can."

"Thanks John, that will be a big help."

SIX

January 7th, 1959

A Wednesday in EL Dorado, Kansas

Anna Harrick is at her restaurant, The Central Avenue Eatery, for the dinner rush. Her son, Harry, is sitting at the booth nearest to the kitchen. He came to the restaurant right from school, where he is a sophomore. He was at baseball practice, first. He is hoping to make the varsity team. He pitches fast and accurately. His height would be the only thing stopping him from making the team. Like his father, Henry, at this age, he hasn't hit his growth spurt, yet. His father grew a foot in his seventeenth year and kept going after that. Like his father, also, at this stage, he doesn't know what sort of sound will come out of his mouth with each sentence. Sometimes he talks high like a girl, sometimes it is low like his father's deep silky voice. Which it will be is a surprise every time.

Anna comes out of the back, "Harry, go make yourself something to eat. Aren't you hungry after all that running around during practice?"

Before he can answer, his father walks into the front door, carrying a large box filled with supplies. "Good, you are here. Grab a box or two, will you, son?"

"Sure, Father." He leaves his books in the booth and goes out to the truck.

Henry walks past his wife of twenty-two years and puts the box on the counter. "Anna, aren't you going to say hello?"

"I am sorry, do I know you, sir?"

"Oh, I am sorry, you looked like a girl I knew back in grade school. She was so pretty. You favor her a lot."

"That's funny, I thought you looked like a boy I knew once, when we had our farm in Hope. He was a short guy, kind of like that young man that is helping you with the boxes." She turns to look closely at him. "Yes, I definitely see a resemblance. Same Roman nose, and wavy hair that is always going into the eyes. Of course, his was almost black, not grey like yours is. I wonder what ever became of him?"

"I heard my friend ended up cooking for a living. Never could get her away from a hot stove."

"I do like things hot, too. My friend was a farm manager for a long time. Now he lives off what his wife makes."

"Is that what they say?"

"Yes, she makes a good living and he is her consort."

"Consort? I like the sound of that. It is better than being called a gigolo. Consort sounds like a royal title. Enough small talk, come give us a kiss." He says in his best low silky tone which still makes her stomach twitter. He grabs her by the arm and pulls her to him.

He bends forward to gently brush her lips with his, when a voice in front of them says, "Will you two ever stop? It is creepy to see your parents smooch. Honestly!"

Henry and Anna do not let their son stop them, and continue with their sweet kiss. When done, Anna turns to look at her boy. "I hope we never stop smooching, son, whether you like it or not. Is that the last of the supplies?" She starts looking in the boxes.

Anna's son, Harry says, "There is one more small box. I will get it. If there is any more smooching to be done, please do it while I am not looking."

"I don't mind if I do." Henry goes behind Anna and kisses the back of her neck. "He's a good kid, and he has some good suggestions."

"Like you need encouraging. Be honest, Henry, do you still want me like you did when we were first married?"

"YES!" he says without a moment's hesitation. "Why would you think otherwise?"

"I am getting so old. We have two daughters in college. I have grey hair coming in and I see some wrinkles

43

starting to form."

"I have all those, too. I was out in the sun, working on the farm for all those years. My face is very lined. Do you still find me attractive?"

"OH! Gross! Now, I want to puke! Must you talk like that in front of God and everybody? There are places you can go, to have these discussions. Any room, with the door closed, where my ears can't hear - would be preferred. Really!"

"Good idea, Harry. Come Anna, let's go to the backroom with these supplies. Harry bring the box in and go back to your studies. Your mother and I will do this *alone.*"

As they head to the backroom, all carrying a box, Henry says, "I heard on the radio that Chicago is being hit with a blizzard. Snow deeper than they've seen in years. We should call the girls to see if they are safe at home. I cannot imagine living in a city that has so much snow."

"I cannot imagine living away from home, period." Anna says. "Now, I am worried. How are those two are going to survive? They have never seen that much snow, their whole lives."

"I imagine them both thinking that it will be a great adventure." Says Henry.

SEVEN
January 8th, 1959
A Wednesday in Chicago

Clara Beth and her little sister Carrie Ann decide to venture out into the snow and get a few things at the Hi – Low Grocery store. They came home with a brown bag each and it was all they could do to keep their balance trudging through the high snow with ice underneath. When they went to leave the apartment, they could barely push the door open. Someone had attempted to clear some snow from the sidewalk but unfortunately it trapped them in.

Once back in the apartment, they put the sacks down to wrestle off their boots. Their phone rings and even though she only has one foot boot-free, Clara Beth hops to the phone. "Harrick girls' residence, Clara speaking. Hi, Mama! Carrie Ann and I are just fine. Blizzard, what blizzard? Dad heard a story on the radio? It made the news in Kansas? It is not that bad, here. Honestly. We just went to the Hi – Low. It's a grocery store. A nice size one, too. Mama really, I will let you talk to Carrie Ann. She has some news to tell you, anyway. No. It's good news. No, I am not going to give you a clue. Let her tell you, herself." She puts the phone down and looks to her sister. "She is worried that we are sitting in the frozen tundra."

"Well, that just about describes it. Why did you tell her about the news? I don't know if I have decided to go?" Carrie says with her hand over the phone's mouthpiece.

"Please, you wouldn't miss it."

"I don't want to worry her about the plane. You know how she is." Carrie says with her hand still covering the mouth piece. "Hello, Mama. How are things going in EL Dorado? No, the snow isn't that bad. I cannot believe you heard about Chicago's weather in Kansas. Oh, she mentioned that I have news? It is just that GW Lewis has asked me to EL Dorado's Valentine Ball. I told him that I would think about it, but I am excited about the thought of going. No mama, if I need to take too many days off school, I won't go. I know how expensive my education is, and I do not want to waste your hard-earned money. That is why I told him, I need to talk with my professors, first. I have not been to school, yet." She looks to her sister and winks. "They have extended the holiday break . . . yes, because of the snow. It is not that bad, since everything is in walking distance for us." Carrie puts he hand over the mouth of the phone, and says to Clara Beth, "She will not let the snow – go."

"Okay, tell her you will be flying into Wichita." Clara chuckles.

"Are you crazy? She will spin completely out of control if she has to worry about that too!" She takes her hand off the mouthpiece, again. "No, Mama, I am still here. Clara Beth was just asking me a question about dinner. We just got groceries. Hey, I met a real nice guy, his family owns an Italian restaurant, here. It is called Como's Spicy Meatball & Pizza Parlor. His name is Gianni Como. He is very cute, too . . . I know I said that I *might* go to the Ball with GW, but I am here now, aren't I? No sense sitting around doing nothing; when I can have a nice guy from a hard-working family, show me the city." She rolls her eyes at her sister who rolled her eyes first.

"I am not sure what we are going to eat, yet. I am thinking I am in the mood for Italian. I could see Gianni, again. Mama, I am a *good* girl, but a little batting of the eye, doesn't hurt anyone."

Carrie finally gets her mother off the line, when the phone rings before she can take her hand off the receiver. "Harrick Girls Residence, this is Carrie Ann speaking. Hey GW, this isn't the weekend yet. I do not have an answer for you. Oh, you heard about our weather on the news in Lawrence? I just got off the phone with Mother. She heard about it in EL Dorado, too. She is a basket case from worrying about us. No, we are just fine. We just picked up groceries. Most everything we need is within walking distance. Oh, you told your parents about offering to pay for my trip to Wichita? I thought you said they knew all ready? Are they mad? No? I am so glad to hear that. I still need to talk to my professors about needing a day or two off. With the snow-days we are being given now, I might not be able to catch up with all the work that they are going to pile up on us. Yes, GW, I am looking forward to it, but there is so much going on here in Chicago . . . The Colonel's letters? Yes, I know about them. Mother always talked about him wooing his Julia through them, while fighting Indians. I was very interested in them. You want to write to me? I don't know if I will have time to respond with class and homework. I think about you often but . . . Okay, I promise I will try to write a letter to you in response, when I get one. I need to go, now GW. Say hello to your parents and siblings for me."

As she puts down the phone, she rubs her ear. "I think I am going to have cauliflower ear from being on the line, for so long."

"I doubt that. Were you telling the truth about going by Gianni's? I wouldn't mind some spaghetti and meatballs."

"Yes, me too. It is funny, we go and buy all these groceries then are too exhausted to stay in and cook."

"There is always tomorrow," Clara says hopefully. "Should we head out, now? This way we won't be home too late.

"Good thinking. That's why they call you the smart Harrick girl."

EIGHT
January 8th, 1896
A Wednesday in Pennysville, Oklahoma

Sheriff Charles Palmer Lewis and Deputy Harkahomé are riding in the stagecoach with the women back to Pennysville. The Sheriff is very quiet at first and just looking out the window. The temperature is dropping again with the onset of nightfall. The women are shivering even though they are each under a stagecoach provided blanket. They are sitting with their back facing the direction they are going, so Chilly and Harkahomé are getting the cold wind in their face.

After a long time of awkward silence, Chilly asks, "What was the first sign of trouble? Was there a shout or a shot?"

"What a funny thing to ask!" Says Aunt Martha. "I was dozing peacefully when the stage jerked hard and I realized we were turning and going faster than before. Then I heard shouting above us and a couple of gunshots. The men were sitting, riding backwards, like we are. The cowboy looking man . . . what was his name, Brenda?"

"Dusty or Rusty Bennet or Banner, I don't recall." She answers in a low tone."

"Well, he looks out the window and shouts, 'We are being attacked by Indians!', then he pulls out his revolver and starts shooting at them behind us."

"Did you ever see who was behind you?"

"No, because the other guy, the businessman Scott Jones yelled for us to take cover and bow our heads down. He carried a revolver in an under-the-arm kind of a holster and started shooting out the window, too."

"Then what happened?" Joshua asks Sadie Miller.

"Well, after they ran out of bullets, they reloaded what they had. The cowboy warned the businessman to save one or two for self-defense. Then the terrain changed.

I could smell a forest smell and our wheels rolled quieter as if we were on grass instead of baked clay. After a few minutes riding like that, everything got very quiet. The men told us to stay down and hidden, but they got out."

"Miss Brenda, can you finish the story?" Chilly asks. "Go slow and try not to leave out any details." He reaches across and takes her hand. "Don't be afraid, the worst is over."

The young blonde in the blue traveling suit looks up at him. She looks him right in the eyes and smiles. The Sheriff takes a breath in. "You have the lightest, blue eyes, I have ever seen. I am sorry, that was rude of me. Please forgive me. Try to pick up the story where Miss Sadie left off. First, do you know the names of the men on top?"

"Yes, Sheriff. They introduced themselves as Mr. Williams and Mr. Scroggins. They were the driver and the guard, respectively. So, we were still hiding in here. The men were yelling to each other. It sounded like Indian or something else foreign to me. It was loud yet muffled at the same time. The coach rocked as they removed the horses and I think they took some things stored on the top. I said to Mother, I hope they steal my luggage because I am tired of what I own. I was trying to break the tension. Mother did not think it was funny. When the business man told us that it was safe to come out, the two employees were gone. We were told they had been wounded in the gunfire, but were going for help. Hours went by and the cowboy said that he couldn't just sit here any longer and that he was going to go back to Bartlesville for help, since that was the opposite direction the employees went. Mr. Johnson stayed until the morning. He left Mother with a gun and three bullets in case the Indians came back. He left, then, to go find help, himself. Then a few hours later, all of you showed up."

"That makes a little more sense than what you said when we first saw you. So, none of you looked out the window at any time?"

"I was afraid if they saw us - they would take us," said Sadie.

Harkahomé reaches across and pats her trembling hand. "That happens with many tribes. Sometimes it is for your own safety, though. That is what happened to my mother and myself. My stepfather saved our lives by taking us captive. He and my Cheyenne people were very good to us. They treated us with respect and kindness, always."

"How old were you when this happened?" Sadie asks.

"I was just eleven. We were very frightened in the beginning because we had not learned the language from them. They had no way to calm our fears except through kindness and smiles."

Martha says, "Well, I was too afraid to look up, I have heard what some Indians do to white women. I did not want that to happen to myself or my daughter. We stayed down and prayed holding onto each other."

Sadie nods her head, "And I am not the kind of woman that usually prays but I did it in this stagecoach that day. I prayed very hard!"

Joshua laughs. "White people tend to call on God when we need him or her but forget to include him when they are thankful for the gifts that they have received. I learned many prayers of thanksgiving. My people thank God for everything that comes to us."

"Well, isn't that fascinating! What sort of things are you talking about?" Sadie leans forward and puts her head in her hand while resting her elbow on her knee.

"We thank God when it rains, and when it stops. We thank God when a good kill of an animal feeds and clothes us. We thank God when our hearts beat for a man or a woman and a marriage is considered. We thank God when we have seed to sow and when the seed comes out of the earth and stretches to the sky. We thank God when the harvest is good and when we find clean water to drink.

Many blessings are sent to us from God. The Cheyenne *must* take the time to thank the One who sends it."

"I have never thought of life or God like that, before. Fascinating, just fascinating." Sadie says again.

"I think you are mocking my nephew, Miss Sadie."

"No Sheriff. I am amazed at the life he must have led. When we get to town, you need to call on me and tell me more about yourself."

Aunt Martha's eyes grow wide as the young woman practically throws herself at the young man raised as a heathen. She exchanges looks with her daughter. Brenda says, "It is very interesting, Harkahomé. I would like to hear more, myself."

This makes Aunt Martha gasp loudly and say, "Brenda, how could you?"

Chilly and Joshua are both looking at Brenda when she says, "I'd like to know more about the sheriff, too. They are fascinating men. Aren't they Miss Sadie?"

"They truly are."

"Well, I never!" Aunt Martha says then crosses her arms, leans back into the seat, then adds, "Never ever!"

Joshua says, "My Uncle here, came to look for me when he was only fourteen-years-old. He braved the snow and ice and tracked my tribe down to Wyoming. He is a very brave good man."

"Is that true, Sheriff?" Brenda asks him then blushes.

"I am glad to see a modicum of modesty from you Brenda. I swear that you have forgotten your upbringing!"

"Mother, I feel like I almost died but have yet to live. I want to change that. It is time to start living. I am to be twenty years old and I have never been kissed. Can you believe that?" Brenda says as looking at Chilly.

"Brenda, why would you say something like that?"

"Because Mother, it is true. I have never been kissed and I almost died. I am tired of being modest and shy and humble. I want to find a good man to fall in love

51

with and make a family. I am tired of waiting around like a wallflower." She turns to Chilly. "Sheriff, do you find me attractive?"

"Very much Miss Brenda." Now it is the Sheriff's turn to blush.

"Sheriff, I would like it very much if you will call on me, when we are settled in at cousin Elliot's." She smiles and he can feel his heart skip a beat and then it picks up the pace and races.

The sheriff awkwardly says, "I would like that very much, too. Miss Brenda. I do have this investigation to wrap up. I will come ask you to dinner the first chance I get. If you would allow it, Aunt Martha."

"It seems I have very little say in the matter!" She says as she breathes in with disgust, cross her arms over the other way and turns her head to stare out the window.

The sheriff watches the mother then turns to Brenda. She is smiling at him as if she didn't even notice her mother's actions. He smiles back, tips his hat and gives her a wink, all the while he is thinking, *Be still my heart!*

NINE
January 8ᵗʰ, 1959
A Thursday in Lawrence, Kansas

Joshua is at the farm office when the phone rings. "Legacy Plantation, Joshua speaking." He says by rote.

"Joshua, it is Henry, how are you, old friend.?"

"Oh, I do not like the way this conversation is starting. Is there something wrong at the Diner?"

"Not at all, we had our best quarter, ever! Anna has hired a great little cook and has trained her on the big grill, all ready. I do not know if you know, but there is a blizzard in Chicago. Anna has talked to the girls, they are fine. They find this all an adventure. I don't remember seeing the world that way. Did you?"

"My college days were fun. But I couldn't wait to get back home. You had it harder with your father losing his farm and all. The Depression was not an adventure for anyone."

"The reason I am calling, Joshua, Carrie mentioned that GW has asked her to the EL Dorado Valentine Ball. Did he mention that to you?"

"He did, actually. He is kind of crazy for Carrie. If you didn't know. Always has been. Is there a problem with her flying out at our expense?"

"Flying out? She didn't mention that."

"GW told her that we would pay for a round-trip ticket to Wichita. This way, she wouldn't miss any school. She didn't tell you that?"

"Well, she talked with Anna. You know how Anna feels about airplanes. Especially, after Matthew's bomber plane went down over the Pacific, in '41. Thank God, he was rescued but planes still scare the bejeezus out of her. Carrie might have just left that part out to keep her from worrying too much. She was concerned about her driving back to Kansas, this time of year, just as she arrived in

53

Chicago, safely, then snowed in. She hasn't even started classes, yet, due to the snow. Well, Carrie has said that she will give him an answer over the weekend. I know she has always been sweet on him, too. We might finally get to be related by blood if things work out."

"They are too young for you to be thinking that far ahead, Henry."

"Really, remind me how old Helen was, when you married her?"

"True, she was just seventeen, but things were different then."

"How is Helen and the other children?"

"Well, Audrey is going to her first formal dance and so the whole house is involved in that craziness. Nothing else is new. How is Harry doing?"

"He made Varsity baseball. He has been working very hard with his pitching. He thought that they might keep him out because of his height, but they saw the speed of his throw and wanted him. He is very excited. He wants to go Pro. Kids these days, dream big."

"That is wonderful, though, Henry. Carrie with her fashion design, Clara Beth with her engineering. I have tried not to push GW into any specific field but thank God, he wants to run the family business and is taking a double major of Agriculture and Business Management. He has a good head on his shoulders. Thank God."

"If he likes my Carrie Ann, he is brilliant!"

"So they got buried in snow in the Big City?"

"And they are loving it, from what I hear."

"To be young, again."

"No thank you. I barely survived my youth. Especially the year Anna was missing. It was a year from hell. I still thank God for your sister Carolyn and you, for taking her in. It still blows me away, all that you've done for her."

"Henry, we loved her at first glance. First Carolyn, then me. We've talked about it many times over the years, she and I. We don't understand it either. She was a sister to us, immediately, even though Anna didn't know herself, who she was. Yes, I was confused by my feelings for her, but when I fell in love with Helen, I was struck by how stupid I was that first year. I never apologized to you for my actions. Better late than never. I am very sorry, Henry, for making your reunion, strained to say the least. When I saw the look on Anna's face when she remembered you, I knew that there was no hope for me."

"Water under the bridge, my old friend. You have more than made up for your actions and those of your jealous bride. We love you both so much. I know I have never said those words to you, but I do. I love you, Joshua, and Helen and Carolyn and her husband Eddie. You have brought us into your family unit, when we were at our lowest. A true friend, indeed!"

"Henry, my dear friend, you are getting mushy in your old age."

"Joshua, my dear friend, we are the same age."

"Let's talk next week. Maybe we'll know more about our children's love life, by then."

"For some reason, I doubt it, but we can hope."

"Hope has been my constant friend, Joshua. Have a good week, give a kiss to Helen for me."

"Same to you and Anna, Henry."

TEN

January 9th, 1896

A Thursday in Pennysville, Oklahoma

At noon, the stagecoach rumbles into town with its posse entourage. Elliot is there to meet it. Before Chilly can open the door, Elliot was yelling, "Aunt Martha? Cousin Brenda? Sheriff did you bring them back safe and sound? I was so worried about you! Is it you?" He has his hand on the doorknob turning it to open it from the outside, but Chilly was trying to turn it from the inside.

Chilly realizes why he could not open the door, and yells. "Damn it Elliot, let go of the doorknob." Elliot lets go and steps back from the stagecoach. Chilly opens the door and puts down the steps as he says to Elliot. "Sometimes I think you don't have the sense God gave flies, Elliot."

"Sorry Sheriff, I am just excited about my relatives' safety. I didn't mean nothing by it."

"Let me present the stagecoach passengers. Miss Sadie Miller, this is our Postmaster and Brenda's cousin." He helps her down from the coach. "Next we have your Aunt Martha Masters. Aunt Martha, sorry to disappoint you but this is your nephew, Elliot."

"Elliot, you're a duplicate of your father. Spitting image, I swear! I am glad you rang the alarm for us. It might have been days before anyone cared that the stage was missing."

"Aunt Martha, I have connecting rooms for you at the Kirby Hotel." Brenda is the last person off the stage. "Cousin? You are beautiful. Are you sure, you were in a lost coach for days? You don't look it at all, you look amazing!"

"Thank you, Cousin. I need to thank you also. The Sheriff speaks very highly of you. He says that you run his office, for him."

Elliot beams. "The Sheriff said that? I can hardly

believe that."

"I never said anything of the sort. I think that she is traumatized by her harrowing experience."

"Sheriff, why are you so rough with my cousin? You were so gentle with us."

"You don't look anything like Elliot, for starters. Plus, he drives me crazy. Always buzzing around."

"Like a fly circling cow pies?" Harkahomé says as he steps down from the coach.

"Wait a minute, that makes me . . ."

"The stink pile, Uncle!" The women and Elliot laugh.

"Nephew, after I gave you a job and everything." Chilly slaps Joshua on the back. "A Deputy should always have his Sheriff's back."

"Only when the wind is blowing in the correct direction, Sheriff."

"Hey, I had a bath just last week. You were there."

"If I wasn't there, I would not believe it."

"He is just teasing you, Sheriff. Did you find the people responsible for the stage mishap?" Elliot changes the subject.

"No Elliot, we have very few leads. The horses and the men are all missing, as well as the strong box. I am waiting for Sheriff Lucas to come to town. He is searching for the men and investigating the surroundings. Has the Tulsa mining men come through yet? We did not see them on the road."

"Yes, sir. They are waiting for you at Penny's saloon. I thought it was very odd that they came all this way but did not want to leave until they talked with you." Explains Elliot.

Chilly nods to him. "Much about this case is very odd. Very odd, indeed. Go and get your womenfolk settled in." Says the Sheriff.

Tom Baker has taken down the remaining luggage. Aunt Martha and the ladies point out which is theirs and several men from the posse, offer to carry them. That leaves two suitcases left. The sheriff nods to them. Put those in my office for me." He calls to the remaining men. "Gentlemen, your assistance was most helpful. The town of Pennysville thanks you. Elliot, do you have the names of all the men who volunteered?"

"Of course, Sheriff. Why?"

"I will ask the town council to put together a fund for them to divvy up and set-up an advance fund for, God forbid, the next posse that I need."

"Great idea, Sheriff. I will suggest that, myself, when the council meets later this week. Come Auntie and Brenda, you must be exhausted from your trip. Let's get you to your rooms. If you are hungry, I can have food sent up to you." Elliot's voice trails off as he and his relatives walk across the road towards the hotel.

Harkahomé looks to the remaining woman. "Miss Sadie, aren't you staying at the hotel?"

"No, I will be living above Penny's Parlor and Saloon. I get free board and a cut of the house winnings that my twenty-one game earns." She says very proudly. "Lee Kirby, himself, saw me work and offered me room and board and a better percentage than what I was making at the dive that I was working in. He seems like a nice enough man to work for, do you know him?"

Harkahomé shakes his head. "I arrived in town just the day before the stagecoach went missing."

"Well, I'd better go to the saloon and get settled. I would really, like it if you came to see me. We can discover what this town has to offer, together." She winks at Joshua. "Sheriff, thank you for the rescue. Give your deputy an order to come see me, will you?"

"That's an order, Joshua. There, Miss Sadie, done."

"Good, then he has no choice in the matter. See you boys, later. Which way to the saloon, Sheriff?"

"It is across the road and five buildings down. You can't miss it. I would send my nephew with you, but I have need of him."

"I am sure one of these gentleman, will carry my bag for me and show me the way." Three men all bend down to grab her suitcase, at once. They give each other looks that could kill but Sadie says, "Now gentleman, no need for a fuss. You in the middle, what is your name?"

"Noah Duncan, Miss Sadie."

"Okay, Noah-Duncan-Miss-Sadie, follow me."

The other two men let go of the handle as Noah elbows them in the ribs. "You heard her, she picked me."

"Noah, tell the men from the mining company that I will receive them at the jail."

Chilly and Joshua turn and walk into the Sheriff's office.

"What do you think happened out at the coach? I do not think it was a tribe of Indians at all." Joshua says.

"Neither do I. The men did a good job of convincing the women of it, though."

The men from Tulsa came to the office minutes later. Tom Baker came in with them. He says, "Sheriff, this is Gordon Mason. He was my boss when I drove the line. He came with the men from the Dawn of the West Mining Company."

"Howdy, Mr. Mason. I am surprised that you didn't come find us on the road." The sheriff says as he holds out his hand for the man to shake it."

"Believe it or not, Sheriff Lewis, we've heard good things about you even as far as Tulsa. We were pretty confident that you'd find our property."

"Yes a stage is sort of hard to hide. It is the strong box that I haven't found yet." Chilly turns around and sits back down at his desk.

"We are not too worried about the strong box, Sheriff." Says a tall dark weathered man next to Mr. Mason.

"And you are?" Joshua asks.

Mr. Mason answers, "Sorry, this is John Henry

Pickford.   He owns the Dawn of the West Mining
Company."

"Okay, Mr. Pickford.   Why are you not worried
about the strong box?" Inquires Chilly.

Mr. Mason interrupts.   "Gentlemen, can we have
the room, we need to talk in private with the sheriff. Please
wait outside." Everyone turns to exit.

"My deputy stays." Orders Chilly. "He is also my
nephew."

"Of course, Sheriff.   This is your office."   Mr.
Pickford says. He waits a minute while his men all leave.
"I am not worried about the strong box because it was a
decoy. My payroll is hidden in the stage, itself. The only
ones who knew about it was myself, Gordon, and my son
who loaded the money in the stage, himself.   He also rode
the stage under the name Scott Jones."

"He went missing the morning after the set-up
robbery. He also acted as if he was shooting at the make-
believe Indians. How do you explain that?"

"He was told if someone approached him or made a
play for the money, he should play along."

"Well, he played along very convincingly. Where do
you think, he is now?"

"That, I do not know.   I am confident that he is
either following the men responsible or on his way here.
Gordon, please go check the hidden compartment and see
if my two thousand dollars is still there. Take the coach to
the livery with my other son, Jason and wait until you two
are alone so that no one else knows where the money is
hidden. I'd like to keep using that stage, if I can."

"Yes sir. I would be very happy if you will continue
to do so. also."

"Joshua, go with Mr. Mason and Jason and stand
guard outside of the livery until they ascertain the
presence of the payroll.   Gentlemen, will you leave it on
board and take the stagecoach with you?"

"That is our plan, Sheriff."

A half an hour later, Mr. Pickford, Mr. Mason and Jason were riding comfortably in the stagecoach driven and guarded by the men that brought them.

***

A little before nightfall, Sheriff Lucas and three men and one prisoner arrive in town. Elliot comes running into the Sheriff's office to warn him that they have arrived. Chilly and Joshua grab their gun belts and hurry out of the office to greet the sheriff outside.

"John, who do you have in custody?" Chilly and Joshua are watching the deputies pulling a man off a horse.

"This is the man who calls himself Rusty Banner. We found him three miles from the site where we found the women. He was on this horse, without a saddle."

"Really, Mr. Banner, the women said that the horses were stolen by the Indians. Where did you get this one?"

"I ran into a small rancher and he sold one to me."

"Let me see the bill of sale." Chilly responds.

"I um, think I lost it." He says as he tries to pat his pockets while his hands are tied.

"We can have someone check with the rancher, you know." Chilly warns. They all walk in the Sheriff's office. Chilly puts the cowboy in the interrogation seat, as he calls it.

"Well, it was more of a ranch hand, I guess. I do not know where he was from, really. I don't know why I am in handcuffs. I was a passenger on the stage that was attacked, not one the attackers, they were Indians."

"What tribe were they, could you tell?" asks Harkahomé.

"I do not know the difference between them. I assumed they were the Creek or Seminole since they are the closest tribes in this area."

61

Harkahomé continues, "Didn't they disarm you when they approached you? Did they speak English?"

"They searched us. They took our guns away but put them on the ground out of our reach until they left. They grunted out a few words that we understood."

Chilly takes over, "Both stage employees were wounded? Where were their injuries and how serious were they that you let them leave for help?"

"Geez, I do not know. It all happened so quickly. The driver had a shoulder wound and the man riding shotgun had his wrist wrapped."

"Which wrist did Jeff hurt?" asks Chilly.

"It was Jeff's right shoulder and Pete's left wrist, I think."

"Did you know the employees well?"

"No, I just met them."

"How did you know their names?"

"They introduced themselves to us before we left Bartlesville."

"I know for a fact, they introduced themselves as Mr. Williams and Mr. Jones. That is the Stagecoach's policy. Why do you know their first names?"

"Are you trying to trick me? They introduced themselves as Mr. Jeff Williams and Mr. Pete Scroggins – not Jones. Why do you think I am guilty of anything?"

"Everyone is under suspicion. How much blood did the employees lose?

"I don't know, a little, I guess."

"There was no blood on the scene or on the top of the stagecoach. If they were shot, there would be blood spray, at least."

"Honest Sheriff, I don't know how to explain that."

"In that case, I hope you don't mind being my guest at the Sheriff's Chez Cell-Avous." He waves to the cells to the prisoner's left. "Just for a night or two until I figure a few things out. Where were you headed, by the way? Here, Tulsa or beyond?"

"I had no destination in mind. Just needed to get out of the crappy town I came from."

"Where was that?" Chilly asks

"EL Dorado."

"Kansas?" Chilly gives a laugh.

"Yeah, are you familiar with it?"

"I've spent some time there."

"It's a dump. I was stuck working on a farm and I ran into trouble with the owner. He thought he owned the town."

"Don't tell me. Grant Johnson?"

"How did you know?"

"He is my brother-in-law and he does kind of own the town."

"Crap! What are the chance escaping one asshole and meeting the asshole's brother-in-law?"

"And his nephew-in-law." Adds Joshua.

"I think that I have heard enough out of you. Time to see the inside of our best-appointed room my Chez Cell-Avous." He stands up and puts his arm under Banner's arm and brings him to a stand. He grabs the keys off the wall and unlocks the door to the cells, and disappears for a moment. The unlocking and locking of the jail cell doors can be heard, then the sheriff comes back into the room and locks the door leading to the prisoner and rehangs the key ring. He turns to say, "Joshua, go to the telegraph office and ask Grant what his problem is with our guest. Tell him not to spare the details."

"Yes, Uncle. I will do that right away, before they close."

Sheriff Lucas looks at Chilly. "Sheriff, I think you owe me a steak. I am starved. We can hash out some of the other details that I have found out while on the road."

"Great idea, John. Joshua meet us at Big Momma's. Shall I order a steak for you?"

"Thank you Uncle. And a tall cold beer to go with it."

"A boy after my own heart. Elliot, see that the prisoner gets some beans and bread. I am sure he hasn't had any food in days."

"Sheriff, why do you always call my jailhouse food, beans and bread? I have never served prisoners the likes of beans. That's trail food."

"Maybe you should, I would not want men misbehaving just for three *great* hot meals and a cot." The sheriff jokes.

ELEVEN
January 9ᵗʰ, 1959
A Friday in Chicago

Carrie Ann is very nervous. School is open for the first time this year. She needs to double check with the registrar to make sure that her records transferred over from EL Dorado. She still doesn't have her schedule either. She has called the office each morning, hoping to find someone that made it in, to assist her. The radio has made the announcement that the public schools, colleges and universities will all be open. So, at seven a.m. Carrie is dressed and ready to go. Her big sister, Clara Beth is going to drive, she starts classes today, also.

She drives down to 58ᵗʰ and Ellis Avenue. The drive takes three times longer than on a snowless day. Much of the snow has been piled in towers on the roadsides. It makes it difficult to see if traffic is coming down from the cross street. Clara Beth travels slowly and carefully to school. They arrive at nine-thirty and Clara drops her sister off at the registrar's office. They agreed to meet up in the Cafeteria when each is done with the day's classes.

Carrie Ann's transcripts from EL Dorado arrived and were filed before the holiday break, thankfully. She receives her class schedule and luckily makes it, on time, to her first Friday class at ten. She has four classes on Friday, and it's overwhelming. She needs to order books and supplies and if she doesn't get them quickly, she will be too far behind to catch up.

She heads to the book store and requests the necessary books, and enquires about her classes on other days, since she has her full class schedule. They gave her most of the textbooks that she needs but two of them need to be ordered. "Unless, you can find someone to sell you them used. There is a bulletin board in the commons area that have many used books for sale by former students."

65

The girl at the bookstore suggests. Carrie Ann thanks her and heads to the commons area.

As she is searching the four bulletin boards, for the books she needs, she is amazed at all the requests for roommates, study partners, furniture, and job postings. She doesn't know how she would be able to handle schoolwork and a job but she wouldn't mind a little extra spending money. A voice behind her says, "Is there anything in particular you are looking for?" She turns to see a tall young man with a shy smile.

"I just came looking for two textbooks but I am amazed at all the posts here. I think there are more people listed here then my whole small town."

"Where is that town?"

"EL Dorado, Kansas. I spent my childhood in Lawrence, Kansas. That is three times bigger but it all pales in comparison to Chicago."

"Would you believe that I am from Wichita? What a small world, two students from Kansas, reading a message board in a school in Chicago."

"Then you know EL Dorado?"

"Of course, it is just a little south of the city. And Lawrence is just south of Topeka. I went on a college tour at the University of Kansas there, but decided on U of C, instead."

"I did the same thing. I also looked at U of K but I would have had to live with my Aunt and Uncle and my six cousins. I chose Chicago, instead."

"And you are rewarded by a blizzard. Lucky you. My name is Mickey. And please – no mouse jokes."

"Darn, I had three of them all ready. My name is Carrie Ann." She juggles the books and her purse, so that she can hold out her hand for him to shake. "Carrie Ann Harrick. What's your last name?"

"Roosevelt. No relations to the presidents. Have you had lunch, Kansas? I am just headed to the cafeteria."

"I actually was going to head there and eat. I am

supposed to meet my older sister, there. I am just overwhelmed with all these books. Today is my first day, here. I don't see anyone else carrying their whole curriculum worth of textbooks."

"I wondered why you had so many. Do you want me to carry some for you?"

"Thank you, Mickey. That is awfully nice of you."

"Not at all, we Kansans need stick together."

Carrie Ann hands him three of the larger textbooks. "I am a freshman, here. What year are you?"

"I am a Junior in Pre-med. What will your major be?"

"I want to be in fashion design."

"So you can sew?"

"Oh, boy, can I? I can make a sewing machine sing!"

They are walking toward the lunchroom. Mickey says, "My mother sews and I am in awe at her ability to make clothing from a pattern."

"Pre-med? You must be smart."

"Well, do you know what they call the person who graduates from Medical school with the lowest grade point average?"

"No, what?"

"Doctor!"

"I guess they would. I cannot imagine that that would be you, though." They enter the cafeteria and she looks around in awe. "This is huge! I am supposed to meet my sister here, but it is so large, how will she find me?"

"I don't think it will be that hard. This place gets smaller the longer you attend school here. What year is your sister?"

"She is a senior. She is majoring in engineering. She is the smart one in the family. Oh, my goodness, here she is now?"

Mickey turns around and smiles. "It is a small

world."

Clara Beth walks up to the table. "Oh, Mickey, you found my sister, already? How do you do it? You know every student at this University. At least, all the female ones." She puts her books down on the table and hugs him. "How have you survived the holidays and the blizzard? Carrie steer clear of this guy from Wichita. He is a Romeo who goes around being a heartbreaker."

"Clara, that is so untrue and you know it. I have had my heart broken, too. I can tell you of a tall dark wavy haired girl that left my hopes dashed because she would not go out with me. Just because I am a year younger. She is seeing some guy named Oliver who is about the same age that I am."

"Yes but he started school younger, so is a senior, he is Pre-Med, also."

"How is Oliver, Clara?"

"He will be joining us shortly."

"Clara, I haven't had a thing to eat. Do we have time for me to get a bite?" Carrie Ann asks.

"Of course, Carrie. I wouldn't want you to waste away to nothing. Mickey, why don't you show my little sister the lunch options, here."

"Carrie Ann, come this way. What do you have a taste for, they have just about everything, you could want."

"Make sure that you bring her back, Mickey. She is not to be one of your conquests." She calls after the couple. She sees Oliver come in from the south entrance and she runs to him. "Oh, Oliver, it feels like a year since I have seen you." He kisses her cheek and she puts her arms around him. "Happy New Year. I hated the holiday without you in them."

"Clara Beth, we have talked for an hour every day we were apart. Your trip back home and the blizzard are to blame for my absence. Please do not blame my heart. It still beats only for you. Was that Mickey and *your* little sister? She looks so much like you. It is sort of creepy. It figures that Mickey has taken an interest in her. She is beautiful."

"And she has a figure to die for!" Clara adds.

"Oh, that I didn't notice."

"Smart answer. Will you be coming over tonight?"

"I heard it is supposed to snow more. And I cannot get snowed in your apartment, now that you have a roommate."

"Say that you'll come, and we can work out the details, later."

"How can I refuse you, my love. I am starving. What's the special, today? I think I almost missed this food."

"I haven't looked yet. Put your books at our table and let's get some food." He drops his books and they head arm in arm to the service counters, as Mickey and Carrie Ann head back to the table with trays filled with great smelling morsels.

TWELVE
An Excerpt from the Letter from Grant Lewis, in Lawrence, Kansas

Jan. 9, 1959

My Dearest Carrie Ann,

My parents have given me, my Great-grandfather, the Colonel's, love letters to read. These were letters that he wrote to my yet-to-be Great-Grandmother Julia. They were very formal, and poetic, as that was the way they wrote back in those days. It was in 1880, after all.

As you might know, since your mother has read all the correspondences, that the Colonel and his Julia were childhood sweethearts just after the Civil War. She moved away when her brother, Grant Johnson the first, inherited the estate in El Dorado. He did not write her after she moved away, but started a few years later, after she agreed to visit his mother, my Great-Great Grandmother, while he went to fight the Cheyenne that killed his brother. They wrote during all the months of his campaign and he asked her to marry him and they did so, just four days after they saw each other for the first time in four years.

I mentioned this because you are in Chicago, so very far from me and I would like to decrease the distance between us, not physically, but in our hearts. We have always had a special bond between us. You admitted to me on the sleigh ride that you have felt that it existed, too.

I will try to be as intimate in my letters as the Colonel was. They each told of special memories from their childhood that meant the most to them. We have those, also. I will admit to you now, that I have loved you from afar, as far back as I can remember. So, I plan on retelling each of my most special memories with you, to prove that my feelings for you are not a flight of fancy or a school boy's crush, but something life long and enduring. As were the childhood memories of your own parents, who grew up with each other and had special feelings for each other but never came to admit them until they were reunited after four years.

Since we are both freshmen in Universities, 600 or so miles apart, I know that we will be separated for years to come. I do not want our hearts separated as your parents and my great-grandparents were. They all admitted suffering from what they thought was unrequited love. Let us not do so, my dearest Carrie Ann. For I do love you with all my heart, and will endeavor to write to you, daily, to convince you of such.

Let me start with a special memory of us. This one is bittersweet. Do you remember your move from Lawrence to El Dorado? I know that we were only six years-old but I remember it distinctly. Your family had all the Little House's belongings on an open bed trailer. Your father brought it and your family to the Plantation House for the final farewell. I remember that everyone was openly crying. Your parents and mine considered each other siblings, and though the reason for the move was a happy one (starting the 2nd restaurant), they were all very, very sad.

I recall that you had a little present for me. Do you remember what it was? I also had a little token for you. I pulled you into the dayroom off the kitchen and gave you my little metal car. When we played together, it was your favorite. That made it my favorite, also. You gave me the slingshot that I took away from that mean boy on the playground. He was threatening you with it and I hit him and grabbed it and we ran away. You asked me for it as proof of my protecting you by standing up to an older and bigger boy. You gave it back to me to have as a reminder of

71

my heroic action. I still have that slingshot and have never used it to shoot as most little boys would have done but I put it in a cigar box which became my memory box, instead.

I am hoping that the shot that never hit you was replaced by Cupid's arrow, that had already pierced my heart. That arrow's elixir is still running in my veins. I think of you non-stop and I am desperate to know if you have been so afflicted.

How was that for my first formal and poetic letter? I miss you like crazy and cannot wait to hold you in my arms on the dance floor at the Valentine's Ball.

Yours very truly,
Grant (GW) Lewis

THIRTEEN
January 10th, 1896 cont'd
A Friday in Pennysville, Oklahoma

Harkahomé has come into Big Momma's diner and nods to Josie before he takes a seat at Chilly's table. Already seated were the two sheriffs and three Bartlesville deputies. "The telegram has been sent, Uncle. Have I missed anything? I see everyone's beer is half empty."

"That is all we've had time for. Sit down and have a pull on your glass. John, what were the other things that you needed to tell me?"

"Well, first, we never did discover any blood from the so called wounded employees. We followed the foot prints away from the stage but they led to hoof prints just a few hundred feet away. This was a 'staged' stagecoach heist. Definitely. We just need to figure out the who and the where."

"Well, the why is the Mining payroll." Chilly adds. "I thought that the ladies were in on it. We thoroughly interrogated them. They did not know the employees first names and they were told to hide in the coach so that the 'Indians' would not find them. I believe their telling of events, and what you found, bears witness to them. Now, the Banner cowpoke, he is a lying snake in the grass, if ever I have seen one. What do you think, Nephew?"

"I agree with your estimation, Uncle."

"A man of few words. Isn't he? I still cannot get over the likeness between he and Will. Almost as tall, too, I think." John notes.

"I am looking forward to seeing my other Uncle, in the spring. It felt odd sending a telegram to another Uncle that I barely remember. I have lots of memories regarding his wife. She is just a year older than our Sheriff, here and we played lots of mean tricks on her, I am afraid."

"And we were not spared the rod, afterward!"

73

"That is true, but I feel that we owe her an apology for our misbehavior."

"Cheyenne living, did change you considerably." Says Chilly with beer foam sticking to his mustache.

Joshua finishes his beer and leans in close to Chilly. "Are we planning on seeing the female passengers tonight? I thought that I would like to go see Miss Sadie at the Saloon."

"I think that you should nephew. IF I see Miss Brenda again, I plan on doing it the right way. I plan on courting her with her mother's permission. What do you think of that?" Chilly says wiping his mustache with his sleeve.

"You are going to become all mushy like the Colonel for his Julia, aren't you?" Joshua says as he finishes his beer.

"Good golly, I hope not. But I cannot get those piercing blue eyes out of my head. I don't feel like I have a choice in the matter." The steaks finally arrive and they end their private conversation. "Eat heartily everyone. We've earned it."

"Hear! Hear!" Sheriff Lucas adds. As all the men heartily attack the meat placed before them.

FOURTEEN
An Excerpt from the letter from Grant Lewis, in Lawrence, Kansas

Jan. 10th, 1959

Dearest Carrie Ann,

I know that you have yet to receive my first post, but I wanted to pen another, while I still have my nerve to do so. It occurred to me (after I mailed the first letter) that I might have come on too strong with my talk of love. Let me assure you that I will not go any further than you allow. I do not want to scare you off before you have decided to come to the Valentine Ball.

I will be calling you tomorrow night but I wanted a chance or maybe a second chance to sway you to accept my offer to fly you out to EL Dorado. I figured that I need to show you how much you would benefit from the trip.

1.) You will be able to spend time with me. I've missed you, so.

2.) You will be able to spend time with your parents and brother.

3.) You will be able to see my parents and siblings, too.

4.) You will get away from all the snow and see that Kansas is still green.

5.) You will get a break from the schoolwork that has been piled upon you. Or I can help you with some it.

6.) You will have a chance to get all dressed up like a princess.

And speaking of princesses. That reminds me of a memory. We were ten years old and your mother gave you

75

a giant birthday party. We came in from Lawrence and you had it at the Farmhouse, since your grandparents and your parents were still living in it at the time. Your mother let you dress like a fairy-tale princess. Everyone was present, my Aunt Carolyn and Uncle Eddie and your aunts and uncles, also. Even my Great-Great Grand Mamá Carolyn was still alive and there. Remember?

You came down the stairs, all dressed up, one step at a time to make the moment last. You knew you looked beautiful and it was all I could do to close my mouth after my jaw dropped watching you with your hand elegantly upon the stair railing. Your hair was piled on top of your head with little flowers in it, just like I read my Great-Grand Mother Julia did. You looked like a dream.

We were told that you drew out the dress and made your mother teach you to sew it on her new sewing machine. You were so proud of the fine job that you did. I still cannot believe that you designed your own princess gown at ten years old. A fashion designer in the making!

I was so proud for you. I heard Aunt Anna talk about you working on it and tearing it apart each time you didn't like the way it came out.

Well, if you say yes, you have a chance to get all dressed up, again. I know for a fact that this is one of your most favorite things to do, especially when you have a month to design and sew a gown. Did you bring your sewing machine with you? I don't imagine you being apart from your sewing machine for any length of time.

That is about all I can think to say, for now. I am hoping that none of these words were necessary because you have already agreed to fly out. Then these words would be just the icing on the cake.

Yours sincerely,
Grant (GW)Lewis

FIFTEEN
January 11th, 1896
A Saturday in EL Dorado, Kansas

Just as the sun is rising, there is a loud knock at the front door. Matilda answers it and accepts the telegram. The young man says that he will wait on the steps. This is the mansion that the Johnson family has called the Farmhouse for years. Matilda puts the telegram on a silver platter and carries it into the Master's study.

"Master Grant? The telegram man iz here for you." She puts the tray on his desk in front of him. "Hez waitin' on an answer if you got one." She turns and steps outside of the room, and waits for further instructions.

Thirty-one-year-old Carolyn, gets off the couch and walks to her forty-one-year old husband of fourteen years. "Who is it from, Grant?"

"It is from Pennysville, Oklahoma so it must be from our brother, Sheriff Chilly." He rips open the envelope. "Oh my Goodness. It is from our nephew, Joshua. He is Chilly's deputy and he wants to know about a farm hand cowboy that left here because of some altercation between us. The problem is I do not recognize the name Rusty Banner. I wonder if he is referring to Jason Williams that left here mad as hell about my not making him a foreman?" He yells to outside of the room. "Mattie?"

She rushes back into the room. "Master? You want the telegram man? I'll run for him." She leaves out before he even says a word.

"Sometimes, I fear she reads my mind. We need to get her married off. She is what? Twenty?"

"More like twenty-one." Red haired Carolyn says. "Isn't she and that man Sullivan from the butcher shop eyeing each other on a regular basis? He is a very nice man. What is my nephew, Harkahomé doing away from his Cheyenne tribe?"

77

"I do not know, but he signed the telegram 'Deputy Joshua Harkahomé Lewis'." He hands her the telegram to read. Mattie brings the man into the study.

"Sir, may I be of service?" He takes off his hat and tips his head to Carolyn. "Ma'am?" He stands for a few moments, hat in hand, while Grant scribbles a few sentences down.

"Please send this reply, immediately."

"One moment, sir." Carolyn grabs a pen and writes her own message. She hands him the note. "This one goes to Lawrence, my good man. Grant, pay for mine, also."

He is counting out some coins. "I am on it, my love." He hands the man a bunch of coins. "This should cover it plus a tip, sir."

The young man puts on his hat, and Matilda walks him out.

"You wired your mother? She will be thrilled to know that Joshua is alive and with Chilly. I cannot wait to hear that story." Grant stands and goes around the desk to his wife. "I hope that he comes this way. I would love our children to hear his life story."

"I will love to hear it, also. If they cannot come here, we can visit them. In a few weeks when the worst of winter clears we can go for a trip to Oklahoma. You will not be needed for the farm that early in the season. Can we go? I am dying to see Joshua. I was only twelve or so when his family went to Oberlin, Kansas. Mother grieved for them, for so long. She will be crying happy tears when she learns the news." Carolyn puts her arms around Grant's neck. "Mr. Johnson, say we can go see Joshua."

"As usually, my love, your wish is my command. If they aren't planning to come here, or to Lawrence that is." He kisses her. "I smell Annabelle's breakfast and I am starving. Are the children getting ready for school?"

"Yes, but I'd better go upstairs and hasten them down. Ada and Ida take so long to get ready, these days.

Thank God, Junior isn't like that. We should have had all boys."

"What fun would that have been? The girls favor you so much. I cannot believe that Ada is almost fourteen? That's the same age that I saw you for the first time in years and fell madly in love with you."

"That feels like a lifetime ago. I'd better go get the children downstairs for breakfast."

As she is about to leave the study, Matilda walks back in. "Mistress, I have the children to the table for breakfast. Mother has made you a second pot of fresh coffee, too."

Carolyn walks out with Matilda. "I do not know what I'd do without you, Mattie. How is that man at Butcher John's place. Sullivan, isn't it? Aren't you sweet on him?"

"Oh Mistress, he is too tall for me. Mama says if I have his baby, it might just kill me." She says with her head down.

"Yes, but do you like him?"

"Very much, Mistress."

They enter the dining room and all three adolescents were sitting eating breakfast. When they see their mother, all three talk at once. Carolyn puts her hand up and they are immediately silent. "Children, I have wonderful news. Your cousin Joshua that has been living with the Cheyenne is now with Uncle Chilly in Oklahoma. Isn't that great? Your father has promised that we will see him. If not, here or in Lawrence, then we will travel to Oklahoma."

All three children start talking again with a dozen questions.

SIXTEEN
January 11th, 1959
A Sunday in Lawrence, Kansas

Carolyn James is helping Helen make an early Sunday dinner in the large kitchen at the Plantation house. She, her husband, Eddie, and their two children have shared a Sunday meal with Joshua's family since they moved into their own home just before the war. They have a large home near the University of Kansas, where Eddie is a Professor. When the children were younger and fewer, the families alternated hosting the dinners but now that there are so many teenagers, they always have it at Legacy Plantation.

The children were all in the large front parlor, entertaining themselves. They were relatively quiet considering that there are eight of them. They range in age from eighteen to eight. The oldest is Grant (GW) Lewis, with Jonathon Edward James just seven months younger. William Johnson Lewis was born the following year. Then two years later, Audrey Jean Lewis and Elizabeth Susan (Bessie) James were born. The last three Lewis children came two years apart. Charlotte Rose (Charlie), Eleanor Leigh (Ellie) with Kevin Joshua being the last.

In the sitting room across the hall from the Parlor, Joshua and Eddie are enjoying a relaxing conversation. "Dinner is starting to smell good, do you know what we are having?"

"Carolyn asked Helen to teach her to cook Anna's pork chops. With this crowd, that's close to twenty-five chops. She will get plenty of practice before this meal is over. I thank God, that Helen took cooking lessons from Anna. Would you believe that old Mattie refused to let Helen in the kitchen at the Farmhouse? Mattie swore it wasn't fitting for a girl of her status, sweating in a kitchen. I am so lucky that she asked Anna to teach her that first recipe, my favorite meal, meatloaf. I would have gone through ten cooks after Anna opened the restaurant, if Helen didn't enjoy cooking. I am very lucky, indeed.

"The Colonel would have said, 'Luckiest Man Alive.' He would have been right, too." Eddie is referring to the Colonel's favorite saying referring to finding the love of his life, his Julia.

"How did your first week back to the classroom go after the holidays?" Joshua changes the subject.

"I must admit it is getting harder and harder to go back after a break. You know, I turn fifty-five this year and I have been teaching for over thirty years. I would retire but I want to see both my children in college. I get a discount if I am still working."

"You have tenure, don't you? They discount for that, I know."

"It's not enough! I have seven more years to teach if I want to be able to pay for Bessie's tuition."

"Carolyn's share of the plantation income is quite substantial. Plus, she has patented more inventions, with customers waiting. The James household is not hurting for money. You love to teach Criminology and you might as well admit it. Blaming the children for 'making' you stay and teach. You should be ashamed." Joshua stands and goes to the door. He looks in on the children across the hall, then he slides the pocket door closed.

Eddie watches him. "What's up, Joshua?"

"Henry called and said that Clara Beth and Carrie Ann are experiencing blizzard conditions in Chicago. Anna is worried sick about her girls. He also said that GW asked Carrie Ann to the El Dorado Valentine Ball. She hasn't given him an answer, yet. Her college classes hadn't resumed, because of the snow. She didn't want to miss any school, having just gotten there."

"Does she have the same affection for GW? They were inseparable before the move, but I thought it was more like brother and sister."

"He says he took her for a sleigh ride during their stay here and admitted his feelings to her. She said she felt the same way. If they start a relationship, it will be a long distance one for three and a half years. Do you think there is a chance it will last?"

"Given that Anna and Henry lasted, the Colonel and his Julia lasted, you and Helen lasted and I and Carolyn lasted, I think they stand a good chance."

"Helen thought that he could write letters like the Colonel did to win her and keep his Julia. She just needs to say, yes. He has to get her to the Valentine Ball, first."

"I understand her hesitance. She started college late and she'll miss classes."

"GW offered to fly her in and out of Wichita Airport, so she would not miss any."

"That boy has class, doesn't he? I cannot believe he took so long to make the first move. Where did the time go? My Jonathon is graduating this year and Bessie is graduating from grammar school. I am still upset that they didn't let her in school when Audrey started. She is such a bright girl, they could have made an exemption, but she had to be five years old by September. Two-weeks shy and she was held back a whole year!" He stops to listen to the sound of voices escalating. "I knew closing that door would invite trouble. Shall we give them a minute or two to settle it by themselves or shall we intervene?"

"I will bet the contents of my pocket that Helen will be on them in less than three minutes." He walks to the side table next to the Professor and empties his pocket. A money clip and a few coins come out."

"You are on." Eddie stands and pulls out the contents of his pocket. They both look at their watches. Finally, Eddie says, "Three, two, one . . ."

"GW, Johnny, Billy! What is all this racket going on. I swear, almost grown and you have no more sense than a babe in diapers. What was so important that you need to fight like this?" Helen says in a loud voice with her hands firmly planted on her hips.

Before they can answer, Joshua slides open the door and calls out, "Helen, you just won me the contents of Eddie's pocket. Have I told you today, how much I love you?" Helen just looks at her husband, dumbfounded.

"Wait just a minute, Joshua. The countdown had ended, I won the bet." Whines Eddie.

"No, you didn't, she was right on time!"

Helen turns to the boy cousins, "See how stupid you look, fighting at your age. Stop it immediately and apologize!" She was now looking at the men.

"I'm sorry." Billy, Johnny, GW, Joshua and Eddie, say all at the same time.

Helen smiles. "That's more like it. Come on, goofballs, dinner is just about ready. I need the dining room table set. All of you, go to work." The children all stop what they are doing and go to the sideboard and or kitchen to get the necessary items to set the table. The men are still standing in the sitting room doorway. "No exceptions! Go, help! Or no supper for either of you!" The men turn and go into the dining room. Helen nods her head. "Circus Wrangled!" She says, then heads into the kitchen to finish preparing the food.

***

After everyone ate until they could not move, the adults go to the sitting room for their coffee, while the children clear the table and clean the kitchen. They do it without being told, and make a game out of the work. Carolyn says, "I do not know how you do it, Helen. All these children and all but Kevin are taller than you but you still rule the roost!"

"She is a natural born drill sergeant! There isn't anything that she cannot do." Joshua says proudly.

"Like I have time to do anything else with this many children." Helen says in a low tone.

"Is there something, you'd like to do, my love? We can afford help to be with the children more, so that you can pursue other interests." Joshua says. "I remember when we were newlyweds, that was very important to you. I never want you to regret our life, together." Joshua adds. Helen puts down her coffee cup, then stands and crosses the room to go to her husband. She takes the cup from his hand, puts it down and puts herself in his lap and her arms around his neck.

"I was a brat! How you put up with it, is beyond me! I have not regretted one minute of our life together. You and our large family is the answer to all my unknown dreams." She kisses him. "I love you so very much. Even if you bet on how I behave!" She pinches his nose with her thumb and index finger. Joshua and Eddie laugh.

"This is something I missed." Carolyn looks at her younger brother, sister-in-law and husband, laughing. "Who bet what?"

Joshua explains then adds, "I still say I won!"

"You would see it that way. I say we are both winners." Says Eddie and he stands and goes to his wife. "My dear, I think it is time that we head home and let the Lewis family have their evening.

***

After the James's family leave, Helen has all the younger children get out their books and papers, so that she can check their homework. After she is satisfied that they have all completed their assignments, she says, "Okay, children. Upstairs. Time for baths then bed."

They all say goodnight to their father and GW and head upstairs, with Helen close behind them. Joshua has stoked the fire and is still in a squatting position when he says, "You know, the Colonel had a fire going, practically year-round. As he got more confused with his illness, he also got colder and colder. He just couldn't warm up." He stands and goes to sit in the chair that was the Colonel's favorite. "No matter how confused or upset he was, we could always distract him with a cup of hot tea and a fire."

"It must have been hard for you, Father. Your parents died before you could remember them, and you had to be raised by your grandparents." GW moves to the chair opposite of his father's. "Then when you were eleven, you had to become the man of the house because your Gram Julia died."

"No, the Colonel was still running things. By the time Carolyn, was a senior in high school, *she* became the man of the house. Running the farm, taking care of me and the Colonel. She almost did not go off to college because she felt responsible for us. Somehow, I convinced her to go to Washburn University in Topeka. They had a great Engineering department there. When she graduated college, I went while she ran the farm, again. It was never anything she wanted to do, but she did it well, and without complaint. Legacy Plantation might not be here today, if Carolyn wasn't so self-sacrificing." He lifts a framed picture of Carolyn on the mantle.

"She found Anna while I was at school. Poor thing, would have died from her injuries, if Carolyn wasn't trying to see if she could use her new irrigation invention to bring water to the drought stricken land."

"Aunt Carolyn is a remarkable woman, father." GW simply states.

"She is! Remind me to tell her that, the next time I talk with her." Joshua is quiet for a moment. "Isn't it time for you to call her namesake, Carrie Ann?"

GW looks at his wristwatch. "I suppose it is, I am so afraid that she will say no. I've written her two letters, all ready."

"There you go, if she says, no, continue doing that. This dance will not be your only opportunity. She is still like family and she will be home, again, for holidays and breaks. If she says no, don't insist. No, could just mean, not now. You must respect her decision."

"Of course, Father. Always."

"Good lad." Joshua stands. "I think I will go help your mother, upstairs. You need your privacy."

SEVENTEEN
January 11th, 1959
A Sunday in Chicago

Clara Beth, Oliver and Carrie Ann go to Chinatown for an early dinner. Carrie follows the couple in and out of stores on 22nd Street. Oliver has been a frequent visitor since he was a boy. He has been to almost every restaurant and has a favorite dish in each. He keeps asking Clara what meal she wants so that he can take her to the place that makes it the best. Carrie Ann is more interested in purchasing the ingredients to make her own at home. "That last place had sesame seeds, red pepper paste and fresh ginger. Here, I can buy fresh bock choy, water chestnuts, pea pods, Hoisin sauce and look at the fresh-made tofu.

Clara Beth looks at her little sister then speaks to Oliver. "I have known her my whole life and she has confounded me on several occasions, but when did she learn to speak another language?" She looks back at her sister. "Do you know how to make stuff out of what you just said?"

"Yes, of course. Last year, when mama and I were in Lawrence, we went to Kim's Cantonese and she talked to the owner, Lee Kim. Well, talked to his son who translated for us. Mr. Kim had come into the Lawrence diner, when we lived there and has had a crush on mama for years. So, when we visited, he was overjoyed to see her. He showed us how to use a wok and when to put in the liquids. It was amazing."

"What is a wok?" Clara Beth asks. Carrie walks to the next aisle, without answering. "Carrie, did you hear my question?"

Carrie grabs a pot that is shaped almost like a funnel and lifts it in the air. "This is a wok. The pointy end fits right into the stoves burner. It gets very hot and

87

cooks everything very quickly. The secret is to keep the veggies moving and cook them until they are tender crisp." She looks at the price tag then laughs. "It is in Chinese! No matter, I am buying this, too. Grocery shopping always makes me hungry. Where shall we dine? As much as I cannot get enough of these stores, we need to eat, now. I am expecting a very important phone call at nine."

"Do you have an answer for GW?"

"Yes, I will go to EL Dorado for the Ball as his date."

"Are you sure it's a good idea?"

"Yes, and do you know who helped me make it?"

"No, who?"

"Oliver." Oliver looks over to her when he hears his name.

"We never talked about EL Dorado, the ball or dating. What makes you say that?"

"I see the way you look at Clara Beth. I do not know if you have told her or not, but you love her and she loves you. I can see it on your faces. I saw that look when GW was looking at me. I want that special feeling that makes my heart twitter and he has always done that to me. Even listening to him on the phone, I can feel it. Why would I not take advantage of it?"

"Don't you think that someone in Chicago can twitter your stomach?" Asks Oliver as he holds the door open for them to exit the store. "You have very successfully flirted with twenty young men that I have witnessed. None of them, twittered you?"

Clara interrupts. "Let's eat at Ming's, they have great Hot-Sour soup." They all head in that direction. "You didn't answer Oliver's question. Didn't any of your flirtations lead to a stomach twitter?"

"Not even close. I think I have it bad for GW. I cannot stop thinking about our sleigh ride and what that meant to me."

The restaurant is three doors down and they get there rather quickly considering the amount of snow and ice left on the sidewalks. It has not actively snowed in two days. The three order full meals which includes soup choices, egg rolls and fried won tons. Little talking is done, while the girls devour their food. Oliver watches them, smiling.

"You two even eat food the same way. Like you haven't eaten in a week and this will be your last best meal, ever. You are the weirdest of siblings. Exactly alike in so many ways that I need to do a double take, but so opposite in others that I am shocked that you never fight. How do you manage this?" He looks from one sister to the other.

"We have our moments, Oliver, believe me. We just don't let them last and we know that we love each other more than the disagreement. Mother instilled this in us. She and Aunt Melinda are exactly like that, also. Not in looks, they are opposites there. Mama has fair skin with a heart shaped face with dark soulful eyes. Auntie has a dark complexion that tans, easily. She has pale blue eyes, like my grandfather Judd. Uncle Matthew has them, also. They disagree about many things but love each other too much to let that get between them. Perfect role models." Explains Clara Beth. "I cannot wait for you to meet them all. On spring break, you'd better come home with me."

"Or what?"

"Or something I haven't thought of, yet. I have time." They all laugh. "Carrie, it is after seven. We'd better head home, it took us a long while to get here and now it is dark."

**

Oliver drops the sisters off at their apartment building. Carrie thanks him for the ride and grabs her three bags of groceries and equipment and goes directly in. Clara stays outside to say good night. "So our little secret is out, for all the world to know. You love me and I love you. How do you feel about that?"

"I love the feeling of love, but I could care less who knows. We were not really keeping it a secret." He gives her a peck on the cheek. "Here, I will prove it." He holds her away from him and yells. "I love Clara Beth Harrick with all my heart!"

"So what?" Says a man, walking up the steps to his apartment, next door.

Clara yells. "I love Oliver Derrick Chapman!"

"That is so nice for you." Says a woman on the apartment stairs on the other side of the man.

Clara and Oliver laugh. Clara asks, "Do you want to come in?"

"I do very much, but I have an exam in chemistry that I must get a good grade in. I have spent most of the weekend here and have not studied. When I meet your family in the spring, I do not want to be a college failure and drop out. I want them to like me."

"That is very important. Give us a long good night kiss then and go study to get an A on your test. You want to be able to say that you get as good or better grades as their daughter."

"You or Carrie?" He laughs, and leans in for a kiss. "Give me a kiss that will last me through my long night ahead."

She puts her arms around his neck and leans in. "Yes, sir." His lips are on hers and they hold them together. She is surprised at how warm they are, despite the chill of the evening. She finally pulls herself away. "I hope that does the trick. I feel if I kiss you any longer, your mind will no longer be able to concentrate on the chemical name for sodium or even water, for that matter."

"You are wise beyond your years, my love." He takes a step down the stairs. "I do not want to leave you."

"But you must, for the good of the grade, my love." She responds as she opens the door and steps into the doorway. "Try not to pull an all-nighter, get some sleep.

90

Promise me, Oliver."

"I will promise you, anything."

She blows a kiss to him and closes the door.

***

The phone rings at nine o'clock sharp. Clara Beth pretends to rush to answer it. "You don't have to seem anxious for his call."

"Why play games? A long-distance relationship is going to be hard enough." She answers on the third ring. "Harrick girl's residence, Carrie Ann speaking."

GW suddenly cannot talk. "Um, a . . ."

"Grant, is that you?"

"I am sorry, Carrie, the cat got my tongue, for a second."

"I received your first letter. It was lovely. I am going to answer it after we hang up."

"I mailed a second one this morning."

"I hope I get it tomorrow. I love getting mail, especially your letters."

"I will write another tonight. No matter what your answer is. It will not change how I feel for you. It will just make the Ball, something I am forced to attend without your presence."

"You do not have to worry about that, GW. I have decided to take you up on your invitation. I will need to fly in, though, so that I do not miss any classes. Are you sure that you have permission to pay for that?"

"Father said that he will make the arrangements tomorrow, if you agree to come out. I am so happy, Carrie. I was so nervous that I could hardly put my fingers in the ring to turn the dial and call you."

"We do not have to be nervous with each other, GW. We have known each other our whole life and have felt similar feelings for each other for most of it."

"I do not remember a time when I did not have

91

feelings for you. I remember after you left, that I wondered why I felt different when I was with you, and why I hurt so bad with you gone."

"That's a lot of feelings for a six-year-old."

"And a lot of thinking! You still pervade my thoughts, daily. Since our sleigh ride, so many times a day, I think 'Oh, I have to remember to tell Carrie'. Or 'Carrie, would love this'. I think I would spend my family's fortune if I called you each time I thought of you."

"Write it all down, I want long extensive letters from you, detailing everything going on in your life."

"I will, Carrie. Will you do the same?"

"I will need to, if I want to stay in your thoughts, don't I?"

"You cannot do or not do anything to stop those thoughts, my dear. I look forward to your first letter, also. I will call you, tomorrow night with the flight information. Are you available? I know the big city has so many activities, day and night."

"Nothing more important than your call, GW. Same time, then?"

"Yes, I am sure that all my siblings are upstairs and in bed or getting ready for bed. Good night, my dear. Talk to you tomorrow."

"GW . . . I love you." Carrie looks down. It is the first time that she has said those words. "I was going to wait until the Ball to tell you but I am about to burst holding it in. I love you." She has a tear fall from her eye.

"I am glad that you didn't wait. I have been waiting for the right time to say the words, also. I love you, Carrie Ann Harrick."

"GW, I am smiling so hard that I think my jaw is going to break."

"Me too! I do have to hang up. I hear my parents coming down the stairs. I cannot wait to tell them the good new!"

"Good night, GW. Tell them that I cannot wait to

see them in February. Talk to you, tomorrow." Carrie hangs up the phone. She looks around the room and her sister has gone into her bedroom. She gets up and calls out. "Clara, I told him that I love him and he said he loves me! I am going to cry. Come here. I need you to cry with me."

Clara looks out of the room and says, "Just write down your feelings in GW's letter. I am very happy for you but I have an exam tomorrow, and I need to cram!"

EIGHTEEN
An Excerpt from the letter of Carrie Ann Harrick
From Chicago, Illinois

January 11, 1959

Dear GW,

I was so nervous for your phone call. When it rang, I practically jumped out of my skin., even though I was expecting it. Then when I heard your nervousness, I realized that we are so much alike. I am so excited!

After classes, tomorrow, I will go downtown to shop for a gown. I would love to sew one of my own design but I am a little overwhelmed with college. I usually have my mama help me with the sewing. She is my sounding board for how the dress looks. She encourages me when I am having doubts about my stitches or the design. I am just at a loss to start one without her. I will see what I like in the stores. If nothing looks good enough or is beyond my means, I will fire up the sewing machine and tackle the project. I want to look just perfect for you.

This afternoon, Clara and her beau, took me to the section of the city called Chinatown. It is so exotic! I bought lots of supplies and I hope to make my first Chinese dish later this week. If you recall, Mr. Lee Kim had shown Mama and I how to use a wok when we ate at Kim's Cantonese, some years back. I bought my own wok, which is a funny shaped pot, to replicate the way I was shown. Someday, I hope to make Chinese food for you. Someday, I hope that we have our own little place and I can cook for you all the time.

I know that we have three-and-a half-years to get through between now and then. I do not know how we can wait that long now that we've declared our feelings for each other. Our weekend together in February will be bittersweet in that way. We will be so happy to be together then so sad when we say good-bye. Just thinking about it makes me happy and sad, already!

I remember the little car that you gave me when my family said good bye to Lawrence. I still have it, in EL Dorado. It is on my window ledge. I used to make believe that someday you would drive up in it and take me back to live with you in Lawrence. It was a little girl's day dream. I do hope that one day, I will live with you, whether in Lawrence or EL Dorado.

I remember an Easter, together, when we were seven or eight. There was an Easter Egg Hunt in EL Dorado. Do you recall it? We were still staying in the Farmhouse, as my Father was helping Grandfather Judd manage the Johnson Family Farm. The Easter Egg Hunt was at the church your parents were married in. They gave us all baskets and the little eggs were filled with candy. Someone blew a whistle and we were off!! You were supposed to help your little siblings but you were helping me instead. You put all your eggs in my basket so that I could barely carry it. When my mama asked me how I collected so much you said, "She is the best one here!" All I could do was smile. You've always made me happy.

I had better sign off for now. I have homework to do. I will mail this in the morning. I cannot wait until we talk tomorrow night. In my next letter, I will tell you a bit about school and my classes. I hope that you will share your college life with me, also. This way we will remain closely connected in each other's lives

Yours truly,

Carrie Ann Harrick

NINETEEN
January 12th, 1896
A Sunday in Pennysville, Oklahoma

The sheriff and deputy have spent another night together in the back bedroom behind the cells in the Sheriff's office. Elliot has gotten a bed for Joshua with a feather tick mattress on it. Both men were out late. Chilly was with Sheriff Lucas and Joshua was with Sadie at the Saloon.

Once again, they are woken up by Elliot pounding on the outer door. "Sheriff, you have a telegram from EL Dorado. I have put the coffee on, Sheriff and I have breakfast for the prisoner. It is nine o'clock. Sorry Sheriff."

Chilly lifts his head and calls out. "Damn it, Elliot! Must you always wake me with your yelling?"

"I said I was sorry, Sheriff." He says.

"Hey, let him in, I am starving." Says the prisoner.

"Like I give a flying cow pie. Everyone, just shut up! I am coming out. Just let me throw some water on my face, will you?"

When Chilly looks over to his nephew, he sees that Joshua is sitting up in his new bed. "Do you like the soft bed?" Chilly asks.

"The bed is great, but all the yelling every morning has got to stop. When I get my pay, I must find different lodgings. One that stays quieter in the mornings, would be much preferred."

"Especially, if you are going to be spending late evening hours with your Sadie Mae Miller."

"Yes, especially."

"Sheriff!" Elliot yells again.

"Elliot, I swear, I am going to use you for target practice if you do not stop with all the noise."

"Sheriff, you do not need target practice, you are a

96

perfect shot!"

"And you are going to be the recipient of my marksmanship, immediately, if not sooner. Now leave the telegram and the prisoner's food in my office and GET OUT!" Chilly is at the wash basin, and pours some water and throws his face into the shallow bowl. He rubs the water all over his face and then scoops some up with his hands and wets his hair. He looks in his little mirror and runs his fingers through his red locks.

"Uncle, I think today, we should go back to the barber for a shave and baths. Even I am starting to smell ripe."

"Let's see what news the telegram has before we make any plans. I would love to get a lead on this case and be done with it." He takes his shirt sleeve and uses it to dry his face off. Then he gets his gun belt and straps it on. "Okay, I am going out." He takes the keys and unlocks the bedroom door. He walks past the prison cells and just nods to the single occupant behind bars.

"I am very hungry, sheriff. The food and coffee smell delicious."

"You'll get your beans and bread, when I am ready to give it to you and not before. Sit down and shut up!" He unlocks the doorway that leads to the office and goes directly to the coffee pot and pours himself a cup. He sees the telegram envelope on his desk and sits down to read it.

"Sheriff?" This startles Chilly.

"Damn it, Elliot! I thought I told you to get out." Chilly says very irritated.

"You did but I have some important information for you." Elliot says very quietly.

"Involving the case?"

"Involving my cousin Brenda."

This makes Chilly give him his undivided attention. "What about her?"

"She has been very unhappy, since she has arrived."

"Why is that? Elliot?"

"She saw you with Miss Sadie, last night. She has been expecting you to call on her. It seems you promised."

"I told her that I would take her to dinner when the investigation is solved."

"Yes, you did, but you've had time for Sadie." Elliot says than looks down. "I am not questioning your actions, Sheriff. Brenda is. She was hoping that you'd call on her by now. Aunt Martha is throwing a fit because Brenda keeps threatening to come call on you, if you refuse to make the first move. Please, do not make her stoop to that, Sheriff. Save her some face, for goodness sake. For some reason, she has her heart set on you and I shudder to think that you'll treat her like you have all the other ladies in town." Elliot looks down.

"You dare talk to me like that, Elliot?" Chilly says in a booming voice as he stands to tower over the man.

Elliot stands taller. "She is my cousin, and someone needs to watch out for her. Are you going to break her heart? Sheriff?"

"Elliot, I have no intention of treating her like the other girls in town because she isn't anything like the other girls in town. I think that she might be the one to break my heart. My cold, hasn't-started-to-beat-until-I-looked-in-her-eyes heart." He looks down. "Don't you dare tell her I said that. Okay, you have spoken your piece, now get out!"

"Yes, Sheriff." He heads toward the door, then turns to add, "Don't forget to feed the prisoner, Sheriff. Good morning, Harkahomé."

Chilly turns to see his nephew. "How long have you been standing there?"

"I think I came in when Elliot asked you if you were going to break Brenda's heart." He smiles a devilish smile. "So, your heart has not beat before you were captivated by her light blue eyes?" He asks as he goes straight to the coffee and pours himself a cup then loudly sips from it.

"I don't have time for falling for a girl, right now. I am trying to concentrate on this stagecoach business. Now let me see what my brother-in-law has to say about our guest in there." He rips open the envelope and reads it. "Don't that beat all. It is a small world." He stands up. "We need a little word with our prisoner." He hands the telegram to his nephew, as he takes a loud sip from his own cup.

"Interesting?" Harkahomé lets the telegram fall to the desk. "Can we finish our coffee first?"

"Coffee is always first. We Lewis's, are nothing before coffee. Except for the Colonel. Something about a Private spilling a cup of coffee on one of his Julia's first letters. He has been an avowed tea drinker ever since.

"I cannot believe that in the short time I have been back how much I need this drink."

"Your Uncle Joseph, the doctor, once explained that there is something in it called callifstine, caffalein, caffenine something like that, and it makes your heart beat faster, your brain think clearer and keeps you awake. He says that it is more addicting than laudanum. If you can believe that?"

"Uncle is a very learned man. Did Aunt Lizzie become a midwife or doctor? She was always talking about it."

"She did. She is a doctor. She and Joseph opened a medical clinic in Wichita. We should visit them on the way to Lawrence. We should also stop and see Grant and Carolyn and you can meet their three little ones."

"Am I going to have my breakfast, before you start this little road trip, Sheriff?" Calls out the man who calls himself Rusty Banner.

"Just for that comment, I think my deputy and I will go OUT to breakfast while yours grows mold!" Yells the sheriff. "Are you hungry, Harkahomé?

"I can always eat, Uncle. Afterward, we should go get that bath and shave. We must keep up appearances,

Sheriff. We do represent the town. Should we take the extra time?"

"I don't see why not?"

"You wouldn't dare!" Shouts the prisoner.

"SHUT UP!" They both yell back, as they drain their coffee cups loudly. Chilly grabs his Stetson hat while Joshua dons his gun belt and the two walk out of the office without another word.

***

After Chilly and Harkahomé have their steak and egg breakfast with two additional cups of coffee. They head to Spence's Barbershop and Bath. He has three bathing rooms. Each have two tubs in them. Spence is a smart man and knows that he can get backed up when it is time for everyone's Saturday night baths. The uncle and nephew are shown to the tubs in the first room. Chilly walks over to the tub and checks the water temperature and cleanliness. "I think we are the first bathers of the day. No bathtub ring."

"Not until, you get in, Uncle." Joshua says as he is removing his buckskins. A small man comes in and takes the clothing out to be laundered and dried. Spence's son, invented a system of drying the clothes quickly in a room with a fan blowing over hot bricks. The fan is powered by a pulley on a large wheel that is turned by peddling a unicycle of sorts. Harkahomé was very intrigued by it the first time he saw the operation. Joshua tests his water and climbs over the edge and eases himself in. "This sure beats a cold river stream, any day."

Chilly is easing himself in his tub, also. "I wouldn't have bothered if that was all that was available." He looks at the doorway and says, "Is that door closed tight? I would like to discuss the case."

Joshua, is closer to the door. He stands up and reaches over to it and turns the deadbolt. "What are your thoughts, Uncle?" He says as he lowers himself back down.

"First, we have the owner's missing son. I find it disturbing that he is gone so long and the owner is not concerned but content that the payroll was still hidden, untouched in the stagecoach. Second, it is obvious that our guest and the driver are related. The man used an alias so that we would not know they had the same last name. Third, if the strong box was a decoy with cut paper instead of real money, why didn't anyone return to the stage or come to town? They had to be disappointed at the haul. They had to know that the women were convinced that Indians were responsible, so they could have stayed undercover for a second chance at a profitable heist? This just doesn't add up."

"I am glad that only we know about the stage's hidden compartment. I am impressed that you did not share that with the other sheriff."

"No use sharing the information. The stage line will need to use it, repeatedly, I have no doubt." Says Chilly.

"I do not understand why the cowboy went off in the opposite direction of the employees." Says Harkahomé as he starts to wash his shoulder length hair. "Unless he doubled back, and took one of the team horses from the employees after they opened up the strong box. He might have just given up or argued with the other two."

"I bet that is what happened. When either they or the son got to the strong box and were told that there was no money. They might have thought that it was a double cross on their part. Words might have been said and someone might be lying out there dead or injured."

"They would not have used guns to kill if they were within three miles of the women. The shots would have been heard. Uncle, I think that I need to go back out there, after we interrogate our Williams fellow."

"Agreed, Harkahomé. I need to stay in town and I am sure that your tracking skills are as good as mine. I think that as careful as the scout was following the original tracks, you might have a harder time after having everyone trampling around."

"I think that my tracking skills are a might better." Joshua smiles. Chilly ignores the comment. "Did you want me to leave directly, or can I spend the evening with Miss Sadie?"

"Our man behind bars, ought to be starving by the time we get done with our leisurely grooming. He might be willing to tell us where you need to look if he wants his beans and bread."

"Even if it were only beans and bread!" Harkahomé laughs. "You have a poetic side to you, Uncle. While I go look for the three missing men, you will have time to dine with Miss Brenda. I know you like her. The door is closed, Uncle. You can confide in me."

The redheaded sheriff turns as red as his hair and beard. "Joshua, she just about took my breath away when I looked in her eyes. Then my heart felt like it wanted to beat right out of my chest. My palms got sweaty and . . . well, let's just say that I had a very hard time concentrating on getting the facts out of the ladies. That is why, I want to wait until this case is closed. If I am with her and cannot think or breathe, I will be of no use."

"Uncle, you are in love. You'd better not waste too much time. You do not want to risk losing her. I have been down that road and I was truly of no use to anyone for a long time, after that happened."

***

After their bath, both men go to Sunday service. It is the first and only church in town but the preacher is only there every third week. Harkahomé has not been to a Christian service since he was eleven. It was before the trip to Oberlin that changed his life. He felt very out of place in his buckskins for the first time since he received his first

102

set. He did not want to turn his back on the Cheyenne people or their way of life but . . . *Maybe I feel this way because of losing Missy's love. Her father, the missionary, thought my embrace of the Cheyenne, made me an unworthy Christian or at least an unworthy white man.* Joshua Nathaniel Lewis thought as he looked down at the clothing sewn lovingly by his white mother. *No, it is not the religion's fault that it's preacher could not see that I am twice the Christian he was, by excepting and loving my adopted family.*

Chilly was beside his nephew and felt the inner turmoil going on behind the otherwise poker faced man. Joshua was his best friend for the first eleven years of his life, and back then, he knew all his thoughts before he thought them. He looked at Joshua and caught his eye. Chilly has the feeling that Harkahomé is uncomfortable here. As soon as Chilly recognized the possible cause of Joshua's unease, he senses that it has resolved itself. His normally very self-assured nephew has regained his do-not-tread-on-me attitude that has served the Lewis men, so well.

After service, the pair head back to the Sheriff's office. Elliot is waiting outside for them. "Sheriff, I have brought the prisoner's lunch. Should I remove his uneaten breakfast?"

"No, he needs to eat them in the order, in which they came." The sheriff unlocks the door to his office, but doesn't open it. He turns to Elliot. "Any other questions or comments?"

Elliot looks up at the man that is 21 inches taller than he. "No sheriff, I know better. Let me know if there is anything else that I can do for you."

"There is something. My deputy will be riding out to do some investigating. See that he has supplies for a week on the road. Do not share this information with anyone. Not even your Aunt or your lovely cousin, got that?

"Of course, always. Sheriff." He turns to leave but

103

stops. "Sheriff, about this morning, it wasn't my place. I should have held my tongue." Again, he turns to leave.

"Elliot?" He waits for the man to turn back around. "You never stood as tall in my eyes as when you stood up to me on *her* behalf." He takes his hat off to him. "Just do not make that a habit. I barely tolerate you as it is. That tall man, I would have to stand up to."

"I understand, Sheriff. I will work on those supplies."

Chilly and Joshua, finally enter the office. Chilly throws his hat at the hat stand and has perfect aim. He looks at the trays of food. "This food looks too fresh for him. I think we should go have our lunch."

"Aw, come on Sheriff. I am starving in here."

"Are you? That's good, Williams. I have questions to ask you? For each answer that I like, I will give you something to eat. You can pick whether it's a bean or the bread." Chilly unlocks the door between the office and the cells. He and Joshua walk through and face the prisoner. Joshua has the breakfast plate in his hand. Chilly say, "Do you understand? If I do not like any answer, I leave the cell area and the office. So, I would answer quickly and tell me true, or we will be able to count your ribs before your next meal!! Now, Williams. Let's start with you admitting your real name, and how you are related to Jeff Williams?"

TWENTY
January 12th, 1959
A Monday in Chicago

Clara Beth and Oliver are cleaning up the kitchen. Carrie cooked Chinese, much to the delight of them both. Oliver was amazed that it tasted just as good as any of the places in Chinatown.

"How did you manage this? I have been eating there my whole life and I wouldn't have a clue how to duplicate any of it."

"She gets that from our mother. When my mother spent a year not knowing who she was, she still knew how to cook!" Clara explains.

"Say that again. Your mother did not know who she was?"

"It's a long story." Clara says. Then she goes into details of the event that started the day after her parents became engaged.

Carrie is in the living room looking through a magazine that she picked up this afternoon. It had all the latest fashions in it. When Carrie came home from school, GW's second letter arrived. Carrie was planning on going downtown to buy a gown but GW's letter convinced her that she should design one. She did leave to purchase the magazine. She plans to go to Goldblatt's for the material and look at the patterns that they have in stock. It is close to the time that GW will call. She is so excited that this is happening.

When she decided to say yes, everything regarding GW seemed to come flooding forward. All the feelings that she learned to ignore, because they lived in two different towns, over a hundred miles from each other. She learned to ignore them, because his family was well-to-do and hers worked for his. She learned to ignore her heart pounding each time she saw him and her sense of loss, each time they had to say good bye. But that is all a thing of the past. She refused to ignore or pretend that it is a dream that could never come true. This is going to be her new reality. GW is now a part of her life, as he has been a part of her heart her whole life.

As if to break the spell, the phone rings. Carrie looks at her wristwatch, it is nine o'clock on the dot. She gets up from her couch and crosses to the phone. Her hand is shaking as she picks up the receiver. "Harrick girl's residence, Carrie Ann speaking."

"Carrie, it is GW."

"I know. I have been looking forward to this all day."

"Me, too!"

"Did your father make the arrangements for me to fly out?"

"Yes, it is all done. You will fly out Friday night at eight o'clock, from Midway Airport to Wichita. You fly back on Sunday at eight again. We will drive you to and from the airport. Can someone take you to and from Midway?"

"I am sure that Oliver and Clara Beth will do it. I can pay them by cooking Chinese. I made some tonight and they were wild about it."

"I cannot wait until you can cook for me. But dancing comes first. I cannot wait to see you."

"I hope my dress turns out. I was going to buy one, but your second letter made me decide to design one instead. What color would you like it to be?"

"I don't know. That is a huge decision. What if the fabric in that color is all wrong for the design?"

"It sounds like you know about designing."

"I have listened to you discuss designs, for forever, and I've learned."

"You were always a great listener."

"You were too. When I told you my idea of modernizing the cow milking, you encouraged me to talk to my father about it. He listened and invested in the

106

equipment that I read about. It was expensive at the time, but we are realizing the benefits, now. I would have kept the information about the article to myself, but you pushed me into believing in myself. Even though we did not see each other but a few times a year, I always felt you were in my corner, to borrow a boxer's term."

"I want to continue the letter writing but I love to hear your voice, too. How often can you call me?"

"I do not think once a week is asking my parents for too much. I know my father called my mother that often when she lived in EL Dorado and he was in Lawrence. Shall it be Sunday nights, then?"

"That will be a great way to start each week."

"That is what I was thinking."

"Grant?"

"Carolyn Ann?"

"I love you."

"I love you, too."

"I am so glad. I always hoped, but never dared to believe it was possible. Did you?"

"I prayed for it. Each time we had to say good bye, I prayed that it would be only temporary and that God would give me the nerve to tell you how I felt, when the time was right. And he did."

"Thank you, God."

"Maybe, I should transfer to the University of Kansas in Lawrence. Mama wanted me to attend school, there."

"Isn't U of C more in line with the fashion design industry?"

"That was my reasoning. It doesn't seem to be that important, anymore. We should be together. The classes that I am taking are just the general classes. They have nothing to do with design, yet."

"Carrie, you are at your second college and it is still our freshman year. Will you want to start all over again? You get overwhelmed with new situations and I am sure that you just got unpacked. I may be sorry later, but you should not talk of changing schools - just to be with me."

"Aww, GW. You are so mean to me!"

"I just don't want you to do something that you will regret! We must be realistic about this. I would love you here, but how will you realize your dream of designing?"

"I can design anywhere. I do not have to be here in this freezing cold. I can live at the plantation house. I would share Audrey's room."

"That move, you would surely regret! She lives in the bathroom, all morning, every morning."

"Clara Beth hogs the bathroom, too. I am used to it."

"My love, no more talk of moving to Lawrence. You will stay in Chicago until you graduate. Then you will be able to design, anything anywhere. Then we will begin our life together. The real question is, will you send me sneak peaks of your dress design or will you keep it a secret until I see you?"

"I am thinking of drawing several choices. Then I will have you pick which one for me to wear for the ball."

"I love it. What a wonderful idea! I look forward to seeing them. I would feel funny picking, though. I will give you my preference but the final choice will be up to you."

"Deal. What classes did you have today? I had math, art appreciation and English."

"Art appreciation? How is that general beginning class?"

"The councilor said that the drawing class that I wanted was full. So, I had to take the appreciation class."

"Do you like it?"

"They are teaching us the work of the masters. So, I appreciate them! It is a better class than math or English. You didn't answer my question. What classes did you have today?"

"I had chemistry, Spanish, business accounting and horticulture."

"Four classes in one day? Are the other days only two?"

"No. I have four classes every day. Don't forget, I am handling a double major. I am very interested in the chemistry of farming. They are making major breakthroughs in propagating. It is fascinating!"

"But that with business accounting and a foreign language? Was your first semester as busy?"

"No, busier. I had five classes on two days. I am trying to finish in three years, even with a double major. I want to begin helping father run Legacy Plantation and the Johnson Family Farms. He has been overseeing both farms for nineteen years. Your grandfather, uncle, and your father have run the EL Dorado holdings since before we were born. I've wanted to take over in your town so that I would have a chance at being with you more."

"Why three years if I will be four years at college?"

"I assumed that I would need to apprentice for a year between Lawrence and EL Dorado before father puts me in charge."

"You've had this all planned out in your mind?"

"Since I was fifteen or so."

"What if I said that I didn't feel the same way about you as you do for me?"

"As my father said, 'a no might just mean not now'. I would just be around to make myself indispensable to you and your family, until you changed your mind."

"Well, you can slow down. That sleigh ride changed everything."

"Thank Goodness. This will make the years fly by, knowing that you feel the same way. I will not slow down. If I stay busy with my heart set on the goal, it will come that much faster."

"Have you told your father about these plans? He might have other ideas in mind."

"We have talked about it over the years. Grandfather Grant's will set your Masters family running the Johnson Family Farms until a male heir can take over. That is me, Billy and/or Kevin. Then father went and bought that six-hundred-acre plantation in Emporia when Kevin was born, so each boy would have farm holdings *IF* we wanted to be farmers."

"What about the girls, what if they wanted to run a farm like Aunt Carolyn did?"

"I am sure father would buy as many farms as he needed to make sure each of us were doing what will make us happy. I always wanted to make things grow. I do not know if Billy is interested or not. He is thinking about going into the military. I think he has a mind to become a Colonel, like his namesake.

"But mother said that the Colonel only did that because he thought he lost his Julia. He wrote her about looking forward to working hard on the farm and watching things grow."

"That's right. I am reading their correspondence, in my spare time."

"What spare time?"

GW laughs, "I have a few moments, just before I close my eyes and dream of you!"

TWENTY-ONE
January 13th, 1896
A Monday in Pennysville, Oklahoma

Harkahomé was ready to get on his horse, to ride out. It was just before daybreak. He and Sadie spent the night together talking in Penny's Parlor, and Sadie walked with him. Elliot had the horse packed for a two-week ride and was waiting for him in front of the Sheriff's office. He looked to Elliot holding the horse's reins. "Make sure that my Uncle takes your cousin to dinner. He is crazy about her. I think falling in love is the only thing that he is afraid of, in the whole world. He is using the 'case' as a reason to avoid falling for her completely." He looks to Sadie. He has a strand of hair that has escaped his hair tie and it was in his eyes. Before he can capture it, she reaches up and tucks it behind his ear. He reaches for her hand, then brings it to his lips. "I will miss our time together. Miss Sadie, will you help my Uncle find his true love? I know that it is Miss Brenda, as sure as I am standing here."

"I could invite them each to dine with me at Big Momma's but not go. They would have to dine together, expecting me to show up."

"That might work. I will leave it in your very capable hands." He is still holding them. "I do not want to leave you, it is so odd for me to be in the white man's world, and, yet, I have come to rely, even need some things as if they have been a part of my life all along."

"Like what things?" She asks with a laugh.

"Coffee, my Uncle's laugh and your presence."

"That is about the sweetest thing any Indian has ever said to me. Hurry back and say some more. Will you kiss me, good-bye?"

"If I do, I might not leave, at all." He bends to kiss her but before their lips meet . . .

"Harkahomé, your bed wasn't slept in! I thought

111

you might have gone in the night without saying good bye." The Sheriff says.

"I was in the middle of a good bye, now. Give me a minute, Uncle and I will come in the office for your last-minute instructions."

"Take your time . . . but hurry, will you? I want you gone before the town wakes up."

"If you and Elliot will give me just a moment of privacy, Miss Sadie will be on her way and you will have my undivided attention."

"You want us to wait inside the office?" Chilly asks incredulously.

"If you can, please." Joshua's eyes are still locked on Sadie's.

"Come on, Sheriff, I will put your pot of coffee on." Says Elliot as he tugs at Chilly's sleeve.

"Elliot, what have I told you about touching me!" He says as he lets Elliot lead him back into the office.

Joshua says to Sadie, "Now, where were we?" Instead of talking, Sadie reaches up and puts her arms around the buckskin wearing white man. He bends down for her to accomplish this, but when he does so, their lips meet. Joshua has never felt such softness as her lips. Her perfume has mixed with her personal smell and he finds it all intoxicating. He forces himself to pull away. "I knew that your kiss would be something that I will never forget, or want to leave."

"Do you say those things because of your Cheyenne upbringing or your Lewis bloodline?"

He tilts his head. "I do not know."

"It doesn't matter. Joshua, I have been around the block, as they say, but I have never felt what I feel for you. I cannot stop thinking about you. Please be careful out there, and come back to me soon."

"You can be sure that I will." He bends to kiss her again. When he pulls away this time, she is holding her hat on her head.

"OH, MY! I better get to my room, so that you can go on your journey. The sooner you go, the sooner you will be back."

"And in your arms, my dear. That is as sure a thing as an Indian on a nickel. Take care, Sadie."

She turns to walk away. After he watches her go a few steps, she turns and says. "Harkahomé, I think that you have just changed my life. I didn't think it needed changing but I am so happy for it."

"I was thinking the same thing, Miss Sadie Mae Miller. Go home and get some sleep, but not too much."

She laughs, "What an odd thing to say. Why not?"

"They call it 'beauty sleep', don't they? If you become any more beautiful, you might not want me. Or, I will need to fight off many other suitors."

"Harkahomé, my heart will stay true to you, I promise."

"I will promise the same. I must talk with my Uncle, now. Or he will come out again, and wake the town."

Sadie doesn't say another word. She blows him a kiss and turns to walk back to Penny's Parlor. Joshua turns to face the office and he sees two faces in the window. One redhead at the top of the window and one balding with glasses at the bottom. He shakes his head and walks into the office. "Did you enjoy the show?"

"It beats looking at Elliot!" Chilly says.

"And it beats being looked at!" Elliot responds.

"So, pour me a cup of coffee. Are there any last-minute things that you'd like to tell me?"

"Just be careful. No stage robbery is worth losing my favorite Indian."

"Aw, I bet you say that to all your deputies." He mock punches his Uncle in the shoulder. "Don't forget our deal, I chase the bad guys, you date his cousin. If I find out that you have not made the first move when I get back, I promise you, you will lose your favorite Indian."

113

"That sounds more like a threat than a promise."

"Yup, I am that serious. If I get any information, I will try to send you a telegram from the next town."

"Good. Don't take any chances. If you find where they are hold up, let me know and I will form another posse to come to you. Do not approach them alone. Promise?"

"Yes, Uncle Sheriff, sir!" Joshua says as he salutes Chilly, who starts to laugh, then Elliot starts to laugh.

Both men turn to Elliot. "Are you still here?" They say at the same time.

***

At around three in the afternoon, Sadie woke up, still in her gown from the night before. She looked at her small watch broach that she wore pinned to her bodice. *Oh, my goodness! I was supposed to ask the sheriff and Brenda to dinner!* Sadie thinks as she sits straight up in bed. Tonight, is her first day off and she promised Joshua that she'll get his uncle to take out Brenda even if she tricks him to do it.

She goes to her trunk for a modest gown. Not the colorful ones that she wears for work but something her mama would say is a Sunday dress. She must go invite the soon-to-be love birds to what will be their first date. *I wonder if old mother Martha will allow her daughter to dine with me at all? It is one thing to hold hands while a stagecoach is being attacked, it is another to be seen in public, together.* She is confident that the sheriff will come out to eat. Especially, if she offers to pay! But the cousin of the Postmaster might be another story.

She quickly dresses and puts on a new hat. She checks herself in the mirror and is out the door in less than twenty minutes. She is going to the hotel first to call on Martha and Brenda.

Sadie is passing the General Store that has the Post Office near the window. She sees that Elliot is at his post. Even though she has taken a few steps past the entrance, she turns around and goes in. Elliot is sorting the latest bag of mail and is oblivious to her presence. She says quietly. "Elliot." He is startled and drops the mail in his hand.

"Oh, Miss Sadie. I did not see you there." He bends to pick up the various envelopes.

"Elliot, you need to drink less coffee. You are so easily startled."

"I make coffee for the sheriff and the store here, but I never touch the stuff. I do not like the taste." He says as he comes up from bending.

"Elliot, I like you but can I say 'You are a funny little man'?"

"The sheriff says much worse, but deep down I think he likes me."

"That would have to be very deep."

"What can I do for you this afternoon, Miss Sadie?"

"I have come for your help in getting your cousin and the sheriff together."

"Brenda would like nothing better. I have talked with Sheriff Lewis about my cousin, but it just made him mad."

"That's because talk is cheap. I need you to take your Aunt out to dinner, while I take Brenda out. Say about 6:30? Can you do that?"

"Aunt Martha did say that she wanted to eat at the Long Horn Restaurant. I can offer to take her there."

"Good, I will take Brenda with me and meet up with the Sheriff. Thanks, Elliot. If all goes well, we might have a match, here." She turns and leaves the store and heads now to the Sheriff's office.

She bursts into the office as if she is a victim and someone needs to run after the bad men. Chilly is at his desk, he looks up, but doesn't move, other than he puts

115

down his coffee cup.

"There you are, Sheriff." She rushes the words out.

"Imagine that, I am where I am supposed to be. How can I help you, Miss Sadie?" He says with a raised eyebrow.

She comes to the desk and plops into the chair on the other side of it. "I am thoroughly enamored by your nephew and I miss him terribly."

"How can I help you, Miss Sadie?" He repeats.

"I do not know. Today is my first evening off and I have no one to spend it with. You sent my beau away just when I have all the time to spend with him."

"I am losing my patience, Miss Sadie. HOW CAN I HELP YOU?"

"Maybe have dinner with me, and tell me stories of my love?"

"Behind his back?"

"It's the only way I can feel like I am still with him, hearing Harkahomé harrowing tales. You have plenty, I am sure."

Chilly raises an eyebrow, "It doesn't feel right. Dining with you and talking about him while he cannot defend himself against my defaming his character."

"You wouldn't do that, you adore him. He is your little brother and side-kick. It doesn't matter how much time you spent apart."

"I am beginning to get annoyed when people keep telling me how I feel about someone."

"Look, I will even pay for your meal, you can buy the drinks."

"Buy both and we have a deal."

Sadie stands up and holds out her hand for a handshake. "Deal, Sheriff." She looks at her watch broach. "It's a little before four. Meet me at seven at Big Momma's. Or do you have another restaurant in mind? It's your choice. Pick your favorite place and order your favorite meal, on me."

"Big Momma's is fine. I will order the most expensive cut of beef on the menu. And I will drink the best whiskey, they sell. This will be the first and last time, we are seen together. I will make it too expensive for you to ask me, again."

"Cunningly, little mind, you have in that oversized head! See you at seven – sharp." Sadie is up and is out the door as fast as she walked in.

***

At quarter to seven, Sadie is at the hotel and seated in Brenda's room. "Come, Brenda. I have it all worked out. The sheriff will be expecting me to wine and dine him for the sake of my broken heart. See, you promised your mother not to make the first move, but I made no such promise. Let's go!"

"Do you like this gown and hat? I don't think it suits me at all."

"Now that you mentioned it, let me look at your selections. Do you have anything dark blue? The Sheriff is crazy about your light blue eyes and a dark blue dress will bring them out." Sadie is rummaging through the small wardrobe cabinet. "Oh, this one is perfect! Royal blue should be your signature color. It not only will bring out your eyes but it will make your light hair even more golden. Hurry, let's get this on you." Sadie helps Brenda remove the dress she has on and assists her into the blue gown. When finished, she stands back, "Oh, this one will surely get his attention. What hat do you have to go with it? The one you wore in the stagecoach will do but surely you have one with more royal blue in it."

Brenda says timidly. "I did buy a hat just yesterday. It is less modest than my mother would like, I didn't even tell her that I bought it." She moves to the pile of hat boxes that she has stacked in the corner. She takes the second one from the bottom and opens it. "I didn't even want her to find it so I moved it lower in the stack. Mother and I have shared hats on occasion." She takes the contents of the hat box and walks over to the small dressing table with a mirror on it. She sits in the chair and puts the hat on her head slightly tilted. "The sales woman says this look is all the rage in the big cities like Chicago and New York. Do you like it?" She turns to Sadie. The hat is royal blue and has many feathers woven into its bonnet. It has a veil that is also royal blue and covers just to the bridge of her nose.

"I was going to ask you how a hat can be immodest, but seeing it on you. . . I see that it gives you a very 'come hither' look. You have all the equipment to get your man, Miss Brenda. And I intend to teach you how to use it all, if you do not know how all ready."

"Mother has never let me have an unchaperoned date. If she does not accompany me, it is because she has someone from his family do it. That is why I am an old maid!"

"Brenda, you are only twenty years old. That is not an old maid by any standards."

"I feel like one. All my childhood friends are married. There was a young man that wanted to start courting me, but Mama came up with this world traveling trip instead. I think she wants me to live with her, her whole life."

Sadie bends down to take Brenda's hands. "Believe me, you do not have to settle for anything that your mother has in mind for you. You have the right to follow your own heart. What does your heart tell you about the sheriff?

"It doesn't have time to say anything. It is beating too hard to get a word in, edgewise."

"Perfect answer. That is how I feel for Joshua. That Indian white man has tomahawked his way into my heart! It is just shameful, how nuts I am about that man, so soon."

"I feel it is too soon, also. We haven't talked except

about the stagecoach robbery. Why am I so drawn to him?"

"I do not know but that's what makes the world go-round!" Sadie chuckles as she helps Brenda to her feet. "The Sheriff might be on his third drink by now. Let's get there. My plan is to order your food then excuse myself to go to the outhouse but you come back to my seat, instead." Sadie reaches into her purse and brings out a $20 gold piece. "As promised, I am paying for the meal."

"Oh, Sadie. I couldn't let you."

"You aren't, Chilly is. Now let's go."

***

Chilly is sitting at his favorite table, drinking his first shot of whiskey with a beer chaser. He looks at his pocket watch. Sadie is twenty minutes late. *I have been stood up!* He grumbles in his own head. He has eyed the memorized menu and has picked out the most expensive steak but has not told Josie, yet. He decides to be a gentleman for once, and wait for his date's arrival before ordering. Josie has met Sadie and will be very upset with him for dining with her, but Chilly doesn't care. Not about Josie, not in the least. *How has my life changed with one ride in a stagecoach?* He wonders, but not for long.

"Sheriff, I am so sorry for being late. I had a problem with a gentleman who saw me at Penny's Parlor. He wanted me to deal cards for him and he would not get it in his thick head that it is my night off." She sits down before he can stand and takes the napkin and wipes her brow. "I must have run the whole way here. Can I have this?" She reaches across and takes his untouched beer and starts to drain the tall glass. "Sorry Sheriff, I will get you another. It was a narrow escape from that man, I tell you." She takes another long drink. "Now, have you ordered food?"

"No, I was waiting for your arrival. I know what I

want, though."

"I know, also. The most expensive cut of beef on the menu. I will have the same. Order for me will you. I like my steak rare. Hot blooded like I like my men. Joshua looks cool on the outside but I am guessing that a very hot male is just under that buckskin. I need to use the facilities, if you do not mind. Please order for us. I will take another beer also."

"Sadie, I can barely keep up with you. You are a mile a minute, today. What is going on?"

"It has been one thing after another. And I am worried about my Indian. Is the deputy in any danger, Sheriff?"

"Not if he does what I said to and not take any undue precautions. He will be in good hands where I sent him because I know the sheriff there."

"Oh, you sent him back to Bartlesville, to Sheriff Lucas?"

"No Sadie, I know more than one sheriff in Oklahoma." He smiles for the first time of the evening. Josie walks over after he catches her eye. "Josie, darling. I need two very expensive rare steaks. Baked potatoes and another round of drinks for the both of us."

"Of course, Sheriff. Coming right up." She hurries off to the kitchen.

Sadie looks from her to Chilly. "She likes you, Sheriff. She is practically sitting in your lap, the way she looks at you."

"Sadie, do you have any filter for your thoughts? Or do they all just come stumbling out, willy-nilly?"

"I am an honest person, for the most part, Sheriff. I call things as I see them. Take Brenda for example."

"What does that mean, take Brenda for example?"

"She is also crazy for you. You, tall ginger goofball. The difference is, you feel the same way for her. Just admit it and let us move on." She looks at him for a moment. "Well, are you going to admit it?"

"Fine, I am crazy for her too. I thought we came here to discuss Joshua."

"That - is because I tricked you." She stands up and without another word leaves the table. A moment later, Josie is bringing the drinks that he ordered. When Josie steps to the side, Brenda is behind her. Brenda does not say a word but sits down in Sadie's vacant seat.

"So Sheriff. It seems this is your Halloween. Sadie was the trick and I am the treat. Or so I hope you think so."

Chilly is stunned beyond speech. He grabs his whiskey and downs the whole thing. To his equal amazement, Brenda grabs the second shot of whiskey and brings it to her lips. Chilly is just watching with his mouth open.

"Sorry, I cannot do it. Whiskey just smells too foul to try!" She says as she puts down the shot glass.

This makes Chilly burst out laughing and he cannot stop. When he finally gets his wind back, he says. "Won't you join me for dinner, Miss Brenda?"

"I believe that I am. Sheriff Lewis."

"My friends call me Chilly."

"Mine leave off the Miss and just call me, Brenda." She is smiling and he can feel his heart race and his stomach twitter at the same time.

"Did you know that Halloween is my favorite holiday?" He asks.

"I didn't. Why is that?"

"I was born on Halloween. That would make you not just a treat but a present, too."

"Sounds about right." Brenda says while looking in his eyes, then she blushes and looks down.

TWENTY-TWO
January 13th, 1959
A Tuesday in EL Dorado, Kansas

Anna has just seen Harry off to high school in his used 1943 Pontiac Convertible. The car is a year younger than Harry but he doesn't care, because it can fit half of his baseball team in it. She is just cleaning up the breakfast dishes.

Henry has gone to the Farm office to help her father with the planning of the crops for next year. Her younger brother, Matthew was her father's assistant until he was in college full time and the Japanese bombed Pearl Harbor. He enlisted in the Air Force, that day and became one of the first pilots trained and released to fight the Japanese. Their whole family was devastated when his plane was shot down and he was presumed dead for several weeks. In the meantime, he became a father again, to Muriel Mae born the same year as Harry.

When the Harrick family moved to EL Dorado in 1946 to start the second restaurant, Henry also became Judd's right hand man, because Judd had had a small heart attack. Matthew was home from war, but decided to work for the airlines flying passenger planes. He was making much more money and as the kid who could drive anything without a lesson, he was very good at driving planes.

As Anna was wiping the counter, the phone rang. She went to the sitting room to where the phone was kept. "Harrick residence, Anna speaking."

"Anna, darling. How is my favorite unrelated sister-in-law?"

"Juliet Helen? I am fine. We haven't talked since Christmas. How are you?"

"I am doing well. I will be ascending down on EL Dorado, soon, for all the work involved in organizing the

Valentine Ball. I have ads to book, posters to have printed and lots of little things to take care of."

"You have been putting this Ball together since you turned eighteen. You have it down to a science. I know that you are not calling me to talk about the Ball. What is going on?"

"Have you talked to Carrie, recently? Do you know that she is coming to EL Dorado for the ball, as GW's guest?"

"She hadn't made up her mind when I talked to her last. So, she said yes? I told her that I didn't want her to miss school and she promised me that she wouldn't."

"She is keeping that promise. We are flying her out on Friday night, and flying her back on Sunday night. The flights are booked and GW will drive to the Wichita airport to pick her up and return her."

"She is going to FLY?" Anna asks a little too loud.

"Yes, but we are paying for the whole thing."

"I don't want my children in planes, you know what happened to my brother in the war."

"Yes, Anna. But he still flies today. He did not let what happened to him, stop his love of flying. He has made a career out of it. Besides, he was shot down. As far as I know, there are no enemy planes from Chicago to Wichita."

"I wish that she would have called me to talk about this."

"You would have tried to talk her out of it. GW is thrilled to death that she is going as his date. They were on the phone last night for over an hour talking, and laughing. I heard GW say 'I love you' to her."

"Isn't he moving just a little too fast?"

"He has had a crush on her since we gave them baths together. It is your fault, really. I distinctly remember, you were always saying, 'Give GW a kiss Carrie Ann,' when they were infants. Don't you remember?"

"I choose not to. I must admit, she has always had

a crush on him also. Every time we'd be together, they were inseparable. Every time we parted, she was in tears. He was her best friend, no matter how far apart the towns that they lived in were."

"Well, just like you and Henry or the Colonel and his Julia, childhood sweethearts are the best. I wish I had known my husband as I was growing up."

"Helen, you met him when you were sixteen, and married him at seventeen. You weren't a real grown-up, yet. Besides, there is the age difference. Six-years is a lot - when you were ten and he was sixteen. You need to be of similar ages to be childhood sweethearts, don't you?"

"I guess you are right. Well, they qualify. We might be finally related by blood, after all these years of calling each other sister. GW says that Carrie Ann plans on designing her gown for the ball. He said that she is nervous tackling that job without your help."

"She doesn't need anyone's help. I just say, 'Oh, that is coming out so nice!'. Sometimes I tell her that the stitches that she hates, look fine or no one will notice. I am just there to give her self-confidence. She is the natural born designer."

"Like you are."

"No, I follow a pattern, or sometimes I know the pattern well enough to sew without one, but I have never designed clothing. Just like Melinda can cook following a recipe but doesn't have a knack for making up recipes, herself. You have mastered the art of cooking, even though you were not allowed to turn on a stove or look in an oven until you lived with me. You have improved some meals, that I taught you."

"That means a lot to me, Anna."

"I am not just saying that. I don't know why you refused to cook at the restaurants. You are good enough."

"Yes, but doing it because you love your husband is different than doing it for a living. That was your passion."

"And thank God, I had the Lewis family to make

sure that I made money at it. All because I taught you how to make Joshua's favorite dish – meatloaf."

"It was a wise investment. Even though we had to wait two years for you to have Carrie Ann and feel comfortable enough to bring her or leave her so that you can run your first place."

"I am glad that it worked out for the both of us. It is too soon to tell but we might become mothers-in-law and down the road share grandchildren."

"I am so happy for them. How could GW not love Carrie? He is so like his father and she is so much like you. If it wasn't for the fact that you were sure that you had a Henry looking for you, my Joshua might have stood a chance at being your husband, before I had a chance to turn his head."

"Thank God, for my insistence, then. We are with the person; we were always meant to be with."

"Well, I will call you if I have any more news to tell on the romance front. I will be down on Thursday and Friday to book and create all the advertising. I hope to grab lunch with you."

"Oh, make it a dinner. Come here and enjoy the peace and quiet of a single child household."

"I would love too. Talk to you then. Have a good day. Anna."

"Oh, you too. Helen. Good bye."

As Anna is walking back to the kitchen, she suddenly gets a sinking feeling in her stomach. Her little girl is going to get on a plane! *I need to call Henry. I am so worried.* She thinks as she regains her composure and turns around to make the call.

"Henry?" She says before he can even say hello.

"Anna? What is wrong?" He can hear it in her voice.

"Carrie is going to FLY in to Wichita."

"I figured that she would except the offer, so that she wouldn't miss any school."

"You knew this was a possibility?"

"Um, yes. I talked with Joshua last week. She hadn't made up her mind, yet. So, there was no use worrying you about it."

"I am not going to sleep until February 16th, you know that, don't you?"

"That is why I didn't want you to know until the last moment."

"Henry, you promised me twenty-three years ago, no secrets between us."

"I figured that promise was made void, when you had become pregnant against medical advice and without my knowledge."

"It's not like I sent out for a stud, Henry. You are the father of all my children."

"And the man who almost lost his wife, four times because of it."

"But look at the beautiful results. Now, I might lose her in a plane crash. You remember what happened to Matthew?"

"Again, Anna, he was shot down, and survived. He flies planes for a living. You are not being realistic. Modern planes are very safe. Listen, I will find out what airline they booked and if it's United Airlines, maybe Matthew can request the run, there and back."

"So you want me to worry double?"

Henry starts to laugh. "Anna, you are so cute. I can just see you standing there with one hand on your hip, the phone wedged between your shoulder and ear, while you are nervously running your other hand through the top of your hair." He pauses for a moment. "Am I right?"

"Henry, sometimes I could slap you for knowing me, so well."

"There are worse things to be slapped for. Anna, don't you need to meet with a supplier at the restaurant? You are late."

She looks at her watch. "Oh, my goodness. I am

supposed to have been there, three minutes ago. Do me a favor and call there and tell them that I am on my way."

"Yes, darling. Drive carefully. I will see you this afternoon." He says but he realizes that she has already hung the phone up. He looks at the calendar. *It is only the 13th. So, I will have a full month of Anna's worrying ahead of me. Thank God, this isn't growing season!"*

TWENTY-THREE
January 14th, 1896
A Tuesday in Collinsville, Oklahoma

Riding out on a tip from the prisoner Williams, that his cousin Jeff is hold up in a town southeast of Pennysville; Harkahomé has made good time. Sheriff Lewis has telegrammed the info to the local sheriff and Joshua is going straight to him before going to the area described as the hideout. Harkahomé doesn't know when he has been more exhausted, in his twenty-eight years. He wishes that he did not stay up all night talking with Sadie, because it is very hard to keep on track for thirty miles if you are asleep on a horse that doesn't know the way.

Though he was riding at a fast pace, his mind tended to drift to his all-night date, Sadie Mae Miller. She is unlike any woman or squaw that he has met. She is smart, and funny with the quickest wit of anyone that he knows, man or woman. She is self-sufficient, and downright pretty to look at. He can imagine spending his life with her. She will be a sparring partner as well as his best friend. When he kissed her good bye, yesterday morning, he wanted to abandon his mission and go to her room and share a blanket with her, as Chilly would put it. He hopes that his mission will not keep him away from her for long.

As lost as he was when he left his Cheyenne family, he feels that he has found a life here with his renewed relationship with his uncle. He feels that the years that they spent apart melted away, the moment they hugged in the bar that first night in Pennysville. He was the happiest being Chilly's little brother in Lawrence, growing up. Finishing each other's sentences, laughing at all their inside jokes has given him a sense of belonging that has been missing since his blood-brother took his first squaw. When his mother passed two years ago, he no longer felt

128

connected but lost and abandoned. He was still surrounded by his adopted family but they were all involved in their wives and children and he was an outsider looking in. Not because of the color of his skin but because of being without a love match, which came so natural to both his blood and step-brother.

It is late at night when Joshua rides into Collinsville. He goes to the livery and stables his horse and asks for directions to the sheriff's office. He also asked for a recommendation for a hotel room. A soft bed is going to feel heavenly after all these hours awake and hard riding.

He walks into the sheriff's office and introduces himself. "I am Joshua Lewis, also known as Harkahomé of the Cheyenne. I am the nephew and deputy of Sheriff Lewis in Pennysville. Did you receive his telegram?" The men standing in front of him are two deputies and the Sheriff. He makes eye contact with all of them. "Sirs? Did you get a telegram from the Sheriff of Pennysville, or didn't you?" The tallest of the men was the sheriff.

"Keep your buckskins on, Deputy Indian. We got the wire, but it doesn't say that an Injun was coming. How do I know that you are who you say you are?"

"Why would I say that I am, if I am not? I do not have time for games. I am looking for two men that held up the stage going from Bartlesville to Tulsa. We have a confession from an accomplice that he was supposed to meet his cousin just outside of this town to split the heist."

The men look at each other. The sheriff starts to laugh. "Harkahomé, is it? Golly, you are the splitting image of Will! How is he? He is taller than you, though, I think." The men around him look as confused as Joshua feels.

"You know my Uncle?" Is all that he can think to say.

"It's a small world in the military/sheriff business. I know both your uncles. I served with Will and Chilly spent some time with me as my deputy. Fine men, both. Both appreciate a practical joke, too. Did that skip a generation?" He has his arm around Joshua's neck. "I was the Private that Will docked a day's pay for spilling coffee on one of his Julia's first letters. My name is Wilcox. Johnny Wilcox. Come, have a meal and I will let you know, what I know about this hideout. We will go to it first thing in the morning." He takes his hat and covers his head as he leads Joshua out of the office.

"Sir, not to seem rude, but I have been awake for thirty-six hours and I need sleep, more than a meal, at this point. I would like to get my things from the livery, check into the hotel and get some food sent to me, if possible."

"Young man, considered it done. What would you have, steak or chicken?" He asks as they walk toward the stable.

"If you're buying sheriff, steak. If it's coming out of my advanced pay, I will take a small pigeon."

"Oh, you still haven't earned your first paycheck? Hard times, then. As a favor to your uncles, whom I respect beyond measure, I will buy you a steak and have it sent to your hotel room. Beer or whiskey?"

"A cold beer, if you please. I cannot tell you how much I appreciate this Sheriff. Little sleep and lots of riding can make even an Indian grouchy!

"Think nothing of it. I have been there, myself. Eat, sleep and come to my office at first light. We will talk then."

TWENTY-FOUR
An Excerpt from the letter of Carrie Ann Harrick
Chicago, Illinois

January 14th, 1959

Dear GW,

I have gone to several dress shops and fabric stores and I have worked on two designs that I like equally. I am at a loss as to which gown, I should create. The designs are very different, as you can see.

The first one that I drew, I see it in a red velvet fabric (it is February). The arms are bare but I would make a matching velvet wrap to wear with a white fur on top so that will be around my neck and shoulders. I would wear long red evening gloves and carry a white muffler to complete the ensemble. I like this design because of the small waist offset by the wide almost hoop skirt.

The second one has my shoulders and arms bare. I see this in light blue fabric for the bodice, like taffeta but that might be too light for the season. This skirting, though just as wide as the previous one would have two different colors (light blue and royal blue?) stripes alternating horizontally from my waist to the floor. I have where the stripes join ruffled. The jacket would complete the look. Royal blue silk with a high collar and long Domain sleeves, but I would bunch the sleeves, just below the elbow, then wear extra-long white gloves bunched up on the forearm. The jacket would be floor length also but be split in five sections at the tight waist then billow out over the skirt.

I love them both and with my figure, I know that they will be perfect. The second one will take longer to sew with all the stripes and will technically challenge

131

me, but my school work might suffer. I really want to make this one but I need to be realistic. I am sending the drawings to mama, also. Her opinion means everything to me.

School has already taken a back seat as I have been doodling the drawings in my classes. Somehow, I do not care. Just don't tell the folks. Today's class was especially boring and I redrew the second design four times in class.

Do you recall your junior prom? I think you and I were very close to admitting our feelings that night. I was so thrilled that you asked me to go. I had such a lovely time hanging out with all my old classmates. With your parents Chaperoning and all our friends surrounding us, we didn't have much time to talk. I was hoping that you'd declare your feelings because I did not have the nerve. What if you did not feel the same way? What if all you felt was I was a best friend that you could dance with? I would have never been able to look you in the eye, again. That's how much it would have hurt and embarrassed me. Going to that dance with you meant everything to me.

Our senior proms were on the same day and we each wanted to go to our own last dance. I was miserable without you. I was so sorry that I did not go to Lawrence for yours, have I ever shared that with you? I regretted it, when he showed up to pick me up, I regretted it during each dance. All that ran through my mind was that I could have been dancing with you. You always meant everything to me and I regret not having the nerve to tell you.

I must end this letter short. Now that the drawings are done and I have both letters addressed, I must get back to the real reason that I am living in this cold chilly city - College! Write back your choice or better yet, call me early, if your parents will let you.

I love you and cannot wait until our next communication: be it letter, phone call or you hop on a plane and come see me. I will relish whatever it is.

Yours with Love,
Carrie Ann

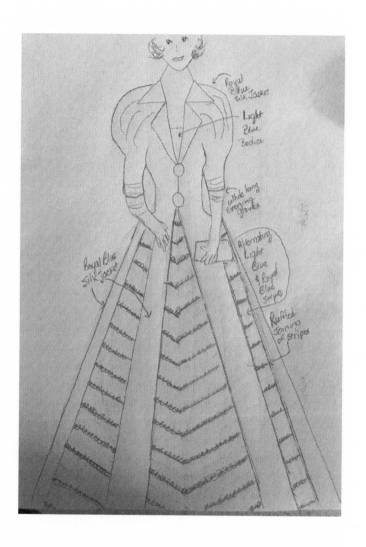

TWENTY-FIVE
January 15th, 1896
A Wednesday in Pennysville, Oklahoma

Chilly is sitting at his desk in the middle of the afternoon when a telegram boy comes in. "Sheriff, this just arrived for you from Collinsville. I will wait on the porch, if you have a response." The teenager hands the sheriff the envelope and he turns to leave.

Before he can get the envelope open, Elliot runs into the office. "Sheriff, there were gunshots fired in the bank!" He runs back out. Chilly has on his gun belt but grabs his Winchester rifle and follows him.

"Sonny, you go back to your office. I'll deal with that telegram later." The boy runs across the street. The bank is on the same side as the sheriff's office but on the next block. With his rifle in hand, he runs to the end of the block and turns down the cross street to go behind the buildings to the alley entrance. Elliot is already there. "What are you doing here, do you want to get yourself killed?"

"I thought I could look in the back window, so I could tell you what is going on in there." They are both advancing toward the bank building.

"Tell me, how many shots were fired?"

"I heard only two, I was sitting on the bench outside the General Store."

"You didn't see anyone going in with guns drawn or anything?"

"No, sir. If I had, I would not have waited for the shots to come get you. You know that." They are at the edge of the bank. There is a gangway between the buildings. "I will look in the window on the side." Elliot whispers.

"Keep your head and your voice down." Chilly takes a few more steps and is under a back window. He slowly peaks in, then ducks down again. He does it again. He sees two female employees hiding behind a counter - hiding from the man waving the pistol in the lobby. The man seems to be talking so Chilly dares tap on the window to get one woman's attention. She is on heightened alert and hears the tiny sound. Chilly motions to her, he points to the back door and makes a makeshift unlock gesture. He was never good at charades. She seems to grasp what he means. He can see Elliot in the side window. Chilly gives the girl a wait signal and he crawls back to the corner and waves Elliot to him.

"Watch me in the window. When the girl starts toward the door, knock on the window and fall flat on your pretty face. I am sure that the man will start shooting at the window, while the girl lets me in the back door." He crouches down again and goes back to his spot. When he peaks in again, the girls are not there. The bandit is holding the girl he was motioning to – by her hair.

Chilly doesn't know if she got to the door or not. He creeps slowly to it and turns the handle. It is turning. He moves in the slowest of motion. He looks up and Elliot is now at the back window. By looking in, Elliot must see that it is not a good time to open the door all the way. He holds up his hand for Chilly to wait. He crawls to the corner of the building. Then he holds up three fingers, changes it to two, then one. He pounds hard on the corner wall, then dives for dirt. As Chilly predicted, shots are fired in the direction of the pounding. Chilly is through the door and has his rifle in the man's back faster than the man could fire his third shot.

"I wouldn't take that next shot. That's our Post Master General you are shooting at. If anyone is going to kill that pain in my ass, it's gonna be me!"

"And who the hell are you?" The robber says with his hand still on the trigger."

"How stupid are you? I am the man with a rifle in your back. Now raise your left hand while you put the gun on the ground with your right. Then slowly stand with both hands raised." He looked to the girl that unlocked the door. "Are you hurt Judith?"

"No, I am not, thank you Sheriff."

"Who did he shoot at the first time? Do we have any injuries?"

Judith answers, "No, injuries, he was shooting in the air to make sure he had all our attention. Not very smart."

"No, it wasn't. He got the whole town's attention." The robber is now standing with his hands in the air. Chilly nudges him. "Mister. Let's both take two giant steps backwards while Judith takes the gun from the floor for me. Don't try anything. I will have no qualms about shooting you in the back, I promise."

Elliot has come in the bank through the back door. "Sheriff, do you need assistance?"

"Yes, Elliot. Take the gun from Judith and hold it on him while I cuff him." Elliot steps forward and takes the gun from the shaking hand of Judith.

"You did very well, Judith. But I will take it from here." Elliot says with all the calm that Chilly has never heard from him.

The Sheriff has the man in cuffs and the rifle still on him and he and Elliot escort the prisoner out the front door. Everyone exits the bank. Naturally, the townspeople all crowd around the sheriff and the prisoner. Good job and congratulations can be heard from everyone. Chilly holds up his hand. "I could not have done it without the brave cooperation of your Postmaster Elliot and the teller Judith. Their actions with no regard of their own safety is the only reason that this man is in custody. They each deserve medals." Chilly says. He continues walking the prisoner to his office while the crowd encircles and congratulates Elliot and Judith.

After he has the man behind lock and key, he begins to ask him questions. For the first time, he is looking at the man's face. He has only one eye. The other eye seems to be sown shut. He also has a long scar that starts above his left brow and ends at his cheek just even with his top lip. He has a handle bar mustache and long dirty brown hair. "Let's start with your name, mister." Chilly says.

"I am called Bart Jackson." He answers.

"Are there other names that you are called by, like the one your momma gave you?"

"I have been recently called, 'One eyed Bart'. I like it, it makes me sound real mean."

"It does. It didn't decrease your stupidity level, though. How did you lose your eye?"

"Bar fight over a girl named Bella."

"Did Bella pick you after you were maimed?"

"Nope, never saw her again."

"So Bart the Bandit goes Blind in one eye in a Bar fight over Bella. Sounds like the beginning of a bad limerick."

"I do not know what that is." Says Bart.

"Figures. Why did you pick this town and this bank?"

"I lost my last dollar at poker last night and I woke up hungry and broke. I didn't plan, nothing."

"That's obvious. Bart Jackson meet Jason Williams. He robbed a stagecoach. You too idiots ought to get along just fine." He turns and goes to his outer office and locks the door between.

He returns to his desk and picks up the unopened envelope. He rips it open and pulls the telegram from it. As he is reading it, Sadie and Brenda rush in, hand in hand. He looks from woman to woman, but smiles at Brenda. "What can I do for you ladies?"

Sadie blurts out. "How can you sit there so calm? You just caught a bank robber in the act. How brave you are, how nonchalant!"

Brenda is just standing there, blushing. "Anyone

hurt, Chilly?"

"No, thank God. You should have seen your cousin. His little crush Judith was a hostage and he finally got the nerve to stand eight feet tall and do something manly for once. He was a real hero, today."

"Elliot? Was a hero? Wait until Mother hears about it!"

"Are we talking about the same little man who is five foot nothing?" asks Sadie Mae.

"That's the one. I would not have believed it if I hadn't witnessed it with my own eyes. I have word from Joshua, here." He waves the telegram in his hand.

"Is he alright? Has he caught up with Jeff Williams?" Sadie says with much concern in her voice. "Is he alright?" She repeats.

"It seems he is fine. Williams gave them the slip but they caught Scott Jones in the hideout. Sheriff Wilcox and his deputy will bring him here, while Joshua stays on the hunt for Williams."

"Why can't Joshua bring the other passenger here?"

"His mission is to get Jeff Williams."

Sadie, unhappy with his answer, plops down into the chair and crosses her arms. "It is not fair. Why don't you have other deputies that can do your dirty work for you. I want Harkahomé back!"

"I wouldn't trust anyone else with this mission. Miss Sadie, are you working tonight?"

"Yes, I start at seven." She answers without thinking.

"Brenda, would you have dinner with me at the Long Horn Restaurant at seven?"

"I would love to. Can you come pick me up? Mother is expecting you to ask for permission to see me."

"Isn't that like shutting the barn door after the cow leaves?"

"It is what is expected of a gentleman." She says looking down and blushing, again.

He stands up and comes from around the desk and puts his arms around her. He lifts her chin, and looks in her eyes. "I would cross the painted desert for you, Brenda. I think I can go get permission from Aunt Martha, as scary as she is." He kisses her cheek as she lets out a small laugh. "After dinner, we can go visit Sadie at the Saloon, if you like."

"I would enjoy that, Chilly." She gives him a return kiss on his cheek. "See you at seven, then. Come Sadie, I want to go shopping. Come help me find something royal blue, please?"

***

The day's harrowing events leaves the Sheriff and the Postmaster shaken for most of the evening. The Bank's hold-up brings Elliot's true feelings for the petite teller Judith to the forefront. The Sheriff is shaken by a different event, entirely. That event is his meeting with Brenda's mother, Martha.

At seven sharp, Chilly is at the hotel in his best clean clothes, with his hair combed flat and his face scrubbed. He is more nervous than when he had his gun to the bandit's back. He has his hat in his hand and he is twisting it round and round as he nervously sits in the overstuffed chair in the hotel lobby waiting with Brenda, for her mother to join them.

"Chilly, if you can, please don't mention our dinner last night. As far as mother knows, I was with Sadie. And she isn't too happy about my being with her. I like Sadie, don't you?"

"She's different from anyone that I've known." He is thoughtful for a moment. "Actually, she reminds me of my sister Carolyn. Though, Carolyn is more refined and a pillar of EL Dorado Society. Just don't get in her way, she could strip a sergeant of his stripes with just her words."

"Sounds like a force to be reckoned with. I'd love to

meet her."

"I have a feeling that you will." He reaches for her hand. "I have never felt this strongly for anyone, in my life. I think you are in my life to stay."

"That's yet to be determined Sheriff." Martha strongly says from across the lobby. "Take your hands off my daughter. You need to show some decorum in public, young man. My girl isn't like the trollops that I've heard you normally see." She has her hands on her hips and crosses the room in a few determined steps. Chilly drops Brenda's hand and stands up before the woman a foot shorter than him comes to him. She holds out her hand and Chilly flinches. "I am not going to hit you. I am saying hello." Chilly takes her hand and shakes it limply.

"I heard that you captured a bank robber in the act, today."

"Yes, Ma'am. Your nephew is the true hero. I could not have done it without him or the teller Judith."

"That's the way I heard it. I still cannot believe it. Please sit." She says as she goes to the chair across from Chilly.

"Ma'am, if I wasn't there, you'd have the dickens of a time, convincing me, too."

"Sheriff, what are your intentions regarding my daughter? I wasn't planning on making Pennysville my last destination. I want us to go to visit Elliot's mother, next."

"Mama, you never said anything about more travel."

"Hush, girl. A letter from your Aunt caught up with me through Elliot. As I have gotten to know him, it makes me miss my sister. She isn't getting any younger. I would like to set my eyes on hers while they are still open and will recognize me."

"But Mama, I am not getting any younger, either. I don't want to keep traveling to see long lost relatives that don't know me. I want to start my life. I want to have my family. I have fallen in love with Chilly, and if he will permit me, I will stay in Pennysville."

"That is out of the question! A young woman of your breeding does not live alone in a strange city! I insist that you accompany me!"

Mother and daughter stare at each other. Chilly says, "I do not want to separate a daughter from her mother." Brenda gasps in despair. "But if the woman that I love wants to live here in town, I will defend her right to do it, even if it is against her mother."

"How could either of you talk of love? You have yet to date." She looks from blushing daughter to blushing sheriff. "Have you?"

The sheriff straightens up. "I love your daughter, and I will court her. After an appropriate time, we will wed. That is all you need to know."

"How dare you talk to me, this way! My daughter is a maiden and her innocence must be guarded. I will not allow her to stay if I leave."

"Then don't leave!" Both Brenda and Chill say. They look at each other and smile.

Chilly stands, puts his hat on his head. "I think that is enough discussion on the subject. Ma'am, your daughter and I have a dinner date. We will be on our way. I will have her back at a decent hour. You have my word." He turns to Brenda and holds out his hand for her to take. "My dear, we are late for our reservation."

***

As Brenda and Chilly walk into the restaurant, they are shocked to see Elliot and demure Judith in a booth in the corner. As they pass the couple, the sheriff, tips his head to the Postmaster. Elliot smiles and blushes.

As they are shown to their seat, Chilly laughs. "When Joshua comes back, he will not believe the change of events, here." They order their meals and drinks but remain silent.

Finally, Brenda speaks. "I am having trouble keeping up, myself. Chilly, may I be honest? I am not sure that I have enough nerve to stay here against mama's wishes. When I go back to the hotel, she is going to give me a huge lecture. Chilly, I have never been strong enough to stand up to mother."

"She hasn't packed her bags, yet. You can stay with Mama Ruth's down the street. The school teacher and Judith both live there. She runs a respectable place. It won't be for long."

"How do you know that?" She asks.

"I know that I will not be able to wait that long." Chilly says as he takes a long drink of his cold beer.

He puts the drink down as Brenda asks, "Wait long for what?"

"Brenda, are you so innocent?" He shakes his head in disbelief.

"I am sorry, Chilly. I must be slow." She is looking down at her hands. "Will you get tired of me, by then? Maybe Mama was right. You are breaking my heart, already. I think that I lost my appetite. I am going back to the hotel, Chilly. Stay and eat your dinner." She stands up to leave.

Chilly is on his feet, in seconds. He grabs her hand. "You can't think that? I have never said 'I love you' to any other woman in my life. I do not want to break your heart. I LOVE YOU. Please sit down." She takes her seat. He sits down, too. "Brenda, I told your mother that I love you and I want to wed you. I know that you are a maiden. I will not make any advances toward you that would be inappropriate. I am dying to kiss you, now. How long will I be able to resist you? NOT LONG! That is what I meant. I am going to marry you." He gets down on one knee. "Brenda Masters, will you marry me?"

She has a tear in her eye. "I am not sure if I . . ."

"Do you need more time?"

She looks in his eyes. "Not more time, I would

marry you, tonight, but. . ."

Chilly starts laughing. "My brother-in-law said that to my sister and before the night was over a preacher was asking them to say 'I Do'. They knew each other for years, though. You don't know anything about me. I am not exactly a pillar in society. I bend rules and take chances. I have always loved the ladies and they have always loved to be with me. I am not worthy of you with your innocence and purity. I am a scoundrel and your mother is correct – I normally see women that like to do more than you even know about. How can I ask you to settle for a man like myself? You can do so much better."

"Chilly, you are talking faster than Sadie. Slow down. I said that I am not sure because I don't know if I *can* be enough for you. I don't know anything about life. You have been around the whole country. You tracked down your nephew in the winter when you were only fourteen years old. You were in the cavalry. You have been a sheriff for years. You can hold a weapon on someone and not shake. How would I be able to keep you interested? As you said, I do not know anything. I can keep your house and have your children, but will you be bored of me for my innocence?"

Chilly gets up from his knee and sits on the chair again. "You are the one that everyone said, will take my breath away. You are the one that makes my heart beat. You are the one! I have never been more sure of anything in my life. I told everyone that I wanted to live before getting 'tied' down. I did a lot of things that I said I wanted to do but I have not lived. My heart did not beat. I have not been a living – breathing being until I met you Brenda. Nothing in my life has meant anything before you. I gave my brother and sister hell for falling in love. It looked to me like their lives were over. I could not have been more wrong! Please believe me, Brenda. I will telegram my sister Carolyn and she will confirm how I always kidded her, Grant and my brother Will."

"I do believe you Chilly. Like I said, I would marry you, tonight."

Just then their meal arrives. As Brenda picks up her silverware, Chilly says, "I know where the preacher lives. We could go see him, instead of Sadie. Eat, my dear. We have a big evening ahead of us.

Before they leave the restaurant, they stop at Elliot's table. Chilly is still holding his hat. "Elliot, will you do me a personal favor?"

"Anything Sheriff. Do you need it tonight?" He looks at his date.

"Judith, Elliot. Would you both do me the honor of being our witnesses at our wedding, tonight? After you are finished eating, can you go get your Aunt Martha? I am sure that my bride would like her mother present at her wedding."

"Yes, Sheriff. I am so happy for you Brenda. The sheriff is a very good man. A little rough around the edges, but I would take a bullet for him." He gives a wink to his cousin.

"You almost took a bullet for me today. I didn't get to thank you, Elliot. You did a fine job, today."

"Sorry Sheriff. I didn't do it for you. I was so worried for Judith. I knew she was working today. All I could think about was her getting hurt."

"You made sure that didn't happen." Judith says in a quiet voice.

"So, I will see you at the Preachers, with Aunt Martha? We have other stops to make. I have to get Tom Baker to watch the prisoners for a night or two and I am sure that Brenda would like Sadie as her maid of honor."

TWENTY-SIX
January 15th, 1959
A Thursday in Chicago

Carrie Ann and Clara Beth are having an early breakfast in the cafeteria at the University. Carrie is swamped with classwork because of the sketch work and fabric hunting. She has decided to get a hold of the backlog and make it disappear. She has brought almost all her textbooks with her this morning, and none of her sketches. She doesn't have a class until three and plans to stay at the table until she is caught up and maybe even ahead in the school work. Clara leaves for her ten o'clock class and Carrie is nose deep in her math workbook. She is stuck on an algebra problem, for 20 minutes.

"I have been watching you struggle and make funny faces for minutes now. I feel if I don't help you, you will end up hurting yourself." Mickey says and he bends over Carrie to look at what is troubling her.

"Oh, Mickey! I could use the help. I am so behind in my work and now I am stuck on this one problem. Can you help? Do you know algebra?"

"Yes, I do. If you can make room for me to sit, I'll help you."

Carrie starts to pile up the books. "What a pickle I have gotten myself into. All because of a ball gown." She has moved the last pile of papers. "There, sit Mickey and help a damsel in distress, please."

"Gladly, but what is this about a ball gown?"

"Oh, I am going back home for the EL Dorado Valentine Ball and I decided to make my dress and it has consumed my life for the last week and I am only in the designing phase."

"You are designing your own gown? How ambitious! Why isn't a store-bought gown good enough when you have a full course load?"

147

"It's a very special dance. My parents are very close friends with the founding family and that puts us in the spotlight also."

"So what is Clara Beth wearing?"

"She isn't going. Only I was asked to attend. I am being flown through Wichita for it. Flying makes me nervous. This will be my first time. Have you flown before?"

"Wait a minute, I am missing something. It doesn't add up. You are being flown there but your older sister wasn't invited to something that your family is in the spotlight for? You are leaving something out my crazy little Kansas Carrie. Who invited you?"

"You caught me. I was invited by the great-great-grandson of the founder. He is even named after him. Grant, but we all call him GW."

"And you've known this GW for years, have you?"

"Yes, I was his date for the Junior prom. We used to take baths together." She adds as he is drinking a coke. He immediately spits it out on her school work.

"Was that before or after the Prom?" He manages to say as he wipes his chin.

"When we were babies. Mickey, honestly. Is your mind always in the gutter?"

"It is when a Kansas girl puts it there. So, you are GW's date. Are you serious about him? I got the impression that you were unattached."

"Things have changed to sort of attached, now. We are starting a long-distance relationship. To be honest with you, Mickey, I have been crazy for him since I was a little girl. My family works for his and we saw each other almost every day until we moved to EL Dorado when I was six. I have kept my feelings to myself while he was doing the same. We've both come out into the open and told each other how we feel. So, it is very important that I look great for the ball."

"I imagine he wouldn't care if you wore a potato

sack."

"My mother owns two restaurants. I can get all the potato sacks, I need. But that doesn't mean I want to wear one."

"Okay, now what about this algebra problem?"

Mickey helps Carrie catch up on all her school work and walks her to her three o'clock class. "Gee, Mickey, I owe you one. I would have never caught up without your help."

"Don't get so far behind next time. Call me, and I will come over to help you, if you need it."

"I don't know if that will be appropriate, now that I have GW."

"But GW cannot help you with schoolwork from Lawrence. I am a friend, Carrie. I just want to help."

He bends down and gives her a peck on the cheek. "And GW cannot do that from Lawrence either." He turns to leave before Carrie can say or do anything.

TWENTY-SEVEN
January 16th, 1896
A Thursday in Pennysville, Oklahoma

After the ceremony is performed by the hastily dressed Preacher, Elliot took Aunt Martha back to the hotel and arranged to have the Bride's things moved to the Bridal Suite. Then Elliot went to the Sheriff's office and packed a few things for him for his wedding night. The Bride and Groom went back with Sadie to Penny's Parlor. The news of their nuptials spread like wild fire and many townspeople came to the Saloon to wish them well and to congratulate them.

After many drinks are bought for the couple, they finally dragged themselves away at midnight. They walked hand in hand to the hotel.

"I am still in shock that I got married tonight. Wait until my family finds out. You will be the talk of EL Dorado and Lawrence. Brenda the woman who finally got Chilly to settle down! I hope you like big families, I am the youngest of seven siblings."

"Let me see if I have their names correct. First is Ian, he died by the hand of the Cheyenne that kidnapped Joshua. Then is Dr. Joseph and Dr. Lizzie. Then is the famous Colonel William born on the same day as you. His wife is Julia, his childhood sweetheart. Her brother Grant married your youngest sister Carolyn. Oh, wait I forgot Marjorie. She is a year older than Carolyn. Did I get them all correct?"

Chilly stops walking. "When did I tell you all their names? I don't remember doing that."

"Elliot told me, but Joshua also filled in some missing information. See, you think I don't know you, but I do. I can tell by all the townspeople, Elliot, Joshua and even that Sheriff Lucas, you are liked, admired, respected and feared. And now you are mine!"

Chilly bends down and picks her up by her waist and swings her around. "And you are all mine!!" He lowers her down. When her face is even with his, she puts her arms around his neck. "Are you going to kiss me, my wife?"

"I was thinking on it."

"I can hold you like this until you do, you know. You weigh nothing. My mother will try to fatten you up."

"Shhh, no talk of mothers, right now." She takes his hat off his head and runs her fingers through his hair. "So red! I didn't know I had a thing for redheads."

"Brenda, my love, kiss me. I cannot wait any longer!" She doesn't answer but lowers her head and places her soft tender lips on his. Chilly starts to turn in circles, again. *Nothing in my life has made me so happy as this kiss.* She lifts her lips from his and he smiles.

"Your kiss is making me dizzy, Chilly."

"That's because I was moving in circles."

"No, it wasn't." She puts her lips on his, again. Chilly stays still this time. She breaks apart. "See I am dizzy and light headed. I think you'd better carry me to the Bridal Suite. My big beautiful redheaded Husband. Carry me in and stop for no one."

Chilly lowers her to her feet but swoops down and with both arms, and picks her back up. With her in his arms he says, "Is this what you have in mind, Mrs. Lewis?"

"Exactly. 'Mrs. Lewis', I love the sound of that almost as much as I love you."

Chilly is walking slowly with her in his arms, not because she is heavy but because he wants to make this last. He knows she has never been with a man and has admitted to being naive about the marriage bed. He is nervous that he will rush her, but he wants her so bad. He needs to control himself and as he is walking he is worried that he won't be able to do that. The last thing he wants to do is hurt her. *If I hurt her by making love to her, will she ever want me to touch her again?*

151

He carefully carries her over the threshold of the hotel doorway. The hotel clerk is waiting. He takes a key from a slot behind him than comes around the desk and wordlessly walks up the staircase while Chilly is following close behind. The clerk, Georgie, is Elliot's closest friend. He opens the door to the room, steps inside, places the key on the side table just inside the doorway. "Is there anything that you need, Sheriff?"

Chilly looks around the room. He sees the extra-large bed and begins to blush bright red. "I don't think so Georgie, I will call you if anything comes up. Put a 'do not disturb' sign on the door knob, will you?"

"Yes, sir." He turns to leave.

"Georgie. If you see Elliot heading up here for any reason, you have my permission to shoot him. I will swear you did it in self-defense."

Georgie chuckles. "Of course Sheriff. Shoot Elliot. Got it." He nods to the husband with his wife still in his arms. "And congratulations."

"Chilly, why are you so mean to my cousin? He admires you so much."

"I am not mean. I like Elliot. My day would be so boring if I could not pick on him. I think he likes it. Truly, I do."

"Do you want to put me down now?"

"Kiss me first?"

"Yes, Dear." She gives him another tender kiss. As she starts to get dizzy, she lifts her head again. "I am not joking, Chilly, I feel dizzy each time, we kiss. I think you should put me down." He places her gently on the end of the bed.

"A bad dizzy? When I kiss you, I feel light headed and my heart races, but it's a good feeling."

"That describes it. But my stomach feels like there are butterflies in it, too. I think I am just nervous." She stands up and goes to the wardrobe closet. All her things have been moved over. "I will change. You can make yourself more comfortable." She goes behind the screen to change into a night gown. "Had I known I was getting married tonight, I would have bought a fancy negligée!"

"Remind me tomorrow, to tell you of my standard comment on that subject. Right now, anything you will have on will be lovely."

"Chilly, I am so nervous, I can hardly unbutton myself."

"Did you need me to help you?" He says and hears her gasp. "I am sorry, I didn't mean to make you more nervous."

She comes out from behind the screen. It doesn't look like she has started unbuttoning anything, yet. She goes back to the edge of the bed. He is just standing in place. "I am sorry. I am too scared. I have a vague idea of what I need to do but . . . I am ashamed of how dumb I am and how dumb I am being. I love you, but . . . I need you to help me. Come here, sit next to me and can we just talk for a while?"

He sits down and takes her hand. "Brenda, we will be married our whole lives and nothing has to happen. I will be glad to sleep on the floor, if you prefer. I just want to see you happy." He reaches for her hand and she flinches away. She raises it to her royal blue hat and with her other hand she removes the hat pin and the hat. "Put this on the dresser for me, please."

He takes it from her gently and stands to take it to the dresser. He turns back to her. He takes the chair from the dressing table and pulls it alongside the edge of the bed and sits down. He reaches for her hand again. It is cold and clammy. He takes her other hand and puts them both together and rubs them. "Your hands have never been so cold."

"I know, Chilly. I think you need to just take me. Do everything a husband needs to do. I am being a ninny and you will change your mind about being married to me before the ink dries on our marriage certificate, if I am not able to be a full wife for you."

He comes back to sit on the bed. He reaches for her face and tilts her head up. "Stop calling my wife dumb and a ninny. She is beautiful and sweet and she takes my breath away." He sits down and kisses her cheek. His hand moves to her hair. The golden long strands are being held up by a few pins. He reaches for them. "May I take your hair down? I have been wondering how long it is." She nods. He is staring into her eyes as his hand expertly removes the six pins holding her hair in place. He runs his fingers through it and brings it all to the front. Its length reaches to her bosom. "Your hair has fascinated me from the start. I do not know many blondes."

"Josie at the restaurant and Judith are blondes."

"Are they? I never noticed." He moves her hair back behind her neck. "Your neck has always enticed me, too. May I kiss it?" His warm lips are giving her small kisses just under her ear. "Do you want me to continue?"

"Mm hmm." Is her consent.

"Good because the other side of your neck is now calling me." He places more small kisses under her ear. "And your throat makes such adorable sounds." He kisses her throat and works his way up to her chin. "Do you know that you have the cutest dimple in your chin?" His kisses move up onto her chin. "And oh those lips! The sweetest lips I have ever tasted. Please tell me they are mine."

"All yours!" She is feeling things that she has never felt before. As he kisses her, she presses harder against him. His hands are still on her face and she takes one and moves it down to her chest. He lightly feels her shape through her dress. His other hand joins the first and they manage to find a button. He undoes her top button, then kisses her neck there. He undoes the next one and his hand slips inside the opening. "May I?" He asks again.

"Kiss me, more." She says

"Where?"

"Lips, neck everywhere you've kissed me, do it again." He does. He takes his time. Nuzzling with his nose as well as his lips. When he gets back to her throat again, manages to undo another button. He starts the process all over again. He gets another button undone. "My dear, I think I have managed to undo all your buttons. Did you want to change your clothing or do you want me to just continue like this?"

She looks down at her open top and sees her camisole. She looks up blushing. "I am at your will, Chilly. Keep doing what you are doing. It feels wonderful." His hands are in her hair again and he takes her by the back of her head and brings her to his lips. She is very warm now and his tongue must have entrance to her willing mouth. She is surprised but she sucks on it slightly. He breaks from her, slightly so he can take his tongue on the journey his lips had just traveled. "OH, Chilly!"

"See my dear. You don't have to know anything. I love you and I am making love to you. I will keep asking 'may I' and I will obey your answer. Shall we continue?"

"Yes, a thousand times, yes."

"That's my girl. I feel it is getting warm in here. Do you mind if I um . . . unbutton my shirt?" His hands leave her body and go to his own shirt. He gets one button undone and he goes back to her. "I must keep kissing you. You taste so good." His lips are on hers again. This time the passion between them is rising. His hands are still on his shirt and he is unbuttoning it as fast as he can. He has never wanted a woman so bad in his life. He gets his shirt off and she reaches for his arms.

"You have such big arms, Chilly. No wonder you can lift me so easily. Lift me up again."

He bends down and scoops her up again. Her hands are on his arms as they are flexing by lifting her. "Like this?"

"Yes, my dear. You can put me down, again."

As he does so, he notices a bottle of something in a tub of ice. "Well, this might help you. Would you like a drink? It seems someone gave us champagne." He goes over to the bottle. "I have never been too keen on the stuff. Too many bubbles but it is the thing everyone uses to celebrate." He manages to pop the cork and he looks around for glasses. "How do they expect us to drink this?"

"Come here, I will show you."

He goes back to her. While he was opening the bottle, she removed her dress and was just in her full-length camisole and stockings. "You can undress rather quickly, when not so nervous."

"I didn't know I would enjoy it so much. Mother always called what happened in the marriage bed 'a woman's duty'! What was I supposed to think?" He hands her the bottle and she puts her mouth on it and takes four large swallows. "That is good champagne. Does that come with the Bridal Suite?" She hands it back to him to drink.

"I don't know, I have never been in a bridal suite, before."

"Good to know. So, I am your first wife, then." She drinks more.

"First and last." He drinks several swallows then hands it back to her. "I've had enough. I want to keep my wits about me. You may drink as much as you like."

She has some more then says. "I think I will have more later. I think this is going to be a long night." She hands him back the bottle. He takes it back to the tub of ice and immerses it again. He turns to her. When she sees him looking at her, she stands taller. "I do think I need help removing my stockings, if you would be so kind. Then you may take me to bed."

"Yes, Brenda, dear, of course." He says with a smile.

TWENTY-EIGHT
January 16th, 1959
A Friday in EL Dorado, Kansas

Anna has read Carrie's letter and is studying both designs. *I can hardly draw a straight line and she draws herself with this wonderful dresses on. What a talent she has! I do not know which one to advise her to wear. They would both be stunning.*

She puts down the sketches and the letter and goes to her husband who is sipping coffee at the counter of the diner. "What are you doing today?"

"I thought I would hang out here with you. That dopey kid that keeps telling us to stop smooching isn't here to bother us. What do you say, my love, shall we go into the backroom and smooch for a while?"

"Oh, Henry. What am I going to do with you?"

"For twenty-three years, the answer is still the same."

"Whatever you want!" They both say at the same time.

"I would like to call Carrie, when she gets home from school. I love her designs and I do not know which one she should make for the ball." The bell to the front door rings and Anna's sister Melinda walks in. She is very short compared to Anna, but like Carrie, she has an hourglass figure. She walks directly to Anna and Henry. They kiss hello.

Melinda sits down next to Henry. "Pour me one, Sis. Oh, Henry, those sketches are divine! Are these Carrie Ann's?"

"Yes, she is going to the Ball with GW. He is flying her in and out of Wichita to attend it, without missing school. She doesn't know which dress to make for the ball."

"Tell her to make me the red one and she can have

157

the stripe one."

"I don't think she has the time to make one gown, never mind two! The stripe one will take her much more time than the red one. But is sooo Carrie!" Says Anna.

"Yes and the red one is sooo Melinda!" I do not know why she is in college. She can design and sew now. And she'd be making money designing for proms, bridesmaids, brides, balls, and gee anything else that a woman needs to look her best for!" says her proud Aunt.

"Did you hear the part about her dating GW?" Asks Anna.

"Are you surprised? They were always nuts for each other. Just like you and Henry. Best friends turned soulmates."

"I know that if I tell her to make the red one, she will think it is because I do not think she can do the blue one because it is so complicated. If I tell her to do the blue one, she will feel obligated to suffer through it. Hey, Helen is coming over for dinner tonight. Can you join us? She came in to do all the ads for the Ball."

"Sure can. But doesn't Harry have a game tonight?"

"Henry is going, isn't Mark?"

"Please, Jude and Mark haven't missed a practice or a game. My boy might be a freshman in college but his heart is still with his old high school team. I am so glad Harry made varsity. He and Jude are so much alike. Baseball means everything."

Anna says, "Well it's a little too chilly out there for me to get excited about the game. I told Harry. I will not miss a game when the temperature is at least 65 degrees."

Melinda looks at her watch. "Oh look at the time! I am late for work! We are getting a new oven in the store. Thank God, Joan still wants to bake after all these years. If she didn't come down to the store every day to bake, I think she would have died the year her crazy Greek husband did. I need to get my quarterly statement to Joshua. The holidays were very good for the store. We turned a nice little profit. I am glad that Joshua and Helen saw the store as a good investment."

"It wasn't a hard sell. You and Mark have been running stores your whole life. Now you are running one store together!"

"Thank you Henry, for pointing that out to the Lewis conglomerate. The grocery store still feels like it is in the same hands with me and Joan still there." She takes another sip of the coffee. "Okay, I am out of here. See you tonight."

Anna looks to Henry. "What shall I make for dinner?"

"The meal that I am not going to be there for? Hmm. How about liver and onions. I hate that meal."

"So does Melinda. You too were always the better match!"

Henry stands up and goes to his wife. "I know it has been almost a quarter of a century since I dated her, but can I say that joke is still not funny?"

"Oh, you are still sensitive about that time? You made a mistake. You fixed it. It stayed fixed even when I was missing for a year. If that doesn't prove you love me, what does?"

"Come here and say that, my love." She looks around the near deserted diner and goes directly in his arms.

"You know, this constant affection is habit forming."

"Are you addicted to me then?"

"Yup, and I never want to be cured, Henry. Never, ever!"

***

Helen is sitting in Anna's kitchen looking over the sketches. "You know she sent them to GW for him to give his opinion but he doesn't know what to tell her."

Melinda says, "I told Anna that she should make

the red dress for me for the Ball. She is wasting her time in college. She has real talent, and is wasting it, taking all those dumb classes. Jude is ready to quit. If it wasn't for Spring tryouts for college baseball, he'd be home helping run the store. He loves it there. And like his father, he is a human cash register. He knows every price without looking and can add it all up in his head."

Helen says, "That is the most amazing thing. I didn't know that about Mark or Jude. GW is taking four or five classes a day. He is trying to graduate with a double major in three years. And he is on track for the dean's list. He is a very determined young man."

"Determined to fly my daughter out!"

"Anna!" Both Melinda and Helen say at the same time.

Anna looks at her sisters. "Sorry. Let's call Carrie Ann and we will all tell her what we think of her designs. Shall we?"

"That is a marvelous idea, this way I can convince her to make me the red velvet number." Says Melinda, only half joking!

Within minutes, the women are in the sitting room, all huddled around the telephone. Anna spins the dial until all the numbers needed are dialed. She waits on the line while it is ringing. Finally, it is answered.

"Harrick girl's residence, Clara Beth speaking."

"Clara, honey, it's Mama. I have Aunt Melinda and Aunt Helen here with me. How is the snow?"

"Gee, Mommy, it's funny you should ask. It is cold and wet and the weirdest thing is, it comes down white and as soon as it hits the city streets, it turns a yucky gray or black."

"Spoken like your father's daughter. I am surprised you are home on a Friday night. No date with Oliver?"

"We were just headed out. If you thought I would be gone, why did you call?"

"We wanted to talk to Carrie Ann about her

beautiful dress designs. Is she there?"

"Well, she is um, is out with a friend, a study partner, really. They were working hard on class work and they just stepped out for pizza pie, down the block."

"I am so glad Carrie is making friends. What is the girl's name?"

"It's not a girl, Momma. His name is Mickey. He is from Wichita."

Anna is looking at Helen and turns bright red. "Um, so will they be back soon? Do you think?"

"I am not sure. Um, they left all the books open so that they can come right back to it. So, maybe?"

"Clara, honey, leave a note for her then to call home. Make sure you say that Aunt Melinda and Aunt Helen all want to talk with her. Okay?"

"I will do that right away. I'd love to talk with my Aunts but Oliver and I are going to see a movie and he doesn't like to miss the cartoons that play before the movie starts. He is just a big kid, my Oliver."

"All men are, honey. They never grow up. They just grow old. Have a great night and don't forget to leave that note, please."

"Okay, Momma. I love you, kiss my aunts and Daddy for me."

Anna hangs up the phone. "Well, I am disappointed. I really wanted to talk with her. Shall I make coffee or tea? She might come home early enough to call us back." Anna turns around and quickly heads into the kitchen. Melinda and Helen are left to look at each other.

Helen says, "Did you see her turn red in the middle of the conversation?"

"I did. What do you think she heard?"

"I know what she heard, Carrie's friend is male. Anna got all embarrassed by it because I am GW's mother." Helen gets up and goes to the kitchen. "Anna, I am glad that Carrie is making friends. What was the guy's name? She is allowed male friends, Anna."

"I guess, it just hit me unexpected. She was out getting pizza pie with him. Girls, these days. I never went out to eat with anyone but Henry." Then she blushes again. "Except for that one time with Joshua. I went on a date with him to tell him that I was spoken for, even though I didn't know his name or mine."

"Thank God for that! My life would have no meaning if you let Joshua be your boyfriend. See men and women can be just friends, especially in college. That is their time to explore their options. That doesn't lessen what she feels for GW. Your living in the house with my Joshua, didn't lessen your feelings for Henry, did they?"

"You are right, I am being silly. Gee, you should be the one upset and I should be the one defending my daughter."

Melinda interjects, "I was going to point that out. Now, did you put coffee on? Less jaw work, more paw work, as I like to say to my employees."

TWENTY-NINE
January 16th, 1959 cont'd
A Friday in Chicago, Illinois

Clara Beth hangs up the phone. "Oliver!" She calls to her boyfriend putting on his coat. "We are going to be late for the movie. We have to stop at Como's to tell Carrie that she has to call EL Dorado."

"Can't you just leave a note?"

"No, I think that Carrie needs to return this call, tonight. GW's mother is with my mother. How does it look that she is on a date?"

"It's not a date."

"I know that but I wasn't raised during the Depression when every date was chaperoned and girls didn't have male friends."

"I think you are overreacting to your mother's possible overreacting. But who am I but the chauffer? Your carriage awaits, my dear." He is holding up her long winter coat. "If we make this fast, we can make it to the last showing of the movie. I will get you home quite late. Well, past your curfew."

"Oliver, you are such a nut. That's why I love you."

"So, that's why? I have been wondering."

***

Carrie has just pushed the pizza pie toward Mickey. "I cannot eat another slice. Where are you putting it all?"

"I am a growing boy."

"You are pre-med. You should consult a text book about that."

Gianni comes into the dining room with his pizza pie warmer bag. "Oh, Miss Carrie. You have graced us with your presence. How was your dinner?"

"Wonderful, Gianni. Compliments to the Chef. This

163

is my friend Mickey."

Gianni holds out his hand for Mickey to shake. "Any friends of the Harrick girls are friends of Gianni. I would love to talk but it is Friday night and I have more deliveries to make. Carrie, have you tried the cannoli?" Carrie shakes her head no. "I will send two over, my treat."

He turns to walk into the kitchen. "Sophia, I want two cannoli for my friends Carrie and Mickey out there. Table six." The door swings closed as his voice trails off.

The front door opens and Clara Beth comes rushing in. "Carrie, Momma just called. You need to get home, right away."

"What happened? Is everyone alright?"

"Everyone is fine, but GW's mother is visiting our mother, and they wanted to talk to you about your dresses. When I said that you were out with a friend, she asked the name of HER. I told her the truth. I could have heard a pin drop over the line. She told me to leave you a note saying that Aunt Helen was over and to call her back."

"Is that all. I will go straight home." Sophia comes with two small plates. "Right after my cannoli. Want a bite?"

"No, I have kept Oliver waiting, as it is. We will miss the first showing and will go to the next time the movie starts, so don't wait up for us, Baby Girl."

"Thanks, Sissy. Have a great time." Carrie doesn't wait until Clara is out the door before she picks up the cannoli. The log shaped delicate fried dough is filled with a sweetened ricotta cheese mixture and has chocolate chips in it. The open ends are then dipped in pistachios. "This looks so yummy. I am glad Clara didn't want any." She takes a nibble on the end. "I love pistachios. I have had cannoli's before but these are the best that I've had."

Gianni comes out of the kitchen. "The recipe is handed down from generation to generation. You like?"

Mickey speaks, "They are unusual, but good. Thanks, Gianni. It was very nice of you to give us these. Carrie and I should hurry back home. Her mother is expecting her to call, right away."

"I hope everything is okay." He turns toward the kitchen. "Sophia, check please, hurry. Table six." He turns back to the two. "Miss Carrie, until I see you again." He lifts her hand and brushes it with his lips. "Have a great weekend." He turns and walks out the door with his heavy warmer bag filled with hot pizzas.

Carrie dabs her lips with her napkin. "He is so sweet."

"You flirt with men, Carrie. Are you aware of that? Or is it just how you are?"

"I do not know what you mean, Mickey." She says with a smile on her lips as he helps her put on her long coat. Mickey throws a few bills down on the table.

Sophia comes out with the check. Mickey doesn't look at it but picks up the money on the table and hands it to her. "This should cover it. Thanks, Sophia. Great food and service. I will be back."

He puts his arm around Carrie and leads her out. "And you say I flirt? You were just short of batting your eyes at her."

"I was just being nice."

"Overly nice. You mean." They step outside. "My, it gets cold when the sun goes down." She turns up her collar.

"That's because you are not in Kansas anymore." Mickey smiles. "How fast can you walk? I think there is a wind chill tonight."

The two run/walk all the way back to the apartment. Carrie has out her key but has trouble getting it in the keyhole, since her ungloved hand is shaking from the cold. "Mickey, can you open my door? I am severely handicapped. I am frozen to the bone. I will put a pot of coffee on, then I will call Mother." They both enter the apartment. She sheds her coat and winter boats, and goes straight to the kitchen. She is working on putting the coffee on the stove. Her hands are still cold as she dials the phone.

"Mama, Hello. You got my letter?"

"Carrie, I am so glad you called. We just wanted to tell you how beautiful the dresses are. Each will look perfect on you."

"Make the red one for me, Carrie." Melinda shouts into the phone from behind Anna. "It will look perfect on me."

"Don't listen to Aunt Melinda. You do not have time to make two dresses. The striped one is so unusual. The details will take a long time to make. You should hold off on that one until you have a break from school. It is so perfect and I know that once you start sewing that you will be up all night, every night, until it is finished. Your school work will suffer and if you burn your candle at both ends like that, so will your health. The red one will be just as beautiful, but will take you half the time. Don't you think?"

"Yes, I think that is correct. The amount of sewing of the stripe one is double. Can I speak with Aunt Helen?"

Anna hands Helen the phone. "Carrie, you are so talented!"

"Aunt, did GW say which one he likes?"

"No, he showed them to me, but he didn't indicate which is his preference. I know it won't matter which one you choose. He will see you with his heart and not his eyes, anyway."

"I mentioned to a friend that I can get potato sacks from mother and sew them together and to GW, I will still look the same."

"Beautiful!" Helen says. "He is so crazy for you."

"I know and I feel the same for him, Aunt. Is Auntie Melinda still there?"

"Yes, sweetheart. Here she is. Stay warm and dry,

okay?" Helen hands Melinda the phone.

"Auntie?"

"Carrie Ann, I was serious about making me the red dress."

"I know, Auntie. You can borrow it. Was my mother weirded out by my friend being a male?"

"You can say that. We've taken an iron to it and all the wrinkles are removed."

"Okay, Auntie. Thank you. I am going to go. I have more school work to get done. My friend is helping me."

"Okay, sweetheart. I will let you go. Anna, did you want to say good bye?" She hands Anna the phone.

"I just want to say 'stay warm, dry and safe, Carrie Ann."

"Thanks Mama. I love you."

"I love you too. Bye-bye." Carrie hangs up the line. She turns to Mickey. "That could have gone worse. The coffee should be ready."

"You are lying to your family and yourself."

"Excuse me?"

"We are more than friends, Carrie. You must feel it, too."

"Mickey, I have been very honest with you."

"You think so, BUT you haven't been honest with yourself." He comes into the kitchen. "Why are you doing this?"

"Making coffee?" She is filling the two cups.

"Lying to yourself." He takes one and sips the hot liquid black.

"You must stop talking like this, Mickey. We are friends. If you think it is more than that, you are wrong."

"You let me kiss you."

"It was on my cheek and I didn't let you. I told you the next day that there will be no more of that. And you agreed."

"We've spent a lot of time together, since then."

"That doesn't mean I have changed my mind. I am

suddenly very tired. Mickey. All that pizza has finally hit bottom. If I can ask you to leave, I will turn in early, I think."

"Chasing me out with the work half done?"

"I have all weekend to do it. I will stay ahead of the work. Thank you for all your help." She takes his cup out of his hand and walks to his coat and lifts it off the couch. "Please, Mickey?"

"Fine, Carrie. I will leave. But please think about what I've said."

"I will, I promise." She helps him into the coat. She walks to the front door and opens it. "Good night, Mickey." Just before he crosses the threshold, he bends down to kiss her cheek. "None of that, now. Mickey, you were told. Respect my wishes."

"Until you realize that I am right." He walks out.

Carrie closes the door quickly and locks it. She goes to the couch. Her hands are shaking.

"What am I going to do, now?" She says out loud.

THIRTY
January 17th, 1959
A Saturday in Chicago, Illinois

Carrie Ann was waiting up for Clara Beth to get home. A little after midnight, she hears the key in the door and when it opens, Clara still had Oliver kissing her good bye. "Clara, Oliver, thank God you are home. I need your advice." Carrie says as she pulls the door open.

Clara can tell that Carrie is very upset. "What's happened?" Clara is already in and has her arms around her little sister.

"It's Mickey. He says that I am lying to myself, that I am really, in love with him. I just refuse to believe it. He is nuts! I have been very upfront with him and my feelings for GW. He kissed my cheek the other day and I chastised him for doing that, uninvited. He tried to do it, again, tonight. I am afraid of him."

"Did he threaten you?" Oliver is taking off his coat.

"No, he was weirdly calm. He is just delusional."

Clara Beth looks at her. "Are you sure that he wasn't playing a joke on you? He is quite the joker. Do you want some coffee?"

"No, I just drank a whole pot. I was making it when he was trying to convince me that I love him not GW." She plops down on the couch.

"I will talk with him. It goes without saying, he is done helping you with homework."

Clara says, "It is so creepy. How can he be so insistent that you love him? But he was calm and non-threatening?"

"That's what made it so creepy. I liked him. He was funny and smart. I was honest with him. I thought he understood my position."

"I am thankful that he didn't try anything." Clara has her arms around her and gives her an extra hug.

"I am afraid of seeing him, again."

"I am too. Oliver, can you call him and talk with him?"

"Yes. I will do it now. Do you have his number, Carrie?"

"Yes, let me get it." She goes to her purse and opens her wallet. "He wrote it down for me. Here." She hands him the paper. Her hand is shaking, violently.

Oliver takes the paper from her and says, "I don't think the coffee has helped you. I think you need a drink, instead. Clara, do you have anything in the house?"

"I have a bottle of Amaretto."

"Pour us all some, please. Put some milk in hers. By the way, I am spending the night on the couch." Oliver is dialing the phone, "It's ringing. Hello, Mickey? It's Oliver. I am calling about Carrie Ann. She is very uncomfortable about your conversation. She feels threatened by what you were saying." He listens for a minute. "I don't care if she is imagining it. I think that your friendship is at an end. I would consider it a favor if you keep your distance from the Harrick sisters." He is listening again. "It was very nice of you to help her but she is concerned for her safety. Even if you meant nothing by it, she is afraid." Oliver's face is turning red. "Darn it Mickey, I was giving you the benefit of the doubt here. She is not secretly in love with you. She is in love with GW. I am hanging up on you. You'd better keep your distance, or my friends and I will find a way to adjust your attitude." He turns away from the girls and says in a low but stern voice into the phone. "Yes, that's a fucking threat. Steer clear, or else!" He slams down the phone and turns to the girls. "Yup, he is fucking nuts."

Carrie turns into her sister's arms and starts to cry on her shoulder. "What did I do to attract a crazy like him? Do I flirt too much? I thought I was just a very nice person?"

"You are a very nice person. Just like our mother.

OH, MY GOD!" Clara puts both hands over her mouth. "This is just like mama's attacker. First he liked Melinda then Mother, then he beat her so Father couldn't have her! OH, MY GOD! Carrie, you should go home. Transfer or quit school for your own safety."

Carrie and Oliver both have their mouths open, looking at her.

Oliver says, "Isn't that a bit extreme?"

"I think she is right. He sounds just like John Walker. He tried to buy mother a drink while she was on a date with daddy and wouldn't take no for an answer. Daddy had to punch him, but that's why he tried to kill mother, to make daddy pay."

"Neither of you girls are making sense. Let's just calm down. Things will look different in the morning. Come, let's drink our drinks so that we can get a good night sleep."

THIRTY-ONE
January 18th, 1896
A Saturday in Nowata, Oklahoma

Harkahomé has rode for two straight days, after finding the owner's son who was being held hostage. Jeff Williams, the disgruntled driver and mastermind of the stagecoach heist blunder figured that holding a business man for cash and the return of his cousin was another bright idea. It was dumb luck that he was outside dumping his chamber pot when Harkahomé, Sheriff Wilcox, and two deputies rode up and tried to get in position to cover front and back entrances.

The Mining Camp's son, Scott Pickford, aka Jones, had put the two thousand dollars in the secret compartment, himself. When approached by Jeff Williams to go along with the robbery or be killed during it, he played along. He felt bad leaving the women stranded with the coach but he felt that the men would get away if he didn't try to follow them. He was found, instead. When he was told that there was no money in the strongbox, he acted dumbfounded. Jeff was desperate and decided to ransom the well-to-do looking businessman. Jeff never found out that his prisoner was Scott Pickford, the heir to the Dawn of the West Mining Company.

Scott had heard Jeff muttering to himself about the town Nowata. Scott did not know where it is, but Sheriff Wilcox did. Wilcox aided the sheriff there with the capture of Cherokee Bill, who was in the headlines for several gruesome murders the year before. He was scheduled to be executed in a month or two.

With the town's name from the lips of the escapee, being Joshua's only lead, he has made the awful ride during the sudden cold snap of January in Oklahoma. Thankfully, Joshua's blood was still conditioned for the harsh elements of his tribe's Wyoming territory. Even so, he was imagining his feather tick bed in the backroom with a fire in the pot belly stove. He can see the town just up ahead. Like an oasis in the desert, it blooms up out of nothing in the middle of nowhere.

He rides up to the saloon in the middle of town. He dusts himself off after he ties up his horse. He goes right up to the bar, and pulls a coin from his pocket. "Whiskey, please. I have to have something to chase the cold away." The bartender takes his coin and pours him a shot.

"What brings you into town? Are you an Indian or a white man?"

"I am here to find my friend and I am a white man incognito." He gulps down the first shot and takes out another coin. "One more of these. Do you serve good food here?"

"What does incog-to mean?"

Joshua leans in. "I am in disguise. I am starving."

"We serve food. Don't know if it's good or not, I have never eaten it." He says as he is pouring the second shot while pocketing the second coin. "Maybe I know your friend. Has he gotta name?"

"How much will it cost me for you to tell me if he's around or not?"

"How much you got?"

"How about a five-dollar bill? I will show it to you and I promise to give it to you, when I have my friend in front of me. Deal?"

"Fair enough, lemme see it?"

Joshua pulls out the bill and shows it to the bartender. He turns it over to show him both sides. "Deal?" He asks as he puts it back in his pocket.

"Deal." He looks around the room to see if anyone is listening. "Who ya lookin' fer?"

"My cousin Jeff Williams. We were supposed to meet up in Collinsville, but he lit out when the sheriff arrived, I heard. Do you know him?"

"Jeff's okay. He was here, last night."

"And where is he now?"

"I think at Lucinda's, she's his girl. She lives above the Nowata Land Trust office. Three doors down. How soon can I get my bill?"

"If I find him there, I will be right back with it. Promise." Joshua turns his coat collar up as he heads back into the cold. He takes his deputy badge and pins it to the outside of his coat. He walks down the three houses and sees the building that holds the land trust. He looks around for an upstairs entrance. Nothing is in front. He goes to the gangway and sees stairs going up to the second floor. There is a light on in the curtained window. He climbs up the stairs and knocks on the door. "Jeff, it's your cousin. Let me in." Joshua draws his gun and waits. The door opens, slightly, then starts to close. Joshua puts his foot in the threshold and points his gun at the surprised face gaping at him.

"Who are you and what in the hell, do you want from me? I ain't got nothing to steal."

"I am a Sheriff's Deputy from Pennysville. You are under arrest. Open the door wider, and come outside with your hands up."

Jeff has his hands raised as Joshua pushes open the door. The last thing he sees is a dark hair girl, holding a rifle aimed at his chest. The blast from the rifle blows the Indian over the banister and he falls to the ground in the gangway.

The Sheriff of Nowata is in the street and he runs toward the gunshot. He finds the unconscious man dressed like an Indian with a whole in his chest. He knows that no one came out of the gangway so he looks up and sees Lucinda holding the rifle and crying. He says, "What happened here?"

"He was gonna rape me, Sheriff. It was self-defense."

"That is a lie. Sheriff." Says the bartender. He offered me five dollars to know where Jeff Williams is. He said he was his cousin. He didn't have time to try to rape her. He just left the saloon."

Joshua starts to awaken. The sheriff says, "Who are you?"

Joshua had just enough strength to say, "Deputy from Pennysville."

"You are Chilly's deputy? He sent me a telegram to expect you."

"I'm Chilly's nephew, too. Jeff Williams is in the apartment. He robbed . . ." He starts to cough.

There is a crowd starting to form in the gangway. "Has anyone gone for the Doctor?" He stands and looks up the stairs. Lucinda is aiming the rifle at him. "What do you think you are doing, silly girl? You are going to kill the sheriff in front of all these people? Put the rifle down."

"You cannot have Jeff. He is the father of my baby. He cannot go to jail." She moves one hand over her swollen belly.

"Lucinda, you are going with him. Doesn't that make you feel better? You shot a Deputy. If he dies, you will be tried for murder. You will have your babe in prison." He pulls his gun out of the holster. "Or you and your baby will die right here. You have a choice."

The fool girl cocks the rifle when the sheriff shoots her. She falls to the broken railing and her rifle falls to the ground. The sheriff goes up the rest of the stairs. "Williams, come out. Do not resist! You didn't kill anyone. We will go easy on you."

Jeff Williams comes out with his hands up. "I didn't know she was going to kill anyone, sheriff. She is a lunatic." Lucinda looks up at the father of her baby. "It's the truth, Lucinda. You are just plumb crazy. You had no reason to shoot this man."

"He had a gun to your forehead."

"Well, there was that." Jeff shrugs. "I am ready to give up. Sheriff."

The sheriff looks down. The doctor is working on the Indian. One of the cowhands in town has Lucinda's

175

rifle pointing upward at the couple. "Alright, to the jail, both of you."

"I am shot. I need the doctor." Lucinda pleads.

"He is busy trying to save an important life. Remember *if* he dies, so do you. I will make sure the Doc will come look in on you. Let's go."

THIRTY-TWO
January 18th, 1896
A Saturday in Pennysville, Oklahoma

Chilly and his bride have been staying in the honeymoon suite since their wedding on Thursday night. Their meals have been brought up and for two hours, yesterday, the sheriff went to his office to check on things.

This morning Chilly woke up and didn't take his bride into his arms. Something was bothering him. He slid out of bed, careful not to disturb his sleeping beauty and crossed the room to look out the window. He moved the curtain over just in time to watch Jones, the telegraph operator, hurry to the sheriff's office. When he leaves that office, still with the envelope in his hands, he heads toward the hotel.

"Crap! This can't be good." He says half to himself. Following Jones is Elliot and Tom Baker. He walks over to his bride. "Brenda, darling, I have to go downstairs. Official business. I will be back as soon as I can."

He is putting on his clothing and gun belt. "Something is wrong, isn't it? I can tell by your jaw. You are Sheriff Lewis and not my Chilly."

"Sorry honey, there is bad news coming up the stairs in a telegram." He says as he puts on his socks and boots. He goes to the pitcher and splashes water on his face. As he looks at himself in the mirror he adds. "I need a shave."

There is a light knocking on the door. "I will be right out." He says as he dries his face on one of the hotel's fancy towels.

He blows a kiss to his wife and opens the door just enough to let himself out. "Gentlemen, can we take this to my office?"

"I think you should open it here, Chilly." Says Elliot, who has never called him by his first name.

"Well, at least let's go down to the lobby. Three men outside the bridal suite is just un-gentlemen-like." He heads down the stairs as he takes the telegram from Jones. "Couldn't send the kid for this message?"

"No, sheriff."

Chilly rips open the envelope, reads it and cries out, "No!! I told him not to take any risks. Damn that fool Indian, getting himself shot over nothing."

"Sorry Sheriff." Elliot says. "Does it say?" He can't bring himself to ask the question.

"He is alive. They fear the wound is mortal, though. Go get Sadie. Tell her that I will bring her to him. I have to tell my bride." He turns to Tom Baker. "Sheriff Wilcox is expected today with Scott Jones. Please ask him to stay here until I return."

"Of course, Sheriff. If you think of anything else." Elliot is getting emotional. "We all love your nephew."

Chilly is on the staircase and pauses to say, "I will need a buckboard. I am bringing Joshua back here." Chilly has tears in his voice when he says, "Dead or alive." Then he goes up the stairs to his bride.

When he opens the door, he sees that she is dressed for the first time in two days. "It's Joshua. Someone has shot my best Indian!" He collapses to the chair and has his head in his hands. "He isn't expected to live. I just got him back. I was going to take him to see his Gram Beth in the spring. Oh, this will kill her, if she loses her grandson before she gets him back! What am I going to do?" Brenda has her arms around him and he is crying into her dress.

"We have to tell Sadie."

"Elliot is doing it. The three of us will take a buckboard to Nowata and get Joshua. If he can get better, he is better off here. If not, I will personally dig his grave, since I sent him to it! What am I going to do? I love him and cannot go on without him."

"Have they caught the person who shot him?"

178

"Yes, they have."

"Good, I wouldn't want you chasing them and getting killed yourself. I like being married to you. So far, at least."

"Brenda, what would I do without you? I am so glad you are here for me."

"I am glad that we married when we did. I would still go with you and Sadie, but my reputation would be ruined. Are you a praying man, my husband? Shall we take a knee and pray for Joshua's full recovery?"

She helps her crying husband down and kneels herself. "Dear Lord, we come to you to pray for the health of our brother Joshua, also known as Harkahomé. He said that he was raised to thank you for everything as it came. He is a faithful man in his own beliefs and to that end, let him recover so that he can pass his wisdom and knowledge of your love for us so that we can become aware of the gifts around us that could only come from you. He means so much to my husband and his family back home. Please see that he can meet them as soon as he is well enough to travel. It is in Jesus's name we pray. Amen."

"Come husband. Enough tears. Let us go comfort Sadie and then pack for the road trip to get our nephew".

THIRTY-THREE
January 18th, 1959
A Sunday in Chicago

Carrie hardly slept a wink. Neither did Oliver or Clara Beth. They have spent the day indoors. They did not venture out to attend Sunday services, either. Carrie has just been pacing back and forth in the apartment all day. She hasn't touched her school work, either.

Clara has tried to get her to watch TV. "Come on, a Milton Burle rerun is on and he is so funny, Carrie. He will take your mind off your troubles."

Carrie tries to sit down but is back up again. "What am I going to do when GW calls at nine? I am so upset and he will be able to tell. Should I tell him? You know mama wanted me to stay in Lawrence and go to U of K. I would live at Aunt Helen's."

"And GW's?"

"I know that doesn't seem right either. Aunt Melinda says that I don't need college, I could launch my designs with her as my model and main purchaser immediately. She is right. I don't need a degree. I just need customers, and ideas. Those I have a plenty. If I marry GW, I will not need to work for money, but for my own fulfillment."

"Aren't you rushing things with GW? Neither of you are ready for marriage. I don't think you should tell GW anything because nothing is going on! Let's see if Mickey behaves himself before you do anything rash like quit school or marry GW." Counsels Oliver.

"He won't behave, I know it. I will look around every minute to make sure he does not sneak up on me. How can I live like that, afraid of my own shadow? I will take a few days off school. I will talk to GW tonight and make the stripe dress. I will go to the fabric store in the morning, instead of school. I can hole up here for days, sewing. He might cool off by then, don't you think?"

"What about your class work?"

"Can you get my assignments from my professors? I will try to keep up with the classes. I don't want to accidentally run into him."

Oliver speaks up, "I would go to your guidance counselor, tell him that you are thinking of quitting due to the inappropriate behavior of one of their students. I can take you to their office at eight am. They must have a way to deal with a situation like this."

"Carrie, that is what you should do. Oliver and I can stay with you. But if you feel uncomfortable, you can take my car home. Oliver will give me a ride."

"I suppose that is better than just quitting and running away. I do feel that I need to tell GW, I don't want any secrets between us."

"I don't think you should, it will just worry him, unnecessarily." Clara is saying when Oliver cut her off.

"I would want to know. You'd keep something that important from me?"

"Yes, why should you lose sleep if you were too far away to help?"

"That's the only reason, because of the distance?"

"Well, his hands are tied, aren't they? He can't walk her to class like you can. So why worry him?"

"Because I don't want to lie! I was stupid to think that I could have a male friend, that wouldn't want more."

Oliver shakes his head. "Don't paint us all with the same brush. I am you friend, but I don't want anything more from you."

"Thank Oliver, but you don't count, you want more from Sissy."

"Carrie!" Clara Beth blushes. "Watch what you say."

"I didn't mean it that way. I meant that he is your beau, not mine. He is a good friend. Thank you, Oliver."

The phone rings and they all jump. "It is too early

to be GW."

Oliver walks over to the phone and answer it. "Harrick residence, Oliver speaking."

"Hi, this is GW Lewis. Is Carrie available? I know I am early but I just couldn't wait."

"Yes, GW. She is here. Hang on." Oliver holds the phone out for Carrie. He takes a few steps and goes to Clara's side. "Maybe I should run home for a change of clothes, while it is still early."

"Yes, maybe this is as good a time as any." He gets his coat on and waves to Carrie, who hasn't started her conversation. She waves back, then turns her back on him.

"Hi GW. How are you this evening?"

"I am doing well. Aunt Carolyn and family just left and my siblings are doing their homework check with mother. So, I thought that I would call early. Did I catch you at a bad time?"

"No, of course not. I am dying to know what you thought of my sketches! Do you like them both?"

"I think you are an amazing designer. Mom said that Aunt Melinda wants the red one for herself. I think that the stripe one is more you. Don't you think that it is too much to sew while in school?"

"I am looking forward to the distraction. There is a small problem. I think we have it figured out, so you don't have to worry but I want to be straight with you."

"I am worried just by the sound of it."

"I don't know where to start. I was getting some homework help from a junior that Clara and Oliver know. I spent more time talking about you than classwork. Well, he was here when our moms called me last night and afterward, he um . . . got a little weird about it. He says that I am lying to myself, that I love him, and I just won't admit it. Well, I got him to leave and Oliver called him to tell him that he needs to keep his distance so . . . I am hoping that he listens to Oliver."

"I don't know what to say, Carrie. I don't like this. You are so far away and you've never had to deal with folks in a big city. They think differently."

"He was born and raised in Wichita!" Clara laughs nervously. "Oliver and Carrie are taking me to the guidance counselor first thing in the morning. If he doesn't keep his distance, I will stay away from school for a while. I keep thinking about what happened to mother. It seems so much like the John Walker thing. Except Mickey is smart and polished and in pre-med."

"Your second semester isn't going as well as you planned, is it? First the blizzards, now this. I am sorry Carrie. I wish there is something I can do. Going to the counselor is the best option. I do hate for you to miss classes but you should do what you feel will be safe. That is most important right now. Follow your instincts, they will keep you protected."

"I am glad I told you, I feel better, now."

Just then a pounding on the door starts. Both girls jump.

Clara goes to the door and looks through the peep hole. "It's Oliver!" She hurries and unlocks the door. "What happened?"

"It's Mickey, he is down the street. I pretended not to see him, then went around the block. He used the time to move just across the street. He was sitting there in the shadow of the building. This guy is not taking no for an answer."

GW is still on the line. "Carrie, what is happening? What was that noise? Are you okay?"

"Oliver just came back. He saw Mickey out front. What do we do now? Can we call the police?"

"He hasn't done anything wrong." Oliver answers. "But maybe they will try to talk sense to him." He walks over to the phone and takes it from Carrie. "Sorry, GW. I am going to call the police. I need to use this line."

"Thank God, you are there. Have Carrie call me

183

after, please."

"Will do. Don't worry, I won't leave them defenseless."

"Do you have a gun?"

"What? Of course, not. This isn't the wild west. Decent citizens don't own guns in Chicago."

"No? Just the indecent ones do? I don't see how that makes sense. I am sorry, Oliver – please call the police. Then call me back, please."

"Right." Oliver says and he hangs up the phone. "He is worried. I told you not to tell him."

"He was fine with our plan until you pounded on the door. Please call the police. I hope Mickey sticks around until they come."

Clara is looking out the window. "I don't see him now. I think he has left, already."

"I am calling the police anyway. I want to get his suspicious activity on record, if nothing else." Oliver picks up the phone and dials O for the operator. When she answers, Oliver says, "I need to be connected to the police. I am at 4937 S. Paulina Street. The non-emergency line, please. Ninth District station? Where is that? 35th and Lowe. Thank you, yes connect me, please.

THIRTY-FOUR
January 18th, 1959
A Sunday in Lawrence, Kansas

GW hangs up the phone, but doesn't move from the spot. He is in the upstairs hall since his brothers and sisters are in the dining room where the other phone is on the sideboard.

His father comes up the stairs. "I couldn't help but hear that someone is calling the police? What is the trouble?"

"Carrie has an admirer who will not take no for an answer. Gosh, she has only been in Chicago less than three weeks! I hate being so far away."

"Who is this guy?"

"He is a junior at the school and an acquaintance of Clara Beth and her beau Oliver. Oliver spotted him watching the apartment after Oliver called him and told him to keep his distance."

"Do they think he is dangerous?"

"Well, they might be reading into it but they are comparing him to John Walker that attacked their mother, while having a crush on her. Carrie says that this guy is smart, though."

"I think we should call Henry."

"Why don't we call Uncle Eddie, first. Do you think he might know someone on the faculty there? He might be able to ask a favor and get this guy pulled out of class. He might let it go, if it is jeopardizes his enrollment."

"Smart idea, GW. I do think we have an obligation to let her parents know, also."

"They are going to call me back, after they call the police. I will ask her if she wants to call them, or if she wants me to do it."

GW is dialing the phone to reach Professor James. "Aunt Carolyn, it's GW. I know that you are just getting

185

home, but may I talk with Uncle for a moment? I need his assistance."

"Sure, let me get him. He is still putting the car in the garage. It will be a moment." GW can hear his aunt put down the phone. He can hear his cousins noisily coming in the house and being told to get their homework out to be checked.

"Hey, GW! We just got home, what's going on?"

"Uncle, it's about Carrie at the University. She is having a very tough time with a fellow there. Can the school do anything to help her? Do you know anyone there to call?"

"What kind of trouble?"

"He says that she is in love with him and not me. He says he will prove it. She has told him no and Clara's boyfriend told him to stay away but he was hanging out in front of her apartment. They are calling the police now. I thought that someone from the faculty could talk to him."

"I do know a member of the faculty in the Criminology Department. I used to know some police when I was working in Chicago with Eliot Ness at the Retail Credit Corp of Atlanta. That was too long ago. I think anyone that I knew would be retired by now. When you talk with Carrie, get this guy's full name and ask what is his major."

"Carrie also said that she is going to her guidance counselor first thing in the morning. Clara and Oliver will stay with her the whole time."

"It seems they are doing all they can. Call me with the rest. No matter how late."

"Uncle, the girls are comparing this guy to Aunt Anna's attacker, John Walker. They are very upset about him."

"That was one seriously crazy person. It is good for them to be aware of the worst scenario. It makes them more aware of potentially dangerous situations."

"Or just paranoid." Responds GW.

The Professor corrects him. "If Clara's boyfriend said to keep away and he isn't listening, that is not paranoid. That is a serious threat. Does Henry and Anna know?"

"I don't think so, I will offer to call them when I talk to Carrie. I want to get off the line. They might be trying to call. Thank you, Uncle."

GW doesn't wait for his uncle to say good bye.

Joshua says, "I think we should go into the dining room now. The little ones will be up here, anytime now."

When they go downstairs, Helen is still looking over Kevin's papers. Joshua goes to her and whispers in her ear. "We need privacy to talk to Carrie, when she is done talking to the police. I will explain more when the children are in bed."

"You'd better." Helen says. "Kevin, this paper looks very well done. Come on, everyone, upstairs. Bath and bed time. Don't dawdle. Father needs to use the phone!"

One by one, each child comes and kisses their father, says good night to their brother and heads upstairs with Helen holding up the rear. Once the chaos dies down, Joshua looks at his watch. "It is just nine, now. Do you think they have talked with anyone? Do you want to call her back?"

"I do, father. But I will wait a little more, give them a chance to sort this out with the police.

THIRTY-FIVE
January 19th, 1959
A Monday in Chicago, Illinois.

Carrie is in the lobby of the guidance office with Clara and Oliver, waiting to see Mrs. Webster. Last night, Oliver called the police, and a patrolman came to the house. A war veteran in his forties came to take the report. Patrolman Arthur Frank was very sympathetic. Not only did the six-foot-four man take the report but he promised to make a house call on Mickey on his way home. It eased Carrie's mind, considerably, and so she slept better.

"GW's idea of calling Uncle Eddie was great. Between the Patrolman's visit and now the school talking to him, he should get the message, don't you think?" Clara asks Carrie.

"Thank God. I feel so much better. So does GW. He wanted to stay on the line longer last night, but he wanted to call Uncle Eddie back with Mickey's information before Uncle retired for the evening," Carrie says.

A young woman comes out of an office and approaches Carrie. "I am Mrs. Webster. Miss Harrick? Please follow me." She leads Carrie down the long corridor to her office. After Carrie sits down, she says, "You are making very serious accusations against a student who has had no previous problems here. He has an admirable grade point average. He is on the board of several charitable organizations on campus, and is very well liked by students and staff. You, on the other hand, have only been here three weeks after you transferred from a first semester in a Kansas school. How do I know you didn't cause trouble for a student there?"

"Call them. Do you want me to pay for the call? I don't like the way this is going. You are practically calling me a liar and a schemer. Talk with my sister Clara and her boyfriend Oliver. They are stellar seniors, and they have both witnessed Mickey's questionable behavior."

"Don't worry, we have a process for these such instances. We do not accuse a good student without a thorough investigation. Having Professor James call Professor Hernandez in the middle of the night, who calls me at six-thirty in the morning, is not the way to do things here at the University of Chicago, Miss Harrick."

"So let me get this straight, I am new in the city and that gives Mickey the right to say that I am in love with him but I don't know it and then stalk me, but you believe him and not me, before you even question him? How would you like it if, after you see him, he decides YOU are the center of his world but you do not know it? What if he is waiting for you, across from your house, or by your car? What if he tries to kiss you because 'one kiss will prove that I am the guy for you'?" as he would say. How would you feel if no one believes you – that all you did was treat him like a friend? All I did was talk about my guy back home who I have feelings for, and Mickey said that I am lying to myself. I just need to realize my true feelings for HIM! How would you feel if he did that to you?" Carrie breaks down in tears. "I am scared out my mind that he will try something! Please, believe me!"

Before the counselor can answer, there is a knock on her door. "Come in." She says.

It is Oliver. "Mrs. Webster? I can hear Carrie all the way in the lobby. I must tell you, I talked to Mickey after he tried to kiss her, and told him to keep his distance. Then when I left their apartment on Sunday, he was across the street but down a few houses. I left but circled back, and he moved to directly across from her apartment. That is called stalking, as per the police officer. You need to take her seriously. I insist!"

"I will do a thorough investigation, young man. Don't worry." Mrs. Webster says coolly.

"Don't talk to him without a witness, for your own

189

safety." warns Carrie. "I will never do that again. Is there anything else you'd like to know? You haven't asked me anything."

"I believe I have the gist of the situation. I have sent for the young man. He should be here shortly."

Carrie starts to shake. "I cannot see him."

"In due process, he has the right to face his accuser," she says.

"You have made up your mind against her. Haven't you?" objects Oliver with his hands on his hips.

"No, I wouldn't say that, but I have seen many young girls go down this road. Not getting the attention she needs, so she makes up some event or events to put herself in the center."

"That is not the case here. I assure you, counselor." Oliver insists.

"We shall see."

There is a light knock on the door. Clara opens it. "Mickey is in the lobby. I didn't feel comfortable alone with him," she says.

"Well, have a seat on my couch. You too, Oliver. I will bring him in." She gets up from behind her large desk and goes to the door, but turns. "I don't want it to be a lynching session here. Carrie does the talking. If I need or want you to corroborate her story, I will ask you. But do not speak unless spoken to, please." She doesn't wait for an answer but leaves the office quickly.

When the door closes, Carrie says, "This is not how I pictured this going. I am the one under investigation, it feels."

Clara has not sat down but stands behind Carrie with her hands on her shoulders for support. "I do not understand the process here. Why did the policeman believe us, but not Mrs. Webster?"

The office door opens and Mrs. Webster has a smile on her face for the first time, this morning. She says, "Sorry to make you miss your first class, Mickey. I will not keep you any longer than necessary. Please, Hon, have a seat across from Miss Harrick." She points to the chair then she sits herself. "So, we have a bit of a misunderstanding here, I believe."

Mickey interrupts. "I agree. I had a visit from a Chicago cop last night. Very unofficial, but he seems to have been misinformed, also."

Mrs. Webster looks at Carrie. "You did not tell me that you called the police!"

Oliver answers, "I mentioned it."

"Mr. Chapman, I told you to only speak when spoken to." She looks to Carrie again. "I believe you have some explaining to do."

Carrie looks down. *Why is she doing this to me? How would my mother handle this? She wouldn't let someone bully her! Well, neither will I!* she thinks silently. Then she looks up. "Mickey made some unwanted advances toward me. Even after I told him that I was involved with someone else. When Oliver intervened on my behalf and told him to keep his distance, he was seen outside my apartment."

"Mickey, what is your side of the story?"

"Miss Carrie is a big flirt and has delusions that everyone has feelings for her. She flirted with the man at the pizza parlor, right in front of me. If she is so interested in a guy back home, why is she flirting right under my nose?"

"What does your nose have to do with it? If I am a sweet and nice person, I am flirting? I am in love with GW. I am not in love with you."

"That is a matter of opinion," Mickey says flatly.

"See, Mrs. Webster? He thinks I love him. Ask him, yourself."

"Mickey, you don't think she loves you, do you? She is obviously a bad choice for you."

"The heart sees what it wants, a man can only follow it."

Carrie asks, "What the HELL does that mean?"

"You love me, you just refuse to believe it. I am not out to hurt you, Carrie. I just want a chance to prove to you that MY love is real and you love me too, I know it."

Carrie does not answer but stands up. "I think he has proven my point. Please, insist that he stay away from me, or I will have him arrested. I am here, missing my family and my boyfriend, to get an education, not to be stalked. If you don't convince him to leave me be, I must leave this college. Oh, and my fiancé is loaded, I might have talked him into giving this school an endowment. Say good bye to that, also."

Mrs. Webster stands. "You are excused, Miss Harrick, and friends. Mickey, we have some serious talking to do," she says with the smile long gone from her face.

THIRTY-SIX
January 20th, 1896
A Monday in Nowata, Oklahoma

When Brenda and Chilly enter Penny's Parlor last Saturday night to get Sadie, everyone was gathered around her. Elliot had told her of the telegram. Her boss, Lee Kirby, was very sympathetic. He not only had taken her off her table and gave her a drink but he offered to take her to Joshua's side, also. Chilly said that he was going to get a buckboard, but Kirby wouldn't allow it. "I have a carriage and a man that can take you to get him. You'd stay as warm as you would on a stagecoach. It is built very similar. When you bring Joshua back, injured, you don't want him in an open buck board!"

"That is so very kind of you, Lee." Sadie said between sobs.

Chilly added, "That will be very helpful. I don't think you need to provide a man to drive. I am perfectly able to . . ."

"No, stay warm inside with your bride. I insist Sheriff!" The unexpected kindness got to Chilly. He turned away from the forty-year-old man, so that he wouldn't see his tears forming.

Brenda put a hand on Chilly's back. "We do appreciate the kindness, sir, in our moment of sorrow. How soon can he be ready to leave for Nowata?"

"I will have him out in front here in less than an hour. I will have provisions packed for your trip, also." Kirby put his hand on Chilly's arm. "I have always appreciated what you have done for this town, Sheriff. And I liked that goofy Indian nephew of yours hanging around. I felt Sadie and my other girls were in good hands when the deputy was here. I pray he mends, quickly."

"Thank you. Lee. Sadie, can you throw some things together and be in the carriage when it gets here?" Chilly asked her.

"I will be waiting outside for it to arrive, Chilly. You won't have to wait for me. I have to see my Indian!" She started to cry again, but got up and wordlessly climbed the stairs to her room.

Brenda said, "Husband, have a drink, I will go pack my things and I will be right back. I will take everything of yours from the suite. Do you need stuff from your office as well?" He nodded. "Then, make it a short drink, we need to get on the road."

With Brenda taking control, they were in the carriage in a half an hour and they rode the whole day. Then they spent one night camped out with a fire but are now approaching the small town.

The driver, Charlie, slows the carriage and yells, "We are coming into the town, Sheriff."

"Stop the carriage, Charlie, I want to climb up with you." The young man listens and Chilly swings up next to the driver. "Do you know this town?"

"Yes sir. I lived here with my Ma, 'til I was fourteen."

"Good, do you know where the Sheriff's office is?"

"Center of Main Street, same as yours."

"I need to talk to the Sheriff, first. Stop there."

Moments later, Charlie pulls up to a building and stops. "Here you go, Sheriff."

Chilly gets down. Brenda opens the door to the carriage. "Chilly, do you know where Joshua is?"

"No, that's why I am stopping here." Chilly turns and is greeted by Sheriff Jubal Walters.

"Sheriff Charles Palmer Lewis! I am so sorry about your deputy. I was waiting for him to come to my office but he took matters into his own hands. Fool thing to do, it has almost cost him his life!"

"Jubal? He is still alive, then?" Chilly has his arms around his friend. "Please tell me he is alive!"

"He was when I looked in on him, last night." Jubal

answers.

"Please take us to him. I have his girl, Sadie and my bride with me."

"You have a bride? The confirmed bachelor bites it. Who is she?"

"Brenda, come dear, meet an old Cavalry buddy of mine. Jubal, meet my Brenda. She and Sadie were on the stage Jeff Williams robbed."

"So, you have just met her, and married her?"

"Something like that. Please Jubal, we are very anxious about Joshua."

"Of course. He is just a few doors down. Come this way." He ushers them to the Doctor's office. The sign in front says Nowata Medical Clinic. Jubal opens the door and calls out. "Doctor Peters, I have your patient's uncle here to see him." There is no sound in return.

"Let me go see where the doc is hiding. He might be out on a house call. Doc's lives are busier than a sheriff's." He says as he walks through a closed door, leaving Chilly, Brenda and Sadie just standing in the lobby waiting. After several moments, he comes back. "No sign of the doc, but I found your nephew. Come this way, I will take you to him. He is sleeping. I don't know if the doc gave him something or not. I also don't know if you'll be able to take him. He had an awful fall from a second story staircase after Lucinda shot him. I kind of think that was more injurious than the .22 bullet. But I ain't the doc, as anyone will tell you." He finally gets to a door and opens it to show Joshua laying down and sleeping. Sadie, runs past Chilly and the sheriff and goes to his side and picks up his hand.

"Harkahomé, are you going to live? Please say yes! Joshua?" There is no answer or movement on Joshua's part.

"Jubal, you said he was awake last night? Was he talking?"

"Yes, he was in a lot of pain, but he asked if I sent

you a telegram. I told him that I did. Then he said that he wanted to send you one. He likes sending telegrams, then he laughed and started coughing, kind of hard. Doc made me leave then."

Brenda steps forward. "Sheriff, might you accompany me back to our carriage. I would like to tell Charlie to take our stuff to the hotel. We will need two rooms."

"Well, Mrs. Chilly, I will see to all that for you. Stay with them." He nods to Chilly and Sadie, each on a side of Joshua, each holding a hand.

"Thank you, Sheriff. I didn't want to presume to ask you to do that for me. It is very kind of you."

"Wow, Chilly, did you notice her eyes? They are the palest of blue!"

"Yes, I noticed Jubal. Stay away from my wife, please. I just got her and I am keeping her."

"Don't fight!" Joshua says with a strain. "You married Brenda?"

"You told me that if I didn't date her while you were gone that I'd lose my favorite Indian. I did better than date her, I married her and you go and almost lose my favorite Indian, anyway."

"Not by choice. Hello, Sadie." Joshua tries to smile, but you can see the pain in his eyes. "I must be bad for you to lose time at the table."

"Harkahomé, you know that I am nuts about you. There is no other place that I want to be, but at your side." She blushes.

Suddenly, Dr. Peters walks in and looks at everyone in the little room. He talks to Sheriff Walters. "Sheriff, this man is very ill. Who are all these people disturbing my patient?"

"Family, Doctor Peters. His family. They came in all the way from Pennysville."

"And I am not leaving his side." Sadie says.

Brenda steps forward. "Doctor, what is his

prognosis?"

"I took the bullet out of his lung. I am surprised he can talk. It did some damage there, that is the worst I've seen. He also took a fall, and cracked some ribs. The worst part is that he has cracked his pelvis bone, I fear. He has little feeling in his feet. I am concerned that he will not walk without pain, even after healing."

"But he'll live?" Sadie asks with tears in her eyes.

"If he hasn't died yet, he will live. He is in extensive pain and I have him on Laudanum. A lot of it. He will need lots of care from this point on."

"He'll have it." Sadie says.

"He cannot be moved for a week, at least. And that is being generous."

Brenda says, "Well, I'd better get us settled in at the hotel. Then we three will go eat something."

"I do not want to leave him. Bring me back a roll. I am not hungry."

"Sadie, you and Chilly and I will take turns staying with Joshua. There is little we can do until he heals a bit more. The pelvis and back are not easy areas to heal or treat."

"You have a medical background, Madame?" Dr. Peters asks.

"My father was a physician. I was his nurse from twelve years old, until his death, a year ago. I've had no formal training other than his medical books and his supervision."

"Brenda, I didn't know that about you. How did you not tell me about this?"

"I didn't see a point to it. No one sought my medical knowledge and Mother didn't approve of my helping Daddy when it was a male patient. So, my experience is limited."

"I think you underestimate yourself young lady. I think you could have the makings of a nurse or a doctor. Formal training is what you lack, nothing else." Joshua begins to moan. "I think that you all should leave, then come back one at a time like Miss, a . . ."

"It is Mrs. Charles Lewis. My Christian name is Brenda. This is my husband, Sheriff Lewis. He is your patient's Uncle. They grew up as brothers, until Joshua was taken by the Cheyenne at eleven years old."

"That will be a fascinating tale to hear, someday. Now I must insist that you leave now. He needs medical attention, not noise."

"Doc, you are making the most noise. Come ladies, let's let the Doctor work, now." He goes to Sadie and takes her under the arm and lifts her gently. "Come Sadie, he is out of danger. We can go get warm food and a hot bath, if you like. Or hot food and a warm bath, if that is more suitable. Come, come." He says as he is physically dragging her out of the office. "For a little lady, you have some real staying power." Chilly adds, trying to lighten her mood.

Once outside the office, both Chilly and Sadie, look at each other and break down crying. "He is going to live!" The say to one another as they hug each other.

Brenda looks at them both and thinks, *Yes, but if he can't walk, will he want to*?

THIRTY-SEVEN
January 20st, 1959
A Tuesday in Chicago, Illinois

Yesterday's meeting with the guidance counselor, left Carrie shaken for the whole day. Several times, she wanted to go to a pay phone and call GW collect and tell him, but she knew that he had classes all day. She wanted to call him when she got home but she remembered that he was going to see his youngest sister, Ellie, at her dance recital. She longed to talk with him.

She picked up the phone, anyway, and dialed her mother's number instead. She had asked GW not to call EL Dorado on her behalf. She wanted a happy ending to tell her mother, before she made her relive the John Walker nightmare. Her mother was proud that she recognized the similarity in the two men and that she went to the authorities, instead handling things herself or ignoring them, thinking that they will just go away on their own. She ended the call assuring her mother that she will be ever vigilant and steer clear of Mickey at all costs.

Today, was Mickey-less, thankfully. Carrie asked Clara to take her to buy the materials for her gown. She had it all measured and cut, in her head and was dying to start it. Both girls looked around going to and from the car. When Oliver came over for dinner, he mentioned that he heard that Mickey had to leave for a few days to visit a sick relative.

This made Carrie feel lighter than she has for days. To celebrate she decided to call GW. So, while Clara and Oliver start cleaning the kitchen, Carrie went to the phone and called Lawrence.

"Good Evening, Legacy Plantation."

"Hello, Aunt Helen. How are you this evening?"

"I am good as gold, Carrie. You sound chipper. I hope that means you are safe and sound."

"It looks good for a while at least."

"Great, I will get GW. He will want all the details. Just one question, have you told your mother?"

"Yes, Aunt. We had a long talk last night."

"Good, I didn't like her not knowing. Okay, I will get GW."

Carrie waits for a few moments.

"Hey, Carrie, it's Ellie. How is college?"

"It's a lot of work, Ellie. How was your recital? Did you have fun?"

"Oh, I had the best time. We were in costume and make-up and everything. I messed up on my steps, once or twice but it was so much fun. Did you ever take tap dancing?"

"No, Ellie, I was born with two left feet."

"That's funny. I remember Aunt Anna once said that she was all thumbs, and they were all green. I didn't know that she was kidding and I made her hold out her hands. She messed my hair instead, and laughed real hard."

"That sounds like my Mama!"

"Well, that's all for now, Carrie. GW is coming. I don't want him mad at me, 'cuz I'm talking to his girlllll frrriendd!" she says as a taunt.

"Go upstairs, it is bath and bed time. Mama is waiting Ellie. Hey, Carrie, this is unexpected. Everything alright?"

"It seems that I have a stay of execution. Mickey has had to go out of town, due to a sickness in his family."

"Please do not use that phrase, especially if he is truly like John Walker. I'm glad he is gone, for whatever reason. Did you tell your mom?"

"Yes, I called her last night. She says that she was proud of me for standing up to that Guidance Counselor."

"What do you mean?"

"Well, she was woken up at 6:30 in the morning by Uncle's friend, Professor Hernandez. That put her in a less than sunny disposition to say the least. She practically said that I was making it all up to ruin a good student's reputation. She was horrible. She brought Mickey in so that he can face his accuser. She didn't believe me or Oliver or Clara. Then when she brought Mickey in, she called him 'Hon'! I knew then, that I had a huge problem. Mickey made it easy, though. He said to her that I love HIM but won't admit it. That floored her. I also said that my rich fiancé will not be sending in any endowments with the way I was being treated. Okay, let's change the subject. I bought the material for my dress today!! It will be so breathtaking!"

"You don't need to make a dress to take my breath away, Carrie!"

"Aww, thank you, GW. Okay. Tell me about your day, quickly. This month's phone bill is going to give my father a heart attack!"

THIRTY-EIGHT
January 21ˢᵗ, 1896
A Tuesday in Nowata, Oklahoma

Brenda was assisting Doctor Peters change the wound dressing. It has started to show signs of infection, but Dr. Peters is not worried. They have had to increase the dose of the pain killer, laudanum, to keep Joshua comfortable.

Brenda says, "I have heard of an invention and they are considering for its ability to help doctors with the diagnosis of broken bones. It is called an x-ray. From what I read in this medical magazine that my father had a subscription to, it shows only bones, not flesh. One can see if they are connected properly or broken. It is years from being available but what a fascinating time to be a physician. Can you imagine, seeing through the body to the bones and seeing the break instead of feeling and guessing?"

"That would be an amazing asset. I am sure that it will go to Universities and Hospitals first. Country doctors will never be so lucky as to have a machine of their own to do that. And what use would it be if the patient needs to travel to a hospital or university just to be treated? I do not think that will come in my lifetime, at least. Hand me the sponge, please."

Sadie walks in and stands there just long enough to turn white. The doctor sees her. "Brenda, take Miss Miller to the waiting room. I do not need two patients here." Brenda puts down the tool she was holding and hurries to Sadie.

"Sadie, let's get some cold water on your face. Are you sick?" Brenda says as she is walking her out of the room.

"No, but all that blood and ooze. Doesn't it bother you at all? How can you look at that then eat steak rare is beyond me?"

"Haven't you ever, slaughtered an animal?"

"God forbid, no! My meat comes cooked before it hits my plate. I don't even like when they bring my fish with its head still on. Or a pig with an apple in its mouth from a slow pit roasting. Goodness, NO!"

Brenda just laughs. "My mother is the same way. She would buy meat, daily at the butcher and cook it but my father would take me hunting and showed me how to skin and chop up the cuts. We would fish together, too. And I know how to scale and filet them."

"Mrs. Brenda Lewis, where have you been my whole life? The more I learn about you, the more I love you!" Chilly says. He had come in quietly while Brenda was leaning over Sadie with a damp cloth.

"Sheriff Lewis, what if your siblings heard you talking like that?" Brenda kidded him.

"Oh, I know that I will be given hell for my non-committal stance, believe you – me! How is your patient doing this morning?"

"I am going to be fine, Chilly. I just do not like the sight of blood." Sadie says.

"I was talking about my nephew, Sadie. I knew you were fine."

Brenda looks down at her bloody hands. "I was helping Doctor Peters debride the wound. Joshua is starting to show signs of infection. The doctor is going to treat it with tree mold."

"He is doing what?"

"It is a common practice with Indians."

"So, Joshua told you to put mold on him?"

"No, husband. Joshua has not awakened. The doctor has increased his laudanum. My father would treat using tree mold all the time. It works best when the patient is immobile like Joshua. Otherwise the smell and itch would make them remove it."

"But that's bad?" Asks Sadie

"The smell and the itch means it is healing and needs to stay in place."

"Chilly please stay with Sadie. I want to assist the doctor."

"By all means, go." Chilly sits down next to Sadie. "Apparently, I married a woman much smarter than myself."

"We all knew that before she opened her mouth, Chilly. Really, you thought I was going to let that opening slide?" She elbows him.

"No, I think that is why Joshua likes you. You are a fast thinker and talker. You were my type, once. Well, you are faster than anyone that I've ever met. And I am saying that as a compliment."

"Thanks?" They both laugh. "I am afraid for Joshua. If he can't walk, what will become of him?" She asks, more serious.

"I do not have an answer for that. I don't think I would want to live, unable to do for myself or the ones that I love. That is the very definition of a man."

"Well, we are going to redefine that definition starting today!" She says very determined. "First, he will remain your deputy. We will get him a chair, to maneuver in. And we will love him just the same as before. He is a proud Cheyenne but we must make him believe he is more than that. His way of thinking, being brought up with the Indians is very interesting. He can do lectures about the different cultures, back in Kansas or even back east where Brenda comes from. The possibilities are endless. We must make him understand that he has gained opportunities. Do you understand, Chilly?"

"I am afraid to say; I agree with your plan. You are a very special woman, Sadie."

"Good enough for your nephew?" She asks shyly.

"More than good enough. I will go in and see if it is safe for you to look. I will come back for you."

The doctor and Brenda are wrapping his chest and

torso with a tight bandage. They are alternately holding him up or wrapping the long cotton strip around him. Chilly asks, "Can I be of assistance?" as he approaches them.

"No, I think Brenda and I are just about through. She is much more experienced and knowledgeable than she admitted. I would be very lucky to have an assistant like her on a permanent basis."

"Like I said to Jubal last night, you cannot have her, she is mine."

"Do not worry about that, Sheriff. I don't think that I can take her from you, if I wanted. She is a glowing young bride. Still in the throes of love, to be sure."

"I am right here, gentlemen. Please do not talk about me like I am not in the room."

"Sorry, Brenda." Says Chilly. "I am getting tired of everyone, liking my girl. And I have 30 or 40 years of it to go. I must get used to being envied for my luck. Can I call Sadie, in? Brenda, will you come have lunch with me? I have a few errands to run, and I want my wife to accompany me. If you can excuse her, Doctor? The needs of Joshua's care come before my own."

"Sadie can come in, and Brenda is no longer needed. I will change the bandage again in eight hours. So right after dinner, I will need assistance."

"I will make sure that WE are back to help you, doctor." The doctor has laid Joshua back down and Brenda is covering him with a blanket. "What happened to his buckskins, Doc?"

"I had to cut them off to examine and treat him. I threw the ripped garments away. Why?"

"They were the last thing that he had from his deceased mother. I think he would have worn them until they hung in torn strips on his body." Chilly explains. "Just one more loss he will face, I suppose. None of this is going to go down easy, I'm afraid."

He goes and gets Sadie and he brings her to the

Indian. She is holding his hand and talking low to him. Brenda cleans her hands, helps the doctor put the tools away or clean them then she puts on her waist coat and turns to Chilly. "Where to, husband?"

"LA Cantina, do you like tacos or tostadas?"

"I do not know. I have never heard of either thing."

"Well, then this is your lucky day!" He takes her and leads her out of the medical clinic.

THIRTY-NINE
January 23rd, 1959
A Friday in Chicago, Illinois

Carrie was staying up very late every night. She was very careful to do her classwork before starting her labor of love. She went into school each day, always looking around, always watchful. She and her sister left the house and returned, in the daylight, overly observant and ever vigilant.

Carrie had all the pieces of the dress measured and drawn and cut. This job, alone, has taken hours and hours. Carrie was measured, multiple times by Clara, so that everything was very exact and form fitting.

This morning, Carrie didn't want to go in with Clara, because she had too much time to herself before class. Time that she could be making her sewing machine hum so that miraculously crescendos into a ball gown! Clara, Oliver and Carrie have breakfast together in the loud Friday-enthusiastic crowd of young people. When Oliver leaves for class, Carrie packs up her things to head to the quiet library to read ahead in her history textbook. She has put all her priorities in NOT becoming behind in her school work, even though it seemed to take, not just a back seat to her project, but it was a nuisance to be packed away and forgotten in the trunk.

Clara is walking her to the library. The sisters are looking around in case Mickey has come back, as they have every minute of every day. As Clara opens the door to the library for Carrie, they see Mickey behind the counter at the check-out desk. They both gasp and turn away and let the doors close without them entering. Carrie whispers, "I knew that it wouldn't last long! Do you think he saw us?"

"No, he was turned away and concentrating on the girl in front of him, most likely his next victim. I think you should come to my next class with me. If you don't want to sit in the class, there is a small study area right across from it that you can use. If I get the right seat, I will be able to watch you through the glass door."

"Perfect! How long can we live like this? Always worried, always watchful. I feel like we are in the armed camp that Uncle Joshua formed when John Walker escaped prison. But he hired security guards!"

"That's what you need. Security guards."

"We don't have the money to hire a guard for me! And who wants a brute following me around all day."

"Oliver knows lots of athletes that are here on scholarships. When they aren't in practice or class, they can take turns guarding you."

"Why would they?"

"Because Oliver and I can tutor them, and you could cook for them. I hear so many athletes need help with their schoolwork."

"I don't know. I still don't like it. I just want to be able to walk around where I want, when I want!"

"I think that ship has sailed, Baby Girl!"

A man's voice speaks in a whispered tone, behind them. "Baby Girl? I like that name. I think that will be my nickname for you."

Both girls tense up, but continue walking. Clara leans into Carrie, "In my class, now. Do not talk to him." Clara links arms with her sister and within a few steps, they walk into her classroom. Clara goes directly to her professor and asks if Carrie can sit in on the class, explaining that a young man is harassing her and has followed them. No sooner does she get the words out and turns – there is Mickey comfortably sitting in a chair in the classroom. "And there he is!" She tells the professor.

The large heavyset man with a determined look about him, crosses the room to talk with Mickey.

"Young man, can I help you?"

"I thought I'd audit your class, today. I know that I

allowed to do that as a tuition paying member of the student body."

"Fine, stay in this seat for the entire class or I will report you for misconduct." The professor leaves him and approaches Clara Beth. "You are excused from class today, Miss Harrick. Call the office later today and I will supply you with the study material and class work that you will need to do on your own. What is this man's name?"

"He is Mickey Roosevelt, a junior. Mrs. Webster of the Guidance office is aware of this situation. If he leaves before class is over, please let her know of what has happened here."

"Of course, Miss Harrick." He turns away from them. "Class, we are going to begin. Textbooks open, please, to page 163." As the class, all search their books for the page, the professor escorts the sisters to the back of the room. Mickey is watching intently. The professor pulls out an empty chair, and whispers, "You may sit here for ten minutes, then quietly leave out the back door. If Mickey Roosevelt leaves before the end of class, I will notify Mrs. Webster immediately. Either way, she will hear of this today." Without another word, he heads back up to the front and starts reading from the textbook with his usual erratic comments thrown into his presentation of the subject.

Carrie's heart is pounding. *What if he follows us out? Clara has another class after this one, will he ask to audit that also? Should I go to the guidance office? Is ten minutes up, yet?* She turns her head to look at the clock on the wall behind her. *It is time.* She stands up and Clara does also. As quietly as they can, they move to the back door. The professor is doing his best to distract the class. He is drawing a diagram on the board and asks Mickey if he understands the concept given. Before he answers, he turns around and sees the girls leave the room.

"No, I don't understand, professor." He stands. "Today is the first day of auditing this class. How could I possibly understand? If this is the way you are going to treat me for trying to learn. I do not need to take this class." He heads toward the door.

"Young man, I will be calling the guidance counselor, if you walk out after those girls. Joe, Harry, please each take a door and stand in front of it. There is extra credit for the both of you if you do not let this young man pass during my class."

"Yessir!" Both Joe and Harry are members of the ROTC program and come to college in their Navy uniforms.

Carrie and Clara go straight to Mrs. Webster's office. They are told that she is in a meeting. The girls sit down but both have so much adrenaline flowing in their systems that they cannot be still. Carrie gets up and walks back to the receptionist. "Can we leave her a note? We are not staying." The note reads:

Mrs. Webster,

Mickey Roosevelt decided to follow Clara and I to her first class of the day. Professor Jordan is aware of the situation and will be contacting you today. We are headed home for the day, as we do not feel safe in this environment. You may call us at home, at your convenience.

If we see him near our house, as I mentioned, the police will be called. As an advisor, please advise him that he will be arrested if he comes near me.

Carrie Ann Harrick

FORTY
January 24th, 1896
A Friday in Nowata, Oklahoma

The days taking care of Joshua have taken their toll on the doctor, Brenda and Sadie. He is awake for longer periods of time, as the doctor is trying to lessen the amount of laudanum given.

Chilly has been in touch with Elliot through telegrams. The one this morning said that the Judge Magistrate will be in Pennysville on Tuesday the 28th to arraign the Williams cousins and Bart the one-eyed Bandit. Chilly heads to the clinic to give Brenda the news.

"Good morning. Doctor Peters, how is our patient this morning?" He says as he walks directly into Joshua's room. Brenda is assisting the doctor, once again, to debride the wound and apply tree moss to it. He sees that Joshua is awake and in pain. He goes closer to see the wound for himself. "It looks much improved for all your administrations doc. My fear is that come fall, he will lose all his hair like trees lose leaves."

Joshua says, "Why don't you make like a tree and leave?"

"Joshua, you wound me with your words. You are sitting up while conscience, how is the pain? One a scale of one to ten."

"Fifteen."

"So, you are getting better. Yesterday, you said twenty. I have news from Pennysville. The Judge Magistrate is coming to arraign all my prisoners on Tuesday. I should leave today with Jeff Williams, so that I can prepare for the court cases. The question is to you, Doc, do you need my bride for assistance or can she accompany me?"

"She has become invaluable to me."

"How long will you be gone, Chilly?" Asks Brenda.

211

"So have you decided to be a nurse versus a bride, then?"

"It depends on your length of stay." She asks, shyly. "You would be traveling with the Williams prisoner?"

"I will be extra cautious to keep him at a distance from you at all times. It might take a week or more to get there, catch up on business, have the court cases heard and get back. That is barring any unforeseen difficulties."

Brenda looks up at the Doctor. "I think that I want to be a bride, Doctor, if you can spare me."

"Of course, my dear. I think this wound is closed enough that Sadie can help maneuver Joshua, with me. We don't want her to faint on us."

Joshua asks, "Doc, how soon before I can travel?"

The Physician thinks about it for a minute. "We haven't got you up, yet. I think if you can stand the pain while fully upright, I will feel confident to release you. Your pelvis is far from healed, so a rough ride would be inadvisable for quite some time."

"Can we see if I can stand for a minute, now?" Joshua asks.

"I am willing if you are. Let me get you wrapped first." The wrapping seems to give him a tremendous amount of pain, but he doesn't moan or complain. After that is done, the doctor looks him in the eye and says, "Still want to try standing?"

"No time like the present. Did you ever wonder why they call 'now' the present? I think it is because God has given us the gift of now as a present. What we do with the gift, is up to us."

"Spoken like a man raised by the Cheyenne." Says Chilly.

"The words for now and a gift are not the same words in Cheyenne, Chilly. You blame everything on my Cheyenne upbringing."

"Joshua, are we having our first fight?"

"Apparently. Okay, Doc. I am rested and ready."

Chilly has one hand under one arm and the Doc has a hand under the other arm. Brenda moves his legs over the side of the bed and repositions his sheets. "I think he needs a pair of underlings, or I need to leave."

"You are no longer a maiden, Aunt Brenda. I am not shy, if you would just keep your gaze averted, please."

"I am not sure that I like being called Aunt by someone older than myself, but I am looking up, you may move him."

The two men, carefully, get him to his feet. He doesn't complain or moan. Chilly asks, "What number on the scale?"

"Twenty-five!" He barely can say, "I think . . . I . . . am . . . going to . . . pass . . ."

Joshua goes limp in their arms. Chilly says, "I got him." He immediately bends down and picks him up into his arms and lays him back down, as gentle as if he was putting a babe to bed. "I guess it will be a while before he can travel?"

"He did better than I thought he would. He has a very strong pain tolerance. Anyone else would not have tried standing for another week, at least. He has come a long way. I think he has a strong chance of making a full recovery. It will be a very long road filled with pain, most likely for the rest of his life, but I do not think that this man will not let that define who he is."

"I have to agree with you doc, if I understood it all." Chilly laughs.

"Husband, you are a very smart man, yet you profess otherwise."

"Wife, I could say the same for you."

The Doctor adds, "And you'd both be correct."

Brenda and Chilly do not wait for Joshua to regain consciousness. They return to their rooms to pack for their journey. As soon as the door is closed behind her, Brenda says, "Husband?"

Chilly has grabbed his carpet bag and has it on the bed, already. "Yes, my wife." Before answering, she moves slowly toward the bed, undressing as she goes. Chilly looks up. "You do not want to travel in that dress, my dear?"

She laughs, "Chilly, when you picked up your cousin and laid him down so gently, it reminded me of our wedding night. I have never wanted to be in your arms as I do right now! Take off your shirt and let me see those strong arms of yours then take me in those arms and have your way with me."

"And you thought I would be bored with your inexperience! You are more than making up for lost time." He says as he quickly throws the carpet bag off the bed and pulls off his shirt. He crosses to her and lifts her up. "Is this what you had in mind?" Her lips on his was her answer. *How I love this woman!* He thinks as he lets her idea take over his mission. He slowly lays her on the bed. "We don't have much time."

"Then you'd better take me quickly. And don't worry about being gentle. Take me like you have something to prove."

"Oh, my young bride, you have me blushing." He says as he removes his pants. He kneels on the bed. "Your bloomers are still on."

"Show them who is boss. Rip them off me. Show ME who is boss!"

"Brenda, don't let my actions fool you, you are the boss of my heart and my every thought." He says as he rips her pants. Then he grabs her neck and kisses her hard. "Say boo, if I am going too far. Promise?" He rips her blouse, now and hungrily takes her breasts and sucks them hard.

Brenda moans, "I promise to say it. But hurry, my love. I want you in me now!"

As he enters her, he says, "I am in charge, you will not speak until I say." He kisses her hard and lightly bites her lip. He puts his tongue in her mouth and she sucks it. "Give me your tongue." He breathlessly orders. Her tongue enters his and he sucks and bites it. He moves down her neck, kissing and biting, as he thrusts with all his might into her. She is moaning under him.

"Oh, Chilly!"

He stops his thrusts, "I told you not to speak! Do you want me to punish you?" She nods consent. "Remember to say Boo? She nods again. He removes himself from inside her and in one movement turns her over and slaps her behind. She gasps. "Do you have something to say?" He asks. She shakes her head no. "Good." He slaps her again. Then he turns her back and enters her again. He is thrusting as hard as he can. She grabs the headboard to keep herself from moving up, under him. "Is this what you wanted?" She bites her lip and nods. "Do you know how much I want you, when you bite your lip?" He doesn't let her answer. His mouth is on hers again and in a few more thrusts, he is finished. He stays in position as he empties into her. "I have never done anything like that. Did I hurt you?"

"No my love. It was exactly what I wanted, but I don't know why."

"Well, in your free time when helping the doctor, you could look for the answer in one of his medical books."

"I will do that, but in the meantime, we need to get going. I have a feeling that I am going to need to purchase several bloomers and camisoles, to have on hand. Not that I will want it like this all the time, but I sure wanted it now!"

"I am glad I was able to do your bidding. I love you, Brenda. You consume my thoughts. I shouldn't be taking you, since I have a prisoner. It could be dangerous, but I cannot stand being without you for two hours. How could I go a week? I would be a wreck of a man."

"Then my plan worked. I hoped that I would mean as much to you as you do to me. I love you so much. It almost scares me." Brenda says as they slowly leave the bed and begin to dress, smiling at each other.

***

Brenda, Chilly and the prisoner, Jeff Williams, are ready to depart Nowata by eleven in the morning. They are taking a buckboard, not Kirby's carriage so the prisoner can be hog tied to the rear of the bed, while Chilly and his bride ride in the front seats. Chilly thinks, *I must keep my bride safe, I am too selfish to spend a moment without her, so I am endangering her. Of course, Jeff has not pulled a gun on anyone or hurt anyone and seems truly worried about Joshua's condition.*

Sheriff Jubal is tying the prisoner while saying, "I think the Judge will come here shortly after his business in your town. Lucinda is lucky that your nephew is recovering but I intend to ask for the maximum penalty. She shot him with no regard to his office or his welfare."

Jeff interrupts. "She has always been crazier than bat shit! But God help me. She loves me and would do anything I ask." He looks at the Sheriffs. "And one major thing I didn't. I swear, I didn't!"

FORTY-ONE
January 24ᵗʰ, 1959
A Saturday in Chicago

Oliver had spent last night on the couch, once again. While Carrie was making them both breakfast. Clara was complaining. "Not that I do not think that your presence wasn't necessary, it was! I am worried about our reputations, having a male living with two single females."

"If you feel that your reputation is in danger, we might as well do what we will be accused of. I am game!"

"Behave yourself! I am not ready to give in, yet."

"Give in to me or your ruined reputation?"

"I refuse to answer that on the grounds it can incriminate me."

"I thought so." Oliver walks over to her and bends to give her a chaste kiss. "Let me know when you are ready, I am always willing."

Carrie comes out of the kitchen. "Willing to do what? Breakfast is served."

Clara looks at Oliver and blushes. "Um, Oliver is being silly."

"I am a third wheel. You never have alone time. I think that you and I would be better off if I went back to EL Dorado."

"Carrie, we have been through this. You are not at fault for trying to be safe while getting an education."

"Well, I think that you two need a date night, minus me. Oliver, take her out for the rest of the day. I will not leave the apartment. I have tons of work to do and I have been very good doing my class work before I get carried away with the dress making. Come, your eggs are getting cold.

***

Oliver takes his girl back to her favorite place, Chinatown. They walk around the different shops and buy some groceries for Carrie. Clara decides what meal she wants, so Oliver can pick the restaurant that would make the meal the best. After a long late lunch, the two use the pay phone to call Carrie and check on her. After Carrie declared herself safe, sound and homebound, they go downtown to catch a movie. After the movie, they stop into a Jazz bar and enjoy music for an hour.

Clara Beth wants to be home before Carrie would want to go to sleep. They are coming down Ashland Ave and turn on 49th St. so that they can go the right way on the one-way-only Paulina block to their apartment. Oliver sees Mickey walking at the middle of the block.

"I do not believe this! How many times does this boy need to be told to stay away! I want to pull over and punch the fuck out of him. Excuse my French." Oliver is turning red from under his collar on up.

"No, Oliver. We need to make sure Carrie is safe and we need to call the police. I want to hurt him myself, but that is not the answer." They drive up to her apartment and a parking space in front is available. "Hurry, he sees us and is running towards us. Oliver parallel parks his car and before he can shift it into park, Clara is out of the vehicle and is up the stairs. Oliver is right behind her. She jiggles the key in the lock. "Oliver, I cannot get it. Before Oliver can help, Carrie opens the door from the inside.

"What's up, guys?" She says as they push their way in. Carrie is still standing there with the open door in her hand. She looks out the door and Mickey is on her stairs. "Mickey, you must stop this!" She yells as she attempts to close the door, but he reaches out and stops it from closing.

Oliver has turned back around and is behind Carrie. "Get the fuck out of here, Mickey! I swear, you will be sorry!"

Clara can be heard on the phone in the background, "Operator, this is an emergency. I live at 4937 South Paulina. I have an intruder in my house and my boyfriend is struggling with him."

Oliver pushes Carrie aside as Mickey pushes himself in. Carrie starts screaming. She looks outside. There are two young men walking across the street. She calls to them, "Help me, please, he wants to kill me." They look at each other and start running to her to help. Carrie looks back into the apartment. "The crew cut guy is the good one. The tall guy with dark hair is the attacker."

The men run past her. Somewhere in the distance, Carrie can hear a siren. She sees Mickey put his hand in his pocket. She sees it in slow motion. "He has a weapon!!!" she yells. She lunges for Mickey's hand as it is coming out of his pocket. Out comes a very small gun, Carrie has her hand on his wrist. She is struggling to keep the gun pointed down. Oliver was punched by Mickey and is on the ground. The two good Samaritans each have an upper arm but his hand is waving even with Carrie trying to hold his wrist. She is too short to combat his reach and strength. Even with both men holding an arm he is practically lifting Carrie off the ground. The sirens were getting closer and she knew that they were coming to help. *If only I can keep Mickey from shooting someone.* Oliver is up off the ground. He is reaching around to help Carrie to control Mickey's hand.

The sound of the gun going off, makes her head feel like it is the clapper of a bell. Clanging from one side to the other. She is temporarily unaware of her surroundings. *Was I shot? Who was shot?* She is forcing herself to think. The world around her is dark and blurry. She is being grabbed by someone. *Is it Mickey?* "Leave me alone! Why won't you leave me alone?"

"Carrie, it's Oliver. Where are you hurt?" She feels for his head and feels the crew cut. The sound of the shot is still booming in her head and she cannot hear Oliver.

"Oliver is everyone alright?" Carrie still cannot focus on anything around her. "OLIVER, ANSWER ME? HELP ME, PLEASE. I CAN'T SEE! I CANNOT HEAR! OH, MY GOD! HELP ME. I CAN'T SEE! She screams. Then, she collapses.

FORTY-TWO
January 27th, 1896
A Monday in Pennysville, Oklahoma

Yesterday, the sheriff delivered his man to a cell. "Jason, say hi to your cousin, Jeff." He puts them in cells on opposite sides of each other. "Jeff meet Bart the one-eyed bandit. He is a failed bank robber. You will be in court Tuesday. All of you. Then I will have empty cells again, and I can concentrate on my nephew and my wife."

This afternoon, Elliot has come in with three lunch trays. "Good to have you back, sheriff. I saw my cousin earlier and she looks very happy."

"OH CRAP" Chilly yells as he slams his fists down on his desk. Elliot gets startled and drops one of the trays. "CRAP, CRAP!!" Chilly adds.

"Sheriff, what is wrong? Do you have some bad news in a letter or something?"

"No, Elliot. You are the Postmaster. Have you delivered a letter?"

"Well, no. But why are you so mad!"

"Because Elliot, we are now related – For life! I will never get rid of you!! Crap! Crap!"

"Sheriff, you had me worried that something is wrong!"

"Something could not be more wrong! Till death do us part, I said. Why did I not think of the consequences? I let that beautiful girl take advantage of me and now I am stuck with YOU!"

"Chilly, stop! I know that you kid me all the time, but I do have some feelings." He is bending down picking up the remnants of the lunch from the dropped tray. When he comes back up, the sheriff is smiling and holding something out. "What have you there, Chilly?"

"I have a badge for you. I would like for you to be one of my deputies. You do so much in an unofficial capacity, already. I should have thought of this sooner. Will you be my deputy, Elliot?"

"Sheriff, I think you were out in the sun too long. You know I am no good in confrontations!"

"You were very reliable in the bank."

"I was just worried about Miss Judith."

"No Elliot, you have always been my assistant and that day, you risked your life for the safety of others. You can think on your feet when danger looms large around you. I want you to be my deputy."

"I don't know if I am allowed. I am a member of the city council, and the Postmaster. I don't know if I can be a deputy, also."

"Well, I will leave it to you to find out."

The door to the office swings open and it is Brenda. Elliot runs to her. "Your husband just offered me the job of deputy. He likes me!" Then he turns to enter the cell area with the trays.

Brenda raises an eyebrow. "Chilly, is there any truth in that?"

"I did ask him to be a deputy. I refuse to admit to anything else."

Brenda laughs. "That sounds more like my man."

"What brings a nice girl like you to a place like this?"

"I thought I would look for my husband to take him out for an afternoon lunch date. I wonder where I put my guy? Have you seen him? He's kind of a tall fella. About your height, I think."

"A class dame, like you, shouldn't be looking for her husband in this kind of a place. There is nothing but bandits and scoundrels and one cousin here." He stands and puts on his hat and walks over to her. "I think I have to investigate this situation."

"You described my husband, I know that he is around. He is the tallest scoundrel anywhere."

"If you were my woman, I might have to make you

pay for calling me a scoundrel."

"Yes, the scoundrel should make me pay, I have been bad!" Brenda is looking up at Chilly. He bends low to kiss her. His lips are just about to touch hers when the locked door to the cells open. Bart the one-eyed bandit has Elliot with a sharpened spoon against his neck. Elliot looks up sheepishly. "I know, Elliot the idiot! I guess your offer to make me deputy has been revoked."

"For starters, yes." Says Chilly. "Brenda leave NOW!" She is frozen with fear and cannot move. "BRENDA!!" She starts moving backward. Then she turns and runs out. Chilly watches the closed door for the count of three. Then he turns to look at the bandit. "Now, Bart. I do not know where you think this is going to lead, but I have a gun and you have a sharp spoon." He pulls his gun and points it. "I am a perfect marksman. You can ask Elliot. I can shoot you between your eyes, from fifty feet away. You are much taller than your hostage. He leaves you no protection to hide behind."

"Look, Sheriff. All I want to do is leave. I never wanted to hurt anyone." He pushes Elliot away. "Let me just leave, will you?" He moves toward Chilly and makes a play to grab Chilly's gun. They wrestle for it for a moment or two.

Suddenly, a metal chamber pot hits Bart in the head and he goes limp. Elliot is standing with the pot still in his hands. "I had to do it, Sheriff. It was my fault that he got out.

"No problem, deputy. Now get him back into the cell and LOCK the door. And make sure you count the silverware going in and out! I have a very frightened bride to find." He adjusts his hat and walks out the door.

As the door closes behind him he calls out, "Brenda?" He starts walking toward the hotel. "Brenda?" He calls again. He walks into the hotel. He looks at the clerk. "Where is my bride?"

"She ran up the stairs, Sheriff." Chilly takes the

stairs two at a time. He enters their new room saying. "Brenda, where are you?" He sees her laid out across the bed. He rushes to her and turns her over. Her face is flushed with her tears. "Brenda, I am fine. Elliot saved me, again. He hit Bart with a chamber pot. Bart never saw it coming because Elliot snuck up on his blind side. Elliot is fine, and I am fine. Please don't carry on so."

She looks up him. "I froze! You had to yell at me. Then I ran like a coward. I didn't stop until I dove on the bed. I am so ashamed!"

"Brenda, it is alright. You have never had a criminal come at you, before. Do you think that I wasn't scared? I thought that he would be taking my reason for living away! I love you so much, Brenda." She wraps her arms around his neck and sobs into his shoulder. "Brenda, I don't understand. You weren't this upset when you were the victim of the stage robbery. That had to seem more dangerous than a one-eyed man with a spoon.

"I didn't think I was with child, then. The babe-to-be was in danger and that was my only thought. I didn't think of your safety or Elliot's. My BABY was in danger, so I ran and ran fast. Then I was so ashamed that I left you and Elliot without looking behind me."

"You are with child, Brenda? My child?"

"I have never been with another man, Chilly. And I think so."

"My lovely little lady." He kisses her. "I am aware that I am your only man. It was only right that you protect our child, first. If you feel bad about it . . ." He continues to kiss her. His kisses are becoming urgent and hungry. "I could spank you for being so selfish, thinking only of the babe in your womb and not of me. Is that what you want?"

"No, Chilly. This isn't fun and games. I was so afraid. I thought our baby would die, then when I got to the room, I thought I left you to die. How could I do that? Just leave?"

"My love, you left because I told you to do that. You have nothing to be ashamed of, you listened to me. I wanted you safe. Had known about the baby, I would have wanted it safe. So, you did what I wanted. Now stop the tears. I would like to celebrate my good fortune. Please get up and come sit with me on the loveseat." He helps her to her feet and takes her face in his hands. "Dry those tears, my dear." He takes a handkerchief from his back pocket and wipes her face. "Now come sit down." He leads her across the room. He sits down and pulls her into his lap. "Now, I am going to hold you like this for the rest of the afternoon. My hand is on your belly and I am protecting my child. You have already protected it. This is my turn." He kisses her neck, sweetly. She turns to face him to kiss him back. He gives her a peck then says, "Turn around, so I can protect my child."

"Yes, husband. Whatever you say."

"Now that sounds more like my sensible level headed wife."

"I am so sorry."

"I don't want to hear it. There is nothing to be sorry for. You used the ultimate survival tactic that God gave you. It is called Fight or Flight. You chose flight to protect the defenseless. Now just sit still and let me hold you. I am going to spend the next hour or two, just sitting here with my hand on my child."

"So, you're happy that I might be with child?"

"My dear, I know that we haven't know each other for long, but this IS my happy look." With that statement, she starts laughing, and laughing. She cannot stop. "Brenda?" He says seriously. "I think you are laughing at me."

"Yes sir, I am. What are you going to do about it?"

"I might have to do something, as soon as I am done with my child, I will be happy to give all my attention to you."

225

FORTY-THREE
January 27th, 1959
A Tuesday in Chicago

The call came just before midnight. When Henry answers, Clara was crying hysterically. They couldn't understand her. Oliver finally got on the phone. "Carrie was shot. She is still unconscious. They have taken her to Mercy Hospital. It is a miracle that she is alive. The bullet just grazed the right side from the temple to the back of her head. It did not enter but ran along the side of her skull cutting it as it went. She didn't know that she was shot. It was Mickey. There were three of us on him and Carrie saw him reach for a gun in his pocket. She tried to wrestle the gun from his hand. She didn't want anyone shot. She kept yelling. 'Don't shoot Mickey. Someone will get hurt.' Her head was so close to the gun when he pulled the trigger. She wasn't in pain but the loudness made her deaf, too. She was in shock. The shot or the event has caused her to go blind. The doctors are leaning toward what they call hysterical blindness. Like I said, she is still unconscious, though."

Henry immediately called his brothers-n-law, Joshua and Matthew. They made sure that a private plane was available before sun-up. Matthew flew the plane carrying Anna, Henry, Joshua and GW to Midway airport. Anna never complained about flying. She wanted to be at her daughter's bedside so bad. While waiting for the plane to be arranged, Anna called Mercy hospital and was given little information. Carrie was stable and they were trying to diagnose the reason for her blindness.

They sat three days at her bedside. They still have very little information. Henry called her school and asked for the guidance office so that he can tell Mrs. Webster that his daughter Carrie will no longer attend the University of Chicago, thanks to their inability to keep her star student under control. She had heard of the incident and had nothing to offer Henry but her heartfelt sympathy.

Mickey has been taken to the Psych ward at Cook County jail. He said that he never meant to hurt her, he just wanted her to realize she loved him.

When the family arrived at the hospital, they were not allowed to go up all at the same time. Her mother, father and GW took turns staying with her. They were told that the brain is swelling from the trauma. That is the reason she is still not awake.

Today, is the third day since she was shot. Carrie wakes up to the sound of someone sleeping. *"I can hear again!* She has pain from the incision that the bullet made. She felt the tubes in her, and her head's large wrapped bandage, covering her eyes. *I must be in a hospital.* She assumes that Clara has called her family. She knows the sleeping sounds of her parents and this is not from them, so. . . "Who is it? Who is there?" *Could Mickey still be at large?* "Mickey, why are you doing this to me? Haven't you hurt me enough, Mickey. Please stop!" She is thrashing in the bed. "You have to leave me alone!"

"Carrie, please stop. It is GW. We've all been taking turns sitting with you. You were sleeping so peacefully. I must have fallen asleep watching you."

"GW, I cannot see. I was shot, wasn't I. I couldn't hear or see. I still have terrible pain on the whole side o my head. Will I have a scar?"

"I don't know. The bullet grazed your temple at your hairline. It ran along the side of your head. I was told that it cut your skull but did not enter it. You might have a small scar there. It won't make you any less beautiful in my eyes. I love you so much Carrie. Can I kiss you? I don't want to hurt you."

"It's not fair. I wanted our first kiss at the ball. Plus, I wanted to SEE you looking at me."

"So, is that a no?"

"A no? No. Please kiss me, GW." She says to clarify

things.

He is at her bedside and leans in and takes her hands. He leads them to his face. "Here, see me with your hands." He leans in closer, "Here it comes." His lips brush hers. "How was that?"

"I was shot in the head and it must have left me numb. I didn't feel your kiss at all. Can you do it again?" He bends down again and brushes her lips. She moves her hands from his face to behind his head and pulls him to her. Just before they meet, she says, "I guess I am taking this matter into my own hands." She pulls him in and kisses him. He is trying to keep it light but she has something else in mind. After a few moments, she lets go of his face. "That felt more like a first kiss, I think. I really do not know since this was my first, first kiss."

"Mine, too. I was picturing it at the ball, also. I have seen the material for your dress and how much you have sewed. It is amazing! Such talent, you have."

"I may never sew, again. If I don't get my sight back."

"Let's not get that far ahead of ourselves. This is 1959 and the miracles of science have made many discoveries. They will figure something out. If not I will take you to Lawrence to our Universities specialists."

Carrie starts to cry. The possibility of staying blind suddenly seems real. "I don't want to be a burden. I was going to be a huge clothing designer, making a fortune and becoming known for my originals! I can't imagine my life blind. NO, I won't!" She thrashes about.

Anna comes into the room. "Carrie, thank God. You are awake. Are you in pain?"

"Mama? I don't want to be blind. Say that I won't stay blind!" Carrie says with sobs.

Anna sits on the bed and puts her hands on her shoulders. "Now listen carefully." She speaks just above a whisper. "Your hearing came back. No one is saying that your vision won't, also.". Carrie concentrates to hear her.

In doing so, her breathing slows and she calms down. Anna continues, "We will find out what is happening. It might be like my amnesia. It is your brain just trying to protect itself. When you feel out of danger, you will see, again. Your father and I were talking and we'd like you to come home, as soon as you can travel. Clara doesn't want to stay here, even though she loves her boyfriend. Oliver says that he'd follow Clara, where ever she goes. There is much to discuss. Uncle Joshua has offered our old little house to you and your sister, if you want to attend school at U of K."

"Do they have a school for the blind, there?" Carrie asks.

"We are not expecting you to remain blind, so stop thinking that." Anna reassures her.

"Mama, you have always taught us to be realists."

"But always with hope! It was a whole year that I didn't know who I was but I never lost hope!! You mustn't either. You have your whole life ahead of you. No one single event or disability defines who you are."

"But Mama. . ."

Anna stops her. "Do you know that I wasn't supposed to have any children after Clara? I suffered so during her birth and almost died. Your father was insistent that we not risk my health. I had Clara Beth to think about as well as him. Your father and I love each other, so very much. We just couldn't avoid getting pregnant. I prayed and had hope that all would be fine. I had the same problems as with my first two pregnancies but I lived. Hope never left me. Then Harry came. Hope was my closest friend. You wouldn't be here, if it wasn't for hope. Believe it, you can achieve it, Baby Girl."

"I like that saying. Is GW still here?"

"I'll never leave you, Carrie."

"Mama, do you think that you can be my eyes and sew my dress? Sight or no sight, I am going to that ball and I want to be seen in my dress."

Anna laughs, "I think I can figure it out."

"Good. GW?"

"Yes, Carrie?"

"Do you mind if I am your blind-date for the ball?" She giggles.

He shakes his head, "Bad, bad pun! But, I would be honored."

FORTY-FOUR
January 28th, 1896
A Tuesday in Pennysville, Oklahoma

The Judge Magistrate convened his court at eight in the morning. Chilly and Elliot have organized all the proof and depositions from the stagecoach robbery and the bank robbery. After Chilly presents the cases, the Judge rules that there is sufficient evidence to take them to Fort Smith for formal Court trials. Court is in session for less than an hour. Judge Nesbitt travels with six U.S. Deputy Marshals. Two will take the prisoners to Fort Smith and the rest will continue to the next town. When the two Deputies drop off the prisoners, they will find the Judge and get another set. The judge has it so that he is not without Marshals and he can keep going from town to town.

Sheriff Charles Lewis and Deputy Elliot Dotson feel very relieved that their cells are finally empty. Chilly plans to head back to Nowata as soon as it can be arranged. He is secretly planning something and getting all the moving parts in place is becoming a headache, but he is sure that it will be worth it. He is expecting a few telegrams and has his deputy Elliot as his partner in crime.

After checking with the telegraph office, once again, Chilly goes home to have his daily lunch date with his bride.

Brenda is waiting for him, in her long camisole. She is laying on her stomach on the bed, pretending to be reading a magazine. When he comes in, she looks up. "Excuse me, sir, I think you are in the wrong room. I am expecting my husband. He will not appreciate you standing there staring at me."

"Does he appreciate what a gorgeous girl you are?"

"I am not sure. I might have to remind him of that when he comes in. In the meantime, is there something I can do for you?"

"I thought I was going to get a bite to eat. Do you have any suggestions? I have a large appetite."

"That fits, you are a large man. But then, I seem to have a large appetite myself and look at how little I am."

"I am looking."

"Can you really see from all the way over there?"

"Brenda, what am I going to do with you? I never know what to expect from you. I cannot believe how lucky I am, that you are all mine."

"At least until that scoundrel husband of mine comes home. Now stop wasting time and come have your lunch." She moves her hand under the pillow and comes out with a bunch of carrots.

Chilly laughs and crawls onto the bed. "I love you! Now take that camisole off and let's have our afternoon fun."

Brenda looks up at him. "I am all thumbs. Can you help me with these?" She rolls over to her back so that the ties are available to him.

He moves to her and begins to untie her top.

She puts her hand on his. "Chilly? Are we normal? I don't think other couples enjoy each other the way we do."

"You mean the games?"

"No, I mean all of it. I don't know any couple that seem as happy as we are just to be in bed."

"It is not something decent folks go around sharing."

"I did have several girlfriends marry and we promised each other that we would tell what it was like, afterward. None of my friends wanted to say. They didn't like it, I think. Are we different?"

"Not from my family! Most of my siblings, who are married have spent the first couple of years, where they couldn't stop touching each other. No let me change that. They STILL cannot stop touching each other. My parents were like that, also. Always hugging, touching, or holding hands. It explains why Momma had eight babies. OR, maybe being sex fiends run in the Lewis family!

"Oh, Chilly. What does that make me?"

"A Lewis, my girl."

"Oh, yeah. That's right!"

When Chilly is back at the office, there were several telegrams on his desk. He eagerly opens them all. He smiles. *Now, there is nothing stopping us from going to Nowata!* He opens the last envelope. He makes a face of momentary disappointment. *Five out of six, is a good showing.* Then he smiles.

Elliot comes into the office. He is proudly wearing the badge that Chilly gave him. "I suppose this means that you are off to see your Indian? You are not leaving me in charge, I hope.

"Tom Baker said that he would . . ."

"Aw, Sheriff leave me in charge, please!"

Chilly laughs, "Deputy – get out of my office. Go do some work!"

"Everything is done, Sheriff. And it is my office until you return." Elliot says with new found confidence.

FORTY-FIVE
January 30th, 1959
A Friday in Chicago, Illinois

Carrie is waiting, impatiently, for the doctors to come remove her head bandage, change her wound dressing, and check her eyesight. Her eyes were bathed in a chemical that they use for newborns, yesterday. She saw light and dark figures but no color - no definition. She was hoping that the solution sitting in her eyes overnight will help her see, again. Another round of head x-rays were taken this morning, but the technicians would not divulge what they saw.

GW spent another night by her side. When Carrie suggested it, Anna did not like the idea. Carrie said, "Mother, with all the tubes on me, I think my honor will be secure."

Anna blushed, "I wasn't concerned as much about that as his comfort and well, I don't know. I guess that I have no real reason. It just seems odd to say good night to a man who will be spending the night with your unmarried daughter."

Carrie said, "Mama, our relationship is still too new. We have not had a first date, yet."

This morning, Henry, Anna and GW are in the small private room that she was transferred to after she woke up. Henry is nervously pacing the floor. Anna says, "Henry, you are going to wear out the vinyl. Please, come sit down." He is about to take a seat when the door opens.

Doctor O'Brien says, "Well, we have a full house, here. Don't we? Carrie, who are all these people?"

"Good morning, Dr. O'Brien, this is my mother, Anna, my father, Henry and my boyfriend, GW. They are hoping that I can see that they are here, instead of just hearing them. What did my x-rays show you?"

The doctor crosses the room to the curtains, and

pulls the drawstring to close them. "The swelling is significantly reduced. If that swelling has put pressure on the optic nerve, that might be reduced also. There is still a chance that nerve damage might take longer to heal. Think of the nerve as a garden hose. Say that it has a kink in it, THEN a car has been parked on the kink for a week. When the car leaves, it may take time for the hose to find it's natural shape and function. Running water through it will force some of the shape back but we cannot simulate that procedure without a dangerous operation. Time, is our best ally to healing." As he is explaining, he is removing the head bandage and examining the wounds. "You are healing remarkably well. I think we can leave this big head bandage off." He rings for the nurse. "I would like to clean this a little." The nurse comes in. "Bring a dressing kit, and saline, please, Nurse Becky." She leaves immediately. He goes to the doorway, where the gloves are kept, and he puts a pair on. He snaps the glove at each wrist as the finishing touch of gloving himself.

Carrie looks like she is laying there, patiently but says, "Doc, I cannot take this. Please, undo my eye bandages. I want to see if I can see."

"So you can sail the seven seas?" He jokes. "I don't want you to be disappointed. Most likely the hose is not unkinked yet."

"I understand but I have been in the dark for almost a week, now. I have a dress that I have designed that I need to sew for a Valentine Ball. I need to get on with my life."

"Kinked hose blind or not, Miss Harrick, your life will go on."

"I understand. It may take days, weeks or even months for the optic nerve to unkink."

Nurse Becky walks in with the dressing tray. "Here we are, Doc." She puts the tray down on the bedside table, then turns to glove up. She comes back to the doctor and opens the tray and is prepared to hand him, whatever he needs. The doctor lays Carrie back down and makes her lay on her left side so that he can clean the wounds and redress them. The two work almost silently. Anna turns away and buries her head into Henry's shoulder. His arms are around Anna but he is watching the medical team closely. GW walks over to the other side of the bed and is bending over Carrie to look carefully at the wound and the work being done.

"Young man, are you interested in medicine?" the Doctor asks.

"No, I am interested in Carrie." He looks up at the pair and smiles. "She is worried about how it all looks. Carrie, the grove that the bullet made is small and almost healed. I do not think you will have a scar. They did cut hair away from your temple on that side, so don't let that bother you when you see it. Hair will grow back and you can wear a hat that covers that side for the ball. This should be all healed over and some hair will come in by then. You have three weeks."

Carrie says, "It won't be so bad. If I still have the top length, I might be able to hide the shaved area with some curls."

"Absolutely." He says. "The doctor is doing a thorough job. Are you in any pain?"

"Well, this doesn't tickle. Are they almost done?"

The doctor answers, "Just a minute or two, my dear."

"You are building up the suspense. It is killing me."

"Me too." Says GW. "You don't appreciate something until it is gone. This should be a lesson learned. Enjoy everything that God gives you, because it is all only here for a little while."

The doctor looks at the eighteen-year-old in front of him. "That knowledge usually takes a lifetime to gain. You are an astute young man."

"Doc, he is mine and you cannot have him." Carrie says and everyone laughs.

"Well, I think you are both very lucky to have each other. I am putting a small wrapping on this and then we will sit you up and look at those eyes of yours."

"Less jaw work, more paw work, Doc. You're killing me, here."

Nurse Becky laughs, "She's got you, there, Doc."

Then he laughs, also. "Okay, I will speed up my process. Can you sit up?" Carrie bounces up as if in an ejector seat. "Easy young lady, you almost knocked the tray out of the nurse's hands."

"If I could see her there, I would not have gotten so close."

Anna is trembling in Henry's arms. She whispers to him, "This is so much like my head injury. I had so many cuts and gashes that they had to keep my whole head shaved so they could clean and treat them. I wouldn't wish that on my worst enemy. Why does my daughter have to endure this also?"

"This too shall pass, Anna. She is your little girl and she has an inner strength that only you can surpass." He gives her a hug and kisses her forehead.

The doctor has taken the tape off her skin around her right eye, but is holding onto the gauze. "Young man, can you dim the light." GW walks to the switches. "Thank you. Okay, Carrie. Here goes." He slowly takes the gauze away from her eye. "Don't open just yet. Light does go through the lid, let your eye adjust to that. Then flutter open your eye, when you are ready."

Everyone in the room is holding their breath. Carrie is blinking. There are tears already falling. "It is brighter, doc." She blinks some more. "GW?" She holds out her hand.

GW crosses back to the bed in two steps and takes her hand. He puts it to his lips and kisses it. "Whatever happens I am here for you."

"I know." She is blinking some more and tearing up. "I think that I can see better but the light really hurts." She tries to look at GW. "I do see you but you are too fuzzy to make out. It is so much better than yesterday. Doc, I will be able to see again! I am not there yet, but it's close. Why does the light hurt?"

"Your eyes are dilated from the medicine. The center of your eye that protectively narrows with light is stuck open. That will lessen in a few hours. Let's uncover the other."

"Yes, please." It takes a few moments, and Carrie keeps her right eye closed while he works on the tape and gauze on the left. Then he lifts that gauze away and she blinks and tears up all over again. "This one is the same. Blurry and bright but I do see things."

"Great news, Carrie. We do not want you to overdo it, until the pupils go back to normal. I am going to put this eye mask on you and I want you to keep this on, or a very dark pair of sunglasses and have no direct light on in the room. If you can obey these conditions, I think we will not need new gauze bandages."

"I'll agree to it, Doc. I will sign an affidavit, if you want. I am going to have my sight back and my hair will grow and I will be able to sew my gown and EVERYTHING will be alright."

"Yes, Miss Harrick." The Doctor says, "I agree completely with your prognosis. Everything will be alright!"

FORTY-SIX
January 31st, 1896
A Friday in Nowata, Oklahoma

"Harkahomé, I don't know where to get you another pair of buckskins. They only sell white man's clothing at the General Store." Sadie says as she is helping Dr. Peters wrap the wound and ribs.

"Doesn't someone know someone who is a member of a Cheyenne tribe, here?" He says through the strain of being held up and wrapped.

"We have Creek, Seminole, Cherokee and a few others in town. I guess to my untrained eye, Cherokee would have the closest buckskins to the ones that I cut off. Sheriff Lewis told me that they were sown by your mother. I apologize for discarding them."

Sadie says. "I do not know how to sew, but if I can buy the material from someone in another tribe, perhaps the tailor in town can put it together for you. It won't replace the loving stitches, Harkahomé, but they would feel like you haven't left the Cheyenne."

"It is of little use. I have left my tribe. I might as well surrender the rest of the way. I will try on the shirt that you bought me. The pants might be another story. I don't think they are long enough and they look too constricting. Wasn't there anything there that was longer? I was the tallest male in the tribe, since I turned fifteen."

"I believe that." Sadie says.

"Chilly is the tallest in my family. He says that he passed my Uncle Will by three inches."

"So all the men in the Lewis family are tall?"

"My father was very tall. Close to my Uncle Will but my Uncle Joseph was not that tall. I seem to remember my father chiding him for just making six foot. He took after Gram Beth's side. I passed her height when I was only ten. That was just before we left Lawrence. I remember thinking what an adventure it was going to be. Going on a cattle drive! My father died so that many Cheyenne could eat. Then many Cheyenne died, anyway, before they reached their northern ancestral home. The family that saved us, split from many of the others. Kanuna, he was my stepfather, he and his second wife argued over which chief to follow and she took one son and one daughter and left Kanuna. I remember that he mourned the loss of his children the way my mother and I mourned the loss of my father. Then came the hungry bear!" The doctor was totally engrossed by the story but laid Joshua back down on the pillow. The pain of moving made Joshua hold in his breath for a moment.

"Sorry Harkahomé. Do you need medicine?" Joshua shook his head no. "Please continue the story. What about the hungry bear?"

"It was during the first spring. It was right after Kanuna's wife left. He became the leader of the Cheyenne that stayed with him. It was still very cold and we found a cave. The young braves checked for any animals but what we did not know was that the bears and their cubs were out foraging. As we were setting up camp, my mother was gathering what twigs and wood that she could. She stumbled over something and fell. A bear cub came to investigate. Mother got to her knees and talked gently to the little guy but the mama came to rescue her baby. When the bear saw my mother, who had just gotten to her feet, she roared up to scare my mother away from her cub.

"Kanuna came running at the sound of Mother's screams and the bear's roars. Without any weapon, other than his arms, he rushed the Mother bear. She backed up a bit but when her cub squealed again, the bear got motivated then attacked Kanuna. He was clawed across the torso and she bit his shoulder. Several other braves gathered and managed to chase her away. Mother felt bad that she was so dumb, and tried to play with a cub, and that it almost cost Kanuna his life. She helped sew his wounds and the tribe stayed in place for a month while he healed. Mother nursed him back to health and things began to develop between them. She became his third wife and I have a younger brother, Avonaco."

"She mentioned the bear story when she gave us a letter for my mother." Chilly says in the doorway. No one had heard him enter the clinic with Brenda.

Harkahomé says, "How long were you standing there?"

Chilly has his arm around his wife's waist. "We were here before you were laid onto the pillow. What number is your pain?"

"I have not had pain medication, today. I am at ten."

"That is a big improvement, Harkahomé!"

"How did court go?" Joshua asks.

"Good. But the day before, Bart the one-eyed bandit, pulled a sharpened spoon on Deputy Dotson."

"Is that one of Sheriff Wilcox's deputies?" He asks.

"Not exactly. I have taken on two new deputies. Tom Baker and Elliot Dotson."

"Brenda's cousin?" Sadie asks.

Brenda interrupts and says, "Thank you for not calling him Elliot the Idiot. Under the sheriff's influence, he has come a long way. He and the teller from the bank, Judith Barnes, are now a couple. He helped Chilly stop the bank robber, and then hit him with a chamber pot when he tried to escape."

"Elliot? The scared little postmaster?" Joshua asks.

"The same one." Chilly says.

"What else have I missed?" Harkahomé asks. Brenda and Chilly look at each other and smile. The look is lost on Joshua but not Sadie.

Sadie says, "Isn't it too soon, to tell?"

"I am pretty sure. I thought that Dr. Peters might be able to confirm my suspicion."

Joshua asks concerned, "What are we talking

about? You need the Doctor? Are you unwell?"

"No, I think that I am about to make Chilly a father and you a big cousin."

"Geez, I take a small trip and everything that I left in Pennysville has changed! How soon can I go back, doc?"

"Do you want to try to stand?"

"Umm, not today. I am trying to kick laudanum. I get stronger and have less pain every day. I will try tomorrow."

"We will be staying here with you. When you go home, so will we." Brenda bends down and gives him a kiss.

"Auntie, you will make my girl Sadie jealous. I have come to rely on her for so much. I just wish that she can sew."

"I can sew. What needs to be sewn?"

"I need new buckskins."

"Chilly knew you would. He found some material and I cut it to his size. I knew that you were slightly smaller but it was a good starting point. I have some of the sewing started."

Joshua turns to his love, "Sadie, you are my dream girl but my Auntie is sure the best."

FORTY-SEVEN
February 1st, 1959
A Sunday in Chicago, Illinois

It has been two days of sitting in darkness or wearing a sleep mask. Today, Doctor O'Brien is going to check her progress and will hopefully allow her to wear sunglasses and walk around the hospital. He had said, that when she can walk unaided and use the bathroom, successfully, she can go home. He means her apartment but she looks at it as one step closer to a full recovery.

As usual, the hall outside her room is filled. Clara Beth, her beau Oliver, Joshua, GW, and Henry are waiting for her to be allowed to walk out of her room. Anna is with Carrie Ann. Dr. O'Brien walks past the family line-up and gives them all a nod. He enters the room to find Carrie and her mother, sitting in the dark. She hears Carrie say, "Mama, with all the time that you have spent here, that dress is never going to be finished in time for the dance."

The doctor replies, "Carrie, I do hope that when you get out of this hospital, you won't be straining your new-found vision, with non-stop fine detail work. You might get headaches and wear yourself out for nothing."

Carrie turns toward the sound of his voice. "It will not be for nothing, Doc. My dress is the best design that I have ever done. When I wear that to the EL Dorado Valentine Ball, I expect to launch my Fashion business."

"That is a lot riding on one dress." He says as he comes to her bedside. "Now, let's see what we have going on. You have been very patient, so far. I do not want you to undo all that you've accomplished so far." He removes her blinders.

"Yes, Doctor. Whatever you say, Doctor. Can I open my eyes, now? The light doesn't seem to be bothering me."

"That's a very good sign. Your pupils must not be

dilated anymore. Go ahead, flutter them open." She follows his directions and she blinks multiple times before keeping them open. There is no tearing. "How does that feel?"

She turns her head to look at her mother. "Mama, I have never been so happy to SEE you." She smiles and her eyes start to tear up.

"Is the light bothering you?" the doctor asks.

"No, doctor – these are happy tears, see my mama has them, too."

He looks from daughter to mother. "You two can be twins." He notices for the first time. They both laugh, while wiping their tears. "Even now, you have the same mannerisms."

Henry says from the doorway, "They do everything alike. You won't have to worry about Carrie working that much on that dress. Anna will be able to sew it for her and will." He crosses the room to his wife. "It will be nice to have both my girls home." He gives Anna a kiss on her cheek. "Can GW come in?"

"When the doctor is finished, I would like to SEE him, alone." Carrie says. Then she turns to the Doctor. "Dr. O'Brien, I presume?" She holds out her hand for him to shake. He takes her hand and shakes it. Then he pulls a small flashlight out of his pocket.

"I need to look in your eyes. This may be bright." He quickly moves the light across her eyes. She holds her eyes steady and does not blink. His light comes back across her face but this time it holds still over her left eye. She blinks but doesn't tear. Then he bends over for a closer look at the eye. "Good, very good." He moves to her other eye. He gets the same results and repeats, "Good, very good. I think you are ready to get out of bed. I would have to say that as far as I can see, things should be operating normally. Let me hold the patch over one of your eyes while you look directly at my nose, then I will hold up some fingers. Tell me how many, but keep your eye on my nose."

He holds up his left hand and holds out three fingers. "Three." She says. Then he holds out his right, above his head. "Two." She says, correctly. They repeat this dance for five more times.

"Good, very good." He says when finished. "Any headache or a feeling of eyestrain?"

"None, so far. Can I look in a mirror at my wound? I want to see if I have scars."

"I do not see why not. I think that you are an extremely lucky young lady. A gunshot grazed your head and you will be walking out of here, with hardly a scar but with a great story to tell."

Anna has given her a mirror and Carrie is looking at herself closely. "I have a great story, all right. And the Mickey in my story is a mouse that shoots. Nothing that Walt Disney would draw, I am sure."

"I would like for you to stand for me. The eyes and ears affect your equilibrium. Let's get you up." Carrie is sitting on the side of the bed. "Give me your hand, I will help you down." She takes his hand and he pulls her to her feet. Then he places a hand on her shoulder to steady her if she is dizzy. "How does that feel? Are you dizzy?"

"No, sir. I feel right as rain."

"All right, then. I think I am done here. You can spend the rest of the day, walking, talking or whatever. If there are no medical complaints, I think that you will be released tomorrow. I think that you can travel to EL Dorado by the end of the week. Drive, not fly. Air pressure in a plane will be very bad for you, now. I suggest no flying for a year, at least."

Anna steps forward. "You do not have to worry about that, doc. I don't believe flying is good for anyone's health."

"OH, Mama!" Carrie says as a complaint. "Are we done, Doc? I have a boyfriend in the hall, that I am dying to SEE."

"Young love! Enjoy it while you can." He turns to leave. "Mom and Dad, will you join me in the hall. I think she deserves a moment or two with her young man." They both walk to the doctor, then precede him out. Once in the hall, he looks to the young man. "GW, your girl is waiting to see you." When GW hurries into her hospital room, everyone is smiling. "He is one lucky fella."

Joshua says, "So is she!"

When GW goes into the room, Carrie is looking in the mirror over the sink, looking closely at her hair and wound. She catches his eye in the mirror and she smiles. "GW, you are a sight for sore eyes. Sorry, that I cannot say the same thing for myself. I cannot wait to get home to a tub and some rollers!"

He walks over to her and turns her around. "I love what I see. My girl looking at me." He bends to her cheek.

"And I can see the love in your eyes. Now, I will take my first real kiss. If I can bother you for it, I mean."

"Bother away." He says as he takes her in his arms and his lips meet hers. She puts her arms around his neck.

"Don't you love first kisses?" She pulls away long enough to say, then her lips are back on his.

GW's head is nodding as he holds her tightly. "There is a hall full of people waiting for you to walk out."

"Let them wait." She says and she pulls him close, again.

FORTY-EIGHT
February 2nd, 1896
A Sunday in Nowata, Oklahoma.

Today, will be the second day that Harkahomé will be attempting to stand. Yesterday, he was on his feet for five whole minutes before asking to lay down. The wound from the bullet is healed. Doctor Peters said that his ribs might still be healing. Most of his pain is in the groin area. The broken pelvis that the doctor accurately diagnosed is the slowest to heal. Joshua does not complain of back pain. His hips forward seem to pulse with pain, though.

The Doctor and Chilly are both ready to help him off the mattress. "Just give me a moment", he says as he is sitting on the edge of the bed. "I need to get up the courage. This is not easy, but if I take some pain medicine, I will have trouble just standing." He takes a large breath in. "Okay, on the count of three, pick me up. One, two, three! UGGHH! I am up. I am going to take a step now. Hold on to me, please."

Chilly reassures him. "We are not leaving you, little buddy."

"I was the tallest in the tribe!" He says as he takes a step, "Oh, what I would give to have not fallen off that damn porch!" He grimaces. "Where is Sadie today? She never misses a morning."

"I am right here, Harkahomé. I went out to breakfast with Brenda. We haven't had a girl's get together in a long time. Did you miss me? I am glad to hear it. Can you walk to me? If you can, I will give you a big kiss."

"Sadie, right here in front of my uncle and the doctor?"

"Yep! Come on Joshua, come give me a kiss. It will be worth your while, I promise."

He looks at the men holding him up. "If I make it to her, please avert your eyes. This will be only our second kiss and I'd like it to be in private."

Chilly says, "I promise. How about you doc?"

"Of course, Joshua, you'll have all the privacy you need. Well, while we are still in the room."

Chilly asks the question. "What's the number?"

"It is at seven, but if I can get to Sadie's lips, I expect that number to go down to a five or three."

Sadie responds, "You honor me. Just get here! Two more steps then I will come two steps, because I love you, you crazy white man who acts like an Indian. I have never said those words to any other man." She takes two giant steps to him and puts her arms around his neck. "Gentlemen, close your eyes. Joshua, keep yours open." She puts her lips on his.

"Yes, this is helping. I think my pain went down to a four. But I'd like to go back to the bed. Sadie, can you sit next to me?"

"I thought you'd never ask."

"Doc, as soon as we get my nephew back to his bed, I think we can let Sadie manage the rest." Chilly says.

"I agree. He will be in very good hands."

When they are alone, Sadie sits down next to Joshua. "Joshua, you know that I am in love with you, right?"

"Yes, you just admitted to it. If you are going to ask me for my feelings . . ."

"No, I am going to go on faith, that you are an honorable man and that when I tell you my secret, you will do what you feel is necessary."

"Sadie, I do have feelings for you. Very strong ones. Why do I feel that what you are about to tell me, is going to try to change that?"

"I pray it doesn't." She gets off the bed, slowly, so not to cause him discomfort. She walks to the other side of the bed to get the wooden chair. She brings it to face him and sits in it. She takes his hands, and holds them. "Nothing went according, to the plan. It was supposed to go without a hitch, but nothing went smoothly."

"What are you talking about, Sadie?"

"The stagecoach, Joshua. I was in on it, also. I was approached in Bartlesville by the man calling himself Rusty Banner. He said that I could earn $50 if I keep any ladies on the coach, out of the way and safe while he pretends Indians are robbing it."

Joshua stands up, by himself. "Sadie, do not tell me anything more. Go get Chilly. I love you, but, I do not want to keep secrets from my Uncle. He will do as he sees fit, and I will abide by his decision. If you were not in on the planning, then you . . . I must sit down. I think I . . . might pass . . . out again."

"Harkahomé, please sit. Let me help you." She manages to get him back to the bed. As soon as his bottom, touches the mattress, he passes out. Sadie manages to get him laid back down, then she yells for the doctor.

With the doctor at Joshua's side, Sadie goes back to the hotel to get Chilly. She looks at the wall clock in the lobby. It is noon. She knows from Brenda that she might be disturbing their lunchtime marital activities. She doesn't want to tell him, at all, but she doesn't dare disturb his pleasure to tell him her dreaded secret.

She sat in the lobby and wiggled in the tufted chair for an hour. Finally, Chilly came down the stairs with a mile-wide smile on his face. When he sees the look on Sadie's face, his smile disappears. "Sadie, what's wrong? Is it Joshua?"

"No, it's me, actually. I would like to talk to you – with Harkahomé and Brenda, present, if possible."

Chilly looks to the wall clock. "She um, might be napping. I will wake her. Go back to the clinic. We will meet you there. Okay?"

"Thank you, Chilly. I am sorry to be bothering you and Brenda, like this. At least, I waited. I have been down here for a while, but I did not want to disturb you."

"Thanks for that, at least. I will be there as soon as possible." He turns to go back up the stairs. He turns back around. "Sadie, we care for you. Not just because we see that you love Joshua, but because you helped us get together. Whatever is going on, we will help you."

"I hope so Chilly. I really do." She turns to leave. She hurries back to the clinic and her nerves take over. She has her hand on the doorknob and her stomach lurches. She suddenly feels very sick to her stomach. *I do not need to vomit, right now!* She thinks. *What am I going to do! If Chilly wants to put me in jail, Joshua will let him, and that isn't the worst thing. I was so stupid! Why did I let those men do this to me! I must get control of myself!* She straightens out her shoulders and turns the knob. She goes through the doorway to Joshua's room. He is laying, peacefully. The doctor is elsewhere.

She walks to the chair across from him and sits, looking at him. *He will hate me, once he knows. I have lied to him and everybody this whole time. What kind of person am I?"* She is wringing her hands with worry.

"A penny for your thoughts?" Joshua says peaking at her. When she doesn't answer right away, he adds, "Are you mad at me for telling you to go get Chilly?"

"No Joshua, I wanted to tell you, privately first. Including Chilly is just more embarrassing, but you are right, I need to tell him, also." She gives Joshua a weak smile. "I just hope . . . well, I hope that we can . . . I just don't want things to change between us. I know that they will and I am already grieving over it."

Joshua goes to move and groans. "Sadie, come closer." She moves the chair back to his bedside. He takes her hand. "You may not have heard me say it, but I love you. That is not something that can be altered easily. We all have had past lives and incidents that we feel someone else could never understand or forgive. I was in love, once before. I did not tell you about her because I was ashamed. She said that she loved me, also, but her actions proved otherwise."

"Harkahomé, you are such a good man. She was an idiot, not to love you, whatever her reasons, that was not your fault. You should not take it personally."

"You have to take it personally if you were the one she was rejecting. It was my Indian lifestyle. Her father did not think it appropriate for his white daughter to marry a white man turned Indian."

"Her loss is my gain. You would still be with the Cheyenne if you had her as a wife and a family, there."

"I felt alone, after my mother died. Everyone else had started families but me. So, I thought that family is what I should seek out. Chilly was always my best pal. It was natural for me to find him first."

"Did you call me, or were you talking about me?" Chilly and Brenda walk into the room arm in arm.

"Uncle, Auntie. So good of you to visit. I think my Sadie has something to get off her chest. As soon as she mentioned the stagecoach, I made her stop talking to get you. Everyone should get a chair. I think this will take a while."

It takes several moments for everyone to get situated. When everyone is seated and Joshua is holding Sadie's hand, he says. "Go ahead, Sadie. Start from the beginning. We will try not to interrupt you."

"Well, you know that Lee Kirby hired me and paid my traveling expenses to get to Pennysville. I mentioned my leaving to some men while dealing blackjack in Wichita. One of the men was Rusty Banner, also known as Jason Williams. He said that he wanted to talk with me before we were to ride the stage. I met with him and he told me that he would give me $50 if I would keep the women on the stage, safe and sound during the hold-up. He gave me $25 then and promised the other $25 after the hold-up. So, when he started shooting out the window and the other man did, too, I screamed about being raped by Indians and told the other women to hide themselves. I kept them down the entire time as directed. Sorry, Brenda. After we stopped and Banner said that we could get out, he asked Brenda and Martha, if they saw anything. When they both said no, he slipped me the other half of what he owed me."

"That does not sound too bad. Why didn't you come forward, before this?" Chilly asks.

"I needed the $50! I knew that I wouldn't be able to work for Lee for very long and I needed the money – I um . . . am with child. I found out just days before I met Lee. Starting in a new town, with no one who knew me, sounded like the perfect way to escape. I was going to pretend that my husband had run off or something. Then the robbery happened and I met you both and well, I never got around to inventing that absentee husband. Now, I am going to be showing in another month, and I will not be able to keep it a secret after that. I wanted to come clean about everything to all of you. If I was going to get into trouble for the stagecoach participation, I knew it should be before my baby comes."

"Did anyone else know about the fifty dollars? Scott Jones or one of the employees?" Chilly asked

"I do not know. Rusty only spoke about it when we were alone."

"Well, I am not going to arrest you or file any charges. If Rusty, I mean Jason Williams mentions it, I will say that I knew and that you donated the money with my blessing." Chilly says as he stands up. "The other matter is not my official concern. You and Joshua need to discuss this without Brenda and I." He holds out his hand for Brenda. "My dear?"

"Chilly, I want a minute with Sadie if I can. Can she and I go into the other room for a moment. Joshua, I will bring her right back."

"I will be here for her, Brenda." Joshua lays his head down. After Sadie and Brenda go out into the hall he says, "I think my head pain is more intense than my pelvis pain."

Chilly looks down at his nephew. "Do you need medicine?"

"After Sadie and I talk for a little bit, please."

"I don't want to be in your moccasins right now."

"Nothing has changed. I love her. She did somethings before she met me. I have done things, also. We will live with the consequences, together."

"Are you sure, you want to raise another man's baby?"

"I was raised by Kanuna. Adoption is a very accepted practice among the Cheyenne. I will not feel any different toward the babe as I would if he were my child. He will be a part of the woman that I love. Period."

"You are an exceptional man, nephew."

"I agree." Joshua says. "But a man with a huge headache."

Chilly sits back down and waits for his bride. A few minutes go by before she comes back into the room. He can tell that she and Sadie have been crying. He stands and goes to his wife. "Shall we give them some privacy?"

"Yes, husband." Brenda says. Sadie has crossed the room to Joshua's side. He holds out his hand for her and she takes it and sits back down next to him. "I do not think that they need our help at this point." Sadie looks up at Brenda and smiles.

"Thank you both." Then she turns to Joshua. "Harkahomé?"

"Yes, my love."

"That is what I needed to hear. I am still your love?" She lets out a big breath as Brenda and Chilly depart.

"Sadie, I cannot see my future without you in it. You and your – no – OUR baby. As soon as we get to Pennysville, will you marry me and share my blanket, for the rest of our lives?"

"I never dreamt that after I lie to you, you would forgive me then ask me to marry you. You are an exceptional man, Harkahomé!"

"I must be, you are the second person that I love, that has told me that today."

"You'd be surprised at how much Chilly and I are alike."

"Yes, but who do you love?"

"Only you, my Indian."

"So, is that a yes to my proposal?"

"I don't deserve you, but yes. I will marry you."

"Come lay down next to me. I have a headache and would like some laudanum but if you massage my temple and whisper that you love me until I fall asleep. I am sure that I will be a new man when I wake." He groans as he moves over in the small pallet for her to lay next to him.

Sadie carefully gets into the bed. "I don't want you to be a new man, Joshua. I love the old one, too much." Joshua smiles. Sadie adds, "What will I tell the Doctor when he comes in and sees me in your bed?"

Joshua gives a small laugh. "Sadie, I don't think anyone has ever had to help you with what to say."

"You know me so well, Harkahomé"

"Not yet, but I have the rest of my life to do so."

FORTY-NINE
February 6th, 1959
A Friday in Chicago, Illinois

The tiny apartment on south Paulina has had a whirlwind of activity from all the Harrick's. Anna and Carrie have been sewing. Clara Beth decided to finish out her school year and graduate with Oliver. Her Aunt Carolyn has offered her a job in her firm. She is an inventor and has patented many farm saving devices and Clara's dream has always been to work for her. She will be moving to the 'little house' that was the Colonel's first home, as well as her parents'. Oliver has said that he will follow her wherever she goes. He will be sending out applications to Medical Schools around Lawrence shortly.

Carrie does not want to continue her studies. She says that she can go back later if she wants, but for now she just wants to design. Anna has been doing most of the sewing, but has not been able to keep Carrie off the machine for long. She has cut the jacket pieces out and has begun the assembly of it.

Anna is amazed that she knows exactly how to size something by looking at it. "Thank God, that your eyes are better. I see how much you love this work. But the doctor told you to not work so much with your eyes. Please listen to him."

"Mama, he also said that my eyes will tell me if I am overdoing it. I will feel strain or get a headache. I have not come close to either of those. Isn't this blue silk fabric beautiful? It is a little difficult to sew but it is so worth the hassle. I wish that I had time to sew the red dress for Aunt Melinda. I think I had her in mind all along."

"You both are the same size and shape. You may look like me, my girl, but from the neck down, you are Melinda. Lucky duck!"

"Clara and I were discussing that during our shut-in days of the snow storm. That seems like a lifetime ago. It took me so much time to unpack and here I am packing it all back up in just a month's time."

"I am sorry, Carrie, that this has turned out like this." Anna says.

"Believe it or not, Mama, I am not sorry. It has made me look at what and who is important. Moving back home for a few months and dating GW here and there is the right move. If I went to Lawrence right away, I would feel like he is second prize. I am not choosing him by comparison. I am choosing him, because I have always been in love with him. Absolutely, always. I feel like moving to Chicago forced us both to examine our feelings and act upon them."

"So much, in such a short time." Anna says. "The University has reimbursed us the tuition, since you attended less than a month's worth of classes and they failed to protect you from Mickey. Your father is using that money to buy a large van, so that we can all drive home together. We will leave this weekend, if you get everything repacked."

"I wish that GW and Uncle Joshua could have stayed longer." Carrie says. "I know that he missed a week of school. With his class load, that's a lot of work."

"He is very smart. He will have it made up in no time. He has always been a hard worker. Very determined, too. Did you hear his plan of finishing in three years with a double major? Then interning for a year with your father and his own?"

"Yes, I could not believe it. I am amazed by him. I didn't know that he was doing that until . . . you know, we started calling each other."

"Carrie, the skirt is just about finished. Look at how beautiful it is. The overstitching at the seams is a great idea. It makes sort of a ruffle but it isn't a ruffle. I don't care how great the school is, they cannot teach creativity like this."

"Thank you, Mama! What do you want for dinner tonight? I think I have everything in the house."

"Anything would be wonderful. I'll ask your father when he gets back. He might want pizza pie. You can go say good-bye to your friend, Gianni."

"Mama, if it wasn't for GW, I would be dating that boy. He is a cutie!"

"Are you sure that you do not want to date other boys, Carrie? You are very young and don't have a lot of experience with the opposite sex."

"Mama, how many boys did you date before you were married? Father and one date with Uncle Joshua? So, do not lecture me on limited experience. You did not marry father because you went shopping around. You married him because He was the One."

There is a knocking on the front door. Carrie gets up and looks through the peephole. "It's Daddy!" she announces. She opens the door for him.

"Do you want to see our chariot? I think I got a very good deal. I even have enough left over to go out to dinner. Italian tonight, Baby Girl?"

"Yes, Daddy, I would love that. Mom just suggested that, also. Clara Beth always has date night with Oliver on Fridays, so it might be just us. Tomorrow, we are having Chinese! My treat, I want you both to see Chinatown before we leave Chicago."

***

At Como's restaurant, Sophia seats them. "I heard about your misfortune. I am so sorry. Who knew that nice looking young man would be so stünod? That means stupid. He is in jail, I hope."

"Yes, Sophia. The police took the gun out of his hand, just as he shot me. It just grazed my skull. I have a neat scar under this hat, if you'd like to see it."

"I will live without looking, please."

"Sophia, these are my parents, Anna and Henry. Is your brother, Gianni, working tonight? I will be moving back to Kansas in a few days and I wanted to say good bye."

"He is out on deliveries. He will be back. I will send him directly to your table. What can I make for the family? Pasta? Pizza? Brizole's? Pasta fageoli? Need time to look at our menu? I will be back. Colas to drink, everyone?" At this they all shake their heads. "Good, I make for you the Sodas." After she walks away, Carrie giggles.

"I noticed that her Italian accent got thicker the more she talked. Her older brother doesn't talk like that."

Henry offers, "Maybe she is around the Italian speaking relatives more."

Anna says, "I am starving. What have you had here, Carrie?"

"I have had pizza and spaghetti and meatballs. They are both so good. I cannot decide which to get. But I know that I am getting Cannoli for dessert. Mama, they are to die for!"

They order food and they eat with hardly saying a word. Everything that they ordered was delicious. Anna says, "I would love to offer some of this type of food in Kansas. Our restaurants could expand their menu to include Italian and Chinese for that matter."

Gianni comes up to the table. "My favorite gunshot victim! Sophia says that you are leaving Chicago. I am very sad. You have been one of our best customers in the short time that you have been here."

"Gianni, this is my mama Anna and my father, Henry. I mentioned that Mama owns two restaurants and she is interested in expanding her menu to include Italian dishes. Could you give her some advice, recipes or actually come out and teach her how to cook these dishes?"

"Go out to Kansas? Will you be there, my little Carrie?"

"Yes, I will be living there. What do you think?"

"I think if your Mama thinks that Kansas needs an Italian restaurant, then Como's needs to open one, for ourselves. Where is your town in Kansas?"

"EL Dorado. It is south of Wichita."

"Leave me all your contact information Mrs. Carrie's mother. I will be in touch. Como's can venture into Kansas, especially if we have a business partner. Leave it to me, I will talk with my father and my uncles. They are the ones that started this business. I am very excited to discuss this with them. I have wanted to start my own place but then I would be in competition with my own family. I have no family in Kansas."

Anna opens her purse and takes out a notebook and writes. Then she tears off the page and hands it to Gianni. "I look forward to hearing from you, Gianni Como. This will be very good for us both, I am sure."

"And then I know that I will see Miss Carrie, again." He says with a blush.

"Gianni, I am practically engaged. I think I have mentioned that to you?"

"Yes, you did. But you are so pretty, like your Mama. I never like to see a pretty woman leave my life. We can still be friends, now." Without another word, he turns around and walks back into the kitchen. The little family can hear Italian being spoken by Gianni and Sophia and some other voices join in.

"I think we have caused a family problem in there." Henry says.

"I don't think it is a problem, Daddy. They always talk like that!" She laughs and when Sophia comes out of the kitchen Carrie calls her over. "Are they upset in there?"

"Oh, that? No, Gianni is missing a pizza for his next order, is all. Why should anyone be upset? Kansas will be a nice place for a new Como's!"

259

FIFTY
February 7th, 1896
A Friday in Nowata, Oklahoma

Lee Kirby's carriage is waiting in front of the clinic. It is time to leave Nowata for good. Harkahomé has been walking every day. His pain level is at a three most days. Dr. Peters has given a vial of laudanum to Joshua to take if traveling becomes too difficult. The doctor has examined Brenda and Sadie and has confirmed both pregnancies to be healthy. Harkahomé is very excited that his child will be older than Chilly's child, he knows that they will be best friends for life.

The driver that brought them has since gone back to Pennysville. Chilly and Brenda are now familiar with the route from Nowata and plan to drive the carriage, themselves. This will leave the whole seat for Joshua to recline and have Sadie attend him. Sadie purchased a small set of pillows and crudely sewed them together for him to sit on. She brought them into the clinic and when he saw them, he laughed. "You were not kidding when you said that you couldn't sew. I think I could have done better with my eyes closed."

"Oh, Joshua! You are so mean. Don't I get an E for effort? I sewed it with love in each stitch as your mother did."

"In that case, the look of the stitches matters not at all. I loved that you thought to do this for me. Thank you." He bends over to give her a kiss on her cheek. She turns to meet his lips and they stay together for a moment. He has been standing for several minutes. "Are you all packed for the trip to Pennysville?"

"Yes, I have given everything to Chilly to put it on the luggage rack on the carriage. I am ready to wipe the dust of this town off my boots. Not that this was a bad place . . . just bad memories. Seeing you so hurt, broke my heart. And during your recovery, I was eaten up inside with the secret that I needed to share. Doc thinks that I lost weight due to morning sickness but I have not been nauseated to the point of vomiting. I have been too nervous to eat anything between worrying over your pain and my secret."

"I would not have had you suffer so, over me." He was standing since she came in, and he was getting fatigued. "I hope I will not hinder our travel with my weakness."

"We are not in any hurry, dear. We will only go as fast as you can handle it." Chilly walks into Joshua's room. "Chilly, tell this Indian that we are not in any hurry and that causing him pain is not what we want."

"We don't want to cause you pain. We will stop at any time you feel uncomfortable. If we need to camp out three nights, to get home, we will. Are you ready to get into the carriage? Brenda has gathered many provisions. We will eat and drink non-stop for the look of the amount of food." Joshua has the pillows in his hand. "I have my love's cushions. So, this is as good a time as any to load up and go."

The doctor has a chair on wheels to convey his patient to the waiting carriage. "I must say that I will miss this little family unit. I am glad to have met you, good luck to you all." He says as he helps his patient into the carriage. Once the pillows are placed across the seat. Joshua gently places his buttocks down. He smiles at the doctor.

"Thank you for all that you did for me. I wouldn't have survived the fall and rifle shot without your expertise."

"Thank you for saying that. We don't get to hear that in cases as bad as yours. I wish that you would wait one more week to travel, but if anyone can handle it, it will be you! You are the strongest person that I have ever met."

Sadie is getting into the carriage on the opposite

side. "He is very strong, but oh, so gentle, too. Did he tell you that we are getting married?"

"I figured you would be at some point, but since your second kiss was just last week, I thought that might take some time. Have you set a date?"

Chilly offers, "How about next Saturday? That will give us a chance to get home, and arrange a nice affair. Brenda and I married within hours of my asking her. I feel like she was cheated out of a grand reception."

Joshua says, "Why don't you get married with us? I missed the first event. How do I know if you are really married?" He turns to his fiancé. "Will you share your wedding with Brenda and Chilly, Sadie? We would have a double wedding for whole town to remember."

"I don't know enough people in Pennysville to have any guests if we didn't share the date. So, Uncle and Auntie, I would love to share my wedding with you." Sadie says, happily.

FIFTY-ONE
February 9th, 1959
A Monday in EL Dorado, Kansas

It is late in the night that Henry pulls into the driveway of their home. They live on the same street as Anna's brother Matthew and his family and her sister, Melinda and her family. Harry has been staying with the Collins family. His cousin Jude is a few years older but are very close. Harry loved having him as an older brother, if only temporarily.

As soon as Carrie gets out of the van, the family descends on them. Anna's parents, Judd and Judy live with Melinda's family, so they were at their house immediately. It was an impromptu block party, even with the chill of February and the lateness of the hour.

Carrie is being kissed and hugged and hugged some more. Her grandmother Judy, is extremely emotional and cannot stop crying. "We were so worried. I barely survived your mother's ordeal, but this my precious little one, almost was my undoing." She strokes her face, coming so close to her newly healed scar. "It is hardly noticeable. Your mother's wounds were far worse. That was the only good thing about her being missing for a year. We did not see her suffer daily from her wounds and scars." Judy says. "It was its own sort of hell, hearing that she was dead but not being able to lay her to rest. Your father could never bring himself to believe that she was gone. His belief kept us hopeful for a full year. Sorry, here I am rambling on like an old fool. God bless you and keep you, my little Carrie. Such a relief that you are back home, where you are loved by many. Come, I baked a cake. You're too skinny."

Anna had Melinda keep an eye on the restaurant for her. She has a fully trained staff so it was just overseeing that everyone came and went as scheduled. "Did anything

263

interesting happen at the restaurant that I need to know about?"

"Nope, everything continued as mundane as ever."

Even with all the aunts, uncles and cousins in the house, Carrie manages to sneak to her parents' room to use the phone to call GW. They have not talked since she left Chicago on Saturday. She wants to let him know that they arrived safe and sound. She dials all the numbers and waits on the line.

Helen answers the phone, "Legacy Plantation, Helen speaking."

"Aunt Helen, I am sorry for the late call, but I just arrived in EL Dorado and I wanted GW to know I am safe and sound."

"We were expecting you to call, Carrie. GW just took the garbage out for me. He will be right in. GW said that the dress that you are making is so very beautiful. Next year, you will be making so many dresses! This ball will be your unveiling. I will make sure that anyone who is anyone will want to wear a gown designed by the newest designer in Kansas."

"That is very nice of you, Aunt. I hope to be able to live up to all the confidence that you have in me."

"You are your mother's daughter. How can I NOT have confidence in you? Here comes your boyfriend. GW, Carrie is on the line. She is in EL Dorado." She hands the phone off and can be heard, "I will give you a little privacy."

"Carrie, it is good of you to call tonight. Is it crazy over there?"

"You have no idea. I have so many relatives on this block! Everyone is here and celebrating. I feel like I am on the 'Queen for the Day' show. Food is coming out of the woodwork. I had to tell my Gram that I was shot, not starving on a desert island!"

"I wish I was there. I love your family."

"Good, cuz I love you."

"Darn, you beat me to saying it. We will all descend

on EL Dorado on Thursday to get ready for the ball. Is your dress finished?"

"I still have the coat to finish. I will work on that tomorrow. The rest is done. I could not have done it without mother. She was my eyes and wouldn't let me do too much."

"As per doctor's orders, I recall. Can I see you for dinner, Thursday? We can make it our first date."

"Yes! Yes! I was wondering if I would have to wait until the ball for our first date. I cannot wait, GW. Now what shall I wear?"

"As I think that I mentioned, a potato sack would look beautiful on you."

"And as I mentioned, I can get a potato sack from Mama's restaurant. And I can make it look heavenly."

"I have no doubt, what-so-ever! I plan on wearing dark trousers and a long sleeve shirt and possibly a tie."

"You'd better wear a tie!"

"Why? So, that I am dressed, properly?"

"No, so if you try to get away, I have something to grab."

"You'll have no trouble with me trying to get away. I am yours for life, as I have been yours for life, so far."

"Sounds just like the Colonel's letters."

"Have you read them?"

"Yes, didn't I tell you that? Mother brought them home for Clara to read when she was sixteen or so. I read them all over, and over, again. Your great-grandfather was a true romantic and not afraid to admit it." Carrie says.

"Once I got the courage up to admit it, I haven't stopped. I have loved you for longer than I can remember. There isn't a happy memory from my childhood that doesn't have you in it. At least until we were six, that is."

"Then it was only sadness." Carrie admits. "I thought that I would die, from missing you."

"Thank God you didn't!"

"GW, I hear my mom looking for me. I must get

back to the party. See you Thursday. Call me when you get in and let me know what time you'll pick me up. I love you!"

"Good night, Carrie. I love you, too."

FIFTY-TWO
February 10th 1896
A Monday in Pennysville, Oklahoma

The road back from Nowata, was bumpy and filled Joshua with pain. He was at ten or twelve after the first hour on the road. Each toss of the carriage would bring new tears to his eyes. He didn't want to have Chilly stop, so he took a few drops of the laudanum. He soon is lulled to sleep. Sadie sat with his head on her lap. She is so relieved that he has not thought less of her because of her past.

They are making good time this morning and Chilly wants to stop and have a long lunch. Joshua is waking up from his morning nap and Chilly lifts him out of the carriage and puts him down on a large tree stump. The women make a pot of coffee. Chilly and Brenda take a stroll to look for game. Brenda sees two small rabbits, and shoots one while Chilly shoots the other one. Chilly had them skinned, put on sticks and in the fire in no time.

Sadie and Joshua are tending the fire while Brenda and Chilly went back out for some alone time. Joshua is awake but feeling no pain as his morning medicine wears off. He is poking at the fire under the rabbits. Sadie looks at him. "Harkahomé, do you want to ask me questions about my condition?"

"I know how it is done, if that is what you mean? I have not shared a blanket myself yet, but I know what happens under it."

"You have never done it?" She asks. "Not with the missionary's daughter, either?"

"No, with her, I wanted to wait until her father said the Christian words over us, making us man and wife. Did you think that you were going to be man and wife, but it didn't work out?"

"I wish." She picks up the stick and turns the

rabbit to get it cooked on the other side. "I was forced. I thought that the man was a man of God. He was trying to get me to have a better line of work, other than working in a saloon. He argued with me over it and followed me to my room. It was there that he beat me and did it to me. I wasn't exactly pure, mind you, but this child is the result of that horrible event."

Joshua moves closer to her. "Did you report the man, who did that to you?" He puts his arm around her.

"It would have been my word against his. He was a bible thumper and I was a saloon girl. He made sure that he only hit me where it doesn't show. He was very mad. He thought that I should have quit my job and go on the road with him and his bibles . . . Me? Can you see me going from town to town, talking about God the whole time? That is as opposite of my personality that he could have chosen for me to be."

"He saw what he wanted to see, then when you refused, he only saw his anger. And yet, a life came from that encounter. A life that will be ours and ours, alone." He caresses her face. "I am sorry that you went through that. Did that man leave the town or did he stay until you left?"

"He came and went. He tried to come after me a few weeks later but my manager caught him trying to pull me up the stairs and he got rough with him. Seems that he didn't like it when the shoe was on the other foot. He left and never came back. Then I discovered I was with child and I met Lee Kirby. Things would have worked out, if it wasn't for the stagecoach robbery. I would have started lying about a husband that ran out on me and no one would have been any wiser. I couldn't do that after I met you. I was fascinated by you. You looked and sounded like a white man but acted and talked like an Indian. My heart beat differently when I was with you. My stomach fluttered. Then I remembered that I was with child and thought that I should try to leave town while you were gone. But you got hurt and all that I could think about was going to you. It tore at me to see you so hurt."

"Knowing that a man hurt you tears me up. How could a man think that he could take a woman like that? The act should be for love not hate. If I ever got my hands on that man, I do not know what I would do to him."

"God forbid that you ever meet him. What a hypocrite he was! Man of God, my Ass!"

"Sadie! You shock me!" He laughs. "It's not the first time, either."

"Sorry, Joshua. You must know, I was not raised genteel-like. I say what I think, and most of the time, that proves that I am NO lady."

"That is why I love you. You are the smartest, no nonsense LADY that I have ever met. White or Cheyenne!"

"Say that again, Harkahomé."

"Which part?" He smiles and reaches out to pinch her cheek. "That is why I love you! You are the smartest, no nonsense LADY that I have ever met. White or Cheyenne! Are you blushing, Sadie Mae Miller?"

"I am not used to real compliments. Or real love. Just an occasional guy pretending to be in love with me to get what he wanted. I am sorry that I have given in and shared a blanket or two, before I met you."

"You know, with my injury, I do not know when I will be able to be a full husband to you. It might not be on our wedding night. It may be too soon. I might not be healed enough."

"Harkahomé, that is completely unacceptable! I demand more from you, if you think I am going to share your blanket, just to sleep!" Then Sadie starts to laugh. Joshua's face still showed shock at her outburst but he begins to laugh, also.

"I thought that I would not lead you on." He tries to say while laughing. "In case, you were expecting something more."

"Joshua, you are an awesome man and I love you so

much. You are giving me your name and a stranger's baby a home. I will love you under that blanket, whether you can ever make love to me or not." She leans over and kisses him lightly at first then with more passion.

He can feel certain feelings rising. He has been attracted to her from the moment they met. He wants to give himself to her, but the pain was too much. He breaks away. "See Sadie, it's too soon." She looks down at her hands but notices something in his lap.

"Joshua Harkahomé Lewis, your love arrow is showing!" They both look down and laugh.

"MOST of me is willing and most likely able. Just not all of me!" He is turning red.

Chilly and Brenda come back to camp. "We found a small stream, not far from here. Are the rabbits ready? After we eat, I'd like to fill our canteens before we journey the rest of the way. Harkahomé, Sadie, I think you both are sitting too close to the fire. You are all red!"

This makes them laugh, all over again.

***

After their leisurely rabbit lunch, the group had some hard traveling to do to get to Pennysville. They arrive just before ten o'clock in the evening. Deputy Elliot is awaiting their arrival. He has Dr. Cassidy meet the carriage as it pulls up to Penny's Parlor and Saloon.

Chilly shouts down from the top of the carriage, "I don't know how you do it, Elliot. You always seem to know when something or someone arrives in town. Do you have a divining rod in your leg, or something?" Chilly is getting down and is helping his bride down also.

"I don't know what you mean, Sheriff. I was just taking a stroll with the doc, here. Then you show up."

"However you knew, Elliot, thank you. Doc, Joshua is in the carriage. I will carry him out for you. He will be either in a lot of pain or unable to talk from the laudanum." He opens wide the door to the carriage to find Joshua in Sadie's arms.

"Close the door a minute, Chilly. We were right in the middle of something." Sadie says.

"Hate to bother you love birds, but I have the doc here to examine your fiancé. Now shall I help him out?"

"Chilly, your timing is awful. Go ahead, take my Indian and have him checked out. I have some wedding planning to do. Tell your wife that I will meet her tomorrow after breakfast for shopping for wedding dresses." She looks to Joshua. "And some lingerie for the honeymoon." Joshua blushes.

"Sadie, you say the darndest things! Do you have a filter? Or does every thought just tumble out of your mouth?" Chilly kids her as he is lifting Joshua.

"Now, Sheriff. We both know that I have kept some things very private. I just like to shock people. It is just so much fun to watch their reactions."

"That is the reason, I do not know if I like the idea of your hanging around my wife."

"On this, you and your mother-in-law agree." Sadie gives him a wink.

FIFTY-THREE
February 10th, 1959
A Tuesday in EL Dorado, Kansas

The last of the relatives left the Harrick home near midnight. Everyone had pitched in and unloaded the van. Most of the boxes were put in their garage, until Carrie decides to unpack them. Anna and Henry were up at their usual time, six in the morning. Anna let the children sleep in. Harry should be off to school at eight, but Anna was going to let him attend only a half a day. The homecoming was very hard on Carrie, after the long hours of being on the road, so Anna has no plans on waking her.

Henry and Anna are sitting at their breakfast nook. After he has his breakfast, he wants to organize the boxes and possibly bring a few inside. Anna says, "Everything is so very taxing on Carrie. I do not want to rush her into unpacking. She was talking about going to live with Clara at the little house in Lawrence. If I unpack for her, she might feel that I am pushing her to stay."

"I don't think she will think that. She knows we like to be organized and that we help her with everything. Besides, Clara doesn't start work with Carolyn until the middle of May, after she graduates." Henry says.

"It seems so odd that they will all be in Lawrence with us in EL Dorado. Carrie's life is repeating my own so closely. Realizing that her childhood best friend is the love of her life, then having another suiter hurt her brain. And because of that she will end up in Lawrence." Anna notes.

"Yes, but thank God she didn't have a year of agony, not knowing who she was, plus she wasn't raped. Again, THANK YOU, GOD."

"Yes, that is a blessing!" Anna says then remains silent.

"Are you going to the restaurant, today?" Henry asks to change the awful subject from the event that haunted Anna's nightmares for years.

"Yes, after Harry goes to school, I thought. It seems so odd to have been away from it for so long. Melinda said that everything flowed well in my absence. No one quit, no one got poisoned. We only broke even on some days but we made a profit on all the rest. I should let her stay in charge, she did so well."

"Like you'd be able to stay away! You don't stay away from the Lawrence Diner for more than two weeks and you have had a great manager there since we left."

"Very true. We should think about going in on the Italian restaurant with Gianni. He seems like a very capable young man."

A voice says from the kitchen doorway. "I know that he wants to get away from doing all the winter deliveries. His Papa and Uncles hardly let him cook, because they love the kitchen, so."

"Carrie, why don't you stay in bed, a little longer. You must be exhausted. Yesterday must have been very taxing. The long hours on the road, then all the family over until late last night." Anna jumps up and goes to her miniature look alike. "Do you want me to make you breakfast?"

"No, Mama. Just coffee for now." Carrie says as Henry has poured her a cup and delivered it to her normal place at the table, as she is sitting down. "Thank you, Daddy. Mama, I think that you should seriously consider opening an Italian restaurant. Como's does a whopping business. EL Dorado is small but if we open it just outside of the city on the north end, we might attract folks escaping the city of Wichita for the day."

Henry says, "That is a very good idea, Carrie. Had you been pondering on it for long?"

"Nope, just came to me. Daddy, can you bring my sewing machine in today? I'd like to finish my jacket. Mama, do you think between the two of us we can make Aunt Melinda's red gown for the ball? She took in Harry and ran your restaurant while you were gone. I'd like to repay her with a gift."

"That is very thoughtful, but she wouldn't want you to take on such a project for her so soon and with so little time before the ball."

"What else do I have to do? I want to keep busy. I didn't sleep very good last night. Mickey kept pervading my dreams turning them into nightmares. As tired as I was last night, I fell asleep quickly but woke from my dreams and then could not fall back asleep. Either I dreamt that he is still on the loose or I relived the struggle with the gun, then it going off." She starts to cry.

Anna goes to her. "I lived through that for years, even when I didn't know what happened to me, I had nightmares. I would wake up not remembering what I dreamt but I would be near panic when I woke. Time, and good memories eventually replaced the bad ones. You should wake me when that happens. I could come hold you. After we were married, is when the full memory of the beating and rape, came back and many nights, your father had to hold me tight after a nightmare."

"Explains why Clara was born so soon, after your marriage."

"Yes, it does." Henry says smiling. "Good came from the bad."

"Daddy!" says Carrie.

"Henry!" says Anna at the same time.

"What? She said it first." He looks at Anna. Then he turns back to his daughter, "You should call your mother. No one understands better, what you are going through."

"I know and I am sorry for that, too. I know that my event has brought back many unpleasant memories."

"They do not haunt me anymore, Baby Girl. Too many good ones have taken their place."

"Good. So, what do you think about Aunt Melinda's dress? We'd have to get her here to get her exact measurements, and she could help sew, if she had to, she is good with sewing."

"That is true, if the three of us work together, it can be done, quickly. Fine, I will call her and see if she wants to participate. If she does not, then NO dress. That is my final decision. It is the three musketeers or nothing." Anna says with her hands on her hips.

Carrie is up and is at the phone in the kitchen, dialing. "I am thrilled." She finishes the number and it is answered on the first ring. "Aunt Melinda, how would you like that red dress for the Ball?"

"Yes. But, how could you?" Melinda asks.

"Mama and I think that if you come here today and we measure you, I could do the calculations for the material we need. Once we have the material, if all three of us cut and sew, you'll have a new dress to wear. Mama says that if you do not help with some of it, the deal is off. I really want to do this, Auntie. Please say yes."

"Why not? I would love that dress, it is beyond gorgeous! I can be there in less than an hour. Luckily, sewing is one of the few domestic activities that I share with my mother and sister. And I like to do it, but I rarely take the time. I am so excited. I am going to be the bell of the ball. Well, after you, anyway. I will make sure that EVERYONE knows that you designed it, too. Your business will just take off, my dear!"

"My thoughts, exactly."

"That is my smart niece."

"I have my family's business sense, at least."

"Very true. Okay, enough chatter, I need to get ready. I have a date with my designer! See you in a bit, Carrie Ann."

"Yup, see you in a bit." Carrie says as she replaces the receiver. "See Mama, I knew that she wanted that dress. I am going to go get dressed. Aunt Melinda will be here shortly."

"You, sly devil, I think I was just played. Did you

and Aunt Melinda talk about this, last night?"

Carrie smiles, "Whatever do you mean, Mama?" Then she shrugs her shoulders. "I really need to get dressed." She turns and leaves.

Henry looks at his wife. "She is one smart cookie. And she always calls Clara the smart Harrick girl. They are smart in very different ways."

"I feel used by what just happened. She is clever at manipulating people."

"Whatever gets the job done. I see all wins in this situation. The three of you get to work together, Melinda will get the dress she wants, and Carrie will get her designs known to all the who's-who's in town. I am proud of my girl and she hasn't started sewing, yet."

"You would be. She has always been your Baby Girl."

"I don't play favorites, Anna."

Anna just smiles. "If you say so, my dear Henry."

***

An hour later, Melinda is in the kitchen of Anna's house, being measured by Anna then Carrie Ann. She is standing with a cup of coffee in her hand and the sketch in the other. Carrie had asked if there were any changes needed to the design. Anna was on the phone in the other room on restaurant business.

Melinda says, "Could I be so daring? I would like the neckline to be more heart shaped. You know that the top half of a heart is two ovals slanted together with a deep v between them. I want my v very deep, if you can do it."

"With your fabulous figure, Auntie, that would work out beautifully."

"Our figure, Baby Girl. You are blessed with my curves, don't forget. We are the lucky ones. You can borrow from my closet, anytime you like."

"I am not as comfortable with my curves, as you

are, Auntie. I think I will keep them safe guarded under lock and key, for now."

"You don't have my adventurous spirt, though. I wanted to get away from everything at your age."

"Auntie, it was the Depression! You had lost your home, and had to pick crops to make a living."

"Roaming the Harvests, Pa would call it. Still, I wanted to travel and see things. I wanted out of this and every other small town. I was tired of being dirty and tired. I wanted glamor and excitement.

"So, how come you never left?"

"My sister died, and it didn't seem important, anymore. Helping my Ma and Pa deal with the pain, was the only thing that helped me deal with the pain. Losing your mother changed my life and my thinking."

Anna walks back into the room. "I am sorry, what did I do?"

"Your missing year. It changed my life." Melinda said.

"It changed everyone's. The Masters', the Harrick's, the Lewis's and of course, the Walker's." Corrected Anna.

"True, little brother was attracted to Susan Walker but when she interrogated her cousin, he fell madly in love." Melinda admits.

"Love can hit at the oddest moments." Anna says. "Henry says that he fell in love with me the first day I went to cook. He said it was when I was talking about taming Big Bertha the grill that he knew."

Melinda is thoughtful for a moment. "When Mark picked me up off the floor at Walker's house, and he cried with me, while holding me. I think I knew. He was so gentle and kind. He was so hurt by our pain. How could I not fall for a guy like that?"

Carrie asks, "When did you know, Mama?"

Anna says, "That's simple. When I let him kiss me. Really, kiss me. Then he said something about his heart smiling. I was done!"

Melinda says, "How about you, Carrie? Did you have a moment?"

"No, I feel almost cheated. I don't remember a time when I didn't love GW. I didn't understand it. I didn't feel that way about any of the other 'cousins'. When I learned that he wasn't a real 'cousin', then I knew that he'd be the one. Oh, my God. I just realized it, now. I do have a clear moment. It was just before we moved from Lawrence. I overheard Daddy saying that 'Anna couldn't love Carolyn and Joshua any more if they were blood relatives'. Then it made sense. Aunt Carolyn wasn't my blood aunt. Uncle Joshua wasn't my blood uncle so GW wasn't my cousin."

Melinda pats Carrie on the head. "Very deep for five."

"I guess so. I walked around in a dream. I could marry GW because he wasn't my cousin!"

The three are quiet for a while. "Let's go get the fabric for this gorgeous dress! Red Velvet or satin?" Anna asks.

"Velvet!" Both women answer.

"Then let's go get it." Anna says as she picks up her car keys.

***

The women went to three different stores that carry fabric before they found the one that was the correct color and feel. Carrie wanted the velvet, the softest that she could find. She had figured out how much fabric that she will need if it was silk, but because velvet needs to be turned so that the infinitesimal nap all lays the same direction, they bought an additional fifty percent.

Once home, Carrie uses tracing paper to draw out each section of the dress to Melinda's measurements. She drew the bodice first and held it up to her own bust. "Is this what you pictured?"

Melinda looks at it. "Like you read my mind!"

FIFTY-FOUR
February 12th 1896
A Tuesday in Pennysville

Yesterday, was filled with shopping and all the arrangements for the wedding. Brenda did excuse herself for a 'lunch' date with her groom. The days on the road put a damper on their afternoon rendezvouses.

Harkahomé is back sleeping in the rear room of the sheriff's office. He is thankful that the travel is over and he can relax the day away in his new feather tick mattress. At half past ten in the morning, Elliot comes to the office and makes coffee. After it is made he pours a cup for Joshua, unlocks the door to the cells. When he gets to the back room, he quietly knocks on the door. "Harkahomé, I have coffee and fresh made coffee cake for you. Would you like me to come in and help you out of bed?"

Harkahomé answers, "No, Deputy Dotson. I will be fine. Is Chilly here, yet?"

"Not yet. I will pour the coffee back into the pot and leave the food out here for you, then. I am going to go meet the stage."

Joshua waits until he can hear Elliot leave the office and turns, "You can get up, my love, he is gone." He puts his hand on Sadie's shoulder. Then he nuzzles her behind her ear. "He has made coffee and brought me coffee cake. I feel like I haven't eaten in days. It must be all the late-night activity."

Sadie turns to face him, "And you thought that you couldn't be a complete husband to me. Do you have any extra pain this morning?"

"No more than any other morning. I think that the exercise is good for me. Shall I let the coffee get cold and we exercise some more?"

"I don't see why not. I don't have anywhere to be until seven tonight." She puts her arms around her

Indian. "So you like sharing a blanket with me?" She gives him a long kiss, so he cannot answer. When she finally breaks apart from him she smiles. "Well?"

"Very much. I knew it would be nice but this is wonderful."

***

An hour later, they were both sipping coffee and nibbling on the coffee cake. They were both still flushed with their afterglow. Chilly walks into his office. "Good morning. Visiting early, aren't you Sadie?"

"Yes, yes, I am." She blushes and smiles. "Well, I will get my stuff and head to my place. I need a long bath and some sleep before I go to work. Are we having an early dinner, together, darling?"

"Of course. Big Momma's?"

She stands and heads to the back room for her stuff. "Sounds grand." She is gone for a few moments.

Chilly smiles. "So not visiting but just wrapping it up?" Joshua does not have time to answer before Sadie comes back in.

"Yes, Chilly. I spent the night. My Indian and I shared a blanket, yet hardly slept under it. As far as I can tell, his pelvis is fully healed." She walks over to Joshua. She gives him a kiss on the cheek. "My love, I will see you later. Uncle Sheriff, have a quiet day." Then she walks out. The door almost closes behind her when it opens again.

Chilly says, "Sadie, what did you forget?"

Elliot answers, "It's me, Sheriff. I have someone here to see Harkahomé. She came in on the stagecoach." He walks in and behind him is a young redhead. She is disheveled and sunburnt.

"Is he here? Harkahomé?" She says in a high voice.

Joshua is up, getting a second cup of coffee when

he hears her voice. He turns to look at her while pouring and he spills coffee all over his leg. He jumps quickly in response to the pain and when he lands it is too much of an impact on his barely healed pelvis. "UUUgggh, the pain!"

Chilly looks to his nephew. He looks pale and about to pass out. He runs over to him to hold him up. "What is the number?"

"Twenty-five!" With that he starts to go down. Chilly with practiced skill, bends down and picks him up.

"Elliot, get the doors, will you? Miss, I am afraid that he is in no condition for visitors. If you still need assistance, I will be with you in a moment. Elliot, hurry with the keys, please. Then go get the doctor to come check on him. He was fine, a minute ago!"

The Sheriff and Deputy Dotson are gone for several moments. The girl walks to the seat across the Sheriff's desk and sits down. As she waits, she removes her bonnet and smooths out her hair.

In the back room, Chilly carefully lays Joshua down on the bed. He is still limp and his eyes are closed. He looks to Elliot and whispers. "Who is she that she made Joshua so upset that he spilled the coffee he was pouring?"

"I don't know. She just arrived on the stage and she said that she knew of a white Indian named Harkahomé that might have passed through here. She has been looking for him for four months, she said."

"Did she tell you her name?"

"I think she said it was Missy."

Chilly straightens up. "Missy? This is not going to be good!" He looks down at his nephew. "What is a man to do? With one fiancé and one girl that he loved but who left him? Did she have her father with her?

"No, Sheriff. She was all by herself."

"Okay, go for that doctor, now. He's been out for too long already." As Elliot leaves the room, Joshua opens his eyes.

"Is it really, Missy? I do not want to see her. I am in too much pain, to think straight. Please tell her to come back later. Or, better yet, find out where she is staying and I will call on her there."

"You are not able to walk across the street, yet."

"Don't tell her that. Go find out what she wants, please. And find out what happened to her father."

"Do you still love her?" Chilly asks before he leaves.

"I don't know. I do love Sadie. Missy is so different from her. I thought I loved her, but now, I do not know."

"Fair enough, I will go interrogate her. I will then send her away. If she has been looking for you for four months, I don't think she will leave without talking to you."

"Most likely not. I just cannot do it, right now. After you get her to leave, can you get word to Sadie to come back. I need to tell her that Missy is in town."

"Are you sure you need to do that before you have even talked with her?"

"I am sure. I think I want Sadie with me when I do."

"Now that is a recipe for disaster, if ever I have heard one."

"Please, Uncle, do as I ask."

"I will, of course. Right away!" He walks out of the back room. When he gets back into the office, she is still seated, waiting patiently.

"So, Miss, who are you and how do you know my deputy?"

"He is a deputy? I didn't know that. My name is Missy Stevens. I met Harkahomé when he was with the Cheyenne. My father and I are missionaries. We were trying to convert the tribe to the one true God."

"Okay." He says flatly. "Is your father with you?"

"No. We are no longer on speaking terms."

"Not very Christian of you." Chilly chuckles.

"My father did not think Harkahomé was husband-worthy. From the time, we moved on from the tribe, I begged him to give me permission to marry Harkahomé, but he refused. I finally told him to go to h . . . well, you know where." She looks down and looks like she was going to cry. She looks up, suddenly. "What is wrong with Harkahomé that he fainted?"

"He was shot and fell from a second-floor balcony. He broke ribs and his pelvis. The pelvis still gives him a lot of pain. Laudanum helps but the stubborn Indian refuses to take it most of the time. It all just happened on the 17th. So, it has been less than a month but both doctors that have worked on him, say that he is doing remarkably well."

"I am glad." She looks down at her hands, again.

"The doctor is on his way. I will send for you when he is ready and able to talk. Where are you staying?"

"I don't know, yet. Somewhere very inexpensive. I have very little funds left. I might need to work for a bit, before I can pay rent of any kind. I will check with the preacher, here, to see if he needs an assistant."

"We don't have a full-time preacher. He only comes every third week. I can wire him to see if he'd like you to work for him. I can also talk with Mama Ruth. She runs the Boarding House. She is a good woman and I can pay for a night or two with her. She is very reasonable and most of the single women in town reside with her."

"Thank you, Sheriff. Um . . . You are Harkahome's Uncle, are you not?"

"I am, as a matter of fact."

"He talked about growing up with you. You look alike except you are a ginger like myself."

"So I am." Chilly looks around, impatiently. "As soon as the doctor and my other deputy come back, I will take you to Mama Ruth's Boarding House. She mother's all her boarders and from what I hear, does scripture reading each night in the parlor with her boarders."

"Sounds wonderful. Thank you, Sheriff." She

stands up and says, "I will wait for you on the bench outside. I wanted to freshen up before seeing Harkahomé, anyway. I was just so thrilled that I finally found him that I couldn't wait to come here." She nods to him then walks to the door. As she opens it, Doctor Cassidy rushes in with Elliot right behind him.

Chilly says, "He is in the back, Doc. See if you can talk him into taking a drop or two of medicine. I'll hold him down so that you can administer it, if you want."

"I hope it doesn't come to that." He says as he rushes past Chilly and heads to the back room.

Chilly looks to Elliot. "Deputy Dotson, I have an errand to run. You are in charge, of the town." Without another word, he walks past him and out the door to get Missy.

***

Chilly has the woman deposited at Ma's, then he sends a wire to the preacher. Finally, he heads to Penny's Parlor to get Sadie. Lee Kirby waves hello. Chilly walks to him, "Lee, I wanted to thank you again for the loan of the carriage."

"Think nothing of it, my boy. Glad that I could help. I think of this town as my responsibility."

"Okay, you got me, why do you think that?" Chilly pauses for the explanation.

"How do you not know? You have been Sheriff of Pennysville for years and you are sitting in Penny's Parlor and you eat at Big Momma's all the time. Did you not know that they are all owned by me?"

"So you own those, the hotel and Kirby Ranch, too. What about it?"

"My beautiful mother was Penny Kirby. She came here as a bride with my father. After I was born, they both started the restaurant for the stagecoach riders to have some good hot food after being on the road for so long.

284

Then during the war, my father died at Shiloh. The town and I grew up around that restaurant. She opened this bar, too. She was an amazing woman. When the town got big enough to incorporate, they decided to name it after my mother. I and the town are about forty years young this year."

"How's come I never knew this story?"

"I am not sure, maybe you were busy fighting the bad guys, for which we are eternally thankful."

"Chilly, I heard your booming voice all the way upstairs. Woke me up! You know that I had a late night and that I have to go to work, tonight." Sadie says.

"I came for you. Joshua wants to see you. It's important."

"Is he alright?" She rushes to him. "I didn't hurt him, did I?"

"Sadie, how would I know? My goodness, you will be my niece-in-law for forty years before I am used to what comes out of your mouth!"

"Sorry, Uncle Chilly. I will try to remember that you and Brenda are my betters."

"I never said that! In fact, you remind me of my sister, Carolyn. She is the only other redhead in the family. She is only a year older than me but we called her the firecracker! She gave me the name Chilly, because my father said that we were as different as fire and ice."

"Harkahomé said that you and he pulled lots of tricks on her. He wants to say he is sorry, when he gets the chance."

They are walking down the street back to the Sheriff's office. "He will get the chance sooner than he thought he would." Chilly says half under his breath.

"Why do you say that?"

"Oh, just a feeling."

"Chilly, you are a horrible liar! I hope that you don't play poker. Or if you do, please let me know so that I could buy in!"

"See, I will never get used to that sense of humor of yours."

"You know what you're good at? Changing the subject." She pokes him in the ribs.

"I learned how to do that early in life. Had to, with all my siblings."

"See – now I forgot what was the original lie!"

"That's how that works. I am that good. Here we are. Listen, Joshua must talk with you. Elliot and I will be out here." He opens the door to the office. "Elliot, come with me, please."

"Yes, Sheriff, coming!"

Sadie steps into the office. "Joshua, where are you?"

"I am in the back room." He calls out.

"Well, here I am, sir. What could not wait until our date, tonight?" She enters the room and sees the doctor still with him. "Oh, my goodness, are you in pain, again? What happened?" She rushes to his side and grabs his hand.

"Stupid accident. I spilled coffee on my leg and jumped to get away from it and landed wrong. Felt like I broke my pelvis all over again."

"I don't think that he did, though. He wouldn't take any medicine until he talks with you about something. Here is the bottle. Four to five drops, at least." He hands her the bottle of laudanum. "Sheriff Lewis offered to hold him down while I poured it, if necessary."

"Thank you, Doc. I will make sure that he takes it." She turns to Joshua. "Now, my husband-to-be, what is so important? I know that you didn't call because of the pain."

Joshua is straining to hear if the doctor has left. When he hears the door close, he says, "Get a chair and sit next to me, please. I have some unexpected bad news."

She gets the chair and pulls it next to the bed. "You are scaring me, Harkahomé. Are you breaking up with me, just when I shared your blanket?"

"Not in the least. I love you and I want to marry you. But . . ."

"I hate that word 'but!'"

"But," He ignores her comment. "Did you see the person with Elliot, when you were leaving this morning? The redhead from the stage?"

"I sort of remember her, why?"

"She was the Missionary's daughter. Missy Stevens."

"You mean the girl you love?"

"Loved."

"What is she doing here?"

"She was looking for me. She left her father to find me."

"What did you tell her?"

"I haven't talked to her. I spilled my coffee, jumped and passed out cold. Chilly carried me to bed, then talked with her. I don't know what she told him, because then the doctor came and he went for you."

"When are you going to talk with her?"

"After I sleep off the three drops."

"The doc said four or five drops."

"I will take three and no more. I want you here when I talk with her, if you can."

"Harkahomé, I think you need to speak to her alone. If I fought my father and left him for the man I loved, I'd deserve a moment alone with the man before I get dumped."

"If you put it like that."

"Think about it, Joshua, she gave up everything she knew for you. You need to let her down, gently. She doesn't need her replacement glaring at her while you are breaking her heart."

"I don't think she loved me that much."

"Why do you say that?"

"She left me."

"My silly man. You do not know how hard it is for women. We are told from birth that we are to serve men and be obedient. It is worse for Bible thumpers. I cannot imagine how much courage it took for her to leave her father and go ALONE to find you."

"It sounds like you want me to marry HER."

"Well, I want you to be honest with yourself and her. I am a new shiny ball. She is the long loved ball. You might think that I am the better ball, but if you search your feelings very hard, I might not be the right one for you. God, I hope you pick me, but I will not have you just because of a promise, if the rest of your life you will want the one that got away."

"You are with child, Sadie. I want to be his or her father!"

"WHAT?" says a high-pitched voice from the doorway. "She is carrying your child?"

Both Sadie and Joshua look to Missy. Both answer at once, but Sadie says, "No." and Joshua answers, "Yes."

Missy looks between the two. "Which is it?"

Sadie looks to Joshua, but says, "I am with child and we are to be married on Saturday. I love him and he says he loved you. I will leave you two, to talk this out. I will abide by whatever Joshua decides." She turns and walks a few steps, then points her finger at Missy. "I just want you to know. You broke his heart, once. If he picks you, you'd better not do it, again. You will have ME to answer to!" She turns back to the man, lying in the bed. "Joshua, I LOVE YOU, you know that, right?"

"Sadie, I believe that with all my heart."

"Good. Then I will leave you to talk. I will be outside to give you your medicine."

"Sadie, I love you, too. Please don't go."

"I am going outside, you stubborn Indian. Then I will give you your medicine. Sleep on the decision and tell us tomorrow." Sadie walks out and slams the door so Harkahomé knows she is gone.

Missy looks at him. Her eyes are beginning to water. "She is some gal. Not exactly God fearing, I think but I wouldn't want to make her mad. I think she would kill for you. I couldn't even stand up to my father for you. I am so sorry that I left you. I can only beg your forgiveness. I had left my father to go back to you, but by the time I got back, you were gone. I swear, I have been just missing finding you by a week at the most. How long have you been here?"

"Not long. You have been traveling alone? That is very unwise for a tenderfoot such as yourself."

"I felt that you were worth the risk."

Joshua tries to sit up, but the pain is too much. "It is too late, Missy. I love her and she loves me and we have the unborn child to think of. We are saying our vows on Saturday."

"Can you honestly say that you no longer love me?" She comes forward and sits on the chair next to him. "After all I have gone through to find you? You owe me that, at least. Tell me that you do not love me and I will leave and never bother you, again."

"Missy, it is not that cut and dry. Of course, I still have feelings for you, but Sadie needs me. I will not let that child go without a father. She and it need me and I love them and want to keep them safe and give them a home."

"Not a teepee?"

"I think that I have grown accustomed to walls, and coffee! I do not think I am who I was when I was still with the tribe. If your father had let us marry, I would have stopped living with them for you. It was time. I needed to try the white man's way, again. As for you, I am very sorry that you separated with your father. That was never my intention, for you to choose between me and him. That is why I did not argue when you told me that you were going with him."

"I was a fool to leave you! Can you ever forgive me?"

"There is nothing to forgive. You saw your duty, elsewhere. Where is your father now?"

"I don't care. When I told him that I wanted to go back to you, he beat me and tied me to the buggy each night. It was awful. I would have never thought him capable of such cruelty." She puts her head down and tears start to fall where they had only threatened before. "I was more determined than ever to go back to the man who loved me."

"Missy, you left him to get away from him. Not to come to me. You always were afraid of him. Too afraid to let yourself fall in love. I see it all as plain as the nose on your face. I was the carrot – he was the stick, of course you think you love me. I am NOT him."

"How can you say that? I . . . am . . ."

"A free woman for the first time in your life. I know that you love your God. I know that you felt something for me. I felt something for you, too. You needed me to plan your escape. Well, you did it, you are free! Go, make your way in the world, for yourself or for your God."

"That is all? You are not tempted at all by my presence?"

"To be honest, no, I am not. I want my shiny new ball."

"What does that mean?"

"It means that I am done talking. The pain is too much and I have delayed taking my medicine for too long. Please go tell Sadie to bring me five drops!"

"You aren't making much sense to me, Harkahomé. I will get her. Can I see you tomorrow?"

"Yes, please visit me, then. My mind is made up, but I would like to see you, again. You are my friend, nothing more. I was raised to value a good friend, above all."

"By the Cheyenne or back in Lawrence?"

"Both. Please get Sadie. I cannot take the pain any longer."

She rushes out the door and says to Sadie waiting outside. "He said to give him five drops and that I am just his friend. I will come say good bye to him tomorrow."

"Five drops? Oh, my poor Indian." Sadie rushes in.

"I am coming Harkahomé! I have your drops here." She takes a small glass and pours a splash of water into it and counts out the drops. "This will help you, my darling. What is the number?" she asks as she is approaching him with the glass.

"One."

"I thought you were in pain?"

"You are number One. The pain is back to twenty-five."

"Okay, do not talk, anymore. Just drink."

"Stay by my side until I drift off." He lifts his head to drink.

"A tribe of wild Indians couldn't make me leave you!"

"That's my girl. I love you, Sadie."

"I love you too. You, big galoot!"

"I am so tired. The medicine is good. I . . ." He closes his eyes and does not finish his sentence.

Chilly walks in and looks from him to her. "I saw Missy leave. How did everything go?"

"This dumb Indian picked me over her! What have I done to deserve this man? He doesn't have the good sense God gave a flea."

"I won't let you talk about him that way, Sadie. Elliot doesn't have the good sense God gave a flea. My nephew has at least twice that."

She looks to him and starts to cry. "He really is too good for me. I should leave and let the church lady have him. She is better for him than I am." She starts to walk out of the back room. Chilly follows her.

"Sadie, don't break his heart like she did. If he has made his decision, who are you to second guess it?"

"I am an unwed pregnant saloon girl."

"And soon to be his wife and mother to his child. If he doesn't think any less of you for what you have been through, why do you?"

"Because of what she has been through to get to him."

"Poppycock! As my sister, Carolyn, would say. She hasn't been through half as much as you, I bet. He told me that she was the first white girl he had seen since he was taken by the Cheyenne. I think he loved the idea of her. He could have gone after her when she left. He felt deserted by her. Her father was a mean man and he felt sorry for the way he treated her but not enough to go after her. We, Lewis men, do not stand idly by when someone we love is being treated wrong. He let her leave. Do you understand? He loved the idea of being white, again. Not being with her. He left the tribe within weeks of her leaving to come find me to take him home to Lawrence. He does not love her. He only loves you!"

"Uncle Chilly, that is the most I have ever heard you say in one breath. I understand what you are saying. I just want the best for him. I see her, next to me and well . . . She looks like a better match to Brenda and you."

"Me? I am a loud mouth, no nonsense, wisecracking, too tall scoundrel. Sadie – you are a shorter ME in woman's clothing."

"Now, that sentence, Chilly, I believe."

FIFTY-FIVE
February 11th, 1959
A Wednesday in Chicago, Illinois

The women worked until late in the evening, yesterday. Carrie has drawn all the pieces. Anna has been pinning and cutting the fabric and Melinda is starting to sew.

This morning, because all the pieces are cut, Melinda brings her table top sewing machine. After a leisurely cup of coffee, all three women are at their machines sewing.

Anna gets a call and needs to go work the lunch shift. She calls her mother to come over. Judy walks in the back door ten minutes after Anna, leaves. "I am here to sew!" She announces. She approaches the fabrics and the sketches. "Oh, my Carrie. This is some project! I do not know how you can bring this all together from scratch! Where are we at and what would you like me to do?"

Melinda looks up from her machine and lets it come to a stop. "Mama, could you make us some lunch? We are knee deep here and starving from all this work." Carrie giggles.

"Melinda, I keep waiting for you to look like what you eat! It is going to catch up with you. I promise, no one escapes middle age spread, who eats like you."

"Nonsense, Mama. I plan on maintaining this figure to my grave! Please, make us soup and sandwiches or whatever you can find in my sister's well stocked larder."

The phone rings. Judy says, "Why don't I answer that first." She walks into the kitchen. "Hello, Harrick Residence, Judy speaking."

"Hello, Gramma Masters, it is wonderful to hear your voice."

"GW? I don't think I have ever heard your voice on the phone. How are you, my dear?"

"I am wonderful. I am coming in for the Ball tomorrow. I cannot wait! Is Carrie available?"

"Of course, sorry GW, for wasting time on your long-distance call, I will get Carrie."

"Gramma Masters?"

"Yes, GW?"

"Is my girl feeling alright? Has she had any physical setbacks from the shooting?

"None that I am aware of. Why are you asking me instead of her?"

"Because, she will lie through her nose, if I ask her. If I take her out tomorrow night, I do not want it to be too much for her."

"Oh, I understand now. You are very thoughtful, for a young man."

"It's just that I am so worried about her and think about her all the time."

"You are in love, GW. Let me go get the object of your affection." She puts down the phone and calls to the girls in the dining room. "Carrie, GW is on the phone!"

"I am coming Gram!" Carrie says. She has stopped sewing and jumps to her feet. "Whoa! Head rush!"

Melinda grabs for her hand to stop her swaying. "Maybe all this concentrated work is not good for your head, Baby Girl."

"I am fine, I just got up too fast." She steadies herself and goes into the kitchen. She picks up the line. "Afternoon, GW. Guess what I am doing?"

"Sewing your ball gown?"

"Please! That was finished in Chicago. I just needed to do the jacket hem here. No, I am sewing the red gown for Aunt Melinda. Mother, Gram, Auntie and I are all sewing to get it done. It is as if I have my business going and I have employees."

Aunt Melinda from the dining room says, "I heard that!"

Carrie takes the receiver farther from the doorway

to the dining room. "Are you still coming tomorrow?"

"Yup, we are taking two cars. Mine and Dad's. Mom will be taking everyone out of school for this. We hope to be on the road before noon. What time do you want me to pick you up for our first date?"

"Are you doing it right – dinner and a movie?"

"Absolutely. Pick something out. I will pick the restaurant."

"Good, pick me up at five-thirty?"

"I cannot wait! Eighteen years is too long to wait for a first date!"

"Don't you count Junior Prom?"

"Not really, we hadn't declared our feelings for each other then."

"I agree. This will be our first date, then."

"I have to go. I am just catching up with all my classwork and I have a class in less than an hour. I am going to miss two more days, that I will need to catch up on, besides."

"And it is all because of me!" She says in a sing-song way.

"ALL for you, you mean. You are worth it my love. I really, must go now. See you tomorrow."

Carrie places the receiver back on the wall phone. She sashays into the dining room and pretends to Waltz around.

Melinda watches her. "Young love." She says amused and half to herself.

FIFTY-SIX
February 12th, 1896
A Wednesday in Pennysville

Joshua slept the day and all night. Twenty-one hours in all. He woke at nine in the morning, stiff as a board but pain free. He opens his eyes and stretches. He feels her warmth beside him. He struggles to turn to face her. Sadie is sleeping soundly next to him. He lifts the blanket to see that she is naked. The thought sends his manhood to attention, or was it in attention and that is why he woke?

He cuddles next to her. He wants to move so badly but he doesn't want the pain of yesterday to return. *Damn, why is she naked? She is trying to drive me wild?* He closes his eyes and tries to fall back asleep. If he could just get a little closer to her. His body moves, before his head thinks it's a good idea or not. He has adjusted himself to be able to feel her against him. *I will just lay here next to her and breath in her deliciousness. God, I want to take her so bad! If I close my eyes and try to sleep, it will be just fine.* He sighs loudly and closes his eyes. He can feel a shift in the bed. She is moving against him.

She says, "I can feel that you want me. Do you want to try? I don't want to hurt you." Before he can answer she repositions herself. He can feel himself between her legs. "There, now let me do all the moving, my love." She reaches for him and shifts again for him to enter her wetness from behind. She moves ever so slowly around him. "Is that okay?" She asks.

"It is better than okay. I didn't know we could do it like this."

"As a matter of fact, neither did I. But, we are. I am not hurting you?"

"Oh, no, Sadie. This is all pleasure. I want to

move. I am afraid of that pain returning." He reaches for her bottom. It is as round and soft as anything he could imagine. She is moving against him slowly but he wants more. He grabs her hips and pulls her hard onto him. He gasps out loud and pushes her away, just for a second. Then he pulls her to him again. Now she moans. "I am not hurting you, am I"

"No, it's good. Keep going." That is all that he needs. He bends his knees under hers and slams her onto him again. And again. "So good" she says with each thrust. It doesn't take long for them both to reach their peak, together. "OH, Harkahomé. That was amazing!"

Just as he is finishing emptying himself into her, he turns his head into the pillow to sneeze. He sneezes three more times. His sneezes have released him from her. "Sorry, Sadie." He says as she says "Bless you." "I think I am allergic to finishing what I start. I have noticed each time that we've done something, I sneeze at the finish.

"I noticed that, too! But don't let that stop you from starting, please. Are you in any pain?" She has turned to face him.

"No, none. I was mad at you for being naked next to me. What a tease you are! My dearest love."

"A tease leaves her man, wanting. I made sure you were satisfied. And if that is what you have in mind for a punishment, please be mad more often." She gives him a long kiss. "And good morning."

"Good morning to you, too."

"I'd better get up and dressed before Deputy Dotson catches me."

"Sadie, don't go! I don't care if he comes. I will tell him to leave."

"Why Harkahomé, will you make an indecent woman out of me to have the whole town know about us?"

"No, I just want to hold you. I felt that I almost lost you, yesterday. I know that she holds my heart no longer. Only you have it in your hands. But you were insisting that I talk to her. You were practically throwing her at me. I do not want her."

"I only want what is best for you, Harkahomé. Are you sure that she is not the better choice?"

"I will only say this, one hundred thousand more times. I LOVE YOU! Now kiss me like you love me, too."

***

The eleven o'clock stage from Bartlesville arrives with four special passengers. They leave the coach and are met by Elliot. He goes up to the Colonel, immediately. "My goodness, the likeness to Harkahomé is uncanny, except for your beard. Let me get you to the Hotel. Chilly and Brenda are waiting for you there." The Colonel, his wife Julia, son, Kevin and Chilly's mother, Elizabeth are all eager to meet the girl that finally unfroze Chilly's heart.

There are other passengers on the coach. One passenger, kept looking at the Colonel. When he overheard Elliot, it all made sense. This is Harkahomé's kin. Of all the towns and territories in the United States, how could his girl and that DAMN Indian be in the same town? As he steps onto the street, he looks up and down. He sees what he is looking for and grabs his bag and heads directly toward the building with the big sign out front.

Elliot says as they are entering the hotel, "We need to keep you folk in here, to surprise Harkahomé on Saturday. Do you think that you can do that?"

Elizabeth Lewis answers. "We made better time than we thought, so we will make the best of it." She is a little woman with a wide gray streak on her left temple. She has her hair up in the fashionable Gibson girl style, as does the demure Colonel's wife Julia.

As they enter the hotel, Chilly runs to his five-foot-tall mother and picks her up and swings her around. "Mama, it is so wonderful of you to come all this way! Come meet my bride."

"Chilly put me down! I am sixty-seven years old! You cannot pick me up as if I were a maiden in my twenties!" He puts her down gently.

Kevin is laughing. At ten years-old, he is soon to pass his grandmother but has never seen anyone lift her up and so easily.

Chilly says, "Sorry, Mama. I was just too excited." He points to the hotel's parlor. "Brenda and her mother are waiting in there. So much has happened since you've been on the road. We've decided to get married again on Saturday in a ceremony with Harkahomé and his girl Sadie. She is a much rougher version of Carolyn. She will shock you by what she says, but she has the best heart and Joshua loves her." When they all walk into the Parlor, his bride and her mother both stand. "Martha, Brenda, it's my extreme pleasure to introduce my mother, Beth, my brother Will, the Colonel and his wife, Julia and their ten-year-old son, Kevin. Kevin has doubled in size since I saw him last." He turns to his mother. "Mama, I received a telegram from Marjorie. She cannot come due to Richard Jr.'s health. Carolyn, and her family will be coming in tomorrow. My siblings, the doctors, will be coming in from Wichita on Friday." He crosses the room and puts his arm around Brenda. "This is my bride, Brenda and her mother, Martha Masters. Isn't Brenda beautiful? Look at her blue eyes. I was done in by those eyes."

Beth speaks first. "So wonderful to meet you both. I still cannot believe that my Chilly is married! I hear that you are repeating the ceremony on Saturday. It seems my last two children have done the same thing. Married without me then had a wedding with me. And Joshua is getting married, also? My little grandson, I just cannot believe it!"

Chilly and Brenda laugh. "He is not so little anymore! He is just a little shorter than the Colonel. In fact, Colonel, if you shave off that beard you and he could be twins."

"Well, rest assured that will not be happening any time soon. I have had this beard since I was seventeen when I joined the Cavalry. Does the hotel have a restaurant? We are starving!" He looks to his wife who is shaking her head. "Okay, I am starving!"

Kevin says, "Me, too, Mama!"

"Yes, there is a little one, this way. Did you want to go upstairs and check into your room and freshen up before you eat? We will join you for lunch, afterward." Chilly offers while his arm around Brenda gets tighter.

"Yes, let's get the dust of the road off before we lunch." Julia says as she puts her arm around her husband while messing up Kevin's hair. "Neither will starve for the next half an hour, I promise."

***

After they all separate, to freshen up, Brenda takes her husband into their room. "I love your family. The Colonel and his little Julia are exactly like you described them." She puts her arms around him. "We don't have much time, my darling. Quick, have your way with me."

Chilly looks down at her. "Brenda, I just left my mother. It seems indecent with her just down the hall."

"Really, and where has my mother been?" She blushes. "So does that mean I will get no loving from you until they leave?"

Chilly is still unmoving. "No, I couldn't ever go that long! But, this feels too soon."

"Well, there is a first time for everything. This will be the first afternoon that we don't do it, since that first day in Nowata." She goes to the mirror and bends over the dressing table to look at her hair. "Do you think that my hair would look good like Julia wears it? I have seen it in magazines but I haven't tried it for myself. I wonder if Julia will show me how?"

Chilly is watching her from behind. "Do you still

think there is time?" He walks to behind her and rubs her in her bent position. "I am thinking of something new to try if you are willing."

"I guess we won't know until we try." She starts to straighten up but he has her hand on her back as he reaches under her skirts and removes her panties. "I think that this is the position that I want you, my girl."

"Oh, Chilly, I don't know."

He has released his pants and they drop to the floor around his ankles. "Just give it a second." His hand is under her skirts again. He is rubbing the area where the panties were just covering. "Do you like this?" She moans a response. He steps closer and positions himself to enter her. He caresses her buttocks. Then he takes her hips and pulls them toward him and he enters her at the same time, but doesn't move. "Oh, Brenda, say this is okay. It feels so good."

"This is more than okay. Move in me, before there is a knock on the door and we have quit before we are started."

"That's my beautiful bride. I am watching you in the mirror. Hold on to something, I am going to . . ." He begins to move slow at first but as she is moaning in delight he moves faster and faster holding on to her hips. "So good. And you thought I would lose interest in you. I never met a more daring partner."

"Chilly, say you love me and want me and nothing else."

"Oh, God, Brenda – you are everything that I could never have dreamed of. I love you so much!"

"I love you too. Now, go harder, pleeaassee! Yesssss!"

***

Brenda and Chilly are the last to enter the small hotel dining room. His family is all at the table as is his mother-in-law. Martha says, "It is about time you showed up Brenda. It is quite rude to keep us waiting to order. Your new brother-in-law and his son are about to starve to death."

The Colonel, whose room is next to the newlyweds heard the noise coming from the other side of the wall. "Nonsense, Mrs. Masters. I and Kevin here had a few crackers in the stage just before arriving. Didn't we boy?" He and Julia look at each other and smile as they had, when they heard the noise. Kevin doesn't have a moment to answer when the waitress comes to take their order. She looks around the table, curiously.

"Yes, Georgia. This is my family. This is my older brother and his wife and son. And this is my mother." He points to Beth.

"Very pleased to make your acquaintance. The resemblance is very strong with all the men in the family. Even you little one. She says to the young boy, in front of her. "Now what'll you have?"

They place their order and have a long luncheon where they get to know each other. Chilly sees Georgia point to the family as she talks with another long-term occupant of the hotel. "I don't think we are going to be able to keep this a secret, with the whole town seeing the resemblance. I am going to have to tell Joshua about you ahead of when I wanted to do. He has a lot on his plate, right now. His first love is in town, also." Chilly goes and gives them a synopsis of the situation.

***

Meanwhile, Frank, the other passenger on the stagecoach, is sitting in the bar having his first drink. He hasn't asked around yet, but he is keeping an eye out. He can see the upstairs rooms from the large mirror over the bar. Decorated, scantily clad women are leading men up and down the stairs. *Evil doings in an evil place. How can she stand living in a den of inequity, such as this?* Just then she comes into the saloon and goes to the man behind the bar and has a few words with him. Frank finishes his drink, turns away from her and heads up the stairs. He leans his back against the bannister so if she looks up, she wouldn't recognize him. A few moments later, she finishes her conversation and starts up the stairs. She looks up before her foot steps on the second stair and recognizes him. Sadie turns and goes back to Lee.

"It's him, the man that raped me back in Wichita! Keep him here. I am going to get Chilly." She rushes out of the saloon and heads to the hotel. *Why do I always have to disturb Chilly and Brenda on their lunch date? God, I hope Chilly can scare this man away!"* She enters the reception area and starts up the stairs. The attendant behind the desk says, "Are you looking for the Sheriff and his wife? They are in the hotel café." He points the way.

"Thank you!" She says as she turns to rush there. She stops suddenly in the threshold of the café. She thinks she is seeing things. There is her Harkahomé with a beard sipping from a coffee cup.

The Colonel sees her agape. He looks to Chilly, "Someone else sees the likeness." Chilly looks to the doorway. He immediately goes to Sadie.

"All my family is coming for the weddings. They didn't know about it when they started out to see Joshua but they are all coming to surprise him. Come meet your new in-laws-to-be." He takes her by the arm. She wiggles out of it immediately.

"Not now, Chilly. Frank, the man who raped me in Wichita, is in the saloon. I need you to get him out of town before Joshua finds out and tries to do something he is not strong enough to do."

Chilly looks to his family. "Sheriff business at the Saloon, I will be right back everyone." He takes Sadie's arm and they head out to the bar without any other explanation. After they leave the hotel, Chilly says, "Is this rapist the father of your baby, Sadie?"

"Yes. How did he find me? I made sure I told no one of my plans to come here, for fear of seeing him, again."

"I will handle him for you." Chilly walks into the bar and Frank is back down the stairs and is having another drink. Lee comes to the doorway to meet him.

"I have just bought drinks for everyone – on the house. Come, have your free drink, right here." Lee leads him next to the rapist. Sadie stays glued just outside the doorway, so Frank will not suspect a trap.

"Thank you, Lee. I don't mind if I do. It has been a hell of a day, so far. My family has just come in on the stage and I am already exhausted." He turns to Frank, "Howdy, friend. I am the Sheriff here in Pennysville. Sheriff Lewis. You are?"

"Just passing through, Sheriff. Thought I would just get a drink."

Chilly leans in to say, "Frank, I know who you are and what you have done to my friend, Sadie. You will leave my town or pay the consequences. Do you understand? Or should I take you outside and beat you until you do?"

"I haven't done anything to that harlot. Why would you listen to the talk of a salon girl?"

"Because she is my friend and soon to be family. She is an honest lady. I would believe her over you, no matter how high the stack of bibles you swear on." Chilly grabs him by his shoulder and gives him a shove to the door. "We have discussed this overly much. Now leave this town. Or have hell to pay for it. I know how you Bible thumpers love to talk about hell."

"This isn't fair!" He pleads.

"Wrong answer!" Chilly has him by his shoulders, again. He doesn't let go but walks forward with him in both hands. Before he can walk out the door with him, the

Colonel walks in with his rifle in hand.

"Sheriff, do you need any assistance?"

"For this puny guy? Nope I am about to kick his ass, outside."

"Whatever you say little brother!" He lets Chilly go past him with his rifle still aimed at the man in Chilly's grasp. Once outside, Chilly turns Frank to face Sadie, cowering outside the doorway. "Is this the man who raped you?"

"And beat me!" She stands up tall to say.

Chilly turns Frank around, again and faces him to the street. He holds him out at arms-length and let's go. He steps backwards and picks his right foot up and kicks him in the back very hard. Frank falls to the ground. "Now, that was me kicking your ass but since I am so much taller, I guess I missed. GET OUT of town now!"

The man gets up from the ground and turns to Chilly. "I have no horse. I came in on the stage. I understand that another will not be through here until tomorrow."

"Then I will just have to lock you up until I can put you on the coach myself. Unless, you start walking and don't stop until sundown. Which will it be?" He steps forward to grab the man again."

"I will not walk out of town into the unknown! That is ridiculous!"

"I really didn't want to lock you up. But I must. Come Colonel, follow us to the office and come meet my deputies."

Sadie steps forward. "You can't let Joshua know that he is the man who raped and beat me. He will kill him, or hurt himself trying. That is what I am worried about. I think Frank should die of a beating, since that is what he tried to do to me, but I can't let Joshua get hurt."

Frank is resisting being taken. He is struggling and the Colonel fires a shot at his feet. "Behave or the next one will NOT be a warning shot."

He stops struggling and reluctantly walks to the Sheriff's office with Chilly holding him and the Colonel behind them. Sadie is following a distance behind. Elliot had heard the shot and has come out of the office.

He sees the prisoner in Chilly's arms and he draws the gun that he has been issued. "What is going on Chilly?" He says as the group reaches the doorway. Elliot's gun is shaking.

"Deputy, put that thing away before you shoot the wrong person." Chilly barks. Elliot holsters his gun. "This man needs to be locked up, until the next stage arrives. Wherever it is going, he is going to be on it! Unless you want to stand trial for the rape and attempted murder?"

"You have no proof of that. Sheriff!" Says Frank as Elliot opens the office door for them to step through.

"I only need proof of her word! Just think of how many bibles you will be able to sell in prison, mister?"

"He doesn't sell bibles. He gives them away." Says Joshua. "What are you doing to Frank? What has he done?" Joshua is standing by the coffee pot.

Sadie brushes past all the men and goes to Joshua. He can tell that she is upset. He puts his arms around her. "What is the matter, Sadie? You are trembling."

"This is the man who raped and beat me! The sheriff will keep him under lock and key until the stage comes to take him away." Joshua looks down at Sadie, and back up at Frank, then to Chilly and then to the man holding the rifle. He looks pale again as he is putting all the pieces together. "Darling, you look faint again." Sadie pulls Chilly's chair out. "Sit down, before you fall."

"I am not in pain, it's just that . . . I don't believe what is happening." He takes the seat, anyway. "THIS is the man that raped you? Are you sure?" She nods. He looks up past Chilly. "Uncle Will, what are you doing here?"

"I am here for the weddings." The Colonel says

simply.

"Yes, that makes sense. But Frank?"

"How do you know him, Joshua?" Chilly asks.

"This is the man who wouldn't let me marry his daughter, Missy."

Now Sadie turns pale and feels faint! "I am carrying the child of your almost father-in-law?" She goes to the other chair and sits. "This is so wrong!"

Joshua looks to Frank. "Did you come here to get Sadie or Missy?"

"MISSY is here?" Frank asks in shock.

"Did someone call me?" Says the high-pitched voice in the doorway. She manages to maneuver past Will and Chilly and is standing across from Joshua. Everyone is staring at her. "What is wrong?" She asks before she turns around to see that Chilly is holding up Frank. "What are you doing here, Father?" She asks. Everyone is too shocked to speak.

Sadie stands up. "No one say a word. Elliot unlock the doors and let Missy and I go to the backroom to talk. Chilly lock up your prisoner. Joshua do not move a muscle." Elliot comes forward with the keys and unlocks the cell entrance door. Sadie takes Missy by the hand and goes to Elliot, "Keys please." He hands them to her. She unlocks the backroom door and throws the keys back to him. "I do not want to be disturbed. This will take a few minutes. Chilly please keep your prisoner quiet!" She and Missy walk into the backroom, then close the door. Sadie turns to Missy. "Let's get comfortable. Do you want the chair or one of the beds?"

"I'll take the chair." Missy walks over to it and sits down, very patiently.

"Good, I might have to pace a little, while I tell you this. The baby that I am carrying is not Harkahomé's. I was working in Wichita when I was raped. This is the rapist's baby but Joshua wants to raise it as his own. He is an amazing man – you missed out on a good one!"

"What does this have to do with my father?"

"I am getting to that." She starts pacing as she predicted. "I met your father up there. As soon as he met me, he was sweet on me but hated where I worked. He tried very hard to convince me to marry him and go on the road to do what he and his 'errant' daughter used to do. 'Give away bibles to heathens and try to win their soul for God.' I practically laughed in his face. The thought of me in that kind of life was absurd. Well, he punched me in the stomach multiple times but I fought him, hard. I scratched his face a few times, you will see the scars. He finally tied me up, saying that he used to do that to his good-for-nothing daughter to make her behave. Once I was tied tight, he raped me. God, that makes my baby, your half-brother or sister." Sadie lets her words sink in and she sits down on the bed. "I am so sorry, Missy. I hope that you believe me."

Missy stands up, and goes to the door. With her hand on the knob, not looking at Sadie, she says, "I believe you. I am so sorry, too, for all of this." She turns the knob, walks past her father, then the men in the office and leaves the building, without looking or saying a word to any of them.

FIFTY-SEVEN
February 12th, 1959
A Thursday in El Dorado, Kansas.

Melinda's dress is nearly finished with all the women working on it. Anna has had to be at the restaurant a few times and Melinda had to do the ordering at the grocery that she owns but Judy filled in where necessary. It is noon and Melinda needs to go to her store this afternoon so she is trying the dress on – inside out so that alterations can be made. Carrie could not see any so she let Melinda put it on the correct way.

"Oh, Carrie – this is just perfect! You are right, the crinoline underneath the velvet was the way to go. I took a scrap of the fabric with me to the shoe store and am having shoes dyed to match. I am just so thrilled. Other than my wedding dress, I have never loved a dress more."

"Aunt Melinda, I'd say you were exaggerating but I can see it on your face. You love this dress. It is sure form fitting enough. It needs that wrap. Did you like the one that I drew? I need it to just fit over your shoulders so as not to block the beautiful bodice."

"I agree. This bodice accentuates my form just perfectly! We don't want anything to hide it. I will leave it in your capable hands. Help me out of this, I must be off. You have outdone yourself, Baby Girl. Your couture line is going to skyrocket if you keep creating dresses like this!"

"So, all that is left to do is the final hem. I will have it done in no time. I will shop for the fur for the neckline and the muffler, tomorrow morning. I have my date tonight and I want to spend some time, primping. Oh, I haven't looked in the paper for what movies are playing! I was supposed to pick the movie and he will pick the restaurant."

Melinda is out of the red dress and is putting on her slacks and top. She says, "Do you know what you are going to wear, tonight? I'd let you borrow my favorite dress but you'd be literally dressed to kill. I think you in this would give your *FATHER* a heart attack if he saw you in this dress!

"I think I will wear a red dress that I made, just not yours."

"Well, I will let you borrow this then. I bought it for the Ball." She goes to her purse and brings Carrie a bottle of red nail polish. "It's called *Drop Dead Red.* Do you like it?"

"You know, Auntie, I think I do. Thank you. I will sew the final hem tomorrow. I am going to go pamper myself."

"You deserve it." Melinda says as she kisses her niece on the forehead. "Have a great time. I'd say don't do anything I would do but being a mother of two, that doesn't limit you, enough!" Melinda gives her a second kiss and is out the door.

The first thing Carrie does is fill the tub with bubbles and bath oils. She brings the polish to the tub with her and gives herself a manicure while soaking. After her hands are painted, she leans her head back on a bath pillow and closes her eyes. *I will just lay here for ten minutes, while my nails dry. This feels so good! I didn't realize that all the hours at the sewing machine has stiffened my shoulders so much. Or is it that I am nervous?*

She can hear someone on the staircase. For just a moment she thinks it could be Mickey. Then she hears the familiar humming from her mother. "Mama, can you come in her a minute? I am in the tub."

Anna opens the bathroom door. "Did you forget your towel, again?" She says as she crosses over to the linen closet.

"No, Mama. I was just thinking about my hair. Can you call Jenny and see if she can fit me in? Now, if possible. Or tomorrow, if today is booked."

"Do you know what you are going to do with it?"

"I think I would like to cut it in a Pixie. My curls should hide the scar wounds. Keeping it long, just for long hair's sake, doesn't make much sense."

"You will look more like Clara Beth than ever."

"There is a down side to everything." She says with a smile. "Please go call."

Anna goes to the upstairs phone that is in the hallway. Carrie can hear her talking but not what she is saying, exactly. Moments later, Anna is back in the doorway. "She says if you can be there within fifteen minutes that she can take you."

Carrie is already standing. "Then let's get going!"

Anna and Carrie are in the car in five minutes and pulling in front of the beauty parlor at exactly one-thirty. They hurry in and ask for Jenny. When Jenny comes forward to get Carrie, Anna follows. She explains, "My daughter had an accident. She has some shaved hair and scarring on the side just behind the temple, it runs across her whole right side. She wants to cut her hair but of course, doesn't want the scars to show. Do you have any suggestions?"

Carrie interrupts, "Thank you, Mama, for explaining it for me. I can talk for myself, now." She turns to Jenny. "I was thinking about something short. A pixie haircut – something like Audrey Hepburn gets in Roman Holiday. I have similar hair to hers, I think, possibly curlier."

Jenny looks at Carrie's shoulder length hair. "That will be very dramatic. I have been cutting your family's hair since you moved here. Clara always wanted short and you always wanted pony tail hair. You realize that you and she will look even more alike?"

Carrie smiles. "I am prepared. Having lived with her for the last couple of weeks, I was jealous at how easy short hair is to take care of. So, a pixie cut? Will it cover my scars, sufficiently?"

Jenny combs through the hair carefully. "Wow, this looks painful. What happened?"

"I was too close to a gun that went off. I was blinded for a week. The guy who did this is in jail."

"Thank God. This happened in Chicago?"

"Yes. So, will the cut work to hide the scars?"

"I think it will work out great. A few pin curls at night and you should be just fine."

"Pin curls! That's a great idea! I was wondering how to control the curls and make it fancy. I am going to the Valentine Ball and I am wearing one of the new dresses that I designed. Aunt Melinda will wear the other one. Do you have pearl pins or something like that for my hair?"

"Carrie, I have just the thing. Now, let me work, quietly. I need to be careful with your head. I don't want to hurt you."

"Jenny, you are a dream!"

***

Carrie is nervously, checking her hair in the mirror. It looks just like Audrey Hepburn's and her scars are covered. She is wearing the red dress that she designed and sewed last year. The color is the only thing it has in common with the one that she is making for her Aunt. This dress is very modest. It has a shirt-like collar and buttons down the front. The waist is very tight but the skirt is very full and swings easily. She is undecided if she will wear her black open toed heels or her shiny black pumps. She looks down at her toes. She should have put the red polish on them. Now there isn't time. Black shiny pumps win. She looks at the clock on the nightstand. "Five-fifteen!" She says out loud. "I forgot about the movie, AGAIN!" She runs to the bannister. "MOM? Do you have today's paper?"

"Yes, Carrie."

Carrie grabs her little red purse and runs down the stairs. When she gets to the bottom, she holds onto the bannister. The room is spinning. The doorbell rings and she jumps. Her mom comes from the kitchen with the paper in her hands and hands it to Carrie. "Go in the parlor. I will show GW in."

Carrie smiles. "Mama, you devil." The doorbell rings again. "He is getting impatient. Hurry." Carrie disappears around the corner. Anna opens the door. "Oh, GW! I didn't know that you were coming tonight. I wonder if Carrie forgot? She never mentioned it to me."

GW stands there, surprised. "What?"

"Don't listen to her. She is playing with you." Carrie says from the threshold of the parlor doorway.

"OH! Carrie, let me look at you. You are stunning! Your dress, your hair. Did you just step out of a glamour magazine?"

"Aw GW, go on." She waves at him. "No, please, go on!"

Anna says, "Well, this is my cue to leave. Have a good night but have her home at a decent time. Her father will be up worrying, otherwise."

"Of course, Aunt Anna. I never want to make Uncle Henry mad."

"GW, I think if you are dating Carrie, you should drop the Aunt and Uncle part. Just call us Anna and Henry."

"I will try. Thank you, Anna." He looks to his girl. "Shall we? My sweet? I have the restaurant all picked out. What movie are we seeing?"

She doesn't answer until they have left the house. "I was thinking that we don't go to a movie. I would just like to sit and talk to you."

"But you are all dressed up. I need to show you off. How about a night club? A jazz club, maybe?"

"They wouldn't let us in, we are too young." She says as he opens the door for her. She waits for him to get in on the other side. When he is behind the wheel, she slides over to him. "GW, after dinner, let's just get to know each other more. She has her hand on his arm and she leans her head on his shoulder.

"Are you tired, Carrie?" He leans over and kisses her forehead.

"No, happy. Just to be with you. I am starving. Where are we going to eat?"

"I thought that this place might bring us luck." He drives to the center of town and turns right. He pulls up to the front of Sally's Diner.

"Here?" Carrie asks.

"Why not? This is where your mother and father had their first date. And she worked here for that week."

"How do you know all this?"

"I called your mother at her diner and she told me. She told me the first date didn't go so well. It wasn't until she started working here that she and Henry started falling for each other. Shall we?"

"I would love to GW. You are so thoughtful."

He exits his vehicle and walks to the other side of the car to open it for her. He takes her hand and helps her out. Once she is standing, he closes the door but she doesn't start walking. "Is there something wrong?" He asks.

"I am waiting for my first kiss. I would like it before dinner, please." He turns to her. She puts her arms around his neck. He bends down, and puts his arms around her waist.

He whispers. "I would love to give you your first kiss. I love you, so, much." He puts his warm lips on hers. She is soft and warm and smells so wonderful. He can feel himself get lost in her kiss. *Oh, my Carrie. I have waited for so long for a kiss like this,* he thinks. He forces himself to pull away from her. "Keep kissing me like that and you'll never get any food." His hands fall to his side.

"I don't mind. Food is highly overrated. Kiss me some more."

GW bends down and once more whispers. "Don't let your mother hear you say that. She makes her living

314

cooking."

"Shush! Another first kiss, please." She stands on her tippy toes to reach his lips. She puts her hands around his neck, once again and kisses him softly at first, then she feels herself breathing differently. She is arching up against him. He cannot resist her and his arms are around her waist again. One hand moves up. The back of his hand slowly brushes past her breast. It moves to her warm neck then to her cheek. She moans slightly when he was at her breast.

He breaks away to ask, "Do you want more?"

"GW let's skip dinner altogether." She takes his hand and brings it back down to her breast. This time it is not the back of his hand but his palm. "Touch me here." She says between kisses.

He pulls away and looks around. He forgot that they are standing in front of Sally's diner in the middle of downtown. "Not here, not like this. I love you and I do not want anything we do to be inappropriate."

Carrie laughs. "Then the appropriate thing to do is to eat. I will have my way with you, just not out in the cold air."

GW laughs, also. "Is the air cold? I never noticed."

Dinner was eaten quickly and quietly. They were holding hands and smiling and looking at each other. Several times, GW took Carrie's hand off his knee. Each time he did, he brought the hand to his lips and kissed it before returning it to the table. The third time he did that, he leans in and whispers. "Now stop that. I am trying to be a gentleman, here."

"Who asked you to?" She says then blushes. "Are you done eating? Let's get out of here."

"I thought that you wanted to talk and get to know each other."

"Did I say *talk*? There are other ways to get to know each other."

GW smiles. "This is a side of you that I did not

know existed."

Carrie sits back in the chair. "I almost died. When I laid in the hospital bed blind, I thought to myself. Why did I waste so much time? If I die tomorrow, I want to know that I did not waste a minute of living."

"I made the opposite promise. I swore to God, that if you came out of that horrible event with your hearing and sight that I would tell you that I love you, every chance I get and be chaste with you so that when we married, you'd be pure before God and our family."

"Now, how are we going to do both those things? I want to love you all the way, GW. Whether it is tonight or our wedding night. My love is pure for you."

"Yes, but . . ." He doesn't know how to respond. "Carrie, let's continue this conversation in the car." She smiles, like she won the grand prize at the fair. "We are going to *discuss* this further, Carrie. You haven't won me over, yet."

"Am I even close?"

"You are very tempting, my sweet." He stands and puts a few dollars on the table for the bill. She stands and puts her arm on his.

"Let me use the ladies room, before we go. Wait for me."

He sits back down and she goes off to the bathroom. As he watches her go, he thinks, *how am I going to resist her? She is an angel from heaven and she loves me.*

When she comes out of the lavatory, he stands up and she puts her arm on his and says, "I am ready, my love." She gives him a smile that takes his breath away.

As they go out to his car, she says, "GW, I feel that I am trying to go farther than you or our relationship is ready to do. I am sorry."

He doesn't respond but opens the door and she gets in. When he slides in behind the wheel, she slides to the middle of the bench seat.

"Do you forgive me?" She asks quietly while looking at her hands.

"There is nothing to forgive. Let's drive around and talk. Shall we?" He starts the car and pulls away from the curb. "It is a bit nippy, out tonight."

"Oh no! We are so bad off that we are discussing the weather?"

"The weather is a good place to start a conversation. I heard that Saturday's weather will be unusually warm. Unlike some years, where we had to chip ice off our windshields and doors."

"If you ask me it is getting chilly in this car."

"Did you want me to turn on the heater?" GW asks.

"That is not what I was talking about."

GW pulls the car into the driveway of the Johnson Family farmhouse. He is the sixth generation to live in the home. The Lewis family only does so part time on weekends, holidays, vacations, and winters when school is out.

"There are no lights on, is everyone asleep?" Carrie asks.

"No one else is here. Did you not know? I came down alone. Kevin caught a fever and Mother and Father did not want to move him. They want to give him a day to rest. If he is still feverish on Saturday morning, they will hire a nurse to stay with him so that they can still come down for the ball."

"So we will be alone in the house?" Carrie asks, sheepishly.

"Yes, ma'am. All alone with six bedrooms to choose from."

Without another word, Carrie has her door open and she is up the front steps to the door. She waits, impatiently, for GW to exit the car and walk up to her. "GW?"

He is putting the key in the front door. "Yes, my love?"

"I love you.

"I think that I know that."

"Can I have my first kiss in the foyer of the farmhouse?"

He opens wide the door. "You can have a first kiss in every room of the house. Foyer first?" GW takes her in his arms.

"Foyer first, for starters." She replies.

"Carrie, I am going to love you, tonight. But if at any point, you don't want me to go all the way. Don't be afraid to tell me. I will not be upset. No matter how far we seem to be. Okay?"

"Just kiss me, GW." He gives her a long kiss. His hand roams a bit, stopping at her breast, again.

"Can I have a first kiss, in the parlor?" She says and she leads him to the couch in the parlor. He sits down with her. She reaches up for his face, and whispers. "I have a surprise for you."

"Oh? Will you tell me if I kiss you?"

"Now you are getting the idea." He leans over and kisses her. She is intoxicating. She is leaning against him and his hand goes up for the third time to feel her breast. She has her hand on his thigh and moves it to his fullness. He moans when he feels her touch him. She then takes his hand from her breast and puts it on her thigh under her dress.

"What happened to your hose?" He asks.

"I took them off in the diner." She continues to lead his hand upward. She has on no panties. "I removed them, also."

GW stands up, abruptly. "Miss Harrick, may I see you in my bedroom? I would like my next first kiss, there, please."

She stands next to him. "GW, I thought you'd never ask!"

***

GW brought Carrie home just little after eleven. Anna and Henry were both waiting up. Carrie was completely put together as she entered her childhood home. She felt different and hoped that neither of her parents would be able to sense it. She is a woman, now.

Anna gets up from watching TV. "Carrie, how was your evening?

"It was perfect, Mama. Absolutely, perfect. Best first date, ever."

Carrie does a little twirl in the foyer. Anna remembers feeling the same way, once she and Henry connected. She had danced the whole way to her room humming 'It had to be you.' by Cole Porter.

After Carrie danced her way to her bedroom, Anna goes back to Henry and sits down and smiles. She looks to Henry, who smiles back at her. "We've lost her now. She is GW's. And she is so happy. She reminds me of me, when I found you."

"That bad?"

"Yup, she's a goner. A girl left this house and a woman just danced her way in."

"We still have Harry."

"Yes, Henry, we still have Harry. He isn't looking at women, yet. Not really. He loves sports, more."

"Say, did you mean Carrie is a woman? Like she and GW. . ."

"I think so."

"Can you go ask?"

"What would I have told my Ma, if she had asked. I would have lied. I am not going to make Carrie do that."

"Say, Anna. How about we dance our way to the bedroom and you can remind me of the things we did that you would not discuss with your mother."

"That Henry, is a long list. We both need to be up early, tomorrow. My mind is on Carrie, anyway. She is so young."

"And how old were we?"

"Weren't we older?"

"Sorry, my love, we were not. Now let me finish my program."

FIFTY-EIGHT
February 12th, 1896 cont'd
A Wednesday in Pennysville

After Missy closes the outer door to the office. Joshua stands up and goes to Sadie in the back room. She is on her stomach on the bed crying hard. Joshua goes to her. "Sadie, you are safe. He is locked up and will not hurt you ever again." He starts to rub her back for a lack of what else he can do. "Please stop crying and come meet my Uncle, the Colonel. It will be all right, I promise."

She sits up and looks at him. "Oh Joshua, I know you love me if you are here comforting me instead of that poor girl. Missy lost both you and who she thought was a good father. All because of me. That poor, poor girl. Where is she?"

"She walked out. She didn't say anything to us but just left."

"Joshua, do you think of her as a friend, at all?"

"Of course, that is what I told her."

"Then go to her, Joshua. She is in shock and has no one to talk to. Are you up to walking to the boarding house? We can borrow the doctor's chair."

"Sadie, my love. You have a rough exterior but the biggest heart that I have ever known." He stops for a second. "That is what Gram Beth always said about Uncle Will."

"If you don't go to her send Brenda, or get the preacher here to counsel her. I am telling you, she will try something desperate. She is not thinking clearly." She gets to her feet and rushes past the cells to the office. "Chilly, I am worried for Missy. Can you get someone to talk with her? Brenda or the preacher?"

"I will go talk with Mama Ruth. She has giving Christian counseling to her girls at the boarding house for twenty years now, and I know that Missy feels very comfortable with her because of her nightly scripture readings." He gets up, puts his hat on his head and says. "Oh, Sadie, this is my brother Will. Will, this is Joshua's wife-to-be! Elliot, keep an eye on our prisoner. Will take Sadie back to the saloon. I am sure that she wants to freshen up before she officially meets the rest of her in-laws. Joshua, I will come back with the doc's wheelchair, so you can see your Gram Beth. She is dying to see you again."

"Yes, Chilly." They all say at once.

Chilly walks to Mama Ruth's Boarding House and walks right in. Mama Ruth is in her chair doing some needlepoint. "Mama Ruth, did Missy come home?"

"Yes, Chilly. She came in and when I said hello to her she walked right up the stairs as if she didn't hear me. What is going on?" She puts her needlework down and is up as she is saying this.

"She just found out that I have her father in my jail. The charge is going to be for assault and rape, if the victim is willing to press formal charges. We are worried about Missy. Can you go to her? She must feel like she doesn't have a friend in the world. The poor thing." He says using Sadie's words.

"Yes, of course. Oh, my what a pity. From what I understand, he has left a few bruises on Missy, himself." She reaches for her bible and rushes past Chilly and heads upstairs. Chilly hears her knock on the door.

"Missy? It's Mama Ruth, may I come in?" He hears her say. He is walking out the door when Mama Ruth starts screaming. "Oh my Lord in Heaven! Sheriff, Sheriff, hurry! Help me someone, hurry!"

He runs up the stairs four at a time and is in the room. Mama Ruth is holding up Missy by her legs. The girl has hung herself. She is still alive because she is struggling. Chilly takes over and holds her up higher. There are several other boarders coming to the room. A man comes and climbs up on the chair and gets the makeshift noose from around Missy's neck. Chilly shouts as he lays Missy down, "Someone get Doc Cassidy. Hurry!" Then, he says half to himself. "Sadie was right to worry." Then he says to Missy, "Wake up Missy, why did you do a fool thing like this for? Your father's crimes are not yours." He looks up at Mama Ruth. "Help her, please." He has a tear in his eyes. "She doesn't deserve to die like this."

Mama Ruth is at her side and is feeling for her heart beat in her bruised neck. "She is not dead, yet. She has just passed out."

"Oh, thank God. If she had died, it would be my fault."

"Why, Chilly?" Mama Ruth asks.

"I arrested her father."

"I think that is more his fault than your own." She pats him on the arm. "Go, Chilly. I will stay with her until the Doctor comes."

Chilly leaves the bedroom and goes downstairs. He remembers that he was going to borrow the doc's wheelchair. He heads toward the Doctor's office when he sees Doc Cassidy coming toward him. "Doc, hurry, she is alive but very bad." The doctor runs past him. "Oh, is your office open? I need to borrow the wheelchair for Joshua." He yells.

"Yes!" is all the doctor says as he enters Mama Ruth's place.

***

Chilly carries the wheelchair to the Sheriff's office. The thought of breaking the news to Joshua and Missy's father is filling him with dread. He enters the office with Elliot and Joshua sitting down. Joshua looks up. "What's happened, Uncle?"

"Sadie was right. I got there in time. Missy tried to hang herself. The doctor is with her now."

Joshua stands up and goes to the door leading to

the cells. "Let him out, Chilly. This is all this that bastard's fault. He doesn't deserve to live and I am going to kill him, myself."

"That won't undo the damage he has done to Sadie or Missy." He has his arm on Joshua and he pulls him back. "I don't want to get rough with you. NEPHEW. Go back to the office and sit down. I will tell him." Joshua hears the seriousness of Chilly's tone and takes a step back.

"I want to be there when you tell him." He stands his ground.

"Fine." Chilly unlocks the door and faces the rapist "Frank Stevens, I just found your daughter with a rope around her neck. She had jumped off the chair and was struggling with her last breath when I got there. I won't let my nephew touch you. I would like the honors. You have wrecked-havoc in my town for what is supposed to be a joyous occasion." He stops talking because the prisoner has sat down and put his head in his hands and starts to cry.

"Her ma killed herself the same way! She couldn't take the beatings no more and killed herself. I swore that I wouldn't lay a hand on another woman and promised God to serve him if he would keep the anger from me. I kept my promise but God did not keep his. My poor Missy. My poor Missy. Gone because of me!"

"Save your damn tears. She was alive when I left her. Tell you what – save us all some trouble. I will go get the noose from her room and bring it to you and you can hang yourself!" Chilly says as he and Joshua walk out of the cell area and lock the door between them.

"Elliot, go to Mama Ruth's and ask her for the noose from Missy's room. Bring it back to the office, please. Do not go into the cell area. Joshua and I are going out and I do not need a dead prisoner on my hands tonight."

"Okay, Sheriff. Have a good family reunion?" He says smiling weakly and shrugging his shoulders.

***

Chilly is pushing Joshua toward the hotel. "This is the worst way to have a wonderful reunion." Joshua says.

"And your Gram Beth has been looking forward to seeing you again since you left in 1878. She has had you in her prayers every night and has included a toast to you at every family occasion with wishes for your safe and happy return to her."

"Let us not mention any of today's events then. Sadie doesn't need everyone knowing her personal business, anyway. When we make Gram Beth a great-grandmother she will be very happy and does not need to know any of the details."

"Agreed. I hope we beat Sadie and Will back. Knowing Sadie, she has told them everything, by now."

They enter the Hotel and go directly to the Parlor where Brenda, Julia and Gram Beth are sitting. They are alone. Chilly wheels Joshua to his grandmother, who has begun to cry the minute she saw them. "Oh, my Joshua! You are a man. Everyone told me, but I could only picture you when you were the same height as me. Can I hug you?" She stands up but Joshua stands, also. He awkwardly hugs her. "It would have been easier if you were still sitting. Goodness, you are as tall as Will."

"Not quite." Chilly and Joshua say at the same time.

"Still finishing each other's sentences, I see. Please sit and let me look at you. So much like Will. Do you want me to call you Harkahomé or Joshua?"

"They are both me. Almost everyone uses both names, interchangeably. Call me what you want but . . ."

"Don't call me late for supper." Says Will behind him at the same time Chilly and Joshua say it. Everyone laughs and Gram Beth cries.

"If only your grandfather were here. He'd be so

happy to see you, again."

"Gram Beth. The Cheyenne believe our ancestors can see us from heaven. I wish I could have seen him, though."

"Turn around. Will is his look-alike as are you. And this must be your fiancée. Sadie, you are beautiful. I hear that you are a very smart lady, by all accounts." She nods to Brenda, who blushes.

"Mrs. Lewis, it is so very nice to meet you. You have traveled such a long way to see your grandson. How wonderful of you! Now, you get to see these two partners in crime get hitched."

"Are they still that?"

"Yes, ma'am. Don't let the badges fool you."

Beth looks at Harkahomé. "Oh, she is smart!"

"Smartest woman I know, white or Cheyenne." He says. "Let me rephrase that – Smartest Lady that I know."

Sadie blushes. "I don't know, Brenda has as much medical knowledge as a Doctor. Plus, she can shoot and skin a rabbit!"

Beth turns to Brenda, "Really, why do you know so much about medicine?"

"I assisted my father. He was a doctor and as I helped him, he would show me the medical books that explained the disease and the treatment for it. I wanted to go to nursing or medical school but mother would not hear of it."

"My daughter Lizzie is a doctor. I couldn't be more proud!"

"We know!" Will, Joshua and Chilly all say at once.

"Stop that boys! I do not play favorites with my children."

Chilly says, "That's true. Except for the Colonel and Dr. Lizbet."

Everyone laughs. Sadie is sitting quietly. She got the subject of her turned off by using Chilly's tactics. She smiles at everyone. *This is an amazing family. I am so honored to be a part of them!*

Joshua sees his Sadie smiling. She looks to him and he beckons her with his index finger. She goes to him and he pats his lap. She blushes and shakes her head no. He says, "Does anyone mind if my Sadie has a seat, here." He points to his lap. "I like to keep her close."

"Spoken like a true Lewis!" Will says.

"Here, here! Says Chilly, Julia and Gram Beth.

FIFTY-NINE
February 13th, 1959
A Friday in EL Dorado, Kansas

Carrie is up very early. She laid in bed almost all night reliving the events of the evening. Today, she must finish Auntie's red dress and the wrap. As soon as she hears her parents rise, she gets out of bed and dresses for the day. She wants to buy the fabric so she can hand everything over to her Aunt this evening.

Since GW was alone in that big farmhouse, she invites him to dine with the family. Now she wonders if that was a wise idea or not. *How are we going to sit there across from each other and not touch,* she thinks?

As she is leaving the fabric store, a wicked thought crossed her mind. Should she stop at the farmhouse and offer to take GW to lunch? *If I do that, we might not make it out to have a meal! I had better not. I have all that sewing to do, when I get home. Then I want to cook a wonderful meal for my man.* She drives her mother's car back home. She's at the sewing machine within minutes. She is so involved in her task she doesn't hear her father come home. He sees that she is in her own world. She is done with the hem of the dress within the hour. She gets up from her machine and fans out the dress. She walks over to the couch and lays it across the back of it. She gets the new material from the bag. It is more red velvet for the wrap and real rabbit fur for the neckline. *This fur will take some time to attach.* She think as she is feeling the fabric while walking.

Her father is walking out of the kitchen with a sandwich and says, "How is the sewing coming along?"

Carrie drops the fabric screaming then yells, "Geez! Dad, you scared me half to death. I didn't hear you come in."

"Sorry, Baby Girl. I wasn't being quiet on purpose."

"No, Daddy. I am sorry, I was just concentrating so hard on how to sew this fur. It is going to be tricky. Hand sewing is my only option. It has to be perfect."

"Hm, mm." was all Henry could say with the sandwich bite fresh in his mouth. "Is that for Melinda, too?"

"Isn't it lovely? It is for around her shoulders."

"You are very talented, Baby Girl. What's for supper? GW is invited, I hear."

"Yes, I want to make meatloaf. It is his favorite."

"His father's favorite, also. If I recall."

"Is that a fact?" She tippy toes to give him a kiss on the cheek. "I want to get this done before I start the meatloaf. Aunt Melinda will be here tonight for the finished product." She brushes past him to sit back down in her spot. She lays the velvet out doubled over, then she covers it with her already measured tracing paper, and begins to pin it. She is back, lost in the work in seconds. Henry shrugs his shoulders and goes back into the kitchen.

***

GW comes for dinner at six-thirty. The meatloaf is just about ready. She also baked an apple pie from the apples in cold storage. She uses a hint of cinnamon, which her mother told her was Joshua's favorite, also.

Carrie is all smiles at the table sitting next to GW. Harry is across from her and is giving her googly eyes. Anna is next to Harry and sees that he is trying to tease his sister so she puts her hand on his arm. When he looks up at her, she shakes her head and he shrugs.

Carrie says, "Thank you, Mother." Anna just smiles.

"GW, how long are you staying here? When's your Mom coming out?"

"I guess not until tomorrow. Kevin is still feverish, I

hear. I will stay until Monday morning. I do not have class until two o'clock, and that's a class that I can miss."

Henry says, "Can you afford that, since you missed so much school after the shooting?"

"I have caught up and I am ahead. Several of my teachers have given me the leeway to work on my own."

"They must like you."

"I help many of them in the classroom. I have earned the right, they feel. I am trying to finish my double major in three years. I imagine that I will apprentice with you and my father in my fourth year. He has been grooming me to take over either the Lawrence or the EL Dorado holdings. Billy has no interest in farming. He wants to join the military like his namesake – the Colonel. Audrey talked about joining the business, especially when she understood that Aunt Carolyn ran the farm while father was in college. Audrey has since decided that boys are more important. Kevin is still a child."

"It seems that you have thought this through."

"I have had this planned out since sophomore year in high school."

"I am impressed." Says Henry.

"I have also planned that I will be your son-in-law."

Carrie was taking a sip of her Coke and spits it out."

"How long have you had that planned?" Carrie asks.

"Oh, that plan is much older. I think that was ten? It was the princess dress making birthday. I decided it then." He says with complete nonchalance.

"Do I have a say in the matter?" Carrie Ann smiles as she asks.

"Of course, you do. You get to pick when. Shall we wait until I graduate? Do you want to have a spring wedding? I assume you will design your own wedding gown. Oh, do you want one or two receptions? One in Lawrence and one in EL Dorado? See you have lots of input."

"So where and when - not yes or no?"

GW gets up from his seat and kneels at her feet. "Carrie Ann Harrick, will you marry me?"

Carrie looks from her father to her mother, then to GW. "We have had only one date. It was an extremely good one, but still."

"Too soon, you are saying?"

"Can I put off my answer until like our tenth date? Just in case you turn out to be um. . ."

Anna interrupts, "not the one? I knew before my tenth date."

Henry says, "I agree, ten dates but not before."

GW stands, "Ten dates, at least, then. I am in no hurry, Carrie, since you have always been a part of my life. Whether you say yes or no, you will always be a part of my life. We are dear cousins, after all."

Cousins never do what we did last night, dear love, Carrie thinks. She just smiles at GW. "Yes, dear cousin, we will always be that."

SIXTY
February 13th, 1896
A Thursday in Pennysville, Oklahoma

After getting to know each other in the parlor of the hotel, the large family unit, including Aunt Martha, went to Big Momma's for dinner. Will very generously picked up the check. When Chilly objected, Will said, "I make much more than a lawman. Tomorrow, we will let Grant pay. He is richer than all of us."

Expect to arrive in this morning's stage, will be Carolyn and her husband and three children. Joshua is getting up out of bed. It is just sun-up. He yawns and stretches, then rubs his eyes. "Come back to bed, Harkahomé." His love calls.

"I will, I just need to use the chamber pot."

He strolls over to the pot and basin. After he goes, he washes his hands and throws water on his face. He dries himself with towels that Sadie bought and crawls back into bed with her. "We need to find our own place. It is not fitting for you to be walking past prisoners to sleep with me. Chilly has three deputies, now. If we rotate who stands guard when a prisoner is in a cell. I would be away from you every fourth night, and that is only when we have guests."

"I don't think that you'd like sleeping in the upstairs rooms at the saloon. Too noisy, too late in the evening." She says as she is playing with his long hair. He in turn starts playing with hers. Her hair falls to the middle of her back, but she wears it neatly tied up. He was shocked that first night that she came. When she took the pins out of hair and the locks fell so long. He knew then, that he could take her without a worry about his pelvis.

"I wonder what Chilly is thinking. He cannot live in a hotel his whole married life. He has never mentioned doing anything different, though."

"Harkahomé, he doesn't pay for the room. The owner likes having in-house protection." She says.

"Why, that dirty rat." He rises from the bed. "I can be just as good of an in-house protector as he is!"

"Of course, Harkahomé. We should propose that to the other hotel." She giggles.

"There is no other hotel." He bites her ear.

"Exactly, so the room goes to the sheriff. Now, quit wasting time. I have to get back to my room and bathe before I meet this Carolyn, I have heard so much about." She takes him in her arms.

***

At eleven o'clock on the dot, the stagecoach arrives. Sadie has pushed Joshua to the depot. The rest of the family is there waiting, also. Hanging out the windows of the coach are Carolyn's three children. Ada is twelve, Ida is ten and Grant Jr. is nine. As soon as they see their cousin Kevin, they start screaming hello and his name. Carolyn puts an end to it quickly by hitting them all in the back of the head. "This isn't recess, children! Compose yourselves."

"Yes, Mamá," can be heard from all three. As soon as the stage stops, the driver gets down from his seat. He puts the step down and opens the door. All three children come stumbling out and run to Kevin to hug him.

Carolyn says, "Please children, there will be plenty time to play. First let's meet our new relatives." They dutifully line up.

Chilly steps forward. "It is so good to see you, Sis. Come meet my Bride. Brenda, this is Carolyn, her husband Grant and Ada, Ida and Junior." Carolyn rushes forward and gives her a big hug. Brenda is surprised that she is as tall as herself. She just assumed that she would take after her mother. "Carolyn, here is Joshua Harkahomé Nathaniel Lewis. And his fiancée, Sadie Mae

333

Miller."

"Fiancée? When is the wedding?"

"Saturday. Can you all come?" Joshua says with a laugh. He stands up and hugs his Aunt Carolyn. "My you've shrunk. How did that happen? Listen Carolyn, I need to apologize for all the nasty things Chilly and I did to you, growing up. I feel so awful for it."

"I don't remember any of it. I felt like dying when we heard about the massacre. I kept praying that you'd come back and put another frog in my bed."

"I can see that your prayer is answered. I just have to find the frog!"

Grant says sternly, "Don't you dare, Joshua. I share her bed now and I will shoot any frog bearing persons."

"Uncle Grant, I have been shot once and that was bad enough!

"Besides, I knew it was always Chilly's idea to do those things to me. He didn't stop after you left. And he has never apologized!" Carolyn says as she gives him the evil eye.

Ada says, "Look out Uncle Chilly. She hits two seconds after that look."

"She'd better not!" Brenda steps forward. "No one hits my husband. No matter how many frog incidents there were!"

Chilly looks at his sister, "I want to thank you for coming. I know you are missing the Valentine Ball for this. Thank goodness that it's not one of the Colonel's. He'd never miss his own Ball."

The Colonel speaks up. "I am missing the Valentine Ball, also! So that's not true!"

"Children, behave!" Beth says in her most authoritative voice.

"Yes, Mama." Carolyn and Chilly say together.

Everyone begins laughing. Carolyn looks at Brenda. "Sister-in-law? I think you are glowing? Are you with child, already?"

Everyone quiets down and looks at Brenda. "Yes, we weren't going to say anything, yet. Not until after the official ceremony on Saturday."

"Chilly, you have always imitated me, haven't you? First the red hair then eloping, getting pregnant immediately then having an official ceremony. Huh?"

"It's not like we planned it that way, sis."

"Speaking of pregnant . . ." Brenda says, "I am eating for two and I am starving! Anyone hungry?" Hands shoot up from everyone. "Good, let's head over to Big Momma's. I told her to expect a huge crowd of excellent eaters."

Gram Beth is the last to walk and stays even with Joshua. As Sadie is pushing him, he takes Beth's hand. She smiles down at him. He says, "Are you happy, Gram Beth?"

"I am deliriously happy. My whole family will be together, except for Marjorie and her family." She looks to her grandson and explains. "Her little boy is a very sick child, from birth. She does very little traveling because of him. It makes me very sad, that he suffers. Just like it made me sad when you suffered under your living condition at such a young age."

He takes her hand and puts it to his lips and kisses it. "I am sorry that my living with the Cheyenne caused you such heart ache."

"I was always worried that you were cold, or hot, or hungry. I longed to see you so much. It wasn't the Cheyenne that I minded – I just missed you and worried for you. I see that a wonderful man has come out of living with them, so I must give them and the Lord, thanks for that. And for Sadie, also. You will be a lovely addition, to our family, dear." She sees Sadie struggling with the chair. "Chilly, come push your deputy before his bride-to-be hurts herself."

***

After a very long lunch, everyone retires to the Hotel to rest. Except Brenda and Chilly. "We can't make as much noise, today, my wife. I know that the Colonel heard us and covered for us."

She is undressing herself. "I am going to take a nap. Care to join me?" When she is naked in the bed, he strips down and slides under the sheets. "I do have some business to take care of at the office. I can't take too long."

"That husband, is all up to you."

Meanwhile, Sadie takes Joshua back to the office but she goes back to the Saloon to also nap. Joshua stands to enter and finds Elliot and Tom Baker both there. "What's going on, guys?"

"A warrant for Frank Stevens came in today's mail. He raped another saloon girl in Dodge City, Kansas. He beat her, too. The man is a menace." Elliot says. "I have wired Dodge, that we have him in custody. They will send two U.S. Marshals to come get him by Saturday. So, Sadie doesn't have to testify, or if she does, they can add her allegations to his count and she can testify in Kansas."

"How is Missy? Has anyone heard, today?" He is looking at Elliot.

"Yes, I stopped in at Ma's. She is awake. Ma and the other boarders are taking turns staying in her room, so that she doesn't try it again. She cannot talk. Doc says that she damaged her voice box. The larynx, he called it. He doesn't know if she will ever be able to speak, again, at this point."

"God, that's just awful. How will she ever be able to communicate?" Tom says.

"Doc says that there is a school for the deaf that can teach her to use a form of communication called sign language." Elliot says.

"I hear she is a pretty gal. Is that true? Harkahomé?" Asks Tom.

"She is beautiful. Red hair, small freckles around her nose."

"I am looking for a wife. If she is pretty and cannot talk, she is the perfect woman for me!" Tom laughs, but he laughs alone.

"I don't think it is funny. But I was raised with the Cheyenne. It may have changed the way I look at things." He unlocks the door to the cell area. "Frank, did Deputy Dotson tell you about Missy or the Warrant from Dodge City?" Frank stands to hear the news. "Missy is awake but the Doc thinks that she may never talk, again. Oh, and you are going to Kansas to stand trial for a few assault charges with rapes added. You have been a busy, sick man since you left the Cheyenne. I hope you hang for it." Just then Joshua notices the rope in his cell. "So, Chilly gave it to you and you are too big of a coward to use it? Missy had more courage than you. You know, I cannot sleep in here with you out here. I am going to Sadie's."

"Fornicating with a whore, you are going to hell. You rotten Indian."

"At least, I am loved by the woman I have sex with. I do not have to take her by force tied up. You sick, bastard. I cannot wait until you get what is coming to you."

With that, he walks out of the Sheriff's office and slowly walks to Penny's Parlor. It is loud and crowded, as usual. He goes to the bottom of the stairs and looks up. He is not sure that climbing stairs is going to be too much for him and his laudanum is at the Sheriff's office.

Lee Kirby can see the dilemma on his face. "Harkahomé, don't strain yourself. I will get Sadie. I can move her to the building in back. My ma used to nap in there. I use it more for a store room but three handy men can clean it out. There is a fireplace for heat and everything. It is not much but your woman will not have to walk past prisoners to see you."

"Lee, that is very generous of you. You have done

so much for Sadie and myself. I cannot ask anymore of you."

"Unless I have gone deaf from this constant noise, I did not hear you ask for anything. As I told your Uncle, I think of this town as my legacy and I care for the good people in it. You, Sheriff Lewis and Sadie are the good people. Now, I will not take no for an answer." He motions to the man sweeping the floor in the corner. "Henry, get John and Mike and get all the boxes out of the back building. Then go upstairs to Miss Miller's room and bring her bed and dresser down, and put it in there. Do a nice job for her, sweep the floor, start a fire, make it homey. Now, go. I want her in there, tonight." He comes back to Joshua. "There, it is done. You look like you can use a drink. Please sit and I will pour you a whisky."

"Make it a beer, Lee. And thank you." He sits down while Lee goes behind the bar and pours a tall glass of beer. He hands it to him, then goes up the stairs to get Sadie.

Joshua can see that Lee is telling her about the small building out back. She smiles and throws her hands around him and gives him a kiss on the cheek. Then she turns to Joshua and waves. She goes back into her room and closes the door. Lee comes back down. "She will be right down. She is all excited about the move. Just stay right here. I am going to go supervise the process." He is gone before Joshua can thank him again. Of course, it looked like Sadie has done that very well.

Joshua is very surprised when he felt a pang of jealousy over her kissing him. He looks up at the stairs again. *If I had made it up the stairs, I would have never made it down!* He thinks. He sees Sadie has changed her clothes to her working outfit. He didn't know that she was going to be on duty, tonight. She comes to him and gives him a kiss on the cheek. "How is my favorite Indian, since I last saw you, less than an hour ago?"

"I was very upset. I wanted to kill Frank. He is

going to Kansas. It seems he beat and raped a saloon girl there and she is pressing charges. So, I came here, instead. I wanted to tell you about Missy, too. She tried to kill herself by hanging, yesterday. Chilly got there just in time. Thanks to your insistence. She might not be able to talk again from the damage done to her throat. I will try to visit her tomorrow. You saved her life, you know." He stands to kiss her cheek. "My big-hearted bride-to-be. I love you."

"That's terrible about Missy. I am sure that I would be the last person on Earth, that she'd want to see. I'd like to take you there. I'll wait outside for you."

"See, you are so thoughtful. I will ask Chilly if her room is on the main floor. I cannot do stairs, yet. Or may-haps, she can come downstairs. I attempted to climb to your room. Lee saw the look on my face and understood my hesitance. Lee is a very generous guy."

"He is wonderful. I told him about the baby, from Frank's rape. He was amazed that you'd raise another's child. He thinks very highly of you, of us. That is one of the reasons that he is moving me to the back building. It is for us to stay in. I don't know how long that I can hide my condition, but I will work as much as I can for him, to pay him in advance of me quitting to give birth."

"Are you not joining the family at the Long Horn restaurant?"

"Of course, I am, wild Indians couldn't keep me from them. They are wonderful folks. It is no wonder you and Chilly have turned out so well. Great loving family. But I want to work up until it is time to go. I feel I owe Lee, so much."

"Sadie, I promised to marry you and raise the baby as my own. Do you think that you will want to work, here, after the baby comes? Who will nurse him or her? You are going to be the food source for quite some time. Have you thought this through?"

"No, I guess, I haven't. I haven't had anyone near

me have a baby. I never thought about what comes next. Can we get by on what a lawman makes?"

"I would imagine. I could get a part-time job. I could deliver mail, for Elliot."

"So I would be home, alone with the baby?"

"That is usually how it is done. He cannot suckle from my teat."

"I guess the little house in the back is out of the question."

"And so is the backroom of the jail."

"We will use the little house for now, my love. Then we will need to build or rent a house or apartment of our own. For just us three."

"Until, the next one comes."

"We are going to have more?

"If God, permits."

"I never pictured myself as the motherly type."

"There is the first time for everything. Sadie, you will be the best little mommy and I will be the best tall daddy. And he or she will have Chilly's little one to get into all sorts of trouble with. It will be a great life! Just like I was raised." He kisses her again. "God, I wish I could climb those stairs. I desperately want to make love to you, again. Another habit in the white man's world, that I have become addicted to, like coffee and walls."

SIXTY-ONE
February 14th, 1959
A Saturday in EL Dorado, Kansas

This is the big day. Tonight, is the Valentine Ball. All the Harrick household will be going. Harry has a date for it, also. Her name is Pearl, and she is very petite. He will go to pick her up at seven, take pictures at her house then come back home to take pictures here. GW will be coming here at seven-thirty.

Melinda had picked up her dress, after dinner, last night. Her eighteen-year-old son, Jude, and lovely sixteen-year-old Gloria Rose have a dates, as well.

This ball has been an annual event since 1883. GW's Great-Great Grandmother, Carolyn and her husband were the founding couple back then. The founding family did miss attending one year. It was 1896, when they traveled to Oklahoma for a family reunion with their long-lost nephew, Harkahomé. The Valentine ball was organized by them but they left two weeks prior and missed the whole event.

Today, the Johnson farmhouse is very busy. Joshua and Helen brought the four children. They left Kevin, whose fever broke but he was still sickly. They hired a nurse to be with him while they traveled to EL Dorado. Helen took over the Ball fundraising and organizing in 1940 when her Great Grandmother Carolyn turned seventy-five. Also, from Lawrence, was the James family. Professor Eddie and his wife Carolyn brought their children Jonathan and Bessie, also. This gathering prior to the ball is a chaotic but practiced dance. Bessie is excited to dance with Melinda's boy, Jude Collins.

Harry leaves at six-thirty to pick-up Pearl. Carrie is ready for when GW arrives. His impromptu proposal at dinner, surprised her. She has wondered for years about marrying GW but she thought it was impossible. Now that they have declared their shared love, and had an intimate first date, she assumed that they would be man and wife, someday. Saying yes this soon seems unwise.

Her gown's skirt is blue and white stripes. The sleeveless bodice is light shiny blue. The skirt has horizontal stripes, and the length is mid-calf. There is a ruffle where each of the blue and white strips meet. Her jacket is a slightly darker satin blue. It's very high and wide lapel leads down to three large buttons. The sleeves are extremely wide at the forearm, but gets tight just below the elbow. She has it adorned with extra-long white gloves. At the waist, the coat branches off in five sections, and all five sections meet at the skirt's bottom. Her curly hair is pinned up on the sides, just like Audrey Hepburn's hair. She is wearing white long cultured pearls around her neck and in her ears. The pins in her hair have cultured pearls on them, also. She had a pair of pumps dyed to the color of the blue jacket.

Everyone is ready at the Harrick house. GW comes a little after seven. "I could not wait to see you Carrie." He explains.

"I could not wait to see you, either." She smiles.

"You look amazing! To wear something, you designed must feel wonderful. This is so gorgeous. Twirl for me." She does so.

Anna says, "Please kids, let me take photos of you. She has her Kodak camera out and the couple pose for several photos. Harry and Pearl arrive just in time and their photos are taken. GW offers to take Anna's and Henry's pictures, as well.

Anna asks, "GW. When will your mother get there? I don't want to get their too early."

"She was leaving the house as I was. As soon as she got into EL Dorado, she headed off to the Opera House to supervise the decorations. Then, she came back to take her twenty-minute power nap."

Anna says, "Yes. She always loved her power naps.

I always hated them. By the time I fall asleep, it is time to get up. It just makes me mad. But your mother has always done that. She started when she was pregnant with you, GW."

"Carrie, Mom was saying that she will want a dress designed by you next year. I told her about Aunt Melinda's. Just wait until everyone sees this dress. It is so perfect on you."

"It is hard not to be when it was made for me."

"A good point. You see, I am out of my element here."

Henry says, "You are in good company."

More pictures are taken and they all deem that it is time to head to the ball. Harry, GW and Henry all drive separately.

***

Helen has ordered giant spot lights in front of the Opera House to bring attention to this grand gala. Many people have chauffeurs bring them in style. GW and Carrie arrive first. The local press was there, snapping pictures and taking names. When asked who they were, GW answered, "I am Grant William Lewis the great-great-grandson of Grant and Carolyn Johnson, founders of the ball. This is my date Carrie Ann Harrick who is an up and coming fashion designer." He lifts her hand and twirls her so that her dress shows its movement. "This is one of her original designs. You will see Mrs. Melinda Collins, who owns the Kroger Grocery Store, is wearing another Carrie Ann original."

Now there is a line forming behind them. The press thanks them but is looking to interview the next couple. Carrie grabs his arm and pulls him away. "GW, you should not have made that about me. You should have talked about your mother, Helen, taking over the Chairmanship or something."

"No, she gets plenty of spotlight." He points to the large lights circling into the sky. As they walk into the crowded ballroom he says, "You should get credit where credit is due. You were just shot but you made your Aunt's dress in five days. I am in awe of you!"

"Are you?" This was the voice of Carrie's nightmare. Her smile disappears as she turns to see Mickey standing next to them dressed as a waiter and holding a tray of hors devours. "Is this the guy that you *think* you love, instead of me?"

Before she can answer, GW steps between her and Mickey. He has his hand in his pocket. "And you must be the punk that shot my girl. Why would you shoot the woman you profess to love?"

"That was her fault. She should not have grabbed my gun. That is how people get hurt."

"So that means that if I pull a gun on you, you wouldn't grab for it?" As he says this he pulls out a small derringer.

Mickey laughs at it. "Is that a toy weapon?"

GW looks to Carrie Ann. "This was the Colonels, he used it to kill your mother's attacker. Mickey, we can walk out of here, get into a waiting police car or I can end this another way. Your choice. What will it be?"

"That little thing couldn't stop me."

GW puts it to his temple. "It will spray your brains all over. That will be hard to put back. Carrie, stay right here. Mickey come with me. There is a patrol car waiting for you."

Carrie interrupts, "GW, how is this happening?"

"I knew that he escaped his jail cell. My father knows a security guard in the facility. He called Father yesterday morning to tell us that Mickey was loose. They have been watching Clara's apartment and his Wichita family's house for him to show up."

"Why didn't you tell me? I went out alone, yesterday. I thought I was safe." She sees her mother and runs to her. Anna can see the very small gun in GW's hand. "Mother, he escaped yesterday morning. I was in danger the whole day, but I didn't know." Carrie sobs as Anna holds her. GW has his attention on the gun and Mickey.

"Anna, please calm her down. I need to remove the riff raff from my family's Valentine Ball. Mickey, do an about face, if you will." Henry sees Anna and Carrie and rushes over. GW has Mickey walking a few paces. "Henry, can you take the tray from your daughter's attacker? I am trying to get him to the police car." Henry takes the tray from him, then dumps the canapes on the ground and brings the heavy tray back up to hit Mickey across the head. Mickey drops to one knee and reaches for the spot that took the most impact. He looks at his hand to see if there is any trace of blood

"Sorry, GW. That tray slipped out of my hand." Henry says. "Is this the asshole that almost killed my daughter?" GW nods as Mickey gets to his feet. No one saw Henry's right hook but it landed perfectly up Mickey's nose. Mickey hit the floor. "Okay, that one I am not sorry for."

GW hands Henry the derringer, and as he is going to Carrie's side he says, "Oh, don't shoot him. He isn't worth the trouble to clean the gun. A patrol car is here to get him if he dared to show up. I cannot believe that he did." He has his arms around Carrie. "I am sorry for not telling you, Carrie. I didn't know until late morning and you said that you'd be back home by then. Also, he needed some time to drive here. We are about 600 miles away." Mickey has gotten to his feet again.

"I know but he spoiled my grand evening." She is crying against his shoulder. "Don't be silly. Aunt Melinda isn't here in your fabulous other creation, yet. Go with your mother and powder your nose, my love. I do need to escort the trash out of the building. When I come back, we are going to dance the night away. I promise." He kisses her forehead. "Now off you go, please." He gives Anna and Carrie a gentle push toward the restrooms.

As soon as their backs are turned and they have gone enough to be blended into the crowd, GW turns on Mickey. He grabs him by the shirt collar, and gives him an upper cut to the stomach. Mickey doubles over. GW then grabs him by one arm and twists it behind his back and holds it high. "Listen here, if you ever cause another tear to fall from my girl's eyes, again, you will wish you were dead. Now, start walking forward. Do not forget that her father has the gun against you and he is also mad enough at you to shoot with only the slightest provocation. Do you want to test him? Let me know so that I can get out of the way of the blood spray, first."

"NO. Don't shoot, please. I will behave." He says. GW senses a slight snicker to his voice, so he kicks him hard behind the knee and Mickey is thrown down on the hardwood flooring for the third time. "My kneecap. I think you've broken it."

"Good. No more snickering then. GET UP! I will have you in that police car, NOW."

"I cannot walk." He uses that as an excuse.

Henry sees a few fellow farm owners and calls them over. "Gentlemen, this is the man that shot my daughter. Between us all, can we carry this menace into the police car? It is just out this entrance." As if a practiced team, they all grabbed an arm or leg and carried him with Henry still holding the derringer. Henry says to GW, "Son, as far as I am concerned, tonight is your TENTH date!"

GW smiles. He doesn't accompany them but heads toward the restroom to find his date. His timing is perfect and she and Anna are coming out just as he gets there. He looks at Carrie. "Picture perfect, yet again. Let me just go wash the criminal off my hands and I am all yours." He walks into the men's room. The music has started.

Carrie looks to her mother, "I wonder what is keeping Aunt Melinda? I hope she isn't having a problem

346

putting on the dress."

Anna looks at her. "Carrie, my sister hasn't been on time for anything her whole life. Why would she start now?"

GW comes out, rubbing his hands as her father hurries up to them. Henry says, "Mickey is on his way downtown and Melinda is outside, creating a huge scene with your gown. She wants you, so hurry!" Everyone rushes to the front doors and there are several flash bulbs going off on Melinda. Not only does she have the red velvet and white fur stole and red pump shoes but her purse and jewelry are all the same color red. Melinda is carrying the white rabbit muffler which matches the stole's neckline. She has her hair up in a chignon and little red variegated miniature roses in her hair. She looks like a model in a fashion magazine.

She sees Carrie out of the corner of her eyes. "There is the designer of this gown, Carrie Ann Harrick. She is my niece but that doesn't stop me from recognizing a genius when I see one." She walks over to Carrie and takes her hand and squeezes it. "Are there any questions for my designer?"

One woman steps forward. "My dear, I am from the Wichita Press, the modern Woman's section. May I have a few moments of your time? Is your dress one of your creations, also? It is just lovely."

"Thank you, of course, you can. But just a few minutes, my date has promised to dance the night away with me and I would like to let him." She looks up at GW and he winks at her.

"Darling, with a date like him, I don't blame you!"

***

The band is playing another waltz. Carrie is dancing with GW. She has her head on his tall shoulder. She tippy toes to whisper in his ear, "I wish that we could be alone. I'd love to show you how much I appreciate your quick action in saving me from Mickey."

"I know of a way to thank me."

"I bet you do."

"Your father said that as far as he is concerned this is our tenth date."

She holds him away from her. "Oh did he now? Why did he say that?"

"I think it had to do with the fact that I kind of beat Mickey up, just a little. I wanted Mickey to know who is in charge, here."

"Beat him up, how?"

"A gut-wrenching stomach punch and a blow to the back of the shin. Each immobilized him enough that he didn't dare try anything on the way to the police car. Your father was very cool about it. He called to some burly friends of his and they carried Mickey out while your father kept the gun on him."

"All this happened while I was in the bathroom?"

"Yes. As soon, as they got him out, I came to you. And that is why your father said he considered this our tenth date. So, do you have a yes or a no, for me?"

"Oh, GW. It has always been a yes! I just didn't want to say it in front of my parents. Do you forgive me for deceiving you that way?"

"I tell you what, Miss Carolyn Ann Harrick. I promise to hold it against you my whole life. Now kiss me!"

Just as their lips were about to touch, the music stopped. GW says, "Carrie Ann? Can I have our first kiss as fiancées?"

"Yes, you can." She takes his face in her hands, bends it down and she kisses him.

He breaks away from her and takes her by the hand and goes to the band as they were about to leave the stand. He asks one of the singers, "My girl just said yes, to my proposal. Can you play an old-fashioned waltz for us?

How about 'And the Band Played On'?"

He nods to GW. He calls out to the band members as they were about to take a break. "Hey guys. We have a very special request." He tells them the song and they shuffle through their sheet music and return to their instruments. He gets on the microphone. "Ladies and Gentlemen, I have a special request from a very lucky gentleman. It seems his young lady has said yes to a very important question. Young man, what is your name and your girl's name?"

"Grant William Lewis and this is Carrie Ann Harrick." GW is beaming with pride.

"Let's give this happy couple a round of applause, if you please." The room starts to clap. Helen and Joshua go to the couple. Anna and Henry do too. Melinda and Mark, Matthew and Susan, Carolyn and Eddie, as well as many cousins and friends of Carrie's, go to them. The announcer says, "I see you have many friends here. Ladies and Gentlemen, please – they wanted to dance a special dance. Grant William Lewis, please take your bride-to-be in your arms."

GW does so and the band starts playing the old waltz song from the early 1890's. GW looks to his gorgeous fiancée, "Happy Darling?"

"The happiest. Happy Valentine's Day." Carrie is smiling from ear to ear.

"We are going to do this every year to celebrate, you know."

"I cannot imagine any better way than to have your arms around me and dancing to this music. Shall we call this our song?"

As he was about to answer, the verse came on, so he answered in the song, "He'd glide 'cross the floor with the girl, he adored and the band played on."

SIXTY-TWO
February 14th, 1896
A Friday in Pennysville, Oklahoma

Today's eleven o'clock stagecoach should have both Doctors Lewis and family. Dr. Joseph, the oldest living sibling is forty-four and Dr. Lizbet is forty-two. Joseph is bringing his wife, Katherine and children. Samuel, is fifteen and Constance, is thirteen. Dr. Lizbet never married but is bringing her long-time friend, Dr. Ezra Scott, who also never married but has accompanied Lizzie to and from EL Dorado since Carolyn's wedding in 1882.

Grant, Carolyn and her children are waiting with Chilly, Brenda, Joshua and Sadie. The children are chasing each other, as the young, usually do. Twice, Carolyn yells to them to calm down and act with decorum. It works for just a few minutes each. Two minutes before eleven, Kevin comes out of the hotel and runs to the depot.

"I am sorry, I am late. Mother had me do my school lessons, first. Thank goodness, I am not too late." He says to the grown-ups then he joins the other children, running, laughing and playing.

At ten after eleven, the stagecoach still has not arrived. Chilly gets a bad feeling. The only other stage that was late more than ten minutes was the one carrying the mining money that was hijacked. Elliot comes down to the depot, he looks at his watch. "Sheriff?"

"I know, Deputy. Let's give it ten more minutes and we will telegram the Bartlesville Depot and Sheriff." Chilly bends down to say this as quietly as he can. He looks to his red-haired sister. "Carolyn, can you give us a song while we wait? I haven't heard you sing in so long."

"I don't like to sing without my piano accompaniment. I am not as in tune as I once was." She says blushing.

"Poppycock!" Both Grant and Chilly say. Chilly

continues, "Come on, Sis. How about a Christmas Carol, then? I know you know those by heart."

"No, Chilly. I am not in the mood to sing, please."

"Then I will, join me, Harkahomé"

"I am afraid that I do not recall the words to Christmas songs. Mother and I tried to sing them the first few years, when we kept track of the holidays. We became so lost in the Cheyenne way, that a few winters went passed where we did not think of Christmas, at all. I would surely love to hear an old fashion song. Chilly sing Silent Night, please."

Chilly started and as off key as he could be, he sang, "Silent Night, Holy Night. All is Calm. All is bright, round yon . . ."

"STOP! You are hurting my ears and not helping Joshua remember one of the prettiest songs ever sung." She says this as she walks up to her younger brother and slaps him on the arm. "You don't fool me, either of you, but it worked. Here goes." She straightens up to her full height and sings the first two stanzas beautifully. Then Sadie joins her as well as Brenda. Both Harkahomé and Chilly look at each other and smile. Both of their women sing, pitch perfect! When the women finish they all blush. Carolyn says, "Ladies, why did you put me through that if you could sing?"

Brenda says, "Chilly asked you, not us. He has never heard me sing. Sadie, did Joshua know you could sing?"

"I didn't know I could sing!" She says and everyone laughs.

Elliot looks at the time, again. It is twenty after. Chilly is looking at him and nods his head to let him know to send the telegrams.

Chilly looks to Harkahomé, "Any other requests?"

"I heard a pretty little tune in Wichita. It is a waltz." Sadie says. "It is called, *The Band Played On.*" Do you want to hear it?" She asks Joshua.

"If you would be so kind." He struggles to stand up. "Can you sing and dance at the same time?"

"I would love to, when you are stronger. Let me just sing it. Carolyn, Brenda? Do either of you know it?"

Carolyn says, "I have heard it but do not know the words. I need to buy the sheet music for it. It is a lovely song. Please sing it, Sadie." So, Sadie sang:

"Matt Casey formed a Social Club
That beat the town for style, and
Hired for a meeting place a hall.

"When payday came around each week,
They greased the floor with wax. And
Dance with noise and vigor at the ball.

"Each Saturday you'd see them
dressed up in Sunday clothes;
Each lad would have his
Sweetheart by his side.

"When Casey led the
First grand march,
They all would fall in line,
Behind the man who
Was their joy and pride.

"For

"Casey would waltz
with the Strawberry blonde
and the band played on.

"He'd glide 'cross the floor
with the girl, he adored
and the band played on.

"His head was so loaded
It nearly exploded,
The poor girl would shake with alarm!

"He'd ne'er leave the girl
with the strawberry curl
and the band played on.

"Such kissing in the corner and
Such whispering in the hall, And
Kissing and love making did his share.

"At twelve o'clock exactly
They all would fall in line,
Then march down to the
Dining Hall and eat.
"But Casey would not
Join them although every
Thing was fine,
But he stayed upstairs
And exercise his feet.

"For

"Casey would waltz
with the Strawberry blonde
and the band played on.

"He'd glide 'cross the floor
with the girl, he adored
and the band played on.

"His head was so loaded
It nearly exploded,
The poor girl would shake with alarm!

"He'd ne'er leave the girl

with the strawberry curl
and the band played on.

"Now when the dance was over and
The band played Home Sweet Home,
They waltz once with the girl
That he loved best.

"Most all the friends are married that
Casey used to know,
And Casey too has taken '
Him a wife.

"The blond he used to
Waltz and glide with on the
Ballroom floor, is happy Missis
Casey now for life.

For

"Casey would waltz
with the Strawberry blonde
and the band played on.

"He'd glide 'cross the floor
with the girl, he adored
and the band played on.

"His head was so loaded
It nearly exploded,
The poor girl would shake with alarm!

"He'd ne'er leave the girl
with the strawberry curl
and the band played on.

"Yes

"Casey would waltz
with the Strawberry blonde
and the band played on.

"He'd glide 'cross the floor
with the girl, he adored
and the band played on.

"His head was so loaded
It nearly exploded,
The poor girl would shake with alarm!

"He'd ne'er leave the girl
with the strawberry curl
and the band played on.

Before she reached the first refrain, Sadie had not just the Lewis family listening but she drew a small crowd, also. When she finished the song, everyone clapped whole heartedly. Harkahomé was still standing and after he applauded he called out. "And this smart, beautiful songstress, is going to be MY wife!" A few people hooped and hollered. The Lewis crowd clapped louder.

Chilly says, "Sadie, with your voice, you don't need to deal twenty-one, you should be an entertainer. We could use a little culture, around here."

"If my singing is it, it would be 'a little'. Say, isn't the stage getting extremely late? The service on this line is bad. How often does this happen?"

"This is the second time since I have been Sheriff." Chilly says.

"Elliot, you keep a mighty close watch on the stage. How many times would you say it's late?" Sadie asks

"I have been here for seventeen years. Postmaster for ten. That is why I meet each stage. I get any mail bag that is on it. In ten years, this is the fourth time it is late more than ten minutes."

"Wow, that's a good record. What is the reason, for each of the delays?" Joshua asks.

Elliot looks around sheepishly before he answers. "Each has been a robbery. Sheriff, I have sent both the telegrams, for you."

"Thank you, Deputy. Please, everyone go back to the hotel. I need to send one more wire, then I am going to the Sheriff's office to wait for them to respond. Deputy, I think we might need to form another posse.

"Yes, Sheriff. I will get on that."

"Carolyn, when you get back to the hotel, can you send the Colonel to my office?"

"Of course, brother." She calls her children to come back to the hotel with her and they object but listen to her.

Brenda puts her hand on Chilly's arm. "I shall go to your mother with your sister. I hope your family isn't going through what Sadie and I went through. Be safe, Chilly. Bend down and let me give you a kiss, my dear."

Chilly looks down at his new bride. "I will be careful, my girl. Now, I'll take that kiss." He bends low and puts one hand on her face and outlines her lips. "God, you're beautiful." Then he puts his lips to hers. "Now go sit with my mother and tell her your life story. I find it fascinating, so will she. It might keep her from worrying."

***

Harkahomé and Chilly are in the Sheriff's office. Will comes in, "The stagecoach is missing? What is the plan?" He is wearing a gun belt and carrying his shotgun.

"We are waiting to hear from the depot in Bartlesville. I need to know if it left on time, who was working, who the passengers are, and what were they carrying besides the passengers. The last missing stage was carrying a mining company payroll to Tulsa. If we need to search for the coach, I will contact Sheriff John

Lucas to head this way while we head his way." Will looks very impressed. "This isn't my first missing coach. This is how Joshua and I met our gals. They were on the last coach to be missing."

Elliot comes in, "Sheriff, I have gone to the same places as last time, looking for volunteers to meet up with us. I have not been able to find Tom Baker, yet. No one seems to know where he's gone."

"I am not too worried. He has the day off. He might be fishing or gone to Barnsdall to see his Ma. We could send a wire to his ma to tell him to come back here." Chilly says.

"How soon did you tell the volunteers to meet here?" Will asks.

"Told them within the next half an hour. I got more of them, seeing that you got the last posse paid."

"I knew that would be an incentive to do the right thing." Chilly says. "I could use a drink." He reaches into his bottom desk drawer and pulls out a bottle. He has a few small glasses that he pulls out also. "Anyone want to join me?"

Will says, "It's a little early for me, little brother."

Elliot starts to laugh. He looks from brother to brother, and laughs more.

Chilly asks in a booming voice. "What the hell is so frickin' funny?"

"He called you little and you didn't blink an eye! You have at least three inches on him."

"Deputy, do you want me to demote you back to 'Elliot the Idiot'? I am his younger brother."

"I know, Sheriff Lewis. It's just funny, sorry."

Will says, "I remember explaining to two-year-old Samuel why I was Joseph's little brother. It is an odd concept."

Harkahomé says, "I did not have that problem. My little half-brother, Avonaco, stayed three inches shorter than myself. Same height as Kanuna. You know, I miss them. Mother, especially."

"That is one thing that upsets Mother Beth, she never got to see Lydia again. She was a true daughter to her. I remember how she cried at the news that you were not coming home with us. She sobbed using both your names. 'Oh, my poor Lydia, I'll never see you again. Oh, my darling Joshua, I'll never see you again!' She took it all so hard."

"I feel very bad about that. My mother asked me if I wanted to go back with the two of you, but I felt that I needed to stay and watch over Mother. Kanuna was a very good man, but I could not imagine leaving her there with him alone. I did not know that my decision caused Gram Beth's such sorrow."

Will puts his hand on Harkahomé's shoulder. "You were wise beyond your years, and acted like a true Lewis. Staying to protect your mother."

"It wasn't just that, I loved the life that the Cheyenne offered me. I loved my blood-brother, Degatoga and little Avonaco. I could not bring myself to leave any of them."

Just then the telegram boy ran into the office. "Sheriff Lewis, I have two telegrams for you." Chilly takes them from him. As a matter of practice, the boy turns and waits outside for a return wire request.

Chilly reads the one from the depot, then he says, "Okay, our family is on this stage as is Scott Jones. The driver is Andy Dalton and riding shotgun is Bruce Donaldson. The strongbox has six hundred dollars again. DAMN IT! I am tired of this. Scott Jones must be in on this. He was a passenger on the last missing stage." He hands the telegram to the Colonel.

Then he reads the second telegram. "Your old friend John Lucas is Sheriff at Bartlesville. He is forming a posse, also. Unless he hears back from us, he will be on the road by twelve-thirty." Chilly looks at his watch. "I guess it is time to ride. Elliot, did you get our provisions?"

358

"Of course, Sheriff." He looks out the window. "I see about fifteen mounted volunteers. I told Petey at the stable to ready two Morgan horses for you. I will send a wire to Tom's Ma. The Marshals for Frank should be here later today. I will keep an eye on the transfer of the prisoner and on Deputy Lewis for you, Sheriff. Anything else?"

Before Sheriff Lewis answers, Joshua says, "I don't need someone to keep an eye on me!" He stands up to tower over Elliot.

"Just a manner of expression, Deputy. I meant no offense."

"Deputies! I demand that you get along." He looks at Will. "See what fun you miss being a farmer?" He laughs.

"Yes, my life seems dull in comparison." He says while laughing, too."

"Sheriff, Petey has your horses. Tallest Morgans in the stable, it seems." Says Elliot.

"Joshua, cable John Henry Pickford of the mining company. Tell him that Scott Jones is missing again. Ask him if the same conditions apply for this ride as the last missing coach. Or words to that affect."

"I understand, Uncle. Be safe out there. Remember, someone else's money isn't worth YOUR life. I wish that I could join you."

"I know Harkahomé. Keep an eye on Deputy Dotson and the town for me."

"Hey!" Elliot says.

Once outside, the brothers mount up. Chilly gives them the talk. "No wondering off on your own. Keep your guns holstered until you see my gun out, not before. Do you understand and can you obey that order?" A few mumbles and grunts are heard. "We will secure the coach and some of us will accompany it back here, then, the rest of us will search for the person or persons responsible for its delay. Let's mount up."

***

It is just at nightfall, that the posse catches up with tracks of the coach leaving the trail. The last coach went off to the west of the trail. This time it is going eastward. "Damn, we are not going to find anything in the dark, even with the two lanterns that Elliot provided. And to top it off, this is the dark phase of the moon. DAMN!!" Chilly is very aggravated. "And there are two children on that coach, most likely scared to death!" He looks to his older brother. "Why don't we leave the others to camp here and you and I continue the search. I couldn't sleep anyway. You and I know how to track and can be quieter than all these guys. Are you willing?"

"More than willing. Let's take one lantern and keep the flame low and hang it between us on the horses. We might be able to at least get close to them. They could not have gotten too far off this road before they had to stop for the night also." Will says.

Chilly nods, then calls out to the posse. "I want you all to camp here and wait for Sheriff Lucas from Bartlesville. At first light, if he is not here yet, leave two men here to show them the way and the rest of you come find us. My brother and I will follow the Coach tracks and try to leave signs for you to find us. Any questions?" No one says anything.

"Good. Give me one of the lanterns and some extra rope. Blacksmith George, you're in charge. Pick sentries, etcetera." He looks to his brother. "Colonel, let's go find our family!"

***

The brothers traveled very slowly. Taking turns watching the track and looking out for a campfire. Roughly two hours later, they could see a small glow

360

coming from the other side of a grove of trees. "Douse the light, Colonel. We may have found them. I'll mark the trail." He had a bottle of mercurochrome. He takes two light wood sticks and rubs some of the medical red liquid on them. Then he puts them down on the trail in a small arrow. Will watches him.

"Very clever." He says.

"The sticks will almost glow in the daylight. Let's go."

They ride up to the tree line about four hundred feet away. They tie up the horses and carefully walk through the forty feet of dense woods. When they get to the clearing, they can see the small campfire. It appears that the coach is there but the team is disconnected. Without talking, the brothers separate to enter the camp from different sides.

Chilly cannot see his family. He assumes that they are asleep in the Coach. He can see a panel of the coach removed on the backside. The real payroll was discovered, he thinks. Will is in place on the other side of the fire. There is a man leaned up against the stump, sound asleep. He must be the lookout. There are two men asleep on their bed rolls near the fire. Chilly walks up to the stump and puts his gun to the head of the sleeping sentry. He wakes but doesn't say anything as he sees Chilly's gun on the side of his nose. Chilly backs away to the first man on the ground. It is the owner's son. He kicks him awake. The look on his face as he faces Chilly's other gun pointed at his nose, tells Chilly that he is in on the robbery. Will has moved around the fire and kicks the third man, who wakes with a rifle in his face.

Chilly says, "You are all under arrest!"

"Not so fast, Sheriff Lewis." Says a voice behind him. "Don't move a muscle. I knew that this was the worst stage to steal with your family being on it, but Scott Pickford was insistent. I told him he was crazy, but he would not be talked out of it." The voice was Tom Bakers.

"Tom, it's you, isn't it?"

"Yes, Sheriff. After those guys messed up the last robbery, and Scott was rescued, he told me that this time HE was going to try it himself and asked for my help. Just couldn't be helped that your family would be on the stage with the biggest purse the mining company has ever moved. Four thousand dollars! Split four ways is enough money to start over anywhere."

"Is my family safe?"

A voice shouts from the coach. "We are all fine, Uncle? Quite the adventure really." It is young Samuel. "Does he have the drop on you, Uncle?"

Will yells back, "You've been reading too many Western dime store novels, Samuel. But yes, currently we are at a Mexican stand-off. Chilly has two guns on two guys and I have a gun on another but someone has a gun to Chilly's back."

Lizzie calls out. "I know that this is the worst timing, but I really have to make water. Is there anyway, your Mexican stand-off could be temporarily frozen while I walk into the woods? I am going to pee here or there and I'd rather it there, please?"

Chilly says, "Come on, Tom. My sister has always had a very weak bladder. It is one of the reasons that she doesn't travel. I mentioned that to you, haven't I?"

"Fine!" Tom says, "But be very quick about it. And no funny stuff or your brother gets his brains blown out."

Lizzie is lowering herself out of the carriage. "Look, Tom, is it? I have a nervous bladder. Threatening me, only makes it worse." She takes a few steps, holding herself in the lower area like a little girl. "OH, OH! Now you've done it! This is so embarrassing!" She freezes a few feet from Chilly and lifts her dress slightly and the ground becomes flooded. She starts to cry out. "OH My God, I want to die. Why does this always happen to me?" She takes a few more steps. "This is all your fault. Look my whole hem is soaked. I told you that I have a condition!"

As he stands transfixed on her hem, she puts down her dress and brings up a small Derringer pistol and brings it to his head. With the calmest of voices, she says, "Lower your weapon from my brother or YOUR brains will be blown out. Don't under estimate the power of this little gun, it will do the trick. I swear!" With that, Chilly turns and grabs Tom's gun.

"Lizzie, that was magnificent! I remember when you pulled that on Johnnie What's-his-name! You were – what twelve?" Asks Will. "You were with Ian and I. God, it worked then, too! I am so proud of you, Sis. To pull that off as an adult is just unbelievable!"

"Thank God, you and Ian told that story enough times over the years. I was prepared. Okay, enough reminiscing, time to tie up the four guys. The rest of the posse will be here a little after sun-up. Joseph, Ezra, Samuel can you come out and give us a hand with the rope. Pretend you have done a surgical procedure and you are sewing up the gapping, pussing hole!" Chilly says.

Everyone is out of the carriage and Joseph and Ezra do tie up the four men as Chilly, Lizzie and Will keep their guns drawn.

When finished, Lizzie looks to Ezra, "Darling, do be a dear and go get my suitcase down. I have to burn this dress and all the evidence of this awful incident."

"Lizzie, my pet. It is Valentine's Day. . . SO. . . With your hem full of urine, bad guys tied up next to us and your three brothers watching," he gets down on one knee, "Will you finally agree to be my bride? We can make it a triple wedding, and make me the happiest man alive, because I love you so much!"

Lizzie is just gaping at him. "Ezra, this is not the most romantic time to propose!" She bends down and kisses his cheek.

"Lizzie, you and I both know, this isn't the first time that I've asked you. Will you do me this great honor and let me be the husband of the most crazy, courageous

Doctor in the West? My knees are killing me, hurry and say yes!"

"I need to, just to get you off your knees." He stands. She puts his head in her hands. "Look who is the crazy one, now!" Then she tenderly kisses him. "So future husband, go get my suitcase down, please!"

SIXTY-THREE
February 15th, 1959
A Sunday in EL Dorado, Kansas

As the band is taking its last break of the evening, Helen takes the microphone and announces "Ladies and Gentlemen. As we are preparing to wrap this evening up, I thought you'd all like to know that the night's fundraising total is twelve thousand dollars for disease research and expansion of the children's ward of the hospital. It is a new record, everyone, thank you so very much for attending and making this all possible. Oh, and all my family and extended family, come back to the farmhouse. I am having breakfast brought in for everyone."

GW looks at his girl. "We are going to be fashionably late for that." He winks at Carrie.

"What is on your mind, fiancé?"

"A little smooching in my Ford truck."

"I like the way you think." Carrie smiles and blushes.

It's now a little after midnight. The crowd has dwindled down. The last one's present are mostly couples in love, slow dancing. Melinda is in her husband, Mark's arms. Anna is in Henry's. Judy is in Judd's. Susan is in Matthew's. Carolyn is in Eddie's. Helen is in Joshua's. Carrie is in GW's. Pearl is in Harry's. Bessie James is in Jude Collins'.

The band announces that this will be the last dance. Boos come from all those standing, holding their partners. The announcer says, "Well, we will make it a repeat. Please get the irony." He calls the song out to the band, who rearranges the sheet music. "Our last song will be 'And The Band Played On.' For you GW." He points to GW holding Carrie. "Luckiest Man Alive"

Everyone applauds as the band starts up. Carrie looks up at GW. "I don't want this night to end. Why does it have to end?"

"Because, if the night doesn't end, we can't marry."

"Oh, that's right. We aren't married, yet. When do you want to do that?"

"I am in no hurry. Tomorrow will be fine."

"GW, that will be the shortest engagement in history."

"Not really. My grandfather's baby brother asked Brenda to marry him in the evening, and they were married that same night. She went from Brenda Masters to Brenda Lewis in a blink of an eye." Says GW.

"She was a Masters?" I wonder if she is related to Papa Judd?"

"Wouldn't that be something? I think they met, when the Colonel was alive and Carolyn gave him that last costume party. Someone would have said something, don't you think?"

GW swings his Carrie close to her grandparents. "Papa Judd, do you have any relatives named Brenda Masters? She married my great Uncle Chilly"

Judy says, "We met her at the Colonel's party." She puts her hand up to her face. "Judd, her eyes were pale blue, remember? We never knew her maiden name. I wonder why she didn't mention it?"

"Judy, dear, I do not think we told her our last name. But my Uncle George, the doctor and Aunt Martha had a girl named Brenda. She was an adult when I was born, I think."

GW says, "I will write my Uncle and ask about his wife. Someday. Right now, the band is playing and I am dancing with my favorite girl."

Judd looks at his wife, "Aren't we all?"

The band stops and everyone is sad that a gorgeous night has come to an end. The Ball was a huge success, yet again. Many people gave generously while having the best time dancing.

As they are leaving, two uniform policemen come in

and ask for Henry Harrick. GW comes forward. "What is wrong, officers?"

"Are you Henry?" GW shakes his head no, as Henry comes to them.

"I am Henry Harrick. Is it about Mickey Roosevelt?" He asks.

"Yes, he has gotten away, again." the taller of the two says,

GW looks at Henry, while his Carrie starts trembling in his arms. "I should have killed him!" GW and Henry say at the same time. Carrie looks between her father and fiancé, and gives a small nervous laugh.

"Now what?" Says Henry to the two officers. "How will you protect my daughter?"

"We were told to escort her home and keep watch on the house."

Carrie looks at them. "NO. I am going to the Johnson Family Farmhouse and be with my family. You can follow us there."

"Our orders were very specific. Take you to your home and sit on the house." Says the shorter of the two.

"I wasn't given any orders. I have a life." She objects.

Henry comes forward. "Carrie, these men are here to protect you."

GW says, "I think it very odd." He looks for his dad. "Father?" Joshua comes to him. GW explains the situation. When he finishes, he adds, "Father, I think she would be safer at our home. Call their Captain and have those orders revoked."

Joshua looks at the officers, "What is your Captain's name?"

They both look at each other. The taller one pulls his gun, and the smaller one does, also, but a second later. The tall one speaks, "This is not how it is supposed to go! Carrie is going with us."

GW still has his arm around her waist. "I am not

letting her go anywhere without me. Why are you insisting?"

The two men look at each other, again. "Orders are orders." Says the taller one. Henry looks at their badges and nameplates.

He addresses the taller one, "Officer Dillard, is it? I am Henry Harrick and she is my daughter. You can protect her by staying with her, not forcing her to go with you. She is not under arrest, for goodness sakes." Henry gets to the officer's elbow. He reaches up and has GW's derringer in his hand. He has it pointed at his head. "Drop the weapons, both of you. Who are you working for?"

The shorter one, with Benson on his nametag says, "I told Mickey this wouldn't work."

Dillard says, "Shut your mouth, Steve."

Carrie looks at them, "Is Mickey in custody, or isn't he?"

"Don't say another word, Steve." The tall one says.

Everyone looks at the officer called Steve. "We were the ones waiting outside and we took Mickey to a secure location. He is waiting for Carrie, there. We are taking her with us. Put your little pea shooter away. We have real guns."

"I think they call this a Mexican stand-off." Says Professor Eddie James. He has a .38 pointed at Steve.

As Steve and Dillard look at Eddie, Joshua pulls out his Colt .44. He points it at Steve, also. "My count is two guns and a pea shooter against two guns. I think the side with the pea shooter wins."

Dillard reaches out to grab Carrie. He tugs her arm as GW holds her. Henry puts the gun up against Dillard's temple. "Is your life worth whatever he is paying you? I am not afraid to end it, right here and now."

Another voice speaks from the doorway. "If you want a job done right, you have to do it yourself." Mickey is holding another gun. "So three guns beats two guns and a pea shooter. Do you want to challenge me? I will take you on. Carrie is mine. All mine. Give her to me."

Dillard still has hold of Carrie. "Come this way! Carrie."

"No. You all can go to hell!?" She wrestles her arm away. "Daddy? Uncles? Take your best shot. I will not have my life dictated to by some punk who is delusional." She walks up to Mickey, while GW was trying to hold her back. "You can go straight to hell!" She strikes him across his face. He is momentarily bent over and Carrie grabs the gun from him so fast that he does not have a chance to stop her. She puts it to his face. "I am sick of you and your delusions. I don't know how you got these men to help you, but they can go to hell, too. My uncles will be very happy to send them there! Now, tell the two officers to put down their guns. Now the count is three guns and a pea shooter to two guns and this game is over." He stands there just looking at her. She reaches up and slaps him in the face, again. "Are you deaf, Mickey? I was the one shot! I said call off your hired help! I will shoot you myself, Mickey! You almost killed me and you are endangering my whole family." He looks up at her again. He has a blank look on his face. Carrie looks at GW. "I don't believe this." She looks back to Mickey. "MICKEY – STOP THIS RIGHT NOW!" She slaps him a third time. When he comes up this time, he has tears in his eyes.

"Drop your guns, Barney, Steve. It's over. She doesn't love me." The two men lower their weapons and her uncles take them. "Why don't you love me, Carrie? I tried everything that I could think of to make you love me. Everything."

Carrie hands the gun to GW. She grabs Mickey's face that she just slapped several times. "I couldn't fall in love with you, Mickey. My heart was already spoken for. I am going to marry GW. I have loved him, my whole life. It is a good love, wholesome and true. You couldn't see that. Wouldn't see that. You need help, Mickey. You will get that help, now." She lets go of him and turns away.

"Will you visit me, Carrie?"

"No, I don't think that would be a good idea, Mickey. It might confuse you again. I am going to be a wife and I am not available for your love. That is the only reason, see. A wife is not supposed to love another man, Mickey. Understand?"

Sirens can be heard coming to the Opera House. Mickey looks at her. "They are coming for me?"

She nods. "You and your officers. They will be serving some time, I imagine."

There is a commotion in the lobby. Twenty officers rush in and the Professor, Joshua and Henry bring the fake officers to them.

Carrie is still standing next to Mickey. GW has the gun trained on him until an officer comes to cuff him. Mickey's face is very red and is showing slap marks. The officer turns him around to get cuffed but Mickey bends down and wrestles with him for a while. GW yells, "He is resisting!" Several other officers come forward. Mickey straightens up and has the officer's gun in his hand. GW takes aim. "Put it down, Mickey! I am a good shot."

Instead of pointing the gun at anyone he brings it to his own temple. "I love you, Carrie!" He yells.

"Nooooo!" Carrie screams but no one can hear her because his gun goes off and a piece of his brain goes off with it. He falls to the floor and the officers are surrounding him. "Let me through!" Carrie yells as she is trying to reach Mickey. When she gets to his side, she can tell that he is taking what must be his last breaths. The back of his head is open and blood is everywhere. "Mickey? I forgive you. Go in peace. Wichita. Go in peace." He breathes in again, but doesn't breathe out. Carrie cries, "There was no need for this. He was a nice guy. Smart, handsome, funny. Why did he end it?"

GW takes her away from his body. "Carrie, let's go outside. I need some fresh air after all this." She follows him without emotion. "Carrie, it is not your fault. He was not well. Clara told me how you talked about me with him. You did not lead him on, it was his mind that failed him."

Anna and Henry come outside, too. The unusual warm February night turned into a frosty morning. Everyone can see their breath but are glad to be out of the Opera House. Anna goes to Carrie, "Are you okay?" She asks. "You were very brave, talking to him that way. Slapping him, taking his gun, away. Brave but crazy. How did you know that he would respond?"

"I do not know Mama. I was just so mad at him. Then I saw sadness in his eyes. Deep, deep, sadness. I knew that I could reason with him. Somehow. I am starved, can we go to the Farmhouse, please?"

SIXTY-FOUR
February 15th, 1896
A Saturday in Oklahoma

When the rest of the posse and Sheriff Lucas find the Coach, they are surprised to see each of the four prisoners tied to a separate wheel of the coach. It was just before nine in the morning. With all the men in there, Chilly says, "John, can I leave you in charge of securing the prisoners and bringing them into Pennysville? My family and I are very late for a triple wedding ceremony. Of course, it cannot take place without one bride and two grooms."

Sheriff Lucas is standing next to his old friend, Will. "I'd be happy to Sheriff Lewis. Who are the happy bride and grooms?"

"My sister, Lizzie and Ezra Scott are the first couple. I and Brenda Masters are the second couple and my nephew Harkahomé and Miss Sadie Mae Miller are the third couple."

Sheriff Lucas is stunned. "You are getting married to that beauty from the first coach robbery?"

"Actually, we are married, already. This will be a do-over for our family members."

"Well don't that beat all!! I am going to bring those prisoners just as fast as I can because I must witness this wedding. Then I need to watch out for hell to freeze over. Chilly takes a bride, don't that beat all."

The Colonel speaks up. "John, you do my brother an injustice. She is a beauty, as you say, and – he couldn't fight it forever – he is a Lewis, after all."

The team is hitched up to the carriage and by nine-thirty, Chilly is cracking the whip over the heads of the animals to make it to Pennysville as soon as possible.

***

Meanwhile, the U.S. Marshals arrive just before noon to pick up the prisoner Frank Stevens. They were greeted by Deputies Dotson and Lewis. Deputy Lewis is using a cane, and refusing any laudanum. He has spent his time equally watching the prisoners, being with his Gram Beth and making love to his Sadie. Marshals Gunther and Briggs check in at the Sheriff's office, then go have a large lunch at Big Momma's. They exchange their two horses and get a third for the prisoner and depart Pennysville by two in the afternoon.

Sadie helps Joshua go to Ma's Boarding house but she waits on the porch while he enters. Missy Stevens is well enough to come down the stairs. Doctor Cassidy is sitting with her in the parlor. When she sees Joshua, she asks for her slate and chalk to write. Her first message was simply: 'Father?'

"U.S. Marshals just came to get him to go to Dodge City to stand trial for assault and rape of the girl there. Sadie has a month to decide to add her rape in Wichita to the charge." Joshua explains.

Her next message was: 'Wedding?'

"Well, that is going to happen when the other groom, Sheriff Lewis, comes back with the posse and our abducted family members."

She uses her hand to erase the board. She writes, again. 'When will I talk?' This time she shows it to the Doctor.

He answers, "There are specialists that can help you in Tulsa. Going to Lawrence would be even better. The Medical school there is on the cutting edge of new discoveries. I think that you should learn sign language. Even when you get your voice back. A hearing person who can sign is a highly needed vocation. You are sort of without a vocation, I understand." She nods.

She looks outside at the porch then at the parlor mantle where the clock is ticking. It is two-thirty. She writes one more time on the board. 'Talk with Sadie.'

The Doctor stands. "I will be going, Missy. I will visit, tomorrow. I will get Sadie for you, if you like." He gets his hat and bows to Ma and walks out the door. Joshua can hear him speaking to Sadie.

Joshua turns to Missy. She is writing something else. "Wait, Missy. I have something I want to ask. Are you in pain?"

She points to her throat and uses her index finger and thumb to show an inch of space. Then she points to her heart and puts down the slate and spreads open her hands. Joshua hangs his head.

"I feel so sorry for doing this to you. If you hadn't followed me here, none of this would have happened to you." She puts her hand on his arm. When he looks up she is shaking her head, no. She erases what is written on the board and writes: 'The women like Sadie.'

Joshua reads it. "I'm sorry, Missy. I don't understand."

Sadie's voice is in the doorway. "She is saying that she is sick in her heart for all the women HE hurt." Missy tugs at Joshua's sleeve and nods her head yes several times. Then she writes, again. She shows him the sign, then kisses his cheek. She wrote, 'Alone with Sadie. Good-bye Joshua.'" He kisses her cheek back and stands up with the help of the cane.

He looks to Sadie, "I will wait for you on the porch." He walks out the door and sits on the porch swing, very carefully. He swings just a few minutes before Sadie comes out, crying. He gets up as quickly as he can and goes to her. "What did she do or say to make you cry?"

"She wrote that she is asking God's forgiveness for her father's deeds and she asked me if I would consider praying with her. I said yes, thinking that it would be silent and quick, she fooled me. She managed to whisper, though I could see that it hurt to do so. She said, "Dear Lord, we are all broken in this world. Please be with me,

Sadie, my step-sibling, my father and Harkahomé. We will all need your forgiveness, but most of all your healing." It took all she had, to do that much. Then she wrote on her slate, 'Please forgive me and my father for your child's sake." I just said, 'I will' and had to leave. Such a dear, sweet child. I will tell you one more time, you deserve her love more than mine."

"And I will tell you, again. I deserve the woman who thinks that her rapist's daughter is a better woman than she is. When I saw you come out in tears, I thought that she was mean to you. Hurt or not, I wanted to go hit her!"

Sadie looks up at her man and smiles. "Harkahomé, will you marry me?"

"I will, but only if you agree to marry me."

"Deal." Sadie kisses his cheek and they walk over to the hotel, to wait for Chilly's return.

Four in the afternoon was to be the time for the ceremonies, but no one has heard from Chilly or the posse. Sadie and Joshua are with Brenda at the Kirby Hotel. Brenda is pacing the lobby floor. "I don't know if I am cut out to be a sheriff's wife. This is killing me, to wait to see if he is coming home or not."

"Don't think about it, that way. As his wife, you are the reason that he wants to come home. Give him something to live for and he will." Says Julia as she enters the lobby, with Beth on her arm.

"That is great advice." Says Brenda.

Beth adds to it. "During the war, that is all we women, could do. Make sure that our men knew what they were fighting for and making sure they wanted to come home to us more than anything else in the world. It is also the reason why so many babies were born, nine months after our men signed up!"

Brenda's mother is sitting in the parlor, too. She gasps when she hears Beth. Brenda just looks at her mother. "Oh, Mama, you act as if you've never spread your legs. How did I get here, then? Immaculate conception?"

Martha's jaw drops. Then she closes her mouth and stands up and walks over to her daughter. Martha's jaw is clenched and an angry brow is knitted. Suddenly, Sadie started laughing. She is immediately joined by Brenda, Julia and Beth and then even Joshua starts laughing. Martha looks at everyone and cannot help but starts laughing herself, also. They are laughing so hard that they do not notice that Chilly and the Colonel are standing in the doorway.

"What is so dang-blasted funny? We are out there risking our lives to make sure all the family is here to attend the weddings, and all you do is stand around laughing?"

Everyone screams and runs to meet all the new arrivals. Chilly looks to Brenda and Sadie. "I know that I am late for the ceremony but do you mind if we alter it just a bit?" The both look at him, quizzically.

"Well, Lizzie and Ezra want to get married with us. A triple wedding in the Lewis family. We will never have a reason to forget the date. Each of us men will telegram the others to remind us of our Anniversaries!"

Gram Beth cries out, "My daughter, my son and my grandson, all getting married on the same day. What a true blessing this is! How soon can you be ready, Lizzie? Brenda? Sadie?" All the brides look at each other. Beth says, "How about in about two hours? So, let's get word to everyone that at six-thirty this evening, THREE weddings are taking place."

Lizzie says, "I don't have a wedding dress!" So, Carolyn and she run to Jane's Couture Shop and look at the selection in her size. Miraculously, the one gown in her size is the one gown that caught her eye, while hanging in the window. Sadie has brought her gown and veil to the Hotel. Lee Kirby has insisted that she and Joshua have the Bridal Suite. All the brides go up to the suite to get ready. Beth, Julia, Carolyn and Katherine all help do up their hair, get the dresses on and apply a little color on their lips.

The men are in the Colonel's room. The Colonel has a bottle of whiskey and pours the three grooms, plus Joseph, Grant and himself a drink. "Here's to the Luckiest Men Alive!!" Everyone says 'Here, here' and takes a drink. "Ezra, how many times have you asked Lizzie to marry you?"

"Gee, I have lost count. I think the first time was 1883 at Marjorie's wedding. Then I asked her at least twice a year since."

"What has been the reason that she has declined you?" Joseph asks.

Ezra laughs as he looks at Chilly. "She always said, 'When Love Consumes the Chill, I will marry you. I guess with Chilly wed, she has no more excuse."

Chilly says to Ezra. "Sorry to have taken so long. You were a good man to have waited around."

"Where else would I be? I have loved her since I joined the practice in 1880. It took me two years to approach her so, who am I to say 'hurry' to her. As long as I have been a part of her life, I have been a happy fool wanting just a bit more."

Chilly looks at the man. "You are a Ladies doctor, like she is?"

"Yes."

"You know that marriage gives you a bit more than 'a bit more?'"

"Yes, I do. We are not children, Chilly." He blushes. "Lizzie and I have enjoyed each other's company intimately, for many years. That is why I have been stumped as to why she would not let me make an honest woman out of her."

Chilly looks down at his drink, "She actually said, 'When Love Consumes the Chill, I will marry you?' What an excuse! Did she want me not to be the only single Lewis sibling? I still don't understand her reasoning."

"You are asking the wrong man, Chilly." Ezra

confesses. "At first, I thought she was comparing it to 'When Hell freezes over'. Just not as bluntly.

"Well, let's have another toast." He waits for the Colonel to fill all the glasses. "Gentlemen, Hell has frozen over because LOVE has CONSUMED the CHILL! And I am loving every minute of it!

SIXTY-FIVE
February 15th, 1959
A Sunday in EL Dorado, Kansas continued

An hour later, everyone is at the farmhouse eating everything in sight. Helen has breakfast catered. Enough for fifty people. All the excitement of the evening's end, enticed more people to come back to the house than normally would.

On the way back to the Farmhouse, Carrie cannot sit still in GW's car. When he pulls up to the home, she jumps out. She starts pacing back and forth. GW tries to let her calm down. He stands and watches her. "Carrie, I have another way to use up all that extra energy. You might just enjoy it." He smiles at her. She doesn't even hear him. "Carrie, you are putting a rut in the grass. Or what will be grass. Will you come here?"

"I can't stay still."

"I noticed."

She is waving her hands like she is trying to shake something off them, all while still pacing. She has just her jacket on. She looks down and notices Mickey's blood on the hem of the dress and jacket. "All the work on this dress and it is ruined." She starts to cry. "Why? Why did he kill himself? I have his blood on my hard work and there was nothing that I could do, it all happened so fast!"

GW goes to her. "That's right, there was nothing that you could do! And it is just the hem of the dress. That can be cut off and a new one sewn on." He tries to hold her but she just moves away.

"It's on the jacket too. I had just put it on to leave when the officers came. I got blood on it, too when I knelt down. Oh! Look at my shoes. They are bloody, too!"

"I hear peroxide takes blood out. You can try that before you throw the whole thing away. Come inside the farmhouse, Carrie. Get something to eat. It is freezing out here. Aren't you cold?"

She suddenly starts to tremble. "I didn't know that I was cold until you said it." He goes to her and she lets him put his arms around her. "You are very warm." She simply says.

He lifts her chin. "We were supposed to be smooching in the Ford, right now." He gives her a light kiss on the lips. "I love you, Carrie."

She puts her arms inside his jacket and hugs him tight. "I want you to make love to me, but they all know we are here."

"I can tell them that we are going for a ride."

"GW, marry me?"

"Yes, Carrie, I'll marry you."

"Can we get married right away? I feel like I used up half of my nine lives. I don't want to waste another minute! I want to bring goodness and love into the world. I want to create beautiful dresses and make beautiful babies with you. I want to be Mrs. Grant William Lewis, as soon as possible."

"I am agreeing to all of it, Carrie. Should we go inside and tell everyone?"

"No, just hold me."

"You've stopped trembling."

"I know." She looks up at him. "Kiss me."

He bends and kisses her. She is leaning against him and practically purring. "Shall I call a preacher and marry you now?" He says.

"Why not? All the family is present. Oh, except Clara Beth. I would need her to be my Maid of Honor."

"She will have spring break off. We could get married then."

"That is not for two months! I want you now."

"Carrie, you have me now. Come into my car. I will hold you and kiss you and make you forget the chill in the air."

"What was the line from your Great Gram Beth's

journals? Love consumes the Chill? It was supposed to be about your Uncle Chilly finally meeting his soulmate, but I think it also means that Love conquers All. Love Consumes the Chill. And you, GW, are my Love. Always have been, always will be. Let's go inside and announce to everyone that we will be married during spring break."

"Carrie, would you like me to transfer to Butler Community College next semester, so that you can build up your business here? I will need to transfer to a university Junior year. Traveling to Wichita State University could be done. After your business takes off here, you can branch out into Lawrence. What do you think?"

"I think that you've been thinking about this for a while."

"I am prepared for whatever was necessary. I had a plan if we married and you wanted to stay in Chicago, also."

"Talk about the cold!"

"Yes, but don't forget, LOVE CONSUMES THE CHILL!"

THE END

TIME LINE FOR
THE PRESENT-PAST SAGAS

- 1805 Clyde Lewis is born
- 1806 Daniel Palmer is born
- 1807 Eloise Chapman is born
- 1809 Charles Palmer is born
- 1812 Carolyn Monnet is born
- 1819 John Caldwell is born (husband to Marilyn, grandfather to Grant & Julia)
- 1820 Marilyn Baker is born (step-mother to Elizabeth)
- 1824 Clyde Lewis marries Eloise Chapman
- 1825 William Lewis is born to Clyde and Eloise Lewis
- 1826 Charles Palmer and Carolyn Monnet are married
- 1828 Oct 18 Elizabeth Palmer is born to Charles and Carolyn Palmer
- 1830 Eloise Chapman Lewis dies
- 1837 July 31 William Quantrill is born
- 1838 John Caldwell marries Marilyn Baker
- 1839 Theodore Johnson marries Gwendolyn Landon
- 1839 Stephen Johnson is born
- 1840 Mary Caldwell is born to Marilyn and John Caldwell
- 1840 Bloody Bill Anderson is born
- 1845 John Caldwell dies
- 1846 Gwendolyn Landon Johnson dies
- 1846 Theodore Johnson marries Antonia Ford
- 1846 Elizabeth Palmer marries William Lewis
- 1847 Lydia Stone is born to Nathan Stone and his wife
- 1849 Ian Clyde Lewis is born to Elizabeth and William Lewis
- 1851 Joseph Lewis is born to Elizabeth and William Lewis
- 1853 Lizbet (Lizzie) Lewis is born to Elizabeth and William Lewis
- 1855 Katherine Henning is born
- 1855 Mary Caldwell marries Stephan Johnson
- 1855 Grant Johnson is born to Mary and Steve Johnson
- 1858 Julia Johnson is born to Mary and Steve Johnson
- 1859 Carolyn Monnet Palmer dies
- 1859 Oct 31 William Lewis, Jr. is born to Elizabeth and William Lewis, Sr.

383

- 1859 Wm Quantrill lives in Lawrence as Charlie Hart & meets Lewis Family
- 1860 Richard Long is born
- 1863 Steven Johnson dies during War
- 1863 Aug 21 Clara Lewis is born to Elizabeth and William Lewis, Sr. and dies in Lawrence Massacre
- 1863 Aug 21 Charles Palmer and Daniel Palmer die in the Lawrence Massacre
- 1863 Aug 21 close to 200 unarmed men are massacred in Lawrence Kansas under Colonel Wm. Quantrill
- 1864 Marjorie Lewis is born to Elizabeth and William Lewis, Sr.
- 1864 Oct 26 Bloody Bill Anderson is killed
- 1865 Carolyn Lewis is born to Elizabeth and William Lewis, Sr.
- 1865 Clyde Lewis marries Marilyn Baker Caldwell
- 1865 June 6 William Quantrill dies
- 1866 Elizabeth Palmer Lewis starts her journals
- 1866 Oct 27 Ian Lewis marries Lydia Stone
- 1866 Oct 31 Charles (Chilly) Palmer Lewis is born to Elizabeth and William Lewis, Sr.
- 1867 May 10 Joshua Nathaniel Lewis is born to Ian Lewis and Lydia Stone Lewis
- 1876 Dr. Joseph Lewis marries Katherine Henning
- 1876 Brenda Masters is born to Dr. George and Martha Masters.
- 1878 Sept 29 Ian Lewis, dies in Cheyenne Indian attack, that killed 41 settlers Joshua Nathaniel is captured by the Cheyenne in Oberlin, Kansas
- 1879 January Cheyenne break out of Fort Robinson – Major Wm Lewis is assigned to capture them.
- 1879 Sat. July 12th - Julia Johnson marries Major William Clyde Lewis
- 1879 Nov Change of venue moves Cheyenne Indian trials to Lawrence, Kansas
- 1880 Samuel Lewis is born to Dr. Joseph and Katherine Lewis
- 1882 Constance Lewis is born to Dr. Joseph and Katherine Lewis
- 1882 December 8th and on the 23rd Grant Johnson marries Carolyn Lewis

- 1883 Ada Johnson is born to Carolyn and Grant Lewis Sr.
- 1883 Mary Caldwell Johnson dies
- 1883 Marjorie Lewis marries Richard Long
- 1885 Clyde Lewis dies
- 1885 Ida Johnson is born to Carolyn and Grant Johnson, Sr.
- 1886 Grant Lewis Jr. is born to Carolyn and Grant Johnson, Sr.
- 1886 Joan Walker is born
- 1886 Kevin William Lewis is born to Colonel William and Julia Lewis
- 1889 Sue Ellen Morgan is born
- 1890 Katherine Henning Lewis dies
- 1890 Richard Long, Jr. is born to Marjorie and Richard Long, Sr.
- 1891 William Lewis Sr. dies
- 1893 Frank Harrick is born
- 1894 Judd Masters is born
- 1895 Judy Evans is born
- 1898 Sheriff Charles (Chilly) Lewis marries Brenda Sharp
- 1898 Richard Long, Jr. dies
- 1899 Elizabeth Lewis is born to Sheriff Charles and Brenda Lewis
- 1901 Marilyn Caldwell Lewis dies
- 1902 Elizabeth Palmer Lewis dies
- 1902 William Charles Lewis is born to Sheriff Charles and Brenda Lewis
- 1903 Edward James is born
- 1904 Grant Johnson, Jr. Marries Joan Lane
- 1905 Grant Johnson (III) is born
- 1907 Mark Collins is born
- 1905 Josephine Lane is born
- 1909 May 30 Kevin Lewis marries Sue Ellen Morgan
- 1910 Grant Johnson, Sr. dies
- 1911 Joan Lane Johnson dies
- 1913 Carolyn Diane Lewis is born to Sue Ellen and Kevin Lewis
- 1915 May 15 Judd Masters marries Judy Evans
- 1915 Joshua Morgan Lewis is born to Sue Ellen and Kevin Lewis
- 1915 Henry Harrick is born to Frank and Ellen Harrick

- 1916 Feb 10 Anna Rose Masters is born to Judd and Judy Masters
- 1918 Kevin and Sue Ellen Lewis die
- 1918 Melinda Masters is born to Judd and Judy Masters
- 1918 August 18 Susan Walker is born
- 1919 Nov 11 Matthew Masters is born to Judd and Judy Masters
- 1921 May 7 Grant Johnson (III) marries Josephine Walker
- 1922 January - Angela Johnson dies (38 years old)
- 1922 Apr 29 Juliet Helen Johnson is born to Josephine and Grant Lewis (III)
- 1923 Richard Long Sr. dies
- 1925 Ida Johnson dies
- 1926 Julia Johnson Lewis dies
- 1929 Grant Johnson, Jr dies
- 1932 May 12 Josephine Walker Johnson dies giving birth
- 1932 May 12 Grant Lewis (IV) dies during his birth
- 1935 Sept 27 Anna Rose Masters is engaged to Henry Harrick
- 1935 Sept 28 Anna Rose Masters is attack by John Walker
- 1935 Sep 29 Jane Doe (Rosanne) is found by Carolyn Lewis
- 1936 Mar 23 Unnamed baby girl is born to Rosanne
- 1936 Sep 27 Anna Rose Masters marries Henry Harrick
- 1936 Nov 21 Melinda Masters marries Mark Collins
- 1937 Apr 17 Susan Walker and Matthew Masters marry
- 1937 Oct 18 Clara Beth is born to Anna and Henry Harrick
- 1937 Oct 29 John Walker is killed by Colonel Wm Lewis
- 1937 Oct 31 Carolyn Lewis is engaged to Professor Edward James
- 1938 Jun 26 Carolyn Lewis marries Professor Edward James
- 1938 Feb 22 Kathryn (Katie) Ann is born to Susan and Matthew Masters
- 1939 Feb 11 Joshua Morgan Lewis marries Juliet Helen Johnson
- 1939 Apr 10 Colonel William Clyde Lewis dies
- 1939 Nov 5 Grant Johnson (III) dies
- 1940 Jude Matthew Collins is born to Mark and Melinda Collins
- 1940 Grant William (GW) Lewis is born to Joshua and Juliet Helen

- 1940 Carolyn (Carrie) Ann Harrick is born to Henry and Anna Harrick
- 1941 Gloria Rose Collins is born to Mark and Melinda Collins
- 1941 Jonathan Edward James is born to Professor Edward and Carolyn James
- 1942 Henry (Harry)Frank Harrick is born to Henry and Anna Harrick
- 1944 William (Bill) Johnson Lewis is born to Joshua and Juliet Helen
- 1944 Elizabeth (Bessie) Susan James is born to Professor Edward and Carolyn James
- 1944 Audrey Jean Lewis is born to Joshua and Juliet Helen
- 1944 Elizabeth (Bessie) Susan James is born to Professor Edward and Carolyn James
- 1946 Charlotte Rose (Charlie) Lewis is born to Joshua and Juliet Helen
- 1948 Eleanor Frances (Ellie) Lewis is born to Joshua and Juliet Helen
- 1950 Kevin Joshua Lewis is born to Joshua and Juliet Helen
- 1959 Mar 28- Grant William (GW) Lewis marries Carolyn (Carrie) Ann Harrick

ABOUT THE AUTHOR

Cherisse M Havlicek writes in the beautiful town of Bridgman, Michigan. She has been married for over thirty years to a now retired Chicago Police Officer. Raised in the suburbs of Chicago, she fell in love and married him in 1985. When he retired from the Police Force in 1999, they had a seven-year-old boy and a two-year-old girl. They knew that they wanted to live in Michigan, where they had been coming up on weekends for many years.

Cherisse has had a very varied work experience. She was a Hairdresser, an interior landscape horticulturist, a clerk at Cook County Juvenile Court, and in Michigan she worked at the daily Newspaper. There, she went from a Route manager to Single Copy manager to the top producer in the Advertising Department while raising her children, and attending their sports activities. She also helped take care of her husband's elderly mother and his disabled cousin, who lived with them.

As they became 'empty nesters', her husband was diagnosed with Lewy Body Dementia with Parkinson's. She knew that she could no longer work full time, but even part-time endeavors took her away from home, too much.

In September of 2016, her grown son, found chapter one of a book she started in high school and gave her grief about not finishing it. She wrote the next forty-five chapters in eight months and her first novel *ANNA AT LAST* was complete. She didn't stop there, though. She wrote *THE LEWIS LEGACY* while her husband had his back surgery and during his rehab. *JUSTICE FOR JOSHUA* and a Children's Christmas story called *A SILENT NIGHT* were all written in 2018. A novella, *CAROLYN'S CHRISTMAS CAROL* was written while her husband spent a few weeks hospitalized in early 2019. This fifth and final(?) installment in the Present / Past Saga series was written in 2019, also. All these works are now available for purchase. She, obviously, is making up for lost time and has no plans to stop.

You can connect with her on her Facebook page:
Author – Cherisse M Havlicek